SPECIAL MESSAGE TO READERS

This book is published under the auspices of

THE ULVERSCROFT FOUNDATION

(registered charity No. 264873 UK)

Established in 1972 to provide funds for research, diagnosis and treatment of eye diseases. Examples of contributions made are: —

A new Children's Assessment Unit at Moorfield's Hospital, London.

•

Twin operating theatres at the Western Ophthalmic Hospital, London.

•

A Chair of Ophthalmology at the University of Leicester.

•

The establishment of a Royal Australian College of Ophthalmologists "Fellowship".

You can help further the work of the Foundation by making a donation or leaving a legacy. Every contribution, no matter how small, is received with gratitude. Please write for details to:

THE ULVERSCROFT FOUNDATION,
The Green, Bradgate Road, Anstey,
Leicester LE7 7FU, England.
Telephone: (0116) 236 4325

In Australia write to:
THE ULVERSCROFT FOUNDATION,
c/o The Royal Australian College of Ophthalmologists,
27, Commonwealth Street, Sydney,
N.S.W. 2010.

Love is
a time of enchantment:
in it all days are fair and all fields
green. Youth is blest by it,
old age made benign:
the eyes of love see
roses blooming in December,
and sunshine through rain. Verily
is the time of true-love
a time of enchantment — and
Oh! how eager is woman
to be bewitched!

THE BLUEBELL POOL

Aubrey Farringdon knows he made a monumental mistake in his first marriage, but when he marries Nancy Gillimore he believes that this time it will work. All is well until they return to Aubrey's Dorset home. Thrown into conflict with Aubrey's mother and his teenage children, Nancy is drawn to the secrecy of the bluebell pool, where Aubrey's first wife, Augusta, had been discovered with a lover. Nancy becomes obsessed by Augusta — and through the pages of Augusta's diary and Nancy's encounters with the gamekeeper, Powers, a disturbing story of lust and betrayal unfolds.

SUE SULLY

THE BLUEBELL POOL

Complete and Unabridged

ULVERSCROFT
Leicester

First published in Great Britain in 1993 by
Headline Book Publishing
London

First Large Print Edition
published August 1995
by arrangement with
Headline Book Publishing Limited
a division of Hodder Headline Plc
London

British Library CIP Data

Sully, Sue
The bluebell pool.—Large print ed.—
Ulverscroft large print series: romance
I. Title
823.914 [F]

ISBN 0–7089–3355–6

Published by
F. A. Thorpe (Publishing) Ltd.
Anstey, Leicestershire

Set by Words & Graphics Ltd.
Anstey, Leicestershire
Printed and bound in Great Britain by
T. J. Press (Padstow) Ltd., Padstow, Cornwall

This book is printed on acid-free paper

Prologue

WHEN he was a boy he had chased the butterflies which flew about the garden. He wanted to capture their bright, flickering movement and keep it. One day he fetched a jar from the kitchens and waited by the flower borders where the butterflies danced; he snatched at them, but they evaded his fingers, until in the end he managed to trap one in his cupped hands and felt the flicker of wings against his palms. He placed his hands over the jar and watched the butterfly fall inside, then screwed down the lid. He watched the creature for a long time, fascinated by the way it persistently beat its wings against the glass. At last the creature settled, resting with its wings spread on the bottom of the jar. It was so beautiful, more delicate than some of the garden butterflies: a painted lady with pale red wings, dappled and tipped with brown and white. He kept it until the next day, and then someone, one of the servants, said that it was 'cruel, Master Aubrey,' to keep a pretty thing like that in a jar. He took the butterfly back to the garden and unscrewed the lid, waiting for the insect to flutter free. But it did not move, and he tipped the lifeless body into the flowerbed.

1

OLD leaves formed pale drifts of colour round the roots of the trees which grew close to the water's edge. They hid the junction of land and water so that, coming suddenly upon the pool, Nancy almost lost her footing. She felt a chill of fear, for the surface of the water was dark; she could not gauge its depth nor see into the reflections of the trees, which spread their black fingers as if to draw her to them. But it was beautiful. Quite, quite beautiful. She wrote in her diary that evening: I know that I have discovered the most wonderful place on the estate. Such an air of secrecy and romance hung over it that it quite took my breath away and I should have thought I had stepped right out of this modern-day world if I had not heard a steam-plough throbbing somewhere across the fields.

"Why didn't you tell me about the pool?" Nancy said to Aubrey at dinner.

There was a long silence. His mother, sharp as the glass-eyed falcons in the wallcases behind her head, allowed her hand to pause for a fraction in mid-air, then continued spooning rice pudding from her dish to her mouth.

"My darling, what is there to tell?" said Aubrey at last.

"How beautiful it is, how absolutely romantic."

"Romantic?" Aubrey's expression hardened. He glanced at his mother, and old Mrs Farringdon's paper-smooth features twisted themselves into a bitter kind of a sneer. Nancy had a swift impression of mother and son being in alliance together at the head of the table.

"Yes, romantic." Nancy smiled engagingly. Her mouth was large, the top lip full and curving and clearly defined, her eyes grey, cat-like under arched brows, which gave her a questioning, slightly amused look.

Aubrey folded his napkin and stood with careful equanimity. "I'm sorry, Nancy dear, I cannot talk about the pool. You will please not go there or mention it again. Mama, if you will excuse me — "

Even now, I guess I'm bound to admire him, thought Nancy. How very composed he always is, that very quality I first learned to love about him. At the same time she felt an exasperation with Aubrey's very gentlemanly control. If he was furious with her for finding the pool, why couldn't he just come right out with it and say so? This irritation with him was new to her; it was something she had not known before he had brought her to live at Midwinter.

The manservant Roberts, impassive and correct, opened the heavy double doors of the dining room and closed them silently behind his master. He stood at the exact centre of the doorway, a human item of furniture, seemingly as stuffed and lifeless as one of Aubrey's glass-cased specimens.

"I dare say it's all connected with Augusta," Nancy said when Aubrey had gone.

Mrs Farringdon offered no response.

Nancy had a habit of making quick judgements. She liked to dramatise a situation, to see it in a brightly coloured light. If the facts did not correspond to her stage directions she could pretend that they did, and very soon it seemed as if they had and what she had invented became real. Maybe the pool had been a special place for Aubrey and Augusta, though that would have been before *It* had happened. Nancy always referred to Aubrey's first wife's breach of faith with a capital letter, or sometimes more luridly — though still in mental capitals — as 'The Foul Deed'. But how in the world could she have been expected to know that the pool would remind Aubrey of Augusta? She had heard the story, of course. It was another point she had admired in him, the fact that he had wanted to tell her everything about his past.

"You're so young." He had touched her cheek with a kind of wonder.

"Your first wife was as old as you, but her advanced years didn't make her any wiser or more faithful." She remembered without compunction his look of pained acknowledgement and her own brief satisfaction. She had not wanted him to be forever reminding her of the difference in their ages, nor that she was uncultivated and naïve. She did not want to be a 'northern lass', 'a child of nature', unspoiled and innocent, nor any of the other labels which had inevitably been applied to her — a mere 'slip of a girl' of eighteen — once their engagement became known among his friends. Nancy saw herself in quite a different light: she was a girl to be reckoned with, independent-minded and open to experience — Nancy's passion for drama frequently featured herself playing the heroine, centre-stage.

Mrs Farringdon continued eating. What a ghastly old bird his mother was. If she had known about his mama, that might have made a difference; she might well have thought twice about becoming the second Mrs Aubrey Farringdon. But his mother, like his children and the long dead Augusta, had been no more than names at first, referred to as if they belonged to the Dorset landscape. She had supposed that their married life would continue in the setting of his London house, that marriage would make little difference to the routine they had established there. Her only doubts had been connected with the subtleties of her change in status from secretary to wife, keeper of his lecture notes and schedules to keeper of his heart and soul. Nancy had no second thoughts about her love for Aubrey — she adored him passionately and without reserve — but she had recently begun to question her role as wife with its subtle erosion of a woman's independence. The fact that Aubrey's first wife had been foolish enough to have an affair with one of his friends had caused her no misgivings. It was vaguely shocking, but also rather romantic. "Poor Aubrey," she had said. He had a secret tragedy in his past; he needed her more than ever.

"Would you like to know why my son does not wish to be reminded about the pool in the wood?" Mrs Farringdon turned to dismiss the butler and waited until he had closed the doors behind him. "I think, Nancy, it might be as well for you to know. Also, I suggest you would be wise to respect my son's wishes and walk or ride only within the immediate grounds or along the lanes in future. There are some very pleasant byways around Midwinter and Winchborne. Far more pleasant — and far less dangerous — than the wood and its quarry pool." She dabbed her mouth with her napkin and reached for the coffee pot which Roberts had left discreetly at her right elbow. She raised her eyebrows inquiringly; she was one of those autocratic women who expected to exert total authority over her household. Nancy indicated with a slight nod of her head that she would have some coffee. Mrs Farringdon poured a thin stream into the tiny cup and waited until Nancy had taken it before she said without expression, "You see, the pool is where Augusta was discovered with her lover."

Nancy had not expected this. She saw that the older woman had scored a minor victory; it was confirmation, if she had needed it, that their relationship was destined to be one of warfare, a series of small campaigns and manoeuvres. She felt a momentary confusion, but hid it with military skill as she sipped the watery coffee. An image of the pool, deep and mysterious, flashed before her. The perfect place for a lovers' tryst.

She murmured with sudden sympathy, "Poor Aubrey." She wondered whether he had gone to his room. She would have liked to follow him and apologise for upsetting him over Augusta. In London she might have done so, she would have quickly charmed him and made him laugh again; but to absent herself now from the table would have gone against the strictly adhered-to codes of behaviour of Midwinter.

"Augusta was high-spirited too," said Mrs Farringdon. "Not so young, of course, but unstable I should say. She was a bad choice from the start."

"Am I a bad choice, would you suppose?" Nancy looked her mother-in-law in the eye.

"I really could not say."

"Aubrey doesn't seem to think so."

"My dear child, Aubrey can be a fool. He thought that Augusta was wonderful too when he married her."

2

NANCY had spotted the advertisement in *The Times* with a leap of excited recognition. Aubrey Farringdon's was a reputation which had been familiar to her from childhood, as far away from academic life and the Royal Geographical Society as the Yorkshire streets of Halifax. She had read his book *The Lonely Voyager* and his series of travel tales from West Africa and had seen his name in the popular periodicals which published articles by famous anthropologists and travellers.

As a child Nancy had been greedy for tales of adventure. She had worked her way along the shelves of her father's limited selection of books, devouring everything from Stevenson and Kipling to Henry Savage Landor's 'Account of a Journey in Tibet' and copies of the *Wide World* magazine with its slogan 'Truth Is Stranger Than Fiction'. Each year around Christmas time her father would bring out the magic lantern. Neighbours and relatives would be packed into the semi-darkened parlour, and Nancy, sitting cross-legged on the carpet with all the neighbourhood children, would thrill to 'Pictures across the Seas' and 'The Wonders of the World', waking as if from a dream when everyone applauded and the lamps were brightened and her mother said, "Well now, I should say you folk are about ready for a bite of supper."

Nancy felt a strong nostalgia for her childhood. She viewed it with the softening glow of hindsight, yet with an awareness of its imperfections and, since she was now alone in the world, she remembered that time with a lingering sense of loss. Her family had known few luxuries, either material or academic, but her mother had been ambitious for her only child, had encouraged her to read and had worked to pay for a secretarial training for her. An appetite for knowledge and adventure and a strong desire to better herself was what had drawn Nancy south to London. It was what alerted her to Aubrey Farringdon's requirement of a secretary one summer's day in 1913.

⋆ ⋆ ⋆

"But you're only a child, my dear."

"I'm getting close on for eighteen."

Nancy had resolved that she would not be ousted, even when the great and awesome Aubrey Farringdon made a tentative move towards her, as if he would escort her personally from his study.

"My dear young lady. This won't do. When you signed your letter of application 'N. Gallimore', without disclosing your sex, naturally I supposed you to be a man." His speech was hesitant, yet his manner was urbane, pleasant, not without authority.

"The references . . ." Nancy was defensive, feeling she had been caught out in a deceit, though none had been intended. She gripped her gloved hands together for courage and began to generate a mood of indignation. Why should he refuse to employ her on the mere grounds of her sex?

"References. Yes. I suppose there must have been such things . . ." Aubrey turned to the muddle of papers on his desk and frowned, trying to remember, then shrugged as if the mislaid references were lost in the swamps of time.

"I'm every bit as qualified as a man to do the work," Nancy volunteered. "And, references or not, you accepted my credentials from my letter."

"But that was before . . ." His embarrassment made him seem vulnerable. They both saw that she was not going to be moved except by force, and clearly he was too much of a gentleman for that.

She had adored him at once. She was attracted to his mild hazel eyes, his very nice dark brown hair, well-trimmed and greying a little at the temples, the good teeth and resolute, well-defined mouth, and the aristocratic, heroic features, with their associations of the distinguished gentleman traveller.

Nancy was something of a snob, she liked to mix with educated and clever people. She envied them the accumulated knowledge and manners which gave them their superiority.

The smell of his study was masculine and learned, a pleasant mixture of cigars and books. The walls were lined from floor to ceiling with impressive leather-bound works on Africa, on Egyptology and zoology; the space between the windows which overlooked the street was filled with a high, glass-fronted cabinet, its shelves taken up with all kinds of curios: African beadwork, carved wooden figures, bowls and blackened shards of earthenware and, on the centre shelf, a pair of jewel-encrusted scimitars, for one of Aubrey Farringdon's many esoteric interests was Arabian art. Nancy had read in *Wide World* about his collection of weapons; he acted in an advisory capacity for the British Museum on them. She let her glance rest on the exquisitely worked hilts of the scimitars and felt faint with pleasure to be there in the great man's study.

True, his house was a little disappointing. The dirty red-brick building in Bloomsbury seemed inappropriately shabby for a man who was a Fellow of the Royal Geographical Society and the British Association for the Advancement of Science, who had lectured at the Sorbonne and had been among the most well-known anthropologists at the turn of the century. His taste in décor was very Victorian and, she had to admit, pretty stuffy: the hall and staircase were dismal, lined with a brown flock paper which looked as if it had seen better days. The curtains of his study were heavily fringed and tassled and dark with London soot. A large padded chair in the corner badly needed restuffing; the carpet too was threadbare, shabbier than her mother's best parlour Axminster had been, and cluttered with files and boxes, piles of manuscripts and learned journals, which jostled for space with a dilapidated typewriter, heaped up with geographical magazines.

Nancy dismissed this deficiency of stylishness in her hero: learned men were renowned for their absence of worldliness, and she decided it was, if anything, a quality to be admired. Already she could imagine working there: she planned where she would have her own corner. She would soon have the jumble organised, a satisfactory system of filing, his work ordered and herself installed with a modern typewriting machine.

She looked for an upright chair and pulled it close to the desk. She gave him one of her brilliant and disarming smiles. "Just hear me through, Mr Farringdon. I'm a good organiser and an accurate typist. I'm also very experienced. More than you'd think. And those references off of my last employer, they spoke really well of my competence. Oh, I just know you won't be disappointed."

* * *

Aubrey had fallen in love with her then, from the moment she sat herself down. She was slender as a wand in a narrow, dark-coloured dress which flared over delicate ankles, and with a jauntily feathered hat perched on her heavy brown hair which was gathered into a knot. Her forthrightness was modern and refreshing. Her cool grey eyes watched him intently from beneath arching brows, almost as if it were she, not he, who had been conducting the interview. She chatted freely and eagerly about her family. Her grandfather had been a ship's captain in Hull, she said, but her mother had married for love and as a consequence had disconnected herself from her family. Nancy's more immediate background was one of genteel poverty: her father, as far as she could remember, had allowed money to slip easily through his fingers. Her mother had believed in female emancipation, and had been one of the first women in the district to ride a bicycle. Widowed young, she had worked as a supervisor at a dairy, putting money by each week to pay for her daughter's secretarial schooling in London. Nancy had set her sights on London from being a tiny girl, and her mother had encouraged her to seek her fortune there. "She died soon after I was sixteen." Aubrey was shocked into pity. An orphan. A mere child. What might not have become of her? And yet, Miss Gallimore had carved out a respectable living for herself by working for a private lending library which had specialised in books about primitive societies and had fed her interest in travel.

Aubrey allowed himself to be captivated.

He could not believe his good fortune, not least in finding an efficient secretary; for, once employed, she arranged his appointments and his speaking engagements with sweeping precision and, without turning a hair, began organising his mountain of travel notes for the book he was compiling on ancient religions of the world.

When a man in his mid-forties falls for a young girl, it is inevitable that he should become a subject for the scepticism and idle speculation of his colleagues. Aubrey flinched from the undercurrent of gossip which had begun to spread among his peers. He had heard it all before, on the lines of 'The man's a fool' or, as he himself had remarked when his fellow geographer, Gilbert Lang, a man ten years his junior, took up with a West End chorus girl, 'She's only after his money.'

Miss Gallimore was no gold-digger: Aubrey had established this much early on. "Miss Gallimore, you have an admirable sense of thrift," he said when, insisting on a new typewriter, she had searched the catalogues for a bargain machine.

"I learned that off my mother," Nancy said, setting a pile of papers on the corner of his desk, "She was a thrifty kind of person. You'd have liked her."

"I'm sure I should," he said gently, "if she had possessed even half your excellent qualities."

"She was much, much better than I'll ever be. She was a wonderful woman." Nancy paused, believing for a moment in the saintliness of motherhood, remembering how her mother had scrimped and saved to educate her.

"And you, Miss Gallimore, are a wonderful girl, for you have come into my crusty, bachelor way of life and lifted me out of the doldrums." He watched her, seeing her cheeks — already flushed with some sentimental memory — redden more deeply with pleasure, and Aubrey knew that he was lost.

"You needed someone to straighten you out a bit, that's all. You've done me a power of good too, letting me work among all these books and learn about ancient cultures." Nancy waved her hand to indicate the book-lined walls, the shelves of curios and piles of manuscript on his desk. "It's *broadened* my horizons — isn't that what they say learning should do?" She tapped the manuscript close to her hand. "Eh — those Egyptians . . . You wouldn't believe, would you, how civilised they were all those years back?"

Aubrey frowned, a small cloud appearing on his own horizon. "I think we should start on your diction. Would you like that, Miss Gallimore, if I were to give you diction lessons?"

Her eyes widened with gratitude. "Would I? I should be that pleased — I'd be over the moon."

Aubrey's heart skipped with pleasure. Was he a fool? He had made monumental mistakes in his first marriage, and Miss Gallimore, for all her youth and inexperience, had a noticeable streak of independence, inherited no doubt from her mother. It smacked more than a little of working class feminism, and might fit uncomfortably in his own circle. For one could not overlook the matter of her class: she was, on her own admission, a 'plainspoken, unrefined kind of person'.

Yet none of her faults were very damning: her tendency to over-exuberance was merely the enthusiasm of youth; her inclination to chatter, even occasionally interrupting him when he was writing — which to some might imply a certain lack of reverence — amused him. She would learn discretion in time. He told himself that under his tuition she would soon iron out her northern idioms and acquire the mannerisms of a lady. Her faults were more than counterbalanced by her innocence, her vitality and her willingness to learn.

"I am thinking of marrying again," Aubrey said to Gilbert Lang one afternoon at his club when they had finished discussing — without much enthusiasm — Asquith and the government, the Dublin strikes and fading hopes for Home Rule. Lang, a collector of ornithological species for a London zoologist, had travelled, like Aubrey himself, in West Africa. He was a man of flamboyant and still youthful good looks. The chorus-girl episode had been brief, but expensive and painful, and Lang still suffered from the notion that he was a man who had been made to look ridiculous. Bouts of melancholia frequently made him turn to drink, when he would rail against his own weak nature. He was a strange choice of confidant, reflected Aubrey, but he had sensed that, of all his colleagues, Lang might be the last to pour scorn.

"Your nice little Yorkshire secretary?" Lang folded his copy of *The Times* and eyed him with a weary smile.

"Do you think I've lost my sense of reason?"

"It's a distinct possibility."

"But she's such a gem. If only you knew."

"Oh, I think I understand perfectly, dear fellow. But why marry the girl?"

Aubrey blinked. Clearly Lang had caught on to the wrong idea. How very distasteful. He should have known better than to confide in someone who had dabbled at the lowest end of the social scale. "I can assure you there's never been anything improper in the relationship. Miss Gallimore lodges with a very respectable widow. She arrives at nine o'clock every day and we spend the mornings discussing my notes, and in the afternoons she often works alone while I'm at the British Museum. I have never once asked her to stay later than five-thirty, and my housekeeper is always in the house during her working hours."

Lang laughed. "Hold on, dear chap. I'm sure it's all very proper. But how extraordinarily dull."

Aubrey relaxed. "Truly though, she's a treasure, Lang. I have never felt so alive. She has taken me over completely. She's organised my research notes and is interested in Egyptology and all my anthropological observations. She has asked me to teach her *all I know* about Africa and even wants to learn Latin and Greek."

"And Hebrew and Sanskrit and Arabic? A rival? I should look to your laurels, Farringdon."

"She *is* very intelligent."

Lang picked up the paper. "No woman is intelligent. If you want my opinion, which you probably don't, you are merely flattered by the girl's youthful interest in your wider experience. You're asking for trouble."

A third figure had joined them. Frank

Singer was an archaeologist who at the turn of the century had worked with Arthur Evans on the Minoan discoveries at Knossos, and grown fat on this tenuous claim to glory. He sat beside them. "Who is asking for trouble?"

"Farringdon is thinking of marrying his nice little secretary."

Singer, who knew of Nancy only by hearsay, studied Aubrey briefly. "Bit rum that, isn't it?"

Lang regarded Aubrey, enjoying his embarrassment. "Well, why not?" he decided suddenly. "You've become too much of a dry old intellectual, Farringdon. A bit of fresh blood will brighten your failing years — now that your travelling days are done," he added with a touch of malice.

A dry old intellectual? His travelling years over? Was that how others saw him? wondered Aubrey. Was that perhaps how Miss Gallimore saw him too? "I may not have travelled for some time, but I hope I still have something to offer."

"Times are changing," said Lang. "A fellowship from the Geographical was a different thing twenty years ago. Travel was taken seriously in your day; mine too. The world at our feet. Cover as much untrodden territory as you could before anyone else got there. And not just for Empire, but the advancement of science. Now, it's all been done before and, in any case, everyone has always been more interested in colonisation than knowledge."

"You'll never hold on to her, of course." Singer returned to the subject of Nancy. The remark was made without reference to Aubrey's first wife, for he had managed to keep that bad business from most of his London friends.

"Young girl. Older man. It's a classic case," said Lang.

Singer flicked Aubrey a rare smile. "Hopeless, I'm afraid."

Aubrey was suddenly tired of their cynicism. He thanked them wryly for their advice and, leaving the club, decided to walk home rather than take a motor cab. Was he getting past it? He was forty-four. Not very old, when one considered his position in society, yet to a lively girl of eighteen he must seem like an old man. He saw younger men all around him, energetic, sharply aggressive-looking young men, who would have no vivid memories of Victoria and Gladstone, Mafeking night or streets without motor cars; he had married Augusta when these young bloods were still babes in arms; he had a daughter, who would in a year or two become a young woman, and a son almost as old as he had been when he first climbed Mont Blanc and drank champagne on its summit. He wanted to stop these young men in their tracks and tell them: when I was your age I made a two-year tour of North Africa dressed in native costume; I have explored the malarial swamps of the Niger and made contact with cannibals; I have had boiled eggs for my breakfast in the crater of Vesuvius.

Was he past it? Travel was such a demanding business. There was all the expense of setting up an expedition, the tiresome procedure of hiring ships and men and the endless planning required. How much easier it was to feed on one's memories, to write about it all and pass on one's experiences to the next generation.

The next generation. Nancy Gallimore. "You'll never hold on to her," Singer had promised. The remark had hurt because of Augusta; Nancy too was a girl who might be difficult to hold down. Why should she agree to marry him? Aubrey knew he looked his age. He was cultured, which women seemed to find attractive, and he had not been short of female company of his own class since Augusta's death, but he was respected in learned rather than society circles these days, not exactly a prize catch. He reached the tall, sooty brick house and thought of his life before Nancy had entered it: he knew he could not exist without her. The decision had already been made.

* * *

I am in love with him, thought Nancy as she read Aubrey's opening notes to his book on ancient religions, a summary of the Pharaohs: *no humility*, *no restraint*, *no deep concept of a spiritual life*. It was the very antithesis of Aubrey himself. She adored his old-fashioned qualities of a Christian gentleman, his self-control, his depth of genius. She was in love with his fine brain, his culture and brilliance, and all the experiences he had acquired which she could never hope to have.

He had said she might take his notes home to read at her lodgings. It was good to have something to warm her thoughts in the evenings. The room was chilly and Kentish Town pretty bleak. She could hear the workings of the plumbing in every corner of the building; the windows rattled too when the traffic passed. The house always smelled of cooking and drains, and the horrid brown curtain at the door of her room cut out none of the draughts, nor the sound of her landlady on the stairs. Mrs Rucinska had a habit of evening wandering, devised to discourage gentlemen callers; but there was only one gentleman Nancy would have wanted to call on her, and he was far too proper to suggest such a thing.

She allowed herself to dream a little, curling deep into the armchair and fingering the thin gold chain which she always wore round her neck. She thought of his strong, handsome face and perfectly structured body. To be desired by a man like Aubrey Farringdon! To be permanently in his presence. Wouldn't that be glorious! She would want nothing in return except his love. Nancy flung down the notes on the Pharaohs in momentary despair. This inner rigidity of his was his only flaw, if flaw there could be in such a perfect human being. Aubrey Farringdon was so honourable that the very idea of her wanting him to desire her would probably shock him to the core. When she told him she had read almost every one of his articles on West Africa he had been surprised — pleased certainly, and flattered by her admiration; but he had suggested, gently, that perhaps her mother should have encouraged her to divert her energies into ladylike accomplishments such as music and drawing. He thought Mary Kingsley, whose *Travels in West Africa* and *West African Studies* Nancy had also read, 'rather unwomanly', and the legendary Isabella Eberhardt, who had lived the life of a vagabond, dressed like a boy among the African desert tribes, 'very peculiar'. "I never met her," he said when Nancy asked him about this Amazon of the Sands, "but she *was* an authority on the desert." He made it clear that he did not entirely approve of women who tried to compete with men.

Nancy stretched and went to the window. Outside, on the pavement, figures walked purposefully, drawn to the public house on their way home from work. She let the curtain fall again, aware that she could be seen from the street and that peering from lighted windows was not genteel. Sometimes she wished she had been born a man, not only a man but a real gent. What if she had studied the Classics alongside Aubrey and had gained a fellowship at Oxford? Then he would consider her his equal. Or to have been born rich enough to be allowed to be eccentric — instead of coming from a town where lower middle-class respectability had allowed little latitude in women's behaviour. She might have learned to hunt and fish and to climb mountains; she could have travelled in Africa, or South America, without being thought 'peculiar'. Sometimes, when she was alone, Nancy would adopt a deliberately unfeminine pose. She did so now, striding about the room and falling again into the easy chair with her legs over the arm, her skirts riding up her calves. She wriggled and slid her body down in the chair. To be married to a famous traveller! To be adored by Aubrey! Aubrey. She closed her eyes, imagining how he would propose to her: Nancy, I worship you. Say you'll marry me or I shall go insane with desire. And her response — Yes, oh yes, my love. He would enfold her in his arms, his lips would meet hers in a kiss of such passion that they would lose all sense of time. She felt her breath rise in her breast and her body grow tense with wanting. Her thoughts were not very clear as to the specifics of what she wanted, but she was alive to an intensely sexual sensation and knew that only Aubrey Farringdon with his strong hands, his heroic looks and athletic, much-travelled limbs could satisfy her need.

★ ★ ★

So it was, the next morning, that when Aubrey left his desk to stand beside her and in a hoarse voice asked her to be his wife, Nancy's breath once more rose dramatically in her breast. True, he had not said that he desired her madly, passionately. What he in fact said was, "Miss Gallimore. You would make me very happy if you would consider the idea of marriage."

Nancy's hand flew to her throat and the gold chain which her mother had given her. "Would you mind repeating that?"

Aubrey's knees had begun to tremble. He sank to the worn carpet beside the chair where she had been typing the first batch of his notes on the Egyptians. "I mean to say, Miss Gallimore, that I would consider myself a very fortunate man if you would consent to be my wife."

She turned towards him. His face was on a level with the pleated jabot of her blouse, his hand rested hesitantly on the coarse dark cloth of her skirt. She could feel the heat of it through the serge and her love for him was almost a pain. "You really want to marry me?"

He nodded. He was incapable of uttering another word and there was no need, for she pressed his head passionately against her breast, filled with the masculine scent of him, feeling the cold, slightly greasy cloth of his coat under her hand and the firm muscle of his shoulder. "Yes, oh yes, my love!" She held him tightly, the buttons of his waistcoat pressing into her thigh, and they remained locked and immobile, Nancy's joy swelling to a pitch which became almost intolerable.

At last Aubrey clambered to his feet. He fiddled with some papers on his desk, more agitated than she had ever seen him. "Well now, we must settle on a date."

"I still can't believe you've asked me." She pressed her hands to her hot cheeks. "Why, only last night . . . Oh, Aubrey — do I call you Aubrey now?"

He laughed, delighted with her and with himself. He began to pace the room, unable to keep still. "I, for my part, can't believe that someone so fresh and innocent and beautiful could actually love an old fuddy-duddy like me."

"Now I won't argue with 'fuddy-duddy'." She turned to the typewriter and handed him a sheet of the freshly corrected manuscript. "Your prose style, Aubrey, leaves much to be desired. Jumbled ideas all crammed into long sentences, thoughts just following on, clause after clause." She affected a briskness, but the violence of her feelings still threatened to burst from her in an explosion of energy.

Aubrey laughed out loud. He ran a hand through his hair. "You hussy! Who is it has been trying to improve your style these past weeks! You dare to presume to teach an English gentleman English style?"

Nancy was serious for a moment, struck by the full momentum of what had taken place. She was going to marry the great and celebrated Aubrey Farringdon. She was the most fortunate woman in all the world. "You know I shall always be your pupil," she said gravely. "How could I ever presume to live up to your brilliance?"

* * *

Their relationship altered in barely definable ways during their engagement. Nancy perhaps allowed a degree of more robust tenderness to enter her secretarial duties; this revealed itself in the way she now corrected his manuscripts. Aubrey would come across scribbled notes in the margins: "I'm sure it would read better thus, my darling . . . " or, "I think what you mean to say is . . . " and even, "I love you, I love you, I love you, but do you really want a paragraph that stretches over three pages!" These messages charmed him, though he found them unsettling: his text on the Pharaohs was hardly the place for frivolous comment. Aubrey had an ambiguous attitude to his own education and knowledge. On the one hand he considered himself to be modest about his achievements; he accepted without any undue sense of pride that he was a scholar and an authority in numerous fields of learning. On the other hand he knew that he was far superior to Nancy. Yet Nancy, although she acknowledged his brilliance, rarely acted with a proper humility. She chatted boldly with his friends in her flat Yorkshire accent, telling them how he was 'ironing her out', and was at ease with friends like Gilbert Lang. But he tolerated her lack of discretion; he would have tolerated anything, so infatuated was he by her. How good she was for him, and how rewarding it was to take her on as his pupil. He enjoyed telling her about his time in Arabia, that place of mystery and adventure. She hung on his descriptions of geese and flamingoes, of burning desert sand and cool palm trees and the sound of water-wheels. She said she could see the colours and smell the heat when he talked and that she did not believe him when he said it was she who had brought colour into his life. She was so bright, she flickered like a butterfly round a flower, taking one sip of knowledge here, one there, hardly resting for more than a moment before she was ready to move on to something else. Sometimes a spasm of fear would seize his heart and he would remember the warning of his friends and a cold, small voice in his head repeated, "You'll never keep her."

* * *

Aubrey first took Nancy to see Midwinter on a day in late September, when a silver-grey mist cloaked the fields. His pulse quickened with anxiety as the car drove from Winchborne and through the wood which lay to the north-west of the estate. Though the pool was hidden down among the trees, painful memories hit him hard under the ribs.

Nancy took his hand in her own. "Is something wrong?" Her grey eyes were serious and concerned. "You look so grim, my darling."

He shook off the mood with an effort. "It's nothing. Absolutely nothing at all." And it was true, he told himself as the car bowled down the hill and entered the green acres of the Midwinter Hall estate. Augusta had been dead more than ten years, and Viner was in the Far East, probably grown wealthy by now on his pay-offs for 'disappearing'. Viner had agreed — what was it? — *never to darken Midwinter's doors again*. Aubrey allowed a bitter smile to touch his lips as the car drew to a halt. Had his mama really said that? How very melodramatic. But then, melodrama was his mother's style.

The domestics had lined up outside the front door to receive their future mistress in the traditional way. Aubrey breathed a deep sigh of satisfaction. Only now did he realise how much he had missed Midwinter. Here were the collections which were a validation of his life's work: here was the study where he had worked as a young man, and the trophies which reminded him of his travelling years. He had wanted to see Nancy in Midwinter's perfect setting. There was a sense of timelessness and continuity in a house in which a family had lived for two generations. He wanted her to experience that atmosphere. Later, when they were married and she grew to love the house as he did, they would forget the past and settle here and Nancy would lose some of her outspoken ways, which, charming though they were, seemed altogether too brash for Midwinter.

"It's all so grand and formal," breathed Nancy as she climbed from the car and linked her hand in the crook of his arm. She seemed amused by the ceremony of the domestics. Aubrey, though he smiled, felt a trace of irritation: she was going to have to learn to take things far more seriously. The dogs ran out from the hall on to the steps, and she cried, "Oh, the darlings! Aubrey — spaniels! You never told me!" She bent down and let the dogs fawn upon her, ignoring the watchful gaze of the servants. His mother came out to stand on the steps with the children, whose autumn school-terms had not yet begun. Hugo looked tall and sunburnt. Connie, pale-skinned even after a summer spent out of doors, stood frowning through her spectacles and biting her lip, and still showed no promise of the grace Augusta had possessed. How splendid his mama looked, dressed in a dark frock and with her silver hair swept high on her head. She had been extremely beautiful when she was young and was, in her sixties, still an elegant woman.

Nancy straightened, and the dogs, wagging their tails, wandered over to Hugo.

"So this is your fiancée." Mrs Farringdon kissed Nancy, as women do, brushing the air with her lips in a cool embrace. The children shook Nancy's hand very formally, and then Aubrey felt his mama's cheek against his own and her brittle shoulders under his hands. "Aubrey, darling." She drew him into the familiar, enveloping gloom of the house.

* * *

I shall never forget my first visit to Midwinter, Nancy wrote in her diary. I detested it at first sight, from its long colonnade of pillars and the flat grey stones to its empty, empty windows. The servants were all lined up in the shadows under the entrance, in their long aprons over stiff dresses; the men in grim uniforms, like soldiers inspecting the new recruit. The only congenial creatures were Aubrey's spaniels, who welcomed me like an old friend, but his mother and children regarded me with so much suspicion. How archaic it all is, and steeped in tradition. There is no electricity at all upstairs, and the bedrooms are lighted by brass lamps and candles, while downstairs the lights flicker and dim because of 'problems with the generator', which is a constant topic of conversation between Aubrey and his mother. The hallway is carpeted with deer skins, and the walls lined with family portraits, which look down disapprovingly at this foolhardy interloper. Aubrey's father made his fortune from rubber and it was he who bought the house. Mrs Farringdon relates her husband's history as if it has made one supreme contribution to Britain's eminence: he was a consultant to the British government in the Far East. At the age of thirty-eight he had done so well for himself that he retired to Dorset. Let British eminence take care of itself. Aubrey says the family have 'investments' in rubber and other commodities abroad. His father was an author, like Aubrey, and used to address the Royal Geographical, though he was not so celebrated as my darling.

How clever and learned they all are. And how small that makes me feel, and Mrs Farringdon wants me to feel, because I'm sure she doesn't care at all for Aubrey marrying so far beneath him.

Everywhere, on the staircases, in the drawing room, the dining room and even

Mrs Farringdon's sitting room, where she invited me to have tea with her, there are the trophies of Aubrey's travels abroad. There is an armoury of spears and clubs, axes and blowpipes, and swords ready to drop on an unwary head. Mrs Farringdon related the history and purpose of each instrument while pouring weak tea from a silver pot and handing me the thinnest potted meat sandwiches you ever saw, which my own mother would have been ashamed to offer to anyone. I longed for Aubrey to return, which he did after half an hour. When I cried "Oh, there you are!" his mother pursed her lips very disagreeably and said, "My dear Nancy, I hope you are not going to be one of those wives who expect constant attention." She and I have got off to a bad start.

The corridors present an ornithological museum: case after case of fulmars and petrels, shearwaters, falcons, ospreys and harriers, one with a little duck between its claws. And the ducks, the poor ducks, stuffed not for dinner, which was a grisly affair of liver and boiled rice and would not keep a canary alive, but preserved in the interests of science: shelducks, teal and widgeon.

In the library sits a collection of fossils — all kinds of fishy creatures. I am dazzled by the extent of it all and at my own darling's vast learning. He is so much cleverer than anyone I have known, but I cannot say I feel comfortable here. I am half starved for want of a decent supper, and the house is just like a mausoleum.

I cannot help but wonder about his first wife. Her portrait hangs in the drawing room. This was a shock to me, I must admit, because, when Aubrey told me about Augusta and the Foul Deed, I supposed she had run off with her lover and left Aubrey and her children in the lurch. Now I discover that she saw the error of her ways and that the lover was bribed to go off to Java or Malaya or somewhere else on the other side of the earth and Augusta stayed at Midwinter until she died.

From a broken heart? But it strikes me Aubrey forgave her. She was very beautiful and he *is* the forgiving kind. I am half afraid he might even cherish fond memories . . .

* * *

"May I come in?"

She had not heard Aubrey's knock at the door.

"What are you writing?"

She closed the diary hurriedly and swung round from the table by the long velvet window curtains to face him. He still wore his evening clothes from dinner and looked very debonair and relaxed as he walked towards her, his face a little flushed from after dinner port.

"It's my diary. I have almost always kept one, right from being a little girl." She was surprised to see him; since their engagement he had always made a point of behaving very correctly. She hoped his mother knew that he had come to her room. She had changed into a Japanese silk robe, his engagement present to her. The gown was soft and graceful and she was conscious of being very alluring in it.

His smile was amused. He was prepared to indulge her any little habit such as keeping a diary.

She swung her body back to the table. "Do you mind?"

He bent down to kiss her neck, running his hands across her shoulders and pinioning her with his arms. "What a funny girl you are, Nancy."

"I don't want to keep anything a secret from you." But she did, she thought as she turned her face to kiss him, for if he asked her to read what she had written, could she honestly tell him that she had immediately hated Midwinter with its miles of draughty corridors and dark, unwelcoming rooms. "Did Augusta keep a diary?"

His grip slackened. "I really couldn't say. If she did, I never saw it."

"Not when she died?"

"Mama dealt with her personal effects."

"Do you mind me talking about Augusta?"

"A little."

"Because you loved her so much — or because of what happened?"

"Nancy . . ."

She pulled his arms round her again, "Please. We have to be absolutely honest with one another."

"All right. To please you. I loved Augusta very much, but things she did hurt me badly and that's why I mind your talking about her."

"She looks so beautiful in her portrait downstairs."

He held her close again. "I promise you, whatever you see in her portrait, she was not so beautiful in spirit as you." His hands moved from her shoulders to her neck and he caressed the skin where the gold chain rested at her throat. She turned her head and pressed her face against his shirt and could feel his body tremble and his breath grow more uneven. She closed her eyes, her desire for him mounting swiftly as it always did when he touched her. "Aubrey, do you have to go?"

He hesitated, his fingers lingered against her throat, then he withdrew his hand slowly. "Forgive me. I should not have come to your room."

She reached for his hand and held it, pressing his fingers passionately to her mouth. "Two whole months . . . "

"It will pass quickly, my love. And then we shall be man and wife." He bent and kissed her tenderly. He was again composed. "Good night, my darling."

He went to the door.

Nancy stilled her disappointment. He was so wise, so *right* about everything. "Aubrey . . . "

He turned with a questioning smile.

"I'm so glad we're going to live in London when we are married."

3

"SO he really has gone through with it." Frank Singer read the announcement from *The Times*. "I'm not surprised he has not wanted to make much of it. Not the sort of thing one is likely to feel too confident about." Singer folded the newspaper. "Farringdon has an exceedingly good brain. Fine classicist, good family, splendid fellow and all that. Then he goes and marries a chit of a girl with neither class, money nor breeding. It's beyond my understanding."

"It's out of character that he should lose his head," agreed Lang. "But Nancy's no ordinary fortune-hunter. She's a clever little thing and rather lovely. And it was she who wanted a quiet wedding." Lang felt a stab of envy, for Farringdon's reputation as a geographer would last long after his own, and everybody, men and women, seemed to come under the man's spell. A room of people, however crowded, would always fall silent in deference to his opinions. He wooed people unconsciously, and he had that allure of power and authority which women found irresistible. Women like Nancy. Women like Augusta.

"I've always thought there was something cold about Farringdon, that he was too much of an intellectual beneath the good fellow impression," said Singer.

"I remember his first wife," Lang replied enigmatically.

"I thought you were too young to have been with the set that went to Dorset."

"I was invited now and then. I was very green, but I remember being knocked for six by Augusta. They had a party after Mafeking." Lang knew Singer was right about Farringdon being a cold fish. He remembered the glitter of that evening, charged with an atmosphere of intense emotion and the strong sexual attraction of the women in their low-cut gowns and frou-frou. He remembered Augusta, glowing with some inner current of excitement all her own, and Farringdon in the midst of them, the perfect host, yet quite calm, quite unmoved by it all.

Lang glanced at Singer. "Did you ever meet John Viner?"

Singer shook his head. "Traveller? Scholar?"

"Of a sort. Bit dubious as to pedigree. He collected butterflies."

"Don't they say Farringdon has a good collection?"

"Viner acquired much of it for him," Lang hesitated. "Viner developed a theory that there is a Roman villa buried on Farringdon's estate."

"Good Lord."

"Thought you'd be interested."

"I'll say."

"Of course, I don't know what real evidence he had."

"I shall tackle Farringdon about it. Perhaps he'll let me have a look."

"I'll put in a good word," said Lang. "I've been invited to dinner next week."

* * *

Nancy enjoyed giving dinner parties in London for Aubrey's colleagues and their wives. "I want to meet all your friends, now I'm your wife," she said when he protested that they were entertaining too frequently. "I feel my lack of culture. I need to get thoroughly mixed in with all these knowledgeable people so that I don't shame you."

"But I shall teach you all you want to know," he said, laughing at her eagerness. He was tutoring her in Latin: in the evenings they studied grammar and the declension of Latin nouns. This evening he was teaching her syntax.

"An adjective agrees in number, gender and case with the substantive to which it is attached. Thus, *Cara est mia patria*, dear is my native land; *habeo multos equos*, I have many horses."

"Do you have many horses?"

"Nancy, I made the remark purely for the sake of an example."

"But do you? Do you ride? Aubrey, there are so many things I still don't know about you."

"Yes, I ride. But we have fewer horses at Midwinter than in the old days."

"Perhaps we could ride."

"At Midwinter?"

"No, here. In Rotten Row. With all the swells."

"I didn't know you could."

Had she detected a trace of condescension? "I learned on a farm. My mother's family were seafarers but my father's family were farming people. Did I never tell you?"

"Nancy, the Latin lesson," he reminded her gently.

Nancy pulled a face. "*Cara est lingua latina*. Dear is the latin tongue."

"Perhaps we could ride together at Midwinter. I should like that," he said, wanting to appease her.

"Do you think I should sit well — considering how I learned on a cart horse?" she laughed.

He kissed her. "My darling, you will always look perfectly adorable."

They returned to the business of syntax, but Nancy felt disappointed. It occurred to her that Aubrey rarely asked her about her childhood or her family or even about the town where she had grown. It was as if her background was no longer of any consequence now he had begun to mould her to the role of his wife. His lack of curiosity hurt her a little, for she wanted to know all she could about his own experiences, every detail of his childhood, his favourite books, pastimes and heroes and what had forged his culture and brilliance.

She quizzed Gilbert Lang at dinner about what Aubrey had been like as a young man.

"Aubrey has never been a young man," laughed Gilbert. "He has always been ancient and venerable, ever since I have known him."

"Which is how long?" pressed Nancy.

"Oh — twelve, fifteen years." He leaned towards her confidentially and rested his chin in his hand with one elbow on the table. Nancy glanced at Gilbert's female companion. Marjorie Benson was an amateur botanical painter, a woman of thirty or so and of 'tremendous patience', Aubrey had said. Marjorie raised her eyes heavenwards, and it occurred to Nancy that Gilbert was a little drunk. "I was a mere boy when Aubrey was establishing his renowned collections at his country seat in Dorset."

Marjorie said with mild asperity, "Gilbert darling, when will you not be a mere boy in comparison with Aubrey?" She turned to Nancy. "Now, tell me. How do you like married life, and are you getting Aubrey out of his dreary routine?"

"I try." Nancy threw Aubrey an adoring look. "But it is an uphill battle."

"Nancy has taken ten years off me," Aubrey declared. "And everyone loves her."

"Of course they do. We all love her," said Marjorie.

Nancy laughed. "Everyone spoils me. And Aubrey worst of all. I've told him he must leave over buying me presents. Do you know he's bought a piano and fixed up a music tutor? And he spends money outrageously on the most beautiful and fashionable clothes." She looked down at the gauze tunic dress which Aubrey had chosen for her; it was printed with poppies and flared, in a kind of lampshade fashion, over a gown of clinging bright blue silk. She felt sophisticated and graceful and she knew the gown suited her, but she found it very shocking to spend so much on clothes; it was not easy to discard the habit of learning to dress on a small budget. She took a swallow of wine and confessed to Gilbert, "Even the servants spoil me. Aubrey's housekeeper, Mrs Mason, won't let me lift a finger. She says she knows all the master's wants by now without I need tell her anything." She let the manservant refill her glass and paused to take another swallow of wine. It was smooth and heavy; she rolled its fruity flavour on her tongue to savour it. "This household is becoming very democratic, I'm glad to say. There's none of your bowing and scraping and giving orders from on high like they have at Midwinter. Which suits me down to the ground, Gilbert, since I'm not right struck with being lady of the manor. Aubrey teases me that I shall have to get used to it one of these days, but I don't see why things shouldn't continue just as they do now."

Aubrey watched Nancy. She was such a child over everything. So natural and vibrant, yet with so much still to learn about his way of life. She looked beautiful in the Bakst design he had chosen for her. She could have rivalled any of the current society beauties, but with none of their tired archness. Her hair framed her lovely face, piled into a luxuriant halo of dark glossy waves. He felt an unanticipated surge of desire for her and was impatient with the evening, wanting it to end. He remembered their wedding night: it had been so long since he had made love to a woman and Nancy was so innocent and open to him, so sweet and unresisting. When it was over she lay for a long time, then told him in a clear and childlike voice that she loved him. He had been overjoyed that his advances did not repel her and that their life was to be one of harmony in every possible respect. He smiled to himself, recalling how he went to his club these days with a spring in his heels, how he made the dusty halls of the British Museum ring as he loudly hailed people to whom he had once only gravely nodded a greeting.

He brought his thoughts back to the present. The dinner was not going as well as usual. Lang had been tipsy when he arrived and had proceeded to drink too much wine during the evening. Now Nancy was tipsy as well, and had slipped back into her north country way of talking. She would learn with time, he told himself, but he wished she was not so amused by Lang's boorishness and that she did not respond to his flirting. Lang should know better. It was such bad form, and it left him to make conversation with Marjorie Benson. Marjorie, as always, looked the discreet and good-natured woman she was; handsome rather than beautiful, in a dark velvet gown which complemented her black hair and high complexion. It was time Lang settled down.

The conversation had almost ground to a halt and Marjorie was looking strained. All at once Nancy rescued the situation with a wicked and less than tactful reference to one of his own stories about Riyadh, where smoking tobacco and drinking alcohol were cardinal offences. Marjorie warmed to her and smiled, and Aubrey breathed a sigh of satisfaction: his apprehension had been groundless, for Nancy had such a splendid knack of winning people over. He remembered with nostalgia the high towers, the palm trees and fertile gardens of Riyadh, and he felt his heart expand as Nancy turned to him and said, "Aubrey never fails to stir up my imagination when he tells me stories about his travels. Don't you think he must have looked romantic in a burnous?"

"Did you really go about dressed in a burnous?" said Marjorie. "How frightfully dashing, Aubrey."

"It's the only practical garment," he asserted. "I shouldn't care to try weathering a desert storm in western dress."

"The Simun." Lang slurred his words. "The most deadly Arabian wind. It comes out of nowhere. First a burning blue sky, next a heaviness in the air and then it strikes."

"Heavens! Whatever does one do?" Nancy laughed.

"You wrap your head in your burnous and crouch low over the neck of your camel. Nothing else for it but to sit it out."

Aubrey frowned. It was a tale he liked to tell. If Lang had experienced the life of the Bedouins at all, it was secondhand, through the writings of men like himself, for Lang's own travel experiences had been restricted to the Gold Coast. But

Lang had abruptly lost interest in the desert. He turned to Aubrey and, with the sudden clarity of the very drunk said, "I was telling Singer about the archaeological find at your place in Dorset. Why don't you let him have a dig around?"

Aubrey stared. He had forgotten that Lang would know that old story. "It was only a theory."

"What sort of archaeological find?" queried Nancy.

"Not a find exactly," said Aubrey. "Someone once suggested there might be Roman remains on the estate."

"How exciting," said Marjorie.

"Perhaps. To an archaeologist. But since the area is very nicely wooded and provides good pheasant cover, I'm none too keen on anyone digging it up."

"Leave the past alone?" said Lang.

Aubrey sipped his wine. "Yes," he said quietly. "Leave the past alone."

* * *

Nancy lay on the bed in her silk nightgown and watched Aubrey undress, impatient for the touch of his body when he slipped down beside her and they could burrow beneath the sheets.

"I hope Lang didn't upset you," said Aubrey. "He's a very decent fellow when he's sober, but he doesn't always know how to behave."

"Not at all. I like him. I like them both. I found the whole evening very amusing."

"Amusing?" Aubrey frowned. "I don't think Marjorie found him very funny."

"Rot. She's the type who would be quite taken with the idea of managing him. Anyone can tell he's a nice man really." She rolled over and wriggled into the bed, holding back the sheet for him. "Tell me again about the Simun."

Aubrey turned out the light and lay down beside her. She wound her legs about him comfortably. How magnificent he must have looked in Arab costume: she pictured him in red leather boots and a coloured head-cloth tied with an elegant band. He caressed her shoulder, holding her close, yet restraining her a little. She sensed that he did not like her to be too eager for him, that a sweet passivity fitted more his image of her as an innocent child. "Patience," Aubrey murmured against her shoulder, and she moved her hand away from him in obedience. "What do you want to hear, my little love?"

"Tell me about the eye of the storm, when the air grows hotter and hotter."

He caressed her breast lightly. "The sky darkens to a heavy purple colour. As the storm approaches the camels turn in circles and prepare to lie down. A stifling blast begins to blow, but the eye of the storm itself is almost totally free from turmoil."

She closed her eyes. "What is it like?" she whispered.

He lifted her nightdress and moved on top of her. "A still heat." He pushed himself inside her. "Like a red hot fire slowly passing through one, before the blast begins again."

She did not cry out at her own rising passion, for she had learned that he preferred her silence, and soon her own need was eclipsed by the gathering urgency of his movements. She was the eye of the Simun, the stillness at the centre of the storm: she tried to slow his impatience, to let their movements become languorous, but his own rhythm was never calm. He climaxed with short jerks, as if he wanted the storm to be done with as quickly as possible, to feel again the sun in a calm blue sky and the clarity of the desert. He lifted himself from her and Nancy lay unsated, aware that something had been missing but not knowing what it was.

"I have been thinking we should consider living at Midwinter," Aubrey said after a while, when she had thought that he was sleeping. "The children see so little of me. And it's very hard on Mama, having to run the estate on her own."

"Hugo and Connie are at school in term-time," Nancy murmured. "They can always come up to London to see us. And your mother has a farm manager and her servants. Even without them, I should think she could run Midwinter backwards. I expect she held the reins even when your father was alive."

"Nevertheless . . . "

After a while she said, "Are you going

to give in and let Frank Singer look for Roman remains?"

He hesitated. "I think not."

"If we live there, perhaps you will change your mind."

"If we live there, Nancy, I hope you will discourage Singer from intruding on Midwinter's solitude as strongly as I shall."

He rolled away from her and soon his breathing became slow and even. Nancy stared into the darkness at the invisible ceiling. She remembered Aubrey's recent hints that she would one day have to get used to Midwinter, and realised that he had been planning to live there all along.

In the end he admitted as much. "The time feels right, Nancy," he said the next morning. "You've given me a sense of starting all over again. At last I can forget the unhappiness of the past — and my proper place is there, it always has been."

She said that for his sake she would do whatever he wanted. And perhaps it will work out, she wrote in her diary. So, what if his mama is a tyrant and his children are hostile brats? I've faced worse, when my darling mother died and I was without a friend in the world, and I wasn't beaten by all that.

* * *

From the moment they arrived, one dark day in February, Nancy felt the oppression of Midwinter. The land around the house was low-lying and, according to Aubrey, damp was a perpetual problem. It should have been built on higher ground to the west, he said, except that the architect had placed a lot of faith in symmetry, from the rows of identical windows in the precisely measured east and west wings, to the fact that the house lay at the exact centre of the estate, some thirty to forty acres of garden, farmland and woodland.

They drove past the farm, the workers' cottages and the kitchen gardens. The Wolseley's wheels crunched the gravel and swept alongside the stables to the pillared front of the house. Nancy watched the chauffeur unload their luggage and squared her shoulders as

Aubrey's mother came down the staircase to the hallway to greet them.

Nancy guessed that Mrs Farringdon had planned her descent with care, dressed in a black velvet gown embroidered with jet beads, with tight cuffs and a graceful sweep to the hem of the skirt as it lightly trailed on the stair. "I was not expecting you so soon. We shall have tea in the drawing room when you have refreshed yourselves and unpacked."

Nancy washed quickly in the bedroom which her mother-in-law had chosen for her. In London she and Aubrey had shared a bedroom, but here, Aubrey explained without meeting her eyes, things were arranged differently.

She laid out a set of ivory brushes, which Aubrey had given her, on the vast dressing table, and hung up a few of her dresses, leaving the rest for the maids to put away. It was not an ugly room, but neither was it inviting, with its heavy furniture and dark curtains, despite a view across the gardens to the south. There was a strange smell, a mixture of new paint from the cream-coloured walls and stale pot-pourri, which filled two huge Chinese jars on either side of the stone fireplace. Nancy changed into an afternoon gown of soft blue wool and, without waiting for Aubrey to come from his own room, she left the bedroom and hurried downstairs.

The main drawing room was empty. A silver tea-service stood on a low table near the fireplace, a tea-kettle, steaming lightly, simmered on its spirit burner. Nancy hugged her arms about her and went to the vast fireplace where a small pile of logs burned in the grate. Beneath her feet sprawled a lion skin, a trophy of one of Aubrey's father's hunting expeditions in Africa; its yellow teeth were bared in a forlorn snarl. She placed one foot on its head, imitating the stance of a big game hunter, and surveyed her new home without enthusiasm, thinking of the comfortable sitting room in Bloomsbury, over which she had begun to exert an influence, with bright chintzes and rugs to replace the threadbare carpets. The overall impression at Midwinter was of muddy-coloured sofas and marble-topped tables, of heavy carving, on the chairs and in the panelling which lined the walls, and of 'things' — there were the collections, of course, but also things made of wood, things made of brass, numerous ugly clocks and pictures, heavy ceramics, and old or outlandish musical instruments.

The room was enormous. It was scented with pot-pourri, but nothing could mask the smell of decay and of old furniture. A large Japanese jar, filled with spring flowers, provided one of the few uplifting aspects in the room, along with the bright, 'dragonfly' Tiffany shades on the electric table-lamps.

One of the spaniels wandered in from the hall and nuzzled round her foot. Nancy bent and patted its head. She looked at the spirit stove. "What do you think? Do I dare make myself a cup of tea?" She touched the cold white marble of the fireplace, above which hung a pair of heavily tasselled spears; two narrow showcases of stuffed birds almost filled the mantelshelf. Nancy turned as Mrs Farringdon came into the room. She removed her foot from the lion's skull, and the dog lay down by the fire.

"Ah, I see you've been admiring the birds."

Nancy glanced again at the glass cases. "They are . . . very pretty." The birds were tropical species, small and exotically coloured, arranged as if flitting among the once brilliant flowers of their habitat. They looked pitiful in their glass prison.

"You didn't wait for Aubrey?"

"I thought it might be warmer downstairs." Nancy spread her hands to the feebly flickering logs, adding silently that she had been wrong.

To the left of the fireplace hung the portrait of Augusta. She was very fine, Nancy mentally conceded. Good bones. A lot of fair hair. The sort of beauty Sargent had favoured in his paintings of society women, haughty and proud-bosomed. She watched Aubrey's mother pour tea from the silver service and guessed that Augusta would not have been in awe of her mother-in-law. The woman of the portrait seemed at home here among the massive furniture and the grandiose museum pieces of the house.

At that moment Aubrey came into the room. "Ah, so there you are." There was an echo of his mother's accusation, a suggestion in his tone that he had been looking for her.

Nancy repeated that she had come in search of a fire.

"Fires in the bedrooms make a great deal of dust and dirt and extra work for the servants," said Mrs Farringdon. "And coal is expensive. As you, Nancy, will no doubt appreciate."

Nancy understood the snub. She raised her eyebrows at Aubrey and did not attempt a reply.

Aubrey smiled and, rubbing his hands together, said placatingly, "Ah — tea."

"I expect it will take some time for you to get used to our ways, Nancy," Mrs Farringdon said. There was no suggestion of kindness in the remark.

Nancy searched Augusta's features, the confident half-smile, the beautiful hair and bones and wide-spaced eyes. The chill of the room made her shiver, and she felt her own confidence suddenly diminish. The sensation was difficult to define: it was less an apprehension than a sapping of vitality, a feeling of being stifled.

4

FINDING the pool had been like discovering a jewel in Aubrey's collections of fossils. Afterwards Nancy thought of its stillness and secrecy with an increasing longing to go there again; it was unreasonable of Aubrey to prevent her from walking there because of something which had happened so long ago. She wondered about the lovers. When she was alone she would stand for minutes at a time before the portrait of Augusta and ask herself why Aubrey's first wife had been unfaithful.

There were afternoons when she rode on the estate, but Aubrey rarely accompanied her: contrary to his promise that they would ride together at Midwinter, he avoided the grounds and preferred to shut himself away in his study.

Nancy usually chose Hugo's horse, a gentle bay called Nelson. Her heart always quickened a little as she neared the wood on the edge of the estate.

When extolling the virtues of Midwinter, Aubrey had concentrated on its more obvious attractions: the tennis court, the stables, the gardens and, from the front of the house, the vista of parkland where she might ride. It was as if the woodland had not existed.

She slowed by the fence, remembering Aubrey's reluctance to let Frank Singer dig there. The trees were dark, dripping with February rain; she bent and patted Nelson's neck, feeling him tremble beneath her. "Don't you like the wood, Nelson?" she whispered. "Do you know about the lovers? Has Radley told you? Do the servants remember the scandal, those oh-so-discreet Midwinter menials?" The wood seemed to be cloaked in mystery beneath its canopy of dripping boughs. Pathways ran through the drifts of leaves, where Nancy could imagine creatures had scuttled in and out around the base of the trees — and the trees themselves — as far as the eye could see, packed themselves closely, sheltering the wood's secrets. How easy it would be to slip along one of the paths and be absorbed by their seclusion. Reluctantly Nancy turned the horse away and rode back to the house.

* * *

The days passed so much more slowly than they had in London; Nancy's life was busy and yet it seemed empty. The house was Aubrey's in name, but his mother had ruled it for years, and she made it clear from the first that she would not relinquish any of her control now that he had returned. Nancy found herself excluded from the daily discussions with the senior household staff and discouraged if she tried to interfere. "You must leave matters to me," Mrs Farringdon said one day after Nancy had given one of the housemaids a letter to take to the village to post. "The girl was delayed a whole half-hour from her duties because of your thoughtlessness. All these little orders and counter-orders are confusing for servants. You only worry them, my dear."

Aubrey looked uncomfortable. "I'm sure Nancy didn't mean to upset the girl, Mama."

"Nevertheless, I think in future she should consult me first if she wishes to burden the servants with extra work."

Aubrey turned to Nancy with a look of inquiry, appealing to her to accommodate his mother's wishes. But why? thought Nancy. Why should he take his mother's side against hers? He smiled. "Nancy?" His soothing manner infuriated her.

She looked away. "It makes no odds. I'll post my own letters next time."

"She's trying to defeat me," Nancy said when Aubrey came to her room later. She sat up in bed and thumped the pillow vigorously before hugging it to her, watching him undress. "She thinks I can be intimidated by her."

"Now, you know that isn't true," Aubrey said mildly. He sat on the bed and stroked her hair from her face. "Mama has an important influence over the servants. She does not want it eroded. They know she is firm and fair."

"Implying I am not?"

He stood and continued to undress. "You are young and not used to Midwinter. The servants like a firm hand. They are worried by informality."

"It didn't worry Mrs Mason in London."
"Well, it worries Midwinter servants."
"I can't believe they think like that." She thumped the pillow again and tossed it behind her. "It's so archaic."
"Then why do they give us such loyal service? No servant would ever dream of questioning Mama's orders."
Nancy laughed in disbelief. "Only because any hint of insubordination would mean instant dismissal." She wriggled down beside him as he climbed into bed. "Aubrey, if I am to become mistress here, some things are going to have to change."
He leaned on one elbow, looking down at her tenderly. "Please tread carefully, my darling. Some of the staff have been with us for years. They are loyal because they know that Mama genuinely cares about their welfare."
"Is that all they get in return for their loyalty — a condescending regard for their welfare?"
"Mama has always given praise where praise is due." Aubrey frowned. "I wish you would try to be friends with her. She only wants to instruct you in the

way things should be done."

He could not see it, thought Nancy in amazement. He really thought it was she who was at fault. She lay in the darkness after he had turned out the oil-lamp and waited for him to touch her. She felt a sullen knot of resentment rise in her chest as he moved his weight on top of her. She turned her head to the pillow, wishing they could talk and resolve the business of his mother first, aware that for the first time she did not want his caresses; she lay like a stone until he rolled away from her and wondered whether he even knew that he had not been welcome.

He put his arm round her and pulled her against him and she rested her face against his neck, breathing the warm familiar smell of him. "You're a wonderful girl, Nancy. Nobody could ask for a sweeter wife." He kissed her sleepily. "I only want you to be happy. I know you're young and lively and it must be boring for you at Midwinter. Just say what you want. Anything."

Nancy was ashamed and pressed her face against his shoulder fiercely, feeling at once a surge of love for him. "I just miss the way things were in London."

He was thoughtful for a while. "Perhaps you miss your piano."

She did not answer, knowing he would not understand if she said that it was not a need for entertainment but Midwinter itself which seemed to threaten their happiness.

"I shall have it brought to Midwinter."

"The piano?"

"Of course. I'll arrange it tomorrow." He turned away from her and his breathing grew heavy and even.

She tried to explain. "I should just like a little more freedom."

"But you are free," he said, half asleep. "You know you are free to do anything you like."

"To go anywhere?"

"Anywhere," he murmured.

She hesitated, afraid of his anger. At last she whispered, "Then let me go to the pool in the wood."

But he was already asleep and did not hear.

* * *

It was true that Midwinter servants were loyal. From the butler Roberts down to the house-boy and Mrs Cassell in the kitchen to the scullery maid, they took a fierce pride in running Midwinter like an efficient, well-oiled machine. As the weeks passed, Nancy grudgingly conceded that they held Mrs Farringdon in genuine respect, if not exactly in affection. Nancy knew that she herself was not popular. The Midwinter staff obeyed all the rules of protocol between mistress and servant, but she detected a resentment beneath their correctness. She was not proper gentry, and they distrusted what they knew of her background. She was 'jumped up'. She had committed the crime of overreaching herself.

Nancy responded by escaping the claustrophobia of the house. She walked to the farm buildings, which reminded her of the Yorkshire farm where she had gone once as a child to help in the hayfield, and where she had first learned to ride the huge farm horses. She wandered in the tangled grass of the orchard or, when it rained, sat with a book in the old summer-house under the apple trees, or she went to the warm-smelling stables where she talked to the horses and Radley, the stableman, who was detached from the prejudices of the indoor staff.

She met Radley one day on the south drive; he was a dour, thick-set man of fifty with hard hands and face but a streak of gentleness in his grey eyes. He rode towards her as she walked past the farmworkers' cottages with their rusted iron fences and long rank grass in the gardens. She picked her way through the mud in her buttoned boots, a spray of hazel catkins in her hand, and Radley reined in his horse. "A fine afternoon, ma'am."

"There's spring in the air, Radley." She glanced behind him to the edge of a copse where a wisp of smoke rose from among the trees.

He followed her glance. "But cold enough still for a fire."

"Are there many more houses on the estate?" Nancy asked, watching the smoke curl against the sky.

"Only Keeper's Cottage."

She turned to him. "Midwinter has a keeper?"

"He doesn't mix much with the other servants."

Nancy paused, wondering briefly why Aubrey maintained a keeper when Midwinter never held a shoot. "Has he been here a long time?"

"Yes, ma'am. I trained Ted Powers as a stable lad when he first worked here. There was a lot more staff in those days."

Nancy felt as if a door had opened a crack upon Midwinter's past, that a world of life and colour might lie just beyond it. "Tell me, Radley. Did Midwinter used to hold shooting weekends?"

"We were known for it, ma'am, in the old master's day."

"And in my husband's time?"

"Yes, ma'am. At least — " he hesitated — "when the first mistress was alive."

"And dinners and parties — were there grand parties?"

He looked uncomfortable. "Best not to talk about the old days. Things are much quieter now, and better that way too, ma'am, maybe."

"But Augusta — my husband's first wife, liked to entertain?" She was sorry for his embarrassment. Of course he knew about Augusta and her lover: Midwinter must have rocked on its foundations with the story when Augusta was discovered with her lover by the pool.

Radley set his mouth and said grimly, "The first mistress entertained a deal too much, ma'am, and that's a fact." He decided he had said more than he should and, flushing deeply, tipped his cap before riding on.

Nancy flicked the catkins in her hand and brushed the dust into her woollen glove. She returned to the house, trying to picture the rooms filled with guests, Augusta receiving them with that enigmatic half smile, and her lover among them. John Viner. A scoundrel, Aubrey had called him, and yet he had once invited him to Midwinter as a friend.

* * *

From her bedroom window, Nancy could see the tops of the trees in the orchard and the gravel paths of the kitchen gardens, sheltered behind their mellow brick walls. Neither Aubrey nor his mother knew that she went to the orchard when she wanted to get away from the house, nor that she talked to Radley in the stables, and to Mortimer in the greenhouses. She preferred the paths between the beds of cabbages and leeks, and the gravel paths of the kitchen gardens to the formal flower borders, the cold grey terrace below Midwinter's windows and the flat expanses of lawn. She liked the warm, mouldy smell of the greenhouses where she watched Mortimer repotting house plants and sometimes helped him, plunging her hands into the rich dark compost, laughing when he said he had never seen any of the family, except young Master Hugo and Miss Connie, get their hands dirty before.

"The first mistress loved flowers," he said one day, watching her cut chrysanthemums for the drawing room.

Nancy paused, then continued snipping the blooms. "You wouldn't entirely condemn her then, Mortimer, with all the rest?"

He considered for a moment, his face furrowed with some recollection. "I'm not saying it wasn't a sin, what she did, but she was always kind to us gardeners. She weren't all bad. I reckon she repented what she did," he added, "or she wouldn't have come to such a sad end."

"A sad end?" Nancy pressed, her curiosity aroused, for Aubrey had told her that Augusta had fallen victim to some sort of wasting disease. "I understood my husband's first wife died after a long illness."

"She lost the will to live, ma'am. It's my notion she died of remorse."

"Yet my husband forgave her," Nancy said, wondering whether Aubrey would have been capable of casting out his wife like some figure from the Old Testament. "He took her back after it was all over." Would he have had to oppose his mother over it, for Mrs Farringdon would surely have rejoiced in pitching Augusta from Midwinter for her crime? Nancy felt a stab of jealousy, remembering how Aubrey always sided with his mother over her own modest sins of omission.

Mortimer looked at her. "Ah — Mr Farringdon's a good Christian man.

Question is — did the poor lady ever forgive herself?"

* * *

Aubrey went downstairs to his study. He saw Nancy through the open doors to the main drawing room and contemplated her slender figure as she knelt on the floor to arrange flowers from the greenhouse. He watched her, half irritated, half amused. The gardener's boy usually did the flowers and, more importantly, he did it without leaving the mess of cut stems which Nancy was scattering liberally on the carpet. Nancy turned as she heard him come into the room. "Aubrey. Were you waiting for me?"

He smiled. "It doesn't matter. When you are ready."

"Don't they look wonderful?" Nancy stood and stepped back to admire the display of brilliantly coloured flowers in the vases.

"Rather bright," Aubrey commented.

"I wanted it to be bright. I'm sick of pastel shades. I asked Mortimer to pick out the colours of the Tiffany lamps. I helped him choose the flowers. He says hardly anyone from the house has taken such a close interest in his greenhouses before." She smiled and knew that Aubrey wanted to ask whether she had his mother's permission to arrange the flowers. She took a perverse pleasure in the fact that his mother had no knowledge of her exploration of the greenhouses. She scooped up the discarded stems, ignoring Aubrey's request that she leave them for the servants and saying, "In London I didn't expect the servants to do every little thing for me. I don't see why I should here."

"Midwinter is different."

"So much so that I might not arrange a few flowers?" She paused, regarding him sadly. "You keep saying I'm free to do as I please, and then I come upon so many petty restrictions."

Aubrey spread his hands apologetically. "You must try to understand how things are done."

"That's what your mother keeps saying. Did Augusta understand how things were done?" She glanced up at the portrait. She saw Aubrey's pained look but she felt unrepentant as she met his gaze. "Aubrey — let me go to the pool again. You can bear to see her portrait on the wall, so why not open up the wood and blow away the ghosts for ever?" She tailed off in confusion, for Aubrey's face had become chalk-white. He opened his mouth to speak, then turned abruptly and left the room.

Nancy followed him to his study. She stood by his desk where he sat with his head bowed over a book, his expression hidden from her.

"I'm sorry. I shouldn't have mentioned Augusta. We'll forget about the pool. I just thought . . ." she made a small, helpless move towards him. "I thought if you really wanted to put the past behind you . . ."

He shook his head and raised a trembling hand as if to brush away her apologies.

"I'm sorry," she repeated.

"It doesn't matter."

Nancy sighed, attempting to lighten the atmosphere between them. "Has it come to this already — bickering over whether or not I should tidy up after arranging a few flowers, or where I may or may not go?"

"It has not come to anything," Aubrey said without looking at her. "I don't know what you mean."

* * *

And yet Aubrey too recognised the increasing distance between them. It was not just because of the pool. He tried to shrug off her fixation with the place, her lack of tact and that dreadful challenge to blow away the ghosts. She was young. How could she know how he had suffered? How could he expect her to understand? He grew calm again as he found solace, as always, in the uncomplicated fascination of his books and notes; yet the question lingered: had he been wrong to think he could come back to Midwinter?

He and Nancy had established a routine, which on the surface worked as well in the country as it had in London. In the mornings Nancy went through his correspondence with him, after which he dictated notes and she would go to the library or one of the sitting rooms and put them in order while he worked on in isolation. In the afternoons and in the hours between tea and dinner, Aubrey read or catalogued his collections and Nancy was left to her own devices: she walked the dogs or rode in the grounds or played her piano which he had fetched from London. She read voraciously; she seemed to want to absorb everything quickly, saying there were so many years of missed learning to recover. If only she and his mama could be friends, it might have been an ideal arrangement, yet his mother found fault at every turn and Nancy complained frequently that Midwinter restricted her.

Aubrey noticed too, with irritation, that a change had come over Nancy's organisation of his work. Her methods, which had been so satisfactory in London, seemed ill-suited to Midwinter. She was too sweeping, expecting him to discard old material, and going at things with bursts of energy which might have been more suited to classifying expedition notes than to arranging research material for a work of serious consideration.

She seemed unwilling to embark on categorising his notes and collections at Midwinter, but increasingly wanted to interfere in his book on ancient religions. She added her own theories, argued points which to him seemed irrefutable, and even suggested he sum up his material on the Pharaohs in one chapter instead of taking three. For the first time he began to question the feasibility of moulding her in the image he had once envisaged.

* * *

Nancy looked out of her window, leaning her arms on the dressing table, recalling Aubrey's anger. To the left, beyond the terrace and green lawns, stretched long herbaceous borders, colourless except for the washed-out yellow and white of spring flowers. Behind them was a high clipped hedge with a wide arch cut into it, beyond which a tree-lined walk led through shrubberies to the tennis court. Open farmland spread in the distance beyond the gardens, and to the right the glass roofs of Midwinter's greenhouses glinted in the sun.

Nancy considered taking Nelson out, then decided that she would walk instead and set out up the steep slope of the main drive to the road which led along the top edge of the Midwinter estate. It was a mild afternoon in March. Pigeons crooned in the trees, which spread traceries of bare branches against the sky with as yet only the faintest hint of green. After some yards the road plunged among trees: to her right they thinned and gave way to open farmland, but to her left, where the land belonging to the estate sloped away steeply, the trees grew more densely, hiding the house and sheltering the romantic quarry pool somewhere below her.

Nancy's attention was held by the sun slanting invitingly through the trees; it would be so easy to change direction and enter the wood. She left the road and slipped through a gap in the thin hedge to find her path obstructed by a low, barbed-wire fence. Hesitating only for a moment, she hitched up her skirt with a renewed determination to gain entry. Her obstinacy was reinforced by a firmer resolution: hang Aubrey's finer feelings, she would take another look at the pool.

* * *

The wood was very still, as if it had been waiting for her. Nancy looked up at the tree-canopy high above and saw the dazzle of the sky through the leaves. There were no sounds except for those of her own footsteps rustling the fallen leaves and the sudden startled call and flurry of a pheasant, whirring its way up from the undergrowth.

She had gone a long way into the wood before she found the pool again; and she did so as suddenly as before, coming to an abrupt halt at the sheer edge of a quarry above a drop of some twelve or fifteen feet.

Nancy clung to the lichened trunk of a tree, breathing hard. The area below her was littered with spoil heaps and ridges. The pool itself lay, flat and still, reflecting the sky and skeletal trunks of trees on its blank surface. The quarry face could not have been worked for years, thought Nancy, peering over its edge, for it was overgrown with brambles and bushes at its base. She thought again of Gilbert Lang's story about a Roman villa. It was hard to give it any credence, and Aubrey was right: with all those trees, the site would be almost impossible to excavate. But it would have been a perfect meeting place for lovers.

Nancy scrambled down the side of the quarry face, clinging to twigs and branches of trees. She had almost reached the foot of the precipice before she realised that she was being watched.

The man looked like a tramp; he carried a cloth satchel over his shoulder: his torn cap and jacket over a grey shirt and patched cords blended with the vegetation as he leaned against one of trees close by the pool.

Nancy let out a cry of alarm and ran down the last slope of bank and came to a halt. She was more than a little frightened, but annoyed too that her clumsy descent of the quarry side had been observed. "Don't you know this is private land?" she called, and then more sharply, "What are you doing here?"

The man was in his late twenties, tough and solid with a rough, fresh complexion and keen, hard blue eyes.

"My husband is Mr Farringdon," Nancy added, feeling that her challenge needed further authorisation.

The man eased himself from the tree and she saw then that he carried a shotgun. "I know who you are," he said with the slow local accent. "I've seen you about."

"You haven't answered my question, Are you employed on the estate?" She glanced at the gun. "Or are you perhaps poaching?"

He looked at his gun then back at her with his extraordinarily intense eyes. "Oh, don't you worry, ma'am. I'm from Midwinter all right." Suddenly he smiled. "I'm Powers, ma'am. I look after the woodland, see off vermin."

"Of course," she said, feeling a swift sense of relief. "You live at Keeper's Cottage." She walked towards him. "What sort of vermin?"

He shrugged. "Rats, foxes, jackdaws, jays. I sometimes clear up a few rabbits.

The farm is plagued with the little devils."

She pulled a face. "Poor things."

"You wouldn't say that if you didn't get your nice fresh lettuce to Midwinter's table. Nor if you saw what a fox will do to pheasant and partridge." He held her gaze and for a moment she was disconcerted again, for though his manner was civil, he had none of the usual deference of the Midwinter staff.

Nancy straightened her beret and tucked her hair under it. "I understand from Radley that you have worked at Midwinter a long time."

"Man and boy."

"You were here in my predecessor's day."

A shuttered look came over his face. "Yes, I remember the first young Mrs Farringdon."

Nancy turned to the pool and he followed her gaze uneasily. She thrust her hands into the pockets of her coat. "Her portrait hangs in the drawing room, you know. She was extremely beautiful."

He sniffed. "Handsome is as handsome does."

Nancy laughed. "You sound like my mother."

"Then she must have been a sensible woman."

"She was." Nancy wondered briefly what her mother would have thought if she could see her now. She would have been proud that she had married the celebrated Aubrey Farringdon, but she would have looked down her nose at her for chatting with Aubrey's gamekeeper as if she were leaning casually over the back wall talking to a neighbour in Ackroyd Street. Not the behaviour of a proper lady. Certainly it was not the way Augusta would have talked to her servants, though Augusta had, in other respects, not always behaved like a proper lady either.

Nancy turned to look at Powers and was startled to see that he was regarding her steadily. "Which side do you take?" she said suddenly. "Do you condemn her for behaving as she did, or do you think she was led astray and was sorry for it?" She was surprised by how much she wanted to know about Augusta, for Mortimer's sentimental talk of remorse had made her curious. She knew she ought to hate her, wanted to hate her, for it was natural for a second wife to hate her husband's first love, especially if she had been both beautiful and wicked; yet the more Nancy looked at Augusta's portrait, the more she found herself wondering about the nature of her wickedness, and the less she felt able to condemn her.

Powers considered the question for a moment then said, "I think it's none of my business, ma'am."

"And that I shouldn't be asking you questions like this — and wouldn't either if I was a proper lady?"

He shifted his bag on his shoulder in preparation for moving off. "I couldn't say about that."

"You're right." She pulled her gloves more tightly on to her wrists. "I'm sorry for delaying you in your duties, Powers."

He nodded. "Ma'am."

She called after him, "Though I should have been interested to hear you give an opinion." He turned, and Nancy added quickly, "You needn't be embarrassed. I should keep it to myself. I do know what happened."

He hesitated only briefly. "I'd be surprised, Mrs Farringdon, if you do."

She stood watching him go. She felt uneasy and unwilling now to linger by the pool with its still secrecy and dark reflections. She walked on through the wood until she could see Midwinter in the distance and, coming to the edge of the trees, she entered the sunny meadow.

* * *

Ted Powers swung his cloth satchel over his shoulder and continued through the wood. So, he had met the new mistress of Midwinter face to face. Pretty enough face, too. Trim figure. Wrong way of going about things to suit the upper ten and the Farringdons, though, hob-nobbing with him like that. Everyone said she was the wrong class, and she looked less than half Farringdon's age. He wondered if she knew what she had taken on. She would have to be tough to get the better of old Mrs Farringdon. Farringdon's first wife had thought she could do it, but time had taught her different. He left the wood and continued down the muddy track. There were some who couldn't help admiring the old witch in spite of all her sins. His father had been one. Sometimes Ted thought that was just what Mrs Farringdon was — a witch. When he was a boy he had believed it too; but others had supposed Viner to be the devil of the piece, the few who had been in the know. Midwinter had always managed to hush up its scandals. They were moving into the future, weren't they? At least, that was what he kept telling himself. Then why did he tolerate working here, just like his father before him?

Ted reached Keeper's Cottage. It was a solidly built house, more imposing than most of the estate workers' cottages. His father had been a man of note all those years ago, head-keeper to the Midwinter estate; it had been a position to be envied in those days, by those who dreamed of raising themselves in the world. Ted swung down the dark, stone-flagged passage to the scullery where he hung his old coat and the gun behind the door and washed his hands at the sink. There was little need to shoot rooks these days, for, with Farringdon living all those years in London, a pheasant shoot had become a rare event. Breeding stock was low: it would have been easy to grow lazy, but habits learned young died hard.

He thought again of Farringdon's new wife. There were plenty would say she had no cause to think herself high and mighty; she was a working girl from Yorkshire who had worked her way into society. The world was not ready for equality of the classes, no more than it would suffer equality between men and women. His father had believed in the natural order of things, but not Darwin's version of it: Darwin had challenged the Bible and was a dangerous heretic — hadn't the preacher in chapel said so? His father's God had been of the Old Testament ilk, who punished evil-doers and smiled only on the righteous; who gave the likes of the Farringdons rights over other men's lives, because the division of man into rich and poor was somehow a part of God's mysterious plan.

Ted went into the kitchen and to the

dresser, where he picked up a book which lay open where he had left off reading. He did not believe in Darwin either, not because evolution was heresy, but because it was no more than a clever idea, thought up to appease the consciences of the upper classes: what better than to discover in the 'survival of the fittest' a proof that the class system was sanctioned by science as well as by God. He sat in the chair by the kitchen stove, but he could not concentrate on the page in front of him, for he kept thinking of Farringdon's young wife. She had stirred him up more than he liked to think, asking whose side he was on, saying that she knew what had happened. He should have kept his mouth shut, he told himself, remembering his response, as deeper memories, one after another, began their insidious patrol through his mind.

* * *

"I shall instruct Browne to drive me to Winchborne tomorrow afternoon," Mrs Farringdon said loudly, ignoring Nancy.

"I shall discuss arrangements with the vicar for your talk on West Africa to the Ladies' Guild." Mrs Farringdon generally addressed her remarks to Aubrey, even talking across Nancy if she sat between them. This disconcerted Aubrey more than it did Nancy. She waited for him to include her in the conversation as usual, tactfully, gently, without drawing attention to what was going on. Why was it that here at Midwinter he seemed so much less impressive, so much in the shadow of his mother?

"Take Nancy with you. She has not been to the village." Aubrey threw Nancy an apologetic smile. "What do you say, my darling? *Would* you like to go?" He spoke patiently, as if he were coaxing a child, thought Nancy. She considered an outing in the Wolseley. Browne was a lively chauffeur, with a gratifying turn of speed on the open highway. She decided that a brief escape to the vicarage, even with Mrs Farringdon for company, might well be preferable to kicking her heels all afternoon at Midwinter.

* * *

The chauffeur eased the car into gear and they bowled up the slope of the drive. Mrs Farringdon tapped him on the shoulder with her parasol as they reached Midwinter's gates. "Rather more steadily, please, Browne." They swung more cautiously into the lane.

Nancy smiled as, after a minute or two, the speedometer again crept to forty. She turned to Mrs Farringdon, determined to make an attempt at breaching the hostility between them. "I suppose it was very dull for you whilst Aubrey was living in London."

"Not at all. I have my friends, my many obligations."

"All the same, I should think it might be fun to put some life back into the house." It was a decision Nancy had come to since Radley had told her that Augusta had held house parties, for she missed their dinner parties in Bloomsbury. "Why should Aubrey hide himself away here in the country? Don't you think the house needs people?"

Mrs Farringdon smiled frostily and turned to look out of the window, cutting off further conversation. "I'm sure Aubrey is quite content with the way things are."

"Perhaps Aubrey is too easily contented," Nancy said crossly, turning to the other window. She watched trees and cottages flit by as they neared the village. They would have summer parties, she decided. Midwinter would throw open its doors as it had done in Augusta's day.

After a while Mrs Farringdon said, "We must find you a lady's maid. But I shall interview her. I will not have a girl who does not suit us."

Nancy was surprised and said lightly, "I didn't employ a personal maid in London. I don't really want one now."

"But you must," Mrs Farringdon insisted with her cold smile. "Whoever heard of such a thing?"

Nancy turned to her, recognising the suggestion of a hand-picked maid as another manoeuvre in the tacit warfare between them, a further means of control. "I'm sincere, Mother-in-law. Besides — just consider the expense."

"There are certain standards which must be maintained."

"Not by me."

"I don't think you understand."
"How things are done at Midwinter? Oh, I think I understand perfectly."
"I shall speak to Aubrey." Mrs Farringdon set her mouth as if to say the matter was decided.
"It won't make any difference."
They were silent for a while. Then Mrs Farringdon said with certainty, "You shall come round to my view. For Aubrey's sake, you and I shall agree."
Nancy looked her in the eye. "And I'm telling you, we shan't."
It was their first open acknowledgement of conflict. They were silent for the rest of the journey and Nancy knew that, in this minor skirmish at least, she had won.

* * *

The village of Winchborne lay at a distance of about a mile. Market stalls filled the square by the church. Sheep, penned among wooden hurdles, added their cries of protest to the mooing of the cattle tied to railings. The road was crowded with men and women, horses and carts, which jostled and made way for the Wolseley as it crawled to a halt and Browne jumped out to open the doors.

Nancy followed Mrs Farringdon along the main street with its limestone cottages and handful of shops: a blacksmith's, the neat post office store, a butcher's, grocer's and draper's. She enjoyed the commotion and noise of it all after the oppressive silence of Midwinter, and was conscious that people had stopped to stare at them and were weighing her up as the new mistress of Midwinter. She nodded and said, "Good-day," not sure what was expected, sensing something feudal in the way the women responded to her smile with diffident nods, and old men bared their heads and clutched their caps to their waistcoats as Mrs Farringdon passed.

They entered the draper's shop. Nancy waited as her mother-in-law ordered a few silks and cottons and grumbled over the price. Nancy, though she was in her own way thrifty, found Midwinter's austerity exacting: Mrs Farringdon kept a tight rein on the accounts and believed in all forms of economy, from turning out lights for the sake of the generator, to frugal meals and the preservation of leftovers. She watched every penny, literally, for the servant who washed the loose change each day did so under her personal supervision. "Honesty in a servant is of supreme importance," she had told Nancy, who had questioned the need for this surveillance. "I will not have a servant in my employ who is light-fingered, nor one who is over-curious. Midwinter servants have always been discreet."

They left the shop and ran the gauntlet of reticent stares once more. Thankful to escape them at last, Nancy headed for the car. Some yards beyond it, at the edge of the village square, stood Winchborne's garage, a concession to the age of the motor car, with a large painted sign and shiny petrol pump. A man on the forecourt, dressed in a cycling coat and a leather helmet, was talking over a motor bicycle with one of the mechanics. He straightened and turned in their direction as Nancy and Mrs Farringdon approached the Wolseley. Nancy stared in surprise as the figure in the motor-cycle coat touched his cap to them.

She turned to Mrs Farringdon. "How strange. That man looks like our gamekeeper."

Mrs Farringdon glanced briefly in the direction of the garage then turned away. "Yes, that is Powers. Why are you surprised?"

Nancy saw that Mrs Farringdon was regarding her with suspicion. She hesitated, disconcerted. "I suppose I didn't expect him to ride a motor bicycle. It seems a queer mix of contrasts."

"Not at all. I ride in a motor car."

Nancy fell silent, unsettled by seeing the keeper. Mrs Farringdon, having spotted an acquaintance across the street, had moved away. "It does seem odd," Nancy insisted, addressing Browne as he stood waiting to open the car door for her.

"Ted Powers is paid well as keeper, ma'am." Browne's scrubbed red face deepened a shade beneath his peaked cap, and Nancy detected a note of resentment. Browne glanced towards Mrs Farringdon's retreating back, aware that he had perhaps overstepped the mark; he dropped his gaze and moved aside as Mrs Farringdon turned with an imperious wave of her hand to indicate that Nancy should follow in her wake.

A man of imposing physical presence, more than six feet tall and broad at both waist and shoulder, was leaning on the fence by the sheep pens. He was, Nancy guessed, over seventy, but handsome and ruddy and with a back — when he left the fence to receive them — as straight as that of a man of forty. Mrs Farringdon introduced him as Colonel Gregory. She underwent a strange metamorphosis in the colonel's presence, becoming at once pliant and charming. She said she had wanted to consult him about one of the village boys who had been caught on the Midwinter farm poaching rabbits. The child had been referred to the local magistrates' court, where the colonel was chairman of the bench. Nancy watched in amazement as her mother-in-law flattered and teased and the colonel toadied to her in return.

"So you recommend a birching?" the colonel said at last in response to Mrs

Farringdon's judgement on the poacher.

"Oh, surely not if he only took a few rabbits," interrupted Nancy in distress.

"The lad has to be punished." Mrs Farringdon smiled at the colonel. "A good thrashing will make him think twice about trapping rabbits again."

"But there are too many rabbits anyway," Nancy said, thinking again of the gamekeeper and remembering Powers's comments. "I heard only the other day that the farm is overrun with them. We should be thanking the boy for poaching them."

The colonel laughed, looking Nancy up and down and labelling her, Nancy decided, a racy filly, since most of his metaphors seemed to be connected with horses. "A romping good notion, my dear. And what do we tell the lad — well done for netting what was not yours for the taking?"

"He was probably hungry. I should let him off with a few strong words and tell him he should ask permission next time."

The colonel turned to Mrs Farringdon. "Does she always go for things headlong and tantivy?"

"Nancy's tongue often runs away with her." Mrs Farringdon attempted a frosty smile. "She does not understand the responsibilities of our position in society, and that it is the duty of our class to set an example to the lower orders."

"Your mama-in-law has a rattling good reputation at the local League of Empire talks," said Colonel Gregory, as if in confidence to Nancy. "She has the spirit of a dozen men, I can tell you. I wouldn't have minded having her in my regiment."

Mrs Farringdon embarked on the virtues of the League of Empire. "There's too little attention paid to the Empire these days . . ."

Nancy indulged in her habit of making up little histories about people as they said farewell to the colonel and drove towards the vicarage. The motor bike and its owner had gone from the garage forecourt; she decided that Powers knew all there was to know about Augusta and her lover, and had threatened to blackmail the family over the scandal if they did not pay him a huge salary and buy him a shiny motor bicycle.

As for her mother-in-law — she had made up her mind that the colonel and Mrs Farringdon had shared a romantic attachment in their younger days, but Mrs Farringdon's high moral stance had finally driven a wedge between them. The colonel, unable to compete with duty to Midwinter and Mrs Farringdon's devotion to her God, had never married, but had applied himself to his horses in compensation.

By contrast, the vicar approved of Mrs Farringdon's devotion to God and to her country seat — so long as her priorities were in that order — Nancy decided after half an hour at the vicarage. Mrs Farringdon was a leading light in the business of charity bazaars, the vicar told Nancy. Perhaps she would like to follow her mother-in-law's example? Nancy, wanting to enter into the spirit of the community, for she genuinely hoped to make friends in the neighbourhood, said that she would man stalls, crochet doilies, or even knit socks for distressed sailors, if that was what was required.

She gave an account of meeting the colonel and her visit to the vicarage to Aubrey that evening while he was dressing for dinner. She had developed a habit of helping him in a wifely way to tie his tie, to adjust his cuff-links and generally to perform the little tasks which, in the absence of a valet, would otherwise have been the duty of Roberts.

"Is he your mother's admirer?"

"The colonel?"

"It strikes me they suit one another pretty well."

"Really, Nancy! What a peculiar thing to say. Mama has been a widow for twenty years."

"The vicar has enlisted me for the next bazaar. I think he and his wife found me too disconcerting. They gave almost no time at all to your lecture about West Africa, though I kept on reminding them how *good* it's going to be."

"Such loyalty, my darling." He kissed her tenderly, but without passion, careful not to disturb her dress or disarrange her hair.

Nancy fastened his tie for him and kissed him back. He looked so handsome in his white dress shirt that she entirely forgave him for his lack of vigour in defending her against his mother; for, after all, she decided, she was more than capable of defending herself.

"They talked a lot about being loyal," she said. "There was a quantity of talk too about the Empire, which, it seems, is in danger of disintegrating if your mother does not stir this corner of Dorset into action by her addresses to the League."

"You don't approve?" he said quizzically.

She snapped the lid of his cuff-link box open. "Oh well. It was all so boring."

"Nancy," murmured Aubrey, a little dismayed by her intolerance.

She turned to face him, holding out his cuff-links. "Tell me about Powers the keeper."

"The gamekeeper?" He shook his head, amused by her habit of sudden non-sequiturs.

"I saw him in the village. Radley told me he used to work in the stables." She wished she could tell Aubrey about her encounter with Powers by the pool. She knew that in her conversation with the gamekeeper, as with the other outdoor staff, she had been what Aubrey would call indiscreet, but she was growing tired of Midwinter's requirements of discretion. "Why do you pay Powers so well that he can afford to ride around on a motor bicycle, yet there's hardly enough work to merit keeping him on?"

Aubrey did not answer. He took his cuff-links from her outstretched hand and concentrated on fixing them to his cuffs.

She went to help him. "Is there some mystery?" she asked, already resurrecting her imagined story of blackmail.

"No, of course not. Ted Powers's father used to be keeper at Midwinter. Naturally, Ted took on the job when his father died." He looked up. "He was very good with horses. One of those men who is a natural with animals. He was lucky. Many of the outdoor staff were dismissed when Midwinter became mechanised. He has been an excellent keeper."

"But you never have a shoot."

"Mama wanted him to stay. She pays him well out of respect for his father. Harry Powers was a —"

"Don't tell me. He was a loyal Midwinter servant."

"Mama has her favourites. We must

allow her these little eccentricities. And I am happy with Powers's work as a woodsman. He's an intelligent man and unusually discreet."

He was not discreet with me, thought Nancy, remembering Ted Powers's parting remark, unconvinced still that there was not some truth in her own version of events.

Aubrey smiled, pulling on his dinner jacket. "Now. Shall we go downstairs?"

5

"SHE is totally unlike us," Mrs Farringdon protested to Aubrey, having summoned him to her sitting room. "She has the manners of a shop-girl. And you know how I detest shop-girls. She and I will never be able to understand one another and I don't think we should try."

"I don't feel you have made an effort to make Nancy welcome, Mama." Aubrey was aware that his hopes of the three of them living in harmony were fading, yet he felt at a loss to know how to achieve his ideal.

"I cannot welcome what I do not find agreeable. So, I have decided I shall avoid her society whenever possible." Mrs Farringdon regarded her son's crestfallen expression with a genuine sadness. She loved him with a passion more fierce than a mere maternal affection: Aubrey was the master of Midwinter, living proof of all that her late husband had achieved.

She saw in her son a refinement of all the qualities she had admired in her husband, and none of those she had sometimes found distasteful; for Aubrey had none of his papa's robust, earthy humour, nor his large appetite for the muscular, physical things of life. He rarely held a shoot and would not ride to hounds; he had travelled from a desire for knowledge rather than a lust for adventure. Sometimes she wondered if Aubrey's gentleness was not the greatest flaw in his make-up, for he had proved himself a fool when it came to women, firstly over Augusta and now Nancy. But if he had frailties, she must overlook them. He was her son. It was as much a mother's obligation to love her son as it was a man's duty to love his country. If Nancy was not a fit person to be Aubrey's wife, and if she would not be trained as such, then, for her son's sake, and as mistress of Midwinter, she would have to see a way in time to accommodate herself to his latest matrimonial blunder. Until then . . .

"I shall take my breakfast of toast and tea alone in my room each morning and spend as much time as possible up here in my sitting room," she told him. "From what I know of Nancy, I am sure this will distress her as little as it will distress me."

"But it will distress me, Mama," said Aubrey a little plaintively.

His mother laid a consoling hand on his arm, then, patting his arm lightly, she withdrew her hand. "I've made up my mind. There'll be no more said."

⋆ ⋆ ⋆

Midwinter seemed gloomier than ever in April. It rained for days on end and Nancy was confined to the house. She wandered the first-floor corridors with their walls lined with glass-encased birds. She read Aubrey's neatly penned labels: *Passeriformes*. *Turdidae*, *Fringillidae*, *Emberizidae*. She explored the gloomy, dust-sheeted bedrooms with their heavy furniture, and tried again to imagine Midwinter bursting at the seams with house guests; but she had begun to despair of that monument to taxidermy ever again pulsing with life.

The corridor to her own room was similarly lined with wallcases and lit by dim oil-lamps which glowed in the soft silence and filled the air with a suffocating smell. The cases here were crowded with butterflies, species upon species with rigid wings, their dried-up furry bodies impaled with pins. She usually hurried past these grisly specimens, but one morning she paused and forced herself to study them, reading each label in turn. *New Guinea Blue Mountain Swallowtail*. The brilliant blue tapering wings were black-edged and large and sinister.

One of the housemaids came towards her, silently along the red-carpeted corridor. She bobbed a curtsey and pressed herself against the glass case to let Nancy pass. Neither spoke. The silence of the domestics was a feature in which everyone took pride at Midwinter: they slipped invisibly into rooms, replenishing coal scuttles and water jugs, they glided in the shadows, becoming human only when they reached the sanctuary of the swinging green baize doors, through which one occasionally heard the faint sound of raised voices, sometimes even laughter on long afternoons.

The maid carried a pile of clean bed-linen over her arms, for Aubrey's children were expected home later that week for the Easter holidays. The girl continued on her way.

Aubrey was coming along the corridor. "Ah, so there you are."

Nancy waited until he reached her.

"Studying the butterflies? It's a very comprehensive collection." He moved along the row of cases, as if he were seeing the butterflies for the first time. "It has taken me years. The Black-Veined Whites are now extinct in Britain."

"It's so unnatural to try to preserve their beauty," murmured Nancy. "And to me, they don't look beautiful. They look rather grotesque."

He stared at her in surprise, then laughed. "My darling, their wing patterns can be seen to so much better advantage when they are under glass."

"But the whole essence of their beauty is in the way they are free to fly about." Nancy looked again at the rows of rigid wings, spread to expose their pattern and colour, and felt a wave of revulsion at the squandering of such beauty. "Why do they have to die for you to appreciate them?"

Aubrey frowned. "But Nancy, of course the collector has to kill, in order to preserve."

"Why? To prove how much cleverer man is than nature?"

"Now you're just being silly."

She was stung by the word and by his insensitivity to her feelings. She said wryly, "Why is it that when I disagree with you, it's always because I'm rather stupid or naïve, but when your opinion is different from mine, it's because yours is based on a greater understanding?"

He spread his hands. "How can man hope to understand nature properly if he doesn't study her? It's the whole basis of science."

"But Aubrey — this isn't science." Nancy waved her hand to indicate the row upon row of lifeless bodies. She felt inexplicably close to tears, for it was suddenly important that he should, just this once, understand her point of view. "This is sheer greed. It's a desire to possess all these beautiful creatures, to preserve them, to deny that their enchantment lies in their very freedom." She saw that she had hurt him. She should not have questioned his motive for collecting. She should apologise and declare that she had been sentimentally swayed by the thought of chloroform and pins, and Aubrey would say it was her prerogative as a woman. She fingered the chain at her throat, silent and strangely unrepentant.

There was a marked coldness between them as Aubrey said, "I shall be in my study for a while. Can you amuse yourself this morning?"

She nodded and waited until he had gone downstairs, then followed more slowly, feeling restless and disturbed by their disagreement. She went from step to step down the staircase, leaning her weight on the iron balustrade and letting her arm slide along its length until she reached the half-landing above the entrance hall, where she rested her cheek on her forearms on the cold wrought iron. The rain had stopped. Sunlight streamed across the black and white tiles of the hall floor, lighting up a vase of dyed yellow pampas grass. She could hear Aubrey's mother talking on the telephone in the drawing room; Mrs Farringdon had not yet discovered that there was no obligation to shout to make the caller on the other end of the line hear.

Nancy raised her head and listened, trying to make out what her mother-in-law was saying. Was she planning something with the colonel? Placing a bet at Aintree? Arranging to have one of the maidservants sold to white slavers? It sounded tediously more like some business to do with Aubrey's talk to the Ladies' Guild.

From the stairs, Nancy could see, to right and left, the passages leading off the entrance hall. To the right was the broad, oak-panelled corridor which led to the library, Aubrey's study and the small drawing room. To the left was a longer, narrower passage; this contained the green baize door which sealed off the servants' offices and led on to the dining room and the west wing of the house. The downstairs rooms in the west wing were used chiefly to store surplus furniture. One of the doors at the far end of the corridor was ajar.

Nancy observed how the light from the room formed a wavering wedge of pink on the red patterned carpet. Attracted by the splash of colour, she moved down the stairs and went towards it. She stepped inside the room and closed the door.

A stack of bentwood chairs blocked her way where one of the servants must have hurriedly deposited them. She edged round them and cleared a path to the window. The air was stale and close, heated by the sun which now streamed through the gaps in the curtains on to the carpet and the dust-sheeted furniture. A fly buzzed against one of the panes. She pulled back the green velvet curtain and opened the casement wide, letting in the warm, damp April smell of the garden and the sweet scent of a Daphne bush which grew close to the wall outside.

There was a view from here across the estate: by squinting between the stable buildings Nancy could see as far as the wood. She imagined how the pool would look now, with a pale green haze of young leaves on the trees, and celandines, and perhaps primroses, appearing among the undergrowth. She thought of her encounter with Ted Powers and his enigmatic comment that he would be surprised if she knew what had happened between Augusta and John Viner. There *was* a mystery about Powers; he knew something intriguing. Aubrey's reluctance to discuss him had only confirmed her suspicions.

Nancy turned again to the room. It was prettily papered in a honeysuckle pattern. On either side of the white marble fireplace the alcoves were partly filled in with low cupboards. She opened one of these and saw delicate vases and ornaments stacked on the shelves; Art Nouveau designs and Tiffany lamps of a decade earlier, like those in the drawing room. She closed the doors and leaned with her back against them. She felt that the room was welcoming, a retreat from the sombre atmosphere of the rest of the house. It would make an excellent sitting room: she would suggest to Aubrey that she turn it into her own. She stretched out a toe and lifted one of the dust sheets to reveal a chintz-covered sofa in the same floral pattern as the walls. She crossed the floor to a set of bookshelves and let her fingers trail along the spines of the books, idly scanning the titles. With a shock of discovery she realised that this was not Aubrey's choice of reading, nor she supposed his father's, nor even Mrs Farringdon's. Would any of them have read *Madame Bovary*, H. G. Wells, or Sherlock Holmes? Had this perhaps been Augusta's own sitting room? She searched the titles eagerly, gratified to discover Keats, Browning and Shelley among the poets and, rather surprisingly, Walt Whitman, who had been considered improper at home and surely had been in Midwinter circles too when Augusta was alive.

She lifted the volume of Whitman poems from the shelf and wiped the dirt from its top edge with her finger. Inside the fly leaf there was an inscription: *Augusta Farringdon, 1901*. There was a chair between the corner of the bookshelves and the window. Nancy pulled the dust cover from the mahogany frame and, curling herself into the green velvet upholstery, she began to read.

Some of the verses had been heavily underlined: *I believe in the flesh and the appetites, Seeing, hearing, feeling, are miracles, and each part and tag of me is a miracle.* Had Augusta marked them? Nancy turned the pages with a sense of voyeurism, A line of verse, *Great is death . . . Sure as life holds all parts together, death holds all parts together,* scored under with vehemence, leaped out at her from the printed page. Its simplicity was shocking.

The notion that Augusta could have wanted her own death fitted with Mortimer's assertion that she had faded away with remorse, yet the poems suggested a sensualism which conformed less easily with saintly notions of repentance. The underlined text seemed linked with Nancy's memory of the beautiful but sinister pool, where the discovery of the lovers had ended the affair once and for all. A more romantic version of the story occurred to Nancy. Had Augusta loved Viner so much that when he left her she just wanted to die? Returning to Aubrey with a broken heart, she had pined for her lover, growing paler and more ethereally beautiful before she expired. Oh, yes! Nancy closed the volume of poetry and leaned her head against the chair cushion. She turned and pressed her cheek against the pile. How voluptuous was velvet. The room was very still and silent except for the hum of bees in the flowers outside. Perhaps Augusta had sat in this very chair. Nancy was finding it harder and harder to dislike her for, if she concentrated, she could almost believe Augusta's presence was in the room; not the Augusta of the portrait, nor the daughter-in-law of whom Mrs Farringdon spoke disparagingly, nor the wife Aubrey mentioned with a tender kind of regret, but a woman who believed in flesh and the appetites and who had taken a lover. Had Augusta detested Midwinter too? How had she filled her time? She would not have had the diversion of sharing in Aubrey's work. Nancy imagined her reading poetry and reliving moments of passion with her lover John Viner, under the trees by the pool.

The sound of the luncheon gong made Nancy jump. She stood and stretched, returning the volume of poems quickly to the shelf as a door banged somewhere in the house and she heard Mrs Farringdon speaking to Aubrey. She threw the dust sheet over the chair, closed the window and drew the curtains again. She would say nothing about the room for the time being; she felt she must hide all trace of her visit, dragging the stack of chairs across the carpet to block the way to the window. With a quick glance along the corridor to be sure that it was empty, she slipped from the room and closed the door.

⋆ ⋆ ⋆

Nancy had persuaded Aubrey to invite Gilbert Lang and Marjorie Benson for the weekend. While the men gossiped about mutual acquaintances at the Geographical Society, Nancy showed Marjorie over the grounds; Marjorie told Nancy the latest London scandals, and Nancy did wickedly accurate impersonations of the colonel and Mrs Farringdon and laughed a lot and felt more lighthearted than she had for weeks. In the evening they played and sang in the small drawing room. Aubrey told stories about Africa and demonstrated how to play a South American nose flute, while Gilbert improvised an accompaniment on a Jew's harp. Nancy performed an Arab lament which Aubrey had taught her, and Marjorie sang a plaintive French love song, inappropriate but moving. Mrs Farringdon joined them and said she wished to participate in the music-making. She sat on the sofa, nursing a small African drum which she tapped unrhythmically, but with an abandon which reminded Nancy of her flirtatiousness in the company of Colonel Gregory.

The small drawing room housed Nancy's piano; Mrs Farringdon disapproved of the fact that Aubrey had gone to the expense of transporting the Bechstein all the way from London, and declared with caustic humour, as Marjorie sat down to play to them, that it might have been worth the expense if Nancy performed with any proficiency.

"It was an extravagance," Nancy agreed, watching Marjorie coax a soulful melody from the keys of the grand piano. "And I should have been happy enough with an upright, but Aubrey knows how much it pleases me to play."

The instrument almost filled the smallest drawing room, and the five of them were squeezed into the remaining space in an enforced intimacy.

"This reminds me of jolly evenings years back," laughed Gilbert, when Marjorie returned from the piano to sit beside Aubrey. Nancy felt Gilbert's thigh against hers, his arm along the back of the sofa rested in a restrained embrace of Mrs Farringdon. "Oh, Midwinter has seen some fiendish frolics, Nancy," he continued. "You should have been here for the musical evenings, the conversation, the champagne, the food, the fancy dress parties."

Gilbert must have been ignorant of Augusta's fall from grace, Nancy reminded herself, yet he could not have missed Aubrey's pained look of dismay. He turned to her, and she sensed a gentle malice which flowed from him. "Nancy, dear girl, if Augusta is looking down on us, she would approve of the way you have put life back into Midwinter. Augusta loved frolics." He saw Marjorie's shake of the head and, at the same time, Mrs Farringdon changed the subject, but Nancy picked up the echo of his challenge to the past with a sense of satisfaction rather than of pity for Aubrey. She was glad Gilbert had talked about Augusta. There was too much guarded secrecy about her memory; too much reverence attached to her portrait; an air of hushed shame over the scandal.

* * *

"I never was so happy for months," confided Nancy to Marjorie as they walked from church the following morning. "I'm so glad you came. I feel as if I'm in touch with the world again."

"What do you do all day, you poor thing? It seems to me that Aubrey neglects you terribly."

"No, that isn't true." Nancy leapt at once to Aubrey's defence. "He has kept up my diction lessons and I'm learning all the time about West Africa and about the Egyptians and ancient religions, and he *is*, after all, frightfully busy." She paused, aware that she was trying too hard to convince. "I walk when it's fine, or else I ride in the grounds. I'm exercising the horses in turn while Aubrey's children are away at school. I like Hugo's horse the best. We talk to one another, Nelson and I, as we amble along the Dorset lanes. He misses Hugo and I miss . . ." She shrugged. "I suppose I don't really know what."

Marjorie regarded her with a shrewd look. "Poor Nancy. Look, any time you feel like escaping for a while and coming to London, you can be sure there will be a room for you at my flat."

"She's aiming to marry Gilbert, I reckon," said Nancy to Aubrey that evening when Gilbert and Marjorie had left. "She's certainly reformed him. Did you notice he stayed sober the entire weekend? We should have invited them before. Even your mother has enjoyed herself." She laughed at the memory of Mrs Farringdon hugging the African drum. "Gilbert and Marjorie have transformed us."

"No, my darling, it's you who have

transformed us," said Aubrey, watching her flit about his room.

She flung herself on his bed. "This is only the beginning. We shall ask *all* your London friends." She paused. "I want to be as good a hostess as Augusta."

He sighed. "I wish you would forget all about Augusta."

"I shall only forget her if you do. I have a theory that you forgave her, which is why you make yourself keep her portrait on the wall, to prove to yourself that you are a Christian gentleman, and thus, very forgiving. But I don't believe you've learned to forget how she made you unhappy all those years ago." She kicked off her shoes, wriggling further down on the counterpane. "I shall make you so happy that you're bound to forget her. I shall love you so much that I *drive* her out, and one day, you'll see, we shall talk about Augusta in a quite matter-of-fact way." She spread her arms above her head, smiling at him. "Shall I sleep with you tonight? Would you like me to stay? Come and kiss me."

Aubrey looked at her in despair, yet feeling desire mount in him. Had she any idea how much she hurt him when she talked so flippantly about what had happened? He knew he could never tell her it all. Did he want her to stay? He removed his jacket, seeing her eyes grow heavy and full, and he knew that he would sleep with her that night. He was conscious of her gaze as he undressed. This he did meticulously and calmly, placing his cuff-links in their box, hanging up his tie and cummerbund, maintaining a practised control until the point where their bodies touched. Then, and only then, did he allow that coarse and brutish force within him its free rein, despising that side of his nature, remembering the wantonness with which Augusta too had received him, hearing her voice, an echo of Nancy's, and voluptuous against his ear, "Oh Aubrey! How I love you!"

* * *

Nancy could not settle after Gilbert and Marjorie's visit. Aubrey's attempts to teach her Latin and Greek had not been a success, and her dreams of benefiting from his knowledge were spoiled; for in spite of his classical background, Aubrey had not proved to be a good teacher. He set her long passages of Latin prose to translate, and rambled in his explanations of points of grammar so that she lost the main thread of the lesson in a wealth of irrelevant detail. He hid his impatience well, was always tolerant, yet she sensed that he had somehow closed his mind to her capacity for learning; it was as if, here at Midwinter, he no longer wanted her to progress. "It's so easy," he would say, smiling with that patient expression which exasperated her. "I learned Greek and Latin as a child. How can you find them so difficult?" A despair of ever being able to learn overwhelmed Nancy at times. Aubrey was so much cleverer than she was. How hard it must be for him, she acknowledged, to try to teach a girl of such a meagre education, and yet she felt he had little conception of what it was like for her, nor how much she envied him his years of study and travel.

"I want to be equal with you," she protested angrily one day, when he suggested with his patient smile that they abandon Virgil's *Aeneid*.

"You push yourself too hard," he said. "And you're beginning to look pale, my dear."

"I like work. I really want to understand Latin."

"Too much study is bad for a woman's constitution."

Nancy laughed out loud, but this time Aubrey did not smile.

"Why don't you spend the time before dinner resting on the terrace? It's such a lovely day."

"Oh, Aubrey. I'm not an invalid. Nor am I a child. Do you always have to be so — so patronising?" She left the study with a vivid impression of his surprised look of hurt.

Nancy went upstairs. She imagined how Aubrey would settle down to his books with a resigned, yet perhaps even a relieved expression. Her pace slowed as she reached the bedroom corridor. Had she really spoken to him so peevishly, her darling Aubrey, who never raised his voice when he expressed his own displeasure? She went to her room and fetched her sunhat, but felt a resistance against going to the terrace, as if she had been told to go outside to play. She would go to the greenhouses where it was quiet and colourful and nobody but Mortimer would know she was there. She hesitated on the sweep of the staircase, her glance falling along the corridor of the west wing. She remembered the secrecy of Augusta's disused sitting room. No one saw her as she made her way along the corridor and stepped inside, closing the door.

* * *

Nancy had been reading the Whitman poems for half an hour curled up in the green velvet chair. She rested the book in her lap feeling pleasantly drowsy. She looked at her watch — a whole hour until dinner — then stood and wandered to the window. The trees threw long shadows at the far side of the meadow: deep, dark, mysterious. One of the under-gardeners was crossing the yard with a basket of flowers for the table. Nancy stepped back against the curtain and, as she did so, noticed a second figure standing in the shadow of the stable wall. She watched as he crossed the yard in a shabby jacket and cord trousers and, recognising Powers, she pressed herself further against the wall so that he would not see her. She noticed how he walked with a purposeful stealth, as if he too wanted to avoid being observed. As soon as he was out of sight, Nancy went to the door and opened it a crack. She heard voices from the hall and could make out Mrs Farringdon's lowered yet distinctive tones, but she could not tell whether the man's voice was that of Powers or one of the other servants. Puzzled, for she had not seen the gamekeeper near the house before, she strained to listen as the voices became more muted and a door closed further along the hall.

Nancy, unable to hear anything more, closed the door and went to the bookshelves, searching along the spines for another source of diversion. Keats, Browning, Tennyson, Shelley. None of them particularly appealed. She was thinking about Powers, wondering why he was favoured by Mrs Farringdon and employed to patrol the wood, when she came to the gap left by the Whitman poems and saw the corner of a book half hidden at the back of the shelf. She pulled out a handful of volumes to reach it and revealed not one but three black leather-bound notebooks. Nancy's heart jumped with excitement as, forgetting all about Powers, she pulled them clear and, opening one, read, *January 1st 1900* . . . She turned to the others: *1901*, *1902*, the years between 'The Foul Deed' and Augusta's death. Nancy was trembling. She had discovered Augusta's diaries. She flicked the pages swiftly, searching the spidery, almost illegible handwriting for the name John Viner and, finding it at last, she fell back into the chair with a little whoop of triumph.

Midwinter
Wednesday 16 May, 1900

Thank God for Nanny. I am so dreadfully bored with motherhood. It is wrapped in layers of sentiment as if to fool women into thinking it is agreeable. No one ever talks about the awfulness of pregnancy and of giving birth.

Aubrey looks so distressed when I say that all I need is a little more freedom. He does not see that he can do as he pleases, but that I must always tread the Midwinter line. I am willing to help him all I can about his work, but he smiles, as if to say, What can you, a mere woman do? I comply with acting the lady, entertaining his friends and behaving discreetly. What a den of hypocrisy and oppression is the English family. I tell him I deserve more consideration. I am the mother of his children.

Aubrey invited some of his friends from the Geographical for dinner and, suspecting I was in for a dull evening, I walked into the library where they were congregated. Aubrey went through the usual ritual — I knew most of them already and their wives, my God, the wives! Not an ounce of style between them — and then Aubrey says that I have not met John Viner, have I? Viner collects butterflies. He has brought Aubrey some New Guinea specimens. He is a man with a reputation for ruthlessness and with great personal charm, though he is not at first sight attractive, being slight, dark and olive-skinned in appearance, with very elegant, almost continental manners. But there is an uncommon power in his soft voice and a compelling quality in his brown eyes.

Midwinter
Friday 18 May, 1900

Mafeking is relieved! The village has gone mad, with grown men and women singing and shouting in the streets, and everyone at last feeling as if they can do something by cheering and fetching out the drums and banners. The postman brought the news with him from Winchborne. Tears were pouring down his cheeks and I wept too and held his hands in mine, and there we stood with tears of joy, laughing from sheer relief, until Aubrey came out. Astounded at the impropriety of my clasping hands with the postman, he could not understand what had happened. And then he too let out the exclamation, "Thank the Lord!" when I told him the news.

It is hard for Aubrey, with his secret pro-Boer feeling. He does so hate to be drawn into politics, for he knows it is such a waste of his intellect. It is comical to see him struggling in the face of his mama's fury at the pro-Boers. I sometimes suspect that his real sympathies are not even with the Afrikaners but with the Africans themselves.

Midwinter
Saturday 19 May, 1900

Aubrey was reluctant, but I have persuaded him to hold a party in celebration. His mama is in favour, of course, though I believe she secretly wishes she had been the first to think of it. She has ordered the men to build a bonfire and there is quite a bustle over the possibility of getting up sufficient entertainment at such short notice. Aubrey has decided on a pigeon shoot, and has been engaged all morning with Powers the keeper, who has done nothing but grumble about it having to be done without a proper attention to detail. I have insisted on arranging the menus entirely alone. His mama is sulking, so I placated her by suggesting we get up a guest list together, and we sat in the drawing room, amiably tossing possible names to one another, just as if we are the nicest of friends. The Lennoxes will come, and his mama's pet colonel, and as many others as are not already too firmly settled down in London for the season. And I have suggested to Aubrey that he ask the butterfly collector, John Viner.

Midwinter
Saturday 26 May, 1900

Getting Viner was quite a coup. He is much in demand for the start of this season, being rather more interesting than one's run-of-the-mill traveller. He has been in Malaysia and New Guinea for five years and has an extensive collection of butterflies of which Aubrey is terribly envious. He arrived quite alone this afternoon off the London train, though we had not expected him much before dinner. That type generally likes to create an air of suspense before his entrance.

It was very pleasant in the gardens. The servants had decorated the house with bunting and Union Jacks, strung between the pillars like some outpost of Empire. Colonel Gregory and Aubrey's mama sat with our new neighbour, Mr Lennox, on the terrace together, exchanging bellicose opinions in support of Kitchener et al and saying how the Boers are only half civilised. The children staggered about on the lawn on their fat little legs, Hugo charming everyone. Connie is just beginning to walk. Aubrey retired to the greenhouses to discuss mosquitoes or beetles or some such interesting phenomena with Dr Neaman the zoologist. The rest of us sat in the gloriously lazy heat under sun umbrellas and talked about how agreeable it was not to be in London, though one feared a loss of *cachet* if one tarried too long. Viner said, just think then how much *cachet* one might lose by missing five seasons in a row. Ah, but he and Aubrey make themselves all the more desirable to society by their long absences, I told him. For what could be more of a catch at a party than a man who has travelled extensively?

Daisy Lennox declared, *à propos* of nothing, that it is because we have entered a new century and are afraid of its being as dull as the last that people long for stories of travel and adventure. Her husband manufactures tiles in the Midlands, so she of all people should know about dullness. Aubrey's mama thinks them common: raised by money but not at all refined, definitely not Midwinter people. They are large and rather loud and have two irrepressible children. I find them refreshing. The Lennoxes are new money. They understand success.

Times are certainly changing, was John Viner's opinion: Gladstone and all the old diehards have gone. A new century has an exciting effect upon people; one has a feeling that anything could happen. He has very dark eyes. There is a look in them, as if he could see exactly what one is thinking.

Midwinter
Sunday 27 May, 1900

It is past 3 a.m. and the men are still at their billiards. I can scarcely write, I am so exhausted. And yet I feel I am still riding high on a tide of glory. I must record the whole evening, which was an unmitigated success from the first canapé to the very last firework. There were twenty-eight at dinner: a mix of local codgers, learned professors and writers and a few gems, such as dear Gilbert, our awfully handsome young anthropologist, and of course the *pièce de résistance*, Mr Viner, our butterfly collector. Professor Deakin's wife wore all her diamonds. She said she was afraid to leave them off in case the house was burgled while they were away. Some of the writers have married very pretty girls, all sugar and lace and enigmatic smiles, like pictures in a fashion magazine. Alas, their conversation proves just as enigmatic, not to say vapid. Give me a plain woman like Daisy Lennox any day.

I wore my new ivory silk muslin with its bodice of silver beads and the skirts soft and trailing and very gracefully draped. Rather too revealing around the shoulders, said Aubrey when we were dressing for dinner. He can be so rigid when it comes to what is decent and what is not. I said, one would think all those native women in Africa with their bare bosoms might have made him more tolerant of mere shoulders.

Aubrey looked very elegant this evening as always, and the sugar fondant beauties batted their silly eyes and simpered at him. He wore an ivory waistcoat which matched my gown, and I felt such an untoward burst of passion for him that, even though I was corseted like a trussed pheasant and jewelled up to the ears and the guests would be assembling downstairs at any minute, I could not hide my lust for him in the dressing room.

We did it in great haste. Aubrey ripped the lace of my petticoat in his impatience and was so aroused and inflamed that I cried out with delight. How much more thrilling it is when I know he is racked with guilt and just a little bit angry with me because he is unable to resist his instincts and knows he cannot help himself, I was all in a fever for the first thrust of him inside me. And then ecstasy, ecstasy, until we were done . . .

Nancy slammed shut the diary. Her heart pounded in her chest and choked her throat. Tears stung her eyes. When had she ever known Aubrey be so inflamed with desire for her that he could not consider the practicalities of their actions, could not decide, 'Later, when Mama has gone to bed,' or, 'Tomorrow, my darling, when you are less tired from all your studying'? She should not have read it. She should never have begun the hateful scrawling thing. She flung the book from her as if it were a nest of ants and heard the sound of the dressing gong for dinner.

She watched Aubrey that evening, unable to reconcile the husband she knew with the impatient lover of Augusta's diary. He was cool with her during dinner, though not hostile: he had forgiven her outburst over the Latin lesson, but she must, of course, be shown that he had not yet forgotten. She tried to picture him as a man of thirty in an ivory waistcoat. The image of him with Augusta swam before her eyes. *Ecstasy*, *ecstasy* . . . Jealousy filled her up so that she could not swallow. She picked at the food on her plate and her throat felt hard and tight.

She watched Aubrey all evening, aware of the sleek line of his body, the heavy strength of his shoulders and thighs and the grace of his beautiful, long, lean legs. She was caught up by a current of hunger for him which was violent in its intensity. She wanted to touch him, to feel the solid weight of his thighs and his body aroused, impatient for her. It seemed as if the long period between dinner and supper only increased her agitation. Why couldn't he see the change which had come over her? His mother sat in the drawing room and talked on and on about Hugo and Connie who were expected the next day for the Easter holidays. Mrs Farringdon sat by the log fire, Aubrey on the opposite side. Nancy sat on the sofa alone, her fingers twisting the thin silk cord of the marker in the pages of *Across Widest Africa*.

At last his mother gathered together her shawl and book. "I think I shall go to bed. Goodnight, Aubrey darling," Aubrey stood as she clambered to her feet. She inclined her papery cheek and he brushed it with his lips. She turned with the barest acknowledgement to Nancy.

Nancy stood too, taut and breathless, as Mrs Farringdon moved with terrible slowness to the door. The catch clicked behind her. The electric lights glowed softly under their dragonfly shades. A log snapped in the hearth.

"Well," Aubrey turned to her. "Shall we . . . ?"

She could not move, she was so faint with desire. "I've wanted you all evening. Couldn't you see how much?"

He came to her and kissed her, and she reached her arms round him and pulled him to her, feeling a shock of energy run through her body as she pressed herself against his thigh.

"Nancy?" He laughed, easing her away from him to look into her face. "I think it's time we went upstairs."

She was so heavy with wanting that she could hardly form the words. "Not upstairs." She kissed him. "Here. On the sofa — no, on the floor." Her lips sought his more urgently and she ran her hands down the front of his body. She felt his muscles, taut under the smooth silk shirt, and she wound herself more closely, rubbing herself like a cat, with the length of her body against him. She felt him harden against her. She wanted to tear the clothes from him. "Now," she moaned. "Let's do it now," and she scrabbled for the buttons which fastened his trousers.

Again he pushed her gently from him. "Nancy? Whatever has got into you?"

She stared. His face was strange. The lust in him had quite gone and his expression was puzzled, even hostile.

"Let's make love here, Aubrey. Here by the fire. Not in that ghastly bedroom, or in ten minutes, or when you decide you would like me to come to your bed." But the ache of her desire was already weakening, blunted by the look on his face.

"For goodness' sake, darling — on the floor!"

"Yes! On the carpet."

"Like animals," he said coldly.

"No, Aubrey. Like people who are crazy with love for one another."

He reached out to touch her shoulder, "But Nancy, it's so unlike you. And, quite frankly, I wouldn't have thought it possible for you to be so indiscreet."

"But I *am* indiscreet. And rather vulgar, if you recall."

"Perhaps," he said gravely. "But I knew you would not stay that way. I hoped that with guidance — "

"Guidance? You mean when you and your mother have trained me?"

"No, of course not."

"Like breaking a horse?"

"Now you're just being silly."

"Aubrey, I am not silly. I am *not* a child. I am your wife!"

Again he reached to touch her, but she put her hands firmly against his chest and pushed him away.

He staggered backwards a little, then recovered himself and walked to the door. He hesitated, trying to smile. "I can see I've upset you. Look — if you want me to come to your bed — "

"Oh, go away!" Nancy shouted. She heard the door click gently behind him.

She knelt on the carpet when he had gone, warming herself at the fire with her arms wrapped tightly round her, feeling the tension in her body. At last she clambered to her feet, drained of both desire and anger. She switched out the table-lamps and walked slowly to the door. She turned before she left, glancing round the room to make sure there was no evidence of the scene which had taken place. The wall above the fireplace was half shadowed in the dying firelight, but the face in the left-hand portrait was clear. Augusta stared at her with the ghost of a smile.

6

TED POWERS stood at the edge of the pool. The place always made the back of his neck tingle in the early morning, when the light stole down through the branches and a mist was on the quarry.

The song-birds at the edge of the wood were battling it out in a dawn chorus, but the sound was muted here at the wood's still centre. The water in the pool was murky; nothing broke its surface, nothing gave a clue to its depth. He asked himself why he was drawn to the place still, observing the same rituals. Habit? Because of the old lady? Or was it in search of his own peace of mind these days? There seemed little chance of that. He released his breath in a shuddering sigh and turned away, swinging his satchel over his shoulder. It was time he left it alone. Let it go.

He halted at the edge of the track which led down to the copse and Keeper's

Cottage. A slim figure was coming up through the trees; the mist and the sunlight made a halo of gold around her. He drew in his breath sharply, for the effect was unearthly and he might have had doubts about her being flesh and blood if he had been superstitious. It was too late to slip away out of sight among the trees for, as she glanced up the slope, Farringdon's wife had recognised him. She paused, confused for a second, before she came on more resolutely in her stride.

"One would think you had nothing better to do, Powers," she said, with a touch of the high and mighty about her. She was learning fast, he thought as she added, "Tell me, do you spend all your time keeping an eye on this part of the estate?"

He touched his cap. "I'm just doing my job, ma'am."

Her wide-set grey eyes narrowed with suspicion. "And what is your job exactly?" A thought occurred to her. "You're not by any chance keeping an eye on *me*, are you? Is that it? Has Mrs Farringdon set you to watch me?"

Ted smiled at her fancy, for he would not have put that past the old lady either, but he was relieved that it was the only suspicion the girl had got into her head.

Nancy turned away impatiently, blushing at his smile. Why did he have such a knack of undermining her pretence of authority.

"I never was set to watch you," he said with a surprising gentleness.

She looked him in the eye. "But you *do* work for Mrs Farringdon rather than my husband?"

Nancy saw him hesitate and felt her confidence return. So, she had unnerved him; there *was* something unusual about his position at Midwinter. Her annoyance at finding him in the wood, when she had wanted to be alone, evaporated as she pressed him further. "You took over the job of gamekeeper after your father died?"

"Yes, ma'am."

He could not meet her gaze, and she was sure that he was hiding something, but what? "My husband says his mother was very fond of your father when he was gamekeeper, that he was a loyal servant."

A look of cold anger flickered for a second in his eyes and then was gone, dismissed as if with a long-practised control, before he said calmly, "My dad was a good worker in the old days."

"Which is why Mrs Farringdon keeps you on?"

He touched his cap. "I suppose so, ma'am."

"That's very touching."

"In this part of the world old ties mean a lot."

She did not believe him, nor did she believe that Mrs Farringdon's chilly soul hid a vein of sentimentality, but she could not bring herself to challenge him directly. Besides, he had seen her in the wood: she did not want him to report their meeting to Aubrey or his mother. She shared a secret with Powers which gave him an advantage over her. She frowned, feeling her face redden as she said, "Powers, I hope you will not mention my early morning walk here when you next speak to anyone at the house." She hesitated. "I mean — since you are *not* spying on me for

Mrs Farringdon, there is no reason at all why she should know that you have seen me in the wood."

She saw him smile, and there was an element of playfulness in his expression which was disconcerting. It seemed to confirm that, however much she might pretend, they both knew she was as far removed from the ways of the gentry as he was. With a sudden revelation, Nancy saw that she would not make the shift of class which was necessary for her authority ever to be more than superficial. Augusta had claimed the right, by birth and upbringing, to become mistress of Midwinter — and in a way she still held on to the position. Augusta had maintained her prior claim on Aubrey too, Nancy thought, remembering her humiliation of the night before.

"If those are your orders, ma'am," Powers said.

Nancy breathed a sigh of relief. "Yes. Those are my orders."

Again he smiled, and this time there was no mockery in his expression. She looked away, aware of a further shift of authority in his favour.

* * *

The servants were emptying the luggage from the car into the hall, and Hugo and Connie were in the drawing room, chatting excitedly to Aubrey and his mother. The dogs ran around, banging their tails against trunks and tables. Everyone fell silent as Nancy came into the room.

Nancy regarded them: Augusta's children, with their mother's wide-spaced green eyes, sandy fair hair and clever, arrogant expression. There was little more than a year between them, yet in the short space of time she had known them, Nancy recognised that there was a world of difference in their temperaments. Hugo, just turned sixteen, was a dreamer; Connie was a temperamental fourteen-year-old. She persuaded herself to a welcoming brightness.

"So you're home for the holidays. What fun."

Connie was seated on the arm of her father's chair, swinging one of her legs under a long navy skirt. She wore a severe-necked blouse and black stockings, and her fly-away hair was tied back with a dark blue ribbon. She looked at Nancy with an expression of sour disdain, then bent to say something to Aubrey, pushing up her spectacles. Her voice was pitched low so that Nancy could not hear.

Hugo's good manners came to the fore. "We are looking forward to them." He frowned at his sister's discouraging glare.

"And what are you going to do with all that freedom?" said Aubrey.

"I hope to add to my geological collection, sir. And to ride of course, and do some fishing."

"Can we invite Stephen and Edith one day?"

Connie flung an arm round Aubrey's neck so that Mrs Farringdon murmured, "Child! Control your exuberance, do."

"Who are Stephen and Edith?" asked Nancy.

Connie gave a snigger, hiding her mouth with her hands. Nancy caught her eye, and the girl stared back insolently over her fingers.

Hugo glanced at his father with a puzzled frown. "Hasn't she met the Lennoxes yet?"

Nancy was aware of a sense of discovery. The Lennoxes. Augusta's diary. Daisy Lennox and her tile-manufacturer husband had been at the Mafeking party. 'Rather loud' with two 'irrepressible children'.

"I've met hardly anyone in the neighbourhood, except Colonel Gregory and the vicar and his wife and a few of the ladies in the village." She had not meant it to be an accusation, yet it clearly sounded like one. She looked at Hugo with his arrogant expression of bafflement, and at Aubrey, who with his customary diplomacy had decided to forget what had happened the previous evening.

Mrs Farringdon said, "If you were lonely, Nancy, you should have told us; though heaven knows we've put ourselves out. Did we not invite your friends from London? My son isn't one for a lot of company when he is in the country. It's something you will just have to get used to."

"The Lennoxes live about three miles the other side of Winchborne," explained Aubrey patiently. "We have known the family for some years. Daisy and Ralph Lennox and their daughter Edith have been in Scotland; the son is at Oxford. Which is why you have not met them." He turned to Connie. "But we will soon put that right. We shall ask them to dinner."

"When Stephen comes down from Oxford? Hurrah!" said Hugo.

Nancy felt her own spirits lift with unexpected optimism. She smiled at Hugo's pleasure and, catching her eye, the boy blushed and looked at the floor.

* * *

Hugo went straight to the stables after tea. He quickened his step as he heard Nelson's excited whinny of greeting. He loved these first hours of the holidays; it was as if a strain had gone from him when he came home to Midwinter. He did not hate school as much as when he had been younger. He had got over the bullying, the homesickness had become bearable, and he was beginning to make a name for himself at cricket and rugger, which was the traditional way for boys to gain friends.

He breathed in the stables' own particular smell, warm and reeking of horses. He could hear the soft sounds of animals shifting in their stalls and champing on the hay, and saw the figure of Radley near Nelson's stall. There were fewer stable-hands now than there had been when he was little. The stables had always been busy and noisy then, with coaches forever being harnessed and unharnessed and horses led to and fro. Now the Wolseley did all the work, and Browne the chauffeur had replaced most of the grooms.

"He smelled me coming," he said, leaning his head against the horse's withers.

"Yes, sir. I reckon they're cleverer than we give them credit."

"Has he been regularly exercised while I've been away?"

"I've taken him out myself. And the mistress has ridden him now and then."

So, his papa had allowed his new wife to ride Nelson. Hugo examined the horse's mouth.

"There's no need for that, sir. The mistress is as gentle as yourself with him — " Radley broke off, for Nancy had come into the yard and had clearly overheard.

Hugo blushed. "I just wanted to make sure."

"Of course you did." Nancy patted the horse's neck and he pricked his ears at the sound of her voice. "I'd have done the same if he was mine."

"You know about horses then?" Hugo had not really intended the note of challenge in the question.

"I learned to ride on farm horses, but I'm improving. Nelson has helped me along no end."

Hugo smiled. He did not really feel hostile to his papa's new wife, not in the same way as Connie. His sister upheld that Nancy was common and that, in any case, stepmothers were by tradition objects of contempt. Hugo had felt obliged to copy her: Nancy was an interloper and there was no denying that she was of a socially inferior class; there was a feeling that one should obey some kind of form in these matters. Nelson clearly had no such scruples. He nuzzled Nancy's skirt pocket, searching for sugar lumps.

She laughed. "I don't have any just now, you silly old thing."

Hugo looked at her and flicked back his hair. She was nice. She was more like Edith and Stephen than his papa and his grandmama. He was glad the Lennoxes were going to come to dinner.

"Thank you for riding Nelson, Step-Mama."

Nancy looked at him and smiled warmly. "The pleasure was all mine. He's a fine horse. And please — you must call me Nancy."

* * *

"I am so much looking forward to meeting the Lennoxes," Nancy said to Aubrey the day the Lennox family were due for dinner.

He avoided her eyes. There had been a tension between them during the past few days, for he had not come to her bed since she had asked him to make love to her in the drawing room. He would kiss her goodnight stiffly in the corridor, and when she said once, "Aubrey, we have to talk about this," he replied, "My darling, we're both tired. Can't it wait until the morning?"

"I'm glad you'll get to know the Lennoxes," he said, searching for the morning's notes with a studied concentration. "The children are extremely fond of Edith and Stephen." He glanced up and his expression was serious. "I've been rather selfish, Nancy. I should have seen that you needed to meet people of your own age."

She wandered about his study, fingering the spines of books on the shelves. "You like them too, don't you?"

He hesitated. "Daisy and Ralph Lennox are decent people. And Stephen and Edith are very jolly young things. I told you, the children adore them."

"But do *you* like them?" she persisted.

He frowned. "Darling, don't be silly. I've told you."

"Yes. You said they're 'very jolly young things'. It sounds a little dismissive."

"Well, Edith and Stephen are not of my generation."

She halted in her restless wandering. "No. They're about the same age as me."

He set aside the notes on which he had intended working, and smiled with an expression of weary amusement which infuriated her. "You seem determined to pick a quarrel this morning. Why don't you come and sit down?"

She went to him and, after a brief hesitation, put her arms round his neck, determined to break down the hostility between them. "Can't you see that I so much want to be more to you than a child-bride?"

"Then perhaps you should cease acting childishly."

She unwound her arms from him. "Aubrey, if I offended your sense of delicacy the other night, I'm sorry, but we have to discuss it, or things will just go from bad to worse."

He sighed. "Why must you always exaggerate?" He seemed unaware of her mounting anger. "Nancy, I am well aware that to you I may seem a little stuffy, too set in my ways, and I have tried to please you — "

"By inviting Gilbert and Marjorie to stay? By fetching my piano? By arranging for me to see friends of my own age? Do you really think that's all I want?"

"Edith is a splendid person and Stephen is becoming a very interesting young man. I'm glad you're going to meet them. It will liven things up for you."

"Oh, you mean it might take my mind off things!" She was gratified to see a faint blush stain his cheek.

"Darling, not now." He lowered his voice as they heard the children come downstairs.

"Tell me then. When? When can we talk about it? Shall I make an appointment?"

"When you are more calm."

"Don't patronise me," Nancy said in a low voice. "I'm warning you, Aubrey, I won't stand for it much longer." She caught the look of exasperation which crossed his face as she turned and slammed from the room.

There was a figure in the corridor outside; Connie lifted a startled face towards her and hurried away towards the main hall. Nancy ran after her and grasped her arm and pulled her round at the bottom of the stairs. "You were spying on us."

"No, I wasn't."

"Don't lie, you smug little toad." She shook her and felt her shoulders, thin and bony under her hands.

"I wasn't spying. I just heard you quarrelling."

"And aren't you mighty pleased about that! Wouldn't you just love it if Aubrey and I fell out?"

"Yes!" spat out Connie. "Because then you might go away and never come back."

Nancy felt her anger leave her. "Connie, what harm have I done you, except marry your father? Is that a crime?"

"Yes," Connie said sulkily.

Nancy loosened her grip on the child's arm. "Wouldn't it be much better if you and I could be friends?"

"Like you are friends with everybody else? Like you got round Hugo by riding Nelson? Grandmama says you're the wily kind. You worm your way in with people."

Nancy gasped. "She did, did she? And

I suppose she thinks I wormed my way in with your father."

"She says one day Papa will come to his senses — or else be brought to them like he was with my mother." She laughed at Nancy's look of dismay. "Oh, I know all about that. Everyone does. Only we've got to pretend we don't. My mama was a tart."

"Oh, but that's a dreadful thing to say about her! There must have been reasons."

"Trust you to think that."

"Connie . . ." Nancy laid a reassuring hand on her arm, but Connie shook it free and flung herself away from her up the stairs.

Nancy stood in the hall, hearing the girl's feet thump along the upstairs corridor and, after a while, the distant slam of a door. A clock ticked slowly on the upper landing. She could hear the cheerful everyday sound of voices from the servants' quarters coming faintly through the green baize door. Someone was whistling 'Alexander's Ragtime Band'. She considered returning to Aubrey and apologising for her bad temper, but she knew she had not been in the wrong, and the thought of his patient acceptance and smothered displeasure at being disturbed after he had settled down to writing deterred her. Why was it so unsatisfactory when they quarrelled? Although she could hardly even call it quarrelling, for he never shouted back, just looked at her with that reproachful tolerance, as if he put her anger, along with her recent 'indiscretion' over their love-making, down to the impetuosity of youth, which one must accept along with youth's charm. She wondered what his attitude to Augusta had been — the same patient mollification? Had he not even raised his voice when he found out about her affair with Viner? The thought was faintly chilling.

The morning stretched ahead. Aubrey would not come looking for her; he would leave her alone, as he always did when he decided she had behaved badly. Mrs Farringdon would assume she was with Aubrey, and Connie would probably not come out from her sulk before lunch.

Nancy walked steadily along the

corridor, past the dining room, until she reached Augusta's sitting room. She hesitated, to make sure she had not been observed, before slipping inside and closing the door.

★ ★ ★

Nancy placed Augusta's diary on her lap and opened it at the page where she had left off reading.

> . . . I wanted to laugh as we entered the drawing room and all faces turned towards us. I should like to have seen the change come over them if they knew that Aubrey and I had been doing it scarcely twenty minutes before. Though perhaps they would not have been so shocked as all that, for there was a wildness in everyone tonight. I could fancy that not a few others had already tasted a little excitement before dinner.
>
> John Viner said, very formally, that he believed he had the pleasure of taking me in to dinner, and I had a strange and wicked desire that he,

more than any of them, should know.

Viner was at first rather serious, not joining in with the boisterous enthusiasm of our rendition of 'Rule Britannia'. I rebuked him, saying I believed he had lost his voice or else his sense of patriotism, and he seemed annoyed. I could sense his eyes on me afterwards, and the thought occurred that he might be one of those men who feels things deeply and that I had really offended him. I apologised, saying I had meant no insult by the remark, and please would he disregard it. He reminded me that he was a collector of butterflies. He said that people sometimes compare women to butterflies, meaning they are quick and beautiful, yet generally implying too a lightness of character, a certain superficiality. He said he did not believe he should like to think of me as a butterfly in that context, but that no butterfly, even the most exotic species from Malaysia, could surpass me for beauty.

What woman could have resisted such a speech? I said that we had plenty of very acceptable butterflies in Dorset, without going all the way to the other side of the world to look for them. He agreed. What could rival the delicacy of a Brimstone or a Blue? I confessed to being very ignorant about species, and he suggested I might care to accompany him on a local expedition and he would teach me. I reminded him that Aubrey has arranged a shoot for the guests tomorrow and there would be no time for chasing butterflies.

Aubrey was talking about Africa. He is planning another trip. This led to a long discussion about our colonies abroad, Aubrey taking the view that we should rule without interference in local customs, his mama that the whole world would be a more agreeable place if it had an unequivocally British flavour, and everyone else somewhere in between. Viner leaned rather more to Aubrey's mama's opinion than to Aubrey's vaguely paradoxical liberalism. How strange. We none of us, not even Aubrey, question the right of an

Englishman to walk into a country and take possession of it, on the mere grounds that he is an Englishman, therefore superior to the lesser breeds. And yet we would all argue in principle that man has a right to be free, even if he is black. We are all extremely curious about the lives and customs of the natives, and yet we do not consider how, by controlling their government and their education, we might be in the process of destroying those quaint and picturesque customs.

After dinner the men set light to the bonfire in the field. People drifted towards it across the grounds, leaving Viner and myself unexpectedly isolated by the house. We watched the glow of the flames and the sparks shooting up against the black sky, and he asked me again if I would not consent to an expedition with him to instruct me in the more common of the local butterflies. I said we should join the others near the fire. I foresee great danger in this proposition of a butterfly expedition and I have refused.

Midwinter
Sunday 27 May, 1900

I went for a walk to clear my head this morning, having scarcely slept at all, for I knew I was not immune to the attractions of a romantic adventure.

I had set out to inspect the remains of the fire, and was surprised and not a little frightened to meet Viner so early, when not even the outdoor servants were about. As we crossed the grounds together, he confessed that he had fallen in love with me. I could not reply, my heart felt so strange. The air was very still and silent, the tops of the trees a line of dark silhouettes against the sky. A cuckoo called far away in the wood. We stood for a long while regarding the blackened and scorched earth without speaking. He said that there is in New Guinea a special kind of wood, which is used by the Papuans to obviate the need for flint or matches: it has the peculiarity of smouldering for days when once it is ignited. He lowered his voice. "Only a look, one word of hope," he promised, "and I should not merely smoulder but burst into flame."

I trembled at the tone of his voice, and at the pressure of his hand on my arm. As if in a dream I told him that Aubrey is to go to London next week. He replied that, if that were so, there was nothing to prevent us, it only remained to decide where. His gaze fell on the wood, easily reached from the Winchborne road or, on this side, from Midwinter without detection. Excellent cover, he said, for partridge, pheasant or lovers. We are to meet the day after Aubrey leaves. Am I in love or mad? Whatever have I done?

Midwinter
Tuesday 29 May, 1900

I am in a torment of confusion and impatience. Aubrey is going to London to see his publisher about the book he will write as a sequel to *Across Widest Africa*. He now wants me to go with him. He says he will not keep up the expense of a London house if we do not use it to the full without waiting for the excuse of Ascot and

Henley. He thought I would be only too happy to go with him. It's true, I miss some of London society and adore the shops and the theatre and the splendid dinners and seeing the Prince of Wales ride by in his victoria, but how it pales into insignificance and how the absurdity of it all comes to the fore when the attractions of London are pitted against my new adventure.

Aubrey was melancholy after the party. He said he used to think he liked all those people, but now they seem to him to be very tedious. Dear Gilbert he proclaims sound, but he has his doubts about John Viner. He is sulking because I will not go to London with him, and I am in an agony that he suspects something. The children have been fractious and Connie 'needs her mama', says well-meaning Nanny, and this is a satisfactory excuse as far as Aubrey is concerned, but it is the reverse of pleasant when I find I am to be mewed up with a squalling infant while he is away. Everything seems to be going wrong.

Yesterday there was an eclipse of the

sun. We all turned out on to the lawn with our portions of sooted glass. As the earth was plunged into darkness I heard one of the maidservants ask, could it be a portent? Three weeks ago, almost to the day, Mount Vesuvius erupted. Is Nature angered by the new century? Could the darkening of the sun be a sign? I feel so superstitious and nervous.

Midwinter
Wednesday 30 May, 1900

How beautiful, beautiful were the bluebells. There was the damp smell of wild garlic and of the bluebells themselves, cool and woody. It has not rained for days and yet the earth was moist and dark underfoot and its scent joined with that of the flowers, of bark and leaf-mould and the thousand other aromas of the wood in May.

We walked hand in hand and felt perfectly natural with one another and free from guilt. John talked to me a little about Hairstreaks and the Fritillaries which will fly about in the summer, and he pointed out Speckled Woods, pretty, mouse-brown little butterflies with cream-flecked wings.

While he lectured me I was able to study him. He has a very thick smooth skin over high cheek-bones. His lips are fleshy, his top lip curling, dark with the suggestion of a moustache. His ears are rather small. His hands, with neatly shaped nails, are slim, and he uses them to illustrate points while he talks. His eyes and manner are extremely seductive.

Our path led us to the pool. I told him how the land around had formerly been quarried and that the locals used to extract the stone in an earlier time. Is it deep? he wanted to know. He seemed wary of standing too close to the edge. I said that it goes down for ever. To hell? he wondered. The look in his eyes made my heart quicken again. He turned me round to face him and asked, "Is that where we shall end?" I said I did not care, and truly I did not. He touched me then, his hand caressing my stomach and moving downwards, pressing hard into the folds of my skirt. He asked with a low insistence, should we do it naked? He said he was mad for the touch of my body, and I was immediately filled with desire for him.

He is smooth and olive-coloured, heavier and more beautiful than his clothes make him appear. He spread his coat and my petticoats to form a counterpane among the bluebells and we lay side by side, examining one another, tracing the lines of one another's form, tormenting a little, until we could neither of us bear to hold back any longer and he entered, not in a mood of agitation like Aubrey, but smooth, like an olive fish, and patient until my storm was over.

The bluebells had left green stains on my petticoat. I said, "What will they say at the laundry?"

Midwinter
Thursday 31 May, 1900

He came to the house with the excuse that he has brought Aubrey a case of butterflies. He is staying in Dorchester. He says he will come to Midwinter often, if he can avoid suspicion. He tells Aubrey's mama he has decided to see more of the West Country. The danger is terrific. We sat drinking tea and making polite conversation and admiring the butterflies. I remarked on how much happier they are when they are free. He asked, could I know that for certain? I said, of course, for now they are dead. Their lives are brief anyway, was his opinion, and happiness and misery are diversions reserved exclusively for humans. He seemed cold with me, and I was annoyed, but soon I saw that his aloofness was for Mrs Farringdon's benefit only. When she was not looking he gave me the sweetest, most loving glance, and when he left he whispered the words, "Tomorrow afternoon. Among the bluebells." I forgave him at once, and am now in an agony of anticipation and don't know how I shall bear to wait.

Midwinter
Friday 1 June, 1900

To have lain among the bluebells and know that I am loved!

We walked all in a dream through the blue carpet at our feet. Sweet delirium of love. To be so worshipped and so exquisitely desired! We were filled with the stillness of the wood and filled one another with silent rapture. The smell of his flesh was the smell of the wood and together we drowned in the scent of the bluebells.

Midwinter
Saturday 2 June, 1900

To the wood, to the wood. Love among the bluebells!

Midwinter
Sunday 3 June, 1900

He sent a message after church under the pretext of giving me notice about some more butterflies for Aubrey. He wants me to go to Dorchester. Is he mad? The wood is safe. We have only to look out for the keeper. But Dorchester. Heaven knows who might not see me there. The Lennoxes. The colonel. I replied that I could not get away and am now in deepest despair in case he grows tired of me.

Midwinter
Monday 4 June, 1900

Drove to Dorchester in the carriage. We walked by the river. He was angry because I would not go to his hotel. He says the wood is spied on. The keeper, for all we know, prowls there night and day. We cannot trust anyone, not even my maid (for he is not pleased that I have entrusted Charlotte, with whom I would trust my life, with the task of delivering messages). I was miserable and dazed with desire for him.

He says he does not believe in marriage and that no commitment should be binding. He says lovers should be free. He thinks that he will never worship me and says that total devotion only imprisons the one who is worshipped.

Midwinter
Tuesday 5 June, 1900

He has written a letter, handed to Charlotte at great risk this afternoon while she was on her way from an errand in Winchborne. He must have lain in wait for hours in hope! He begs my forgiveness for his pique yesterday. He says it is the way of lovers to be cruel to the one they love, that he adores me all the more because of my acceptance of his ill-humour. He swears he will throw himself at my feet and I may trample his face among the bluebells or treat him in any way I desire: he will not resist or complain.

Midwinter
Wednesday 6 June, 1900

Oh my love, my tender god! How sweet is reconciliation.

I made him take me at the edge of the pool, knowing how the water frightens him. I said I wanted to see how much he loved me. He stood with his bare heels overhanging the edge of the bank and his arms outspread as if to fall back into the depths and sacrifice himself. He looked like the god he has become to me, like Pan himself. When I came to him we knelt by the pool and he held me over the water, so that my hair brushed the surface and only his arm beneath my waist prevented my falling. But I was not the one who was afraid.

Midwinter
Thursday 7 June, 1900

We were sad today. Tomorrow Aubrey comes back from London. The bluebells are over.

Nancy heard the sound of the luncheon gong. She looked up from the diary. Nothing had changed. The sun streamed in at the window. Birds sang in the garden. The house reverberated with the sound of the gong. And yet the sun hurt her eyes, the bird-song seemed loud and intense and the stillness of the room seemed menacing. The gong rang inside her head, so that she felt it must burst it open. She covered the chair with the dust sheet and put Augusta's diary back in its place on the shelf. And with an unaccountable headache she went to lunch.

7

"I EXPECTED you to look like what Pa used to call a northern lass — all red-cheeked and eh-bah-gum."

"Stephen! You make poor Nancy sound like a mill girl," laughed his mother.

Mrs Farringdon's expression implied that the description would not have been far wrong.

"She's a bonny lass, right enough," said Mr Lennox.

Nancy, following her habit of making quick judgements based on little except instinct — a feeling of, I like this person or, I must be wary of this one — had warmed to the Lennoxes at once. Ralph Lennox was a large, shapeless kind of a man with a handsome face and small moustache; he talked in a loud Midlands voice as if addressing a sizeable audience, and, when he spoke, Mrs Farringdon narrowed her eyes against the sound as if she were eating lemons. It was clear that Mrs Farringdon looked down on the Lennoxes — who had made their money too conspicuously in trade — almost as much as she looked down on Nancy. The realisation made Nancy warm to them further: they were joint allies against the pretensions of Midwinter. Daisy Lennox was as large as her husband; a handsome, full-bosomed, homely woman who reminded Nancy pleasantly of bread-making; this impression was reinforced by her hairstyle, like a well-risen cottage loaf.

The Lennoxes clearly adored their children. Nancy could understand why everyone adored Stephen; he was a little older than herself, perhaps twenty, though he looked younger, with dark hair and intelligent eyes. He was eager and athletic, and he reminded her of a puppy just discovering it has turned into a young dog.

Edith was older than her brother. Her black hair was cut in a straight low fringe above steady blue eyes. "We *did* rather expect someone very independent and bumptious," she said candidly as they sat down to dinner.

"Don't be so sure you're wrong," said Aubrey's mother with a barbed pretence at good humour.

"She's delicious." Stephen beamed at her, and Nancy, captivated by their exuberance, saw that Connie had overheard the remark and was sulking because of it.

"Do you like ragtime?" Stephen demanded and, before Nancy had time to reply, "Can you do the Turkey Trot?"

"No," said Nancy, laughing.

"Edith will teach you. She's a capital dancer. Do you like poetry?"

"Oh, yes!"

"I think Aubrey looks like a poet," said Edith. "Don't you?"

Her mother scolded them. "You are confusing Nancy when you both talk at once."

"Not at all," Nancy said. She smiled wryly. "Though I must admit, I'm not sure what Edith means about Aubrey."

"He's so *fine* and self-contained. He would make a poet in the heroic vein," said Edith. She turned to Aubrey's mother. "You must agree, Mrs Farringdon."

"My son has a fine, Christian character,"

she acknowledged. "Though he's not, I think, poetical."

Nancy glanced at Aubrey who looked acutely embarrassed.

"Some men have a natural heroism. I can't imagine Aubrey making fun of the Pankhursts." Edith turned to Nancy. "Do you believe in equality and women's rights, Nancy?"

Stephen groaned. "Don't let my sister get on her pet hobby horse."

"You young women don't know when you are fortunate," said Mrs Farringdon, though even she had begun to smile.

Stephen raised his glass to her. "Well spoken."

He really is a charmer, thought Nancy. They both are. Why, they've got the old girl almost lying down and waving her legs in the air.

"I'm not going to be a feminist," declared Connie fiercely; the bravura was clearly intended for Stephen's ears.

"Oh — so you'd rather let your more revolutionary sisters win the vote for you, would you?" laughed Nancy.

"I can just see Connie breaking windows," said Hugo.

"Those suffragettes' behaviour is outrageous, and so unfeminine," declared Daisy Lennox; her distress was genuine, for she was in principle, she said, a suffragist.

"We ought to deport the law-breakers. Far from making fun of women like the Pankhursts, I should tell them to look to their proper womanly duties," remarked Mrs Farringdon. She watched Aubrey, who toyed with his fork and said nothing.

"Which side do you take, Nancy?" Stephen was regarding her closely.

Aubrey glanced up with a slight frown, as if her reply was of grave importance. "Yes. Where do you stand, Nancy darling?"

Nancy looked at him. Did he really not know? They had been married almost six months and yet he did not know that she was at heart a feminist. Surely it was the sort of thing a husband and wife *should* know about one another. "I support the suffragists in principle." Aubrey's frown deepened. "I mean, I think women should have their chance in everything, the same as men. But I'm against the methods which the militant suffragettes have used. I could never go along with violent ways to achieve an end."

Aubrey nodded, as if, after some consideration, he approved of her reply. Mrs Farringdon, with an enigmatic, shuttered expression, lowered her eyes.

"We may all have to condone violent means before long," Stephen said soberly. "When it's our patriotic duty to take up arms against the Hun."

Aubrey felt uneasy when people talked of hostility against Germany. For years it seemed the great powers had been getting ready for a war in Europe, pulling one another into alliances. He could remember only too well the last war, people declaring themselves 'pro-Boer' and 'anti' and all the hysteria of Mafeking. He stared at the tablecloth. How unexpectedly memories could strike at one's emotions. Why did everything always come back to Augusta?

He looked at Nancy and wondered again whether he had been wrong to bring her to Midwinter. They had been so happy in London. She was talking to Edith about the possibility of a war, saying in her engagingly naïve way that someone or other had proved that nobody could win in modern warfare, so it followed that nobody would be so crazy as to start hostilities. He recognised her rapport with the Lennoxes, who were of a different class and generation. Hugo, the young idiot, looked almost disappointed at the prospect of missing out on a European skirmish. War, to a sixteen-year-old, fed on the patriotics of the *Boy's Own Paper*, sounded like a romantic adventure. Aubrey felt as old as Methuselah as he listened to their conversation. Romantic. It had been Nancy's word for the pool in the wood. An innocent enough impression, and the secret the wood concealed had happened all so long ago, but for him it had been for ever poisoned because of that devil who stole Augusta from him.

* * *

"How I detest war talk." Daisy Lennox arranged her skirt about her plump thighs as she settled herself on one of the sofas in the drawing room. "How nice it always is to leave the men to their port and silly gossip." She beamed at Nancy and patted the seat beside her. "And to have a chance to get to know one another a little better."

Nancy smiled and sat next to her. The talk of war had depressed her a little. She sensed that, however much one argued that it could not happen, a war in Europe might one day be inevitable.

"Tell us about your home and your family," pressed Mrs Lennox. "Ralph and I consider ourselves honorary southerners these days, but you cannot imagine the nostalgia we still feel for the north."

"Personally, I have little interest in the north," interrupted Mrs Farringdon. She had seated herself opposite, near one of the Tiffany lamps; the light did not soften her face with shadows, but made her features look harsh. "North and south belong to such different worlds culturally. We don't think in the same way."

"That's true." Connie, awkward and bony in a pink V-necked party frock, was setting out a chessboard on a small table. She looked up with a smirk, and

Nancy felt a sense of despair. She could ignore Mrs Farringdon's insults, but how could she hope to become a mother to this disagreeable child when less than four years separated them? And yet she felt a perverse sympathy as she watched Connie's thin hands lift the chessmen from the box. There was something of herself in the rebellious girl — not in looks, for she knew she had been a pretty child and she had known how to charm — but with the same vehement flashes of emotion.

Nancy's own childhood seemed long ago now; her memories of her mother were already blurring. She had been a profoundly down-to-earth woman of uncertain temper, but loving — that much Nancy would always remember — and lovely, with a clear skin and large dark eyes. She had worn long black skirts and high-necked blouses pinned with a modest brooch in the severe style of her Nonconformist upbringing. Her wonderful chestnut hair was always pulled into a smooth round chignon at the nape of her neck. Nancy sometimes wondered whether, having done her duty, there had been nothing left for her to live for. She blinked back sudden tears. Her mother had not lived long enough to see her dream come to fruition. It seemed such a small ambition now — to give her daughter an 'education'; and how meagre that schooling had proved to be, compared to Aubrey's background. For an instant she longed to be back in the easy-going, no-nonsense atmosphere of her childhood, where there had been no claustrophobic country houses and correct ways of doing things, no stuffy upper middle-class tradition.

"We are all very fond of the north," asserted Daisy Lennox, drawing herself up a little in response to Mrs Farringdon's disparagement of her birthplace.

"I sometimes feel rather homesick," confessed Nancy. "My mother died only two years ago."

Mrs Lennox's eyes filled with ready tears. "And your papa?"

Nancy, seeing Stephen and Hugo come into the drawing room, replied, "My father died when I was small."

"You poor child. No brothers or sisters?"

Nancy shook her head, and at once found herself enfolded in Mrs Lennox's arms, her face pressed by a soft, consoling hand to her beaded lace corsage. She heard Mrs Farringdon's stifled intake of breath and, catching Stephen's eye on her release from his mother's embrace, saw him wink.

Hugo, coming into the drawing room with Stephen, saw Nancy clasped against Mrs Lennox's bosom, and reflected that the women seemed to have been having a more interesting time of it than the men. It was the first time he had been allowed to join in the men's after-dinner conversation and the passing of port, and he was frankly disappointed. Stephen had led him to believe that when men were alone the talk became risqué, but his papa and Mr Lennox had discussed nothing but strikes and politics, and how Lloyd George and his unemployment and insurance schemes were ruining the country. There had not even been any of his papa's famous travel tales to enliven the half-hour. He could hear his father's voice in the hall; the two men were still discussing the government and Asquith, whom Mr Lennox thought 'very sound'. He suspected his papa was only lingering out of politeness.

Stephen was watching Nancy as, smiling, she struggled free from Mrs Lennox's embrace, and Hugo wondered if his friend was gone on her. He hoped not, for he wanted Stephen all to himself this holiday. How strange that his best friend and his step-mama should be just about the same age. She had said they must call her Nancy, but you could tell his papa disapproved. It probably made Papa feel old, and reminded him that he had picked her out from the wrong class. And yet how could he and Connie possibly have called her 'Mama'? He wondered disloyally what Nancy had seen in his papa. Was she after his money? Somehow he thought not.

Connie was looking at him through her spectacles, trying to signal to him to go over and play chess with her. He supposed a game with his sister was preferable to keeping up boring conversations with the adults. He sighed and went to join her.

Stephen leaned over the back of the

sofa where Nancy was sitting. He was persuading his sister to show them how to dance the latest ragtime steps. Edith turned to Nancy. "You must join in, Nancy."

"Just so long as you don't ask me to do the tango."

"Good Lord, I hope not," said Daisy Lennox. "Girls throwing themselves about like a lot of gypsies. What is the world coming to?"

Nancy, leaving Mrs Lennox's side, tried out a few steps with Edith. She had loved to dance as a child, but it had not been ragtime then. A strong memory flooded her mind, one of the few of her father: she was waltzing round and round with him on the parlour carpet while her mother played the battered old upright piano. She pushed a strand of hair behind her ear and halted, laughing with Edith to the Lennoxes' applause. Ignoring the combined hostility of Mrs Farringdon's scowl and Connie's stare of derision, she went to the fireplace and spread her hands to the log fire. Edith flopped on to the sofa. "That's warmed us up rather."

Nancy smiled at Edith's frank acknowledgement of Midwinter's shortcomings. She shivered: her thin evening dress was no protection from the cold which breathed through the house in the evenings. She turned and glanced at the carriage clock on one of the small tables, wondering when Aubrey would come in from the hall. She could hear him talking out there to Mr Lennox. Perhaps someone would ask him about taking ship for Africa, so that he might begin on one of his stories about being surrounded by hostile Arabs, or meeting cannibals who supposedly smoked their human victims before they ate them, or about crocodiles which swallowed people in small canoes. She needed to revive her girlish adoration of him. What had shaken it? Augusta and the diary, his recent coldness towards her — or Midwinter itself? Was it Midwinter's chilly influence which prevented Aubrey from coming to her bed at night?

Mrs Farringdon had moved closer to Hugo and Connie, as if taking an interest in their game. Hugo studied the chessboard, a frown creasing his brow; he leaned his elbows on the table and rested his chin in his hands. His hair fell softly over his eyes and every now and then he would shake it back with an irritable flick of the head. Hugo was like Aubrey, thought Nancy; he had inherited his father's intelligence and his reserve. Connie tapped her fingers on the arm of her chair. Every now and then she wrinkled her nose to hitch up her spectacles, and her face worked with impatience for her turn.

Nancy straightened her back, feeling the fire's patchy warmth begin to seep through the silk of her dress. She was very conscious of the portrait of Augusta, gazing down from the wall above her. It was a constant reminder of her own position here as intruder, and that, for all her failings, it was Augusta who had long ago established a place in Aubrey's heart and was the mother of his children. Nancy thought of Augusta and Aubrey together. Augusta and her lover in the bluebells, tormenting one another until they could bear to hold back no longer and then — smooth like an olive fish. She tried to close her mind to it. She would *not* think of it.

Stephen was talking to his mother, and Edith had discovered an album of photographs. Mrs Farringdon had positioned herself with her back to Nancy. Was it a deliberate snub? Nancy lifted her chin. She would not be made to feel an outsider here. She was Aubrey's wife; she would get around him and his children, if only to prove she could not be beaten — not by Midwinter, nor by Mrs Farringdon, nor by Augusta.

She waited for a pause in the game. "Who taught you to play chess? Your father?"

Mrs Farringdon answered for the children. "Of course."

"I don't expect people played chess where you come from," Connie said with her sly smile.

"On the contrary. It was my mother taught me."

"Our papa used to say Yorkshire was a raw, uncivilised place."

Nancy glanced at Mrs Farringdon, who confirmed the statement with a twitch of her mouth.

"Did he now? I dare say he has

changed his opinion a little since then."

"Why?" challenged Connie. "Just because he married you?"

Mrs Farringdon said automatically, though clearly not in defence of Nancy, "Connie! Young ladies who are rude are sent to their rooms."

"Why should he change his opinion?" Hugo was looking at Nancy closely. He flicked his hair from his forehead.

"Well, you know. People do change their minds about things. We're all open to influence."

"Am I open to influence?" Aubrey, mellowed by port, had at last come into the room with Mr Lennox. He strolled to stand affectionately beside her, and she linked her arm in his.

"I'm hoping that you are." She smiled at him and felt the strength of his arm. He smiled back with his eyes and said, "No doubt about it. You could twist the fiercest Hottentot round your little finger if you had a mind to it."

"That's true. We are all totally bewitched," said Stephen with undisguised admiration, and Nancy, flattered by his enthusiasm, and with Aubrey's arm entwined in hers, felt her love for her husband rekindle.

"I think Yorkshire people are common and stupid!" Connie flung her arm across the chessboard, scattering the pieces.

"For goodness' sake, child!" thundered Aubrey, shocked from his normal composure. He released Nancy's arm.

Mrs Farringdon said quietly and coldly, "You have gone far enough, Connie. You must leave us at once and go to your room."

Hugo began to pick up and set out the chess pieces again, red in the face with embarrassment as Connie ran from the drawing room.

"Dear, dear," said Daisy Lennox briskly. "What a little firebrand you have been raising, Aubrey."

"Let us hope it won't be too long before our ugly duckling turns into a swan," said Mrs Farringdon in an attempt to smooth the situation.

"You should never have sent her away to school," remarked Ralph Lennox cheerfully. "It doesn't do girls any good."

Aubrey turned to Nancy. "I'm so sorry."

"It doesn't matter."

"I'm awfully afraid she may take after Augusta," said Mrs Farringdon tersely.

Aubrey jerked his head. "Mama — I hardly think —"

"Oh, you know what I mean."

But *I* don't know what they mean, thought Nancy. In what way might Connie 'take after Augusta'? She thought of Augusta's diaries. What else did they hide?

Edith stood up. She smiled sympathetically at Nancy. "I should like to talk to Connie if I may."

* * *

Connie flung herself on her back and placed her hands behind her head. The pillow was wet where she had cried into it and it felt cold against her wrists. She stared hard at the ceiling. "I hate her." She felt the creak of the mattress as Edith sat on the edge of her bed. She knew that she had behaved abominably, that she looked awful and ugly and her nose was running. She scrabbled under the pillow for a handkerchief.

Edith pretended not to notice. She picked up Connie's spectacles from the bedside table and polished them on her dress before she handed them to her, "Don't you think you are being rather silly? You're not a child any more, Connie, even though everyone treats you like one." She did not smile, but her clear blue eyes were calm and kind, like a nurse or some of the nicer teachers at school, and Connie wished her papa had married someone like Edith instead of the hateful and common Nancy.

"She's not my mother," Connie said sulkily.

"No one could replace your mama," Edith said. "And I'm sure Nancy is too sensible a person to try."

"I hardly remember my mama."

"Well then. All the more reason to give Nancy a chance." Edith paused. "I like her. I really do. And so does Stephen."

Connie's mouth worked to control a fresh bout of weeping. So that was it, thought Edith. Or part of it, for who could tell what was going on in that mixed-up head? "She seems awfully nice to me. If your papa can ignore her background, so can you. She's a decent person who would make a good friend."

"Oh, go away!"

"Very well." Edith stood up. "But I think you should apologise to her. We would all think the better of you for it."

Nancy met Edith in the corridor. "Is she all right?"

"She'll get over it. You might even get an apology."

"I don't care about that. I just hoped they might take to me. Hugo is half-way there, but I don't think I'll ever win Connie over."

"I shouldn't try too hard. The little beast doesn't deserve it."

"Unlikely though it may sound, I almost feel a kind of affection for her. Aubrey's mother said she is like Augusta. Do you remember her?" They had reached the stairs. A murmur of voices drifted through the half-open drawing-room door. Nancy sat on the top step and Edith sat beside her. Nancy drew up her knees and rested her chin in her hands. "I've got this terrible curiosity to know what Augusta was like."

Edith regarded Nancy for a moment. "To tell the truth, I don't really know. I wasn't very old when she died. But I think that what happened wasn't altogether her fault. The story is that Viner was a bad egg." She frowned. "It was a dreadful time for Aubrey by all accounts. Is it wise to dig around?"

"No," sighed Nancy. "But I get so bored." She wanted to tell Edith about the pool and meeting Powers, and about Augusta's diary and the long hours when Aubrey ignored her and there was nothing at all to do except delve into things which were best left hidden. "Aubrey is so good and full of restraint, and he is — oh — so much cleverer than I am. I felt, when we lived in London, that I might have a chance to catch up a little, to develop myself. I never thought I should have to get used to living at Midwinter."

"I should have thought you would be only too glad to go where Aubrey goes."

"I am. And I'm not ungrateful," declared Nancy. "I used to dream about marrying a husband who was cultured and interesting and moved in educated society."

"You admire him a lot."

"He's the most admirable man in the world to me," Nancy said passionately. And it was true. But Edith's silence posed the question: was admiration enough?

* * *

Hugo felt a surge of pure joy as the wind buffeted his ears and the afternoon sun, flickering through the line of oak trees, made light and dark patterns in front of his eyes. He urged Nelson into a canter as he saw a figure on horseback come towards the house. Stephen had promised to ride with him today. He was grinning at him as he reined to a halt.

Stephen was all that Hugo wanted to be when he was twenty. He gave an impression of bouncing through life with complete self-confidence, never having a care in the world.

"Where to then, young master?" Stephen touched his hat, imitating the local accent.

"Winchborne Hill," Hugo said breathlessly. "I want to collect some fossils."

They cut across the estate and rode the horses hard over the fields. Hugo felt hot with pleasure because Nelson could keep up with Stephen's larger hunter. They slowed the animals to a walk as they came to an open limestone quarry cut into the hillside, about a mile from the estate.

"All these years we've lived in Dorset, and I've hardly ever been here," Stephen said, dismounting.

"There's no stone been extracted for decades," said Hugo. "There's another quarry in the wood at Midwinter, but that one's supposed to be dangerous. There's a pit filled with water. No one knows how deep it is." He fell silent, remembering his father's aversion to the quarry in the wood.

"Well, we're fortunate here. No water. Not even any rain. What glorious weather," Stephen watched Hugo clamber with a leather bag and small hammer over the boulders to the quarry face. "You really take this seriously, don't you?"

"I want to be a geologist." Hugo

turned to smile at him. "Do you like it at Oxford?"

"Very much. I expect you'll like it too."

"It seems an awfully long time to wait."

"The years will pass quickly, my child." Stephen's gravity was less mocking as he added, "Unless there's a war, of course."

"If there's a war, I shall miss out and you'll have all the fun."

"We need a war, don't you think? We need something to shake us up. I've joined the Officer Training Corps at Oxford with some chums. I feel as if I'm just waiting for something to happen and for my life to start in earnest."

Hugo began chipping at the fossiliferous stone. If Stephen felt as if he were waiting for something to happen too, when did anything ever begin? He extracted a modest piece of ammonite and put it in his bag. He thought of his papa, for whom life seemed to have stopped permanently since he had given up travelling, buried by his books and collections; yet his life must once have been full of romance and adventure. He looked up. "What do you think of my step-mama?"

Stephen whistled through his teeth. "She's ravishing. But Midwinter must be a bit dull for her."

"I suppose it is." As much as he loved his home, Hugo could see that it was not exciting. Implied in Stephen's statement was the fact that his papa was a bit dull too.

Would he become as hidebound by Midwinter one day? Fossilised on the estate? For when his papa and grandmama were dead and gone, Midwinter would be his. The notion was not unpleasant as he thought of the museum he was going to establish there. He became preoccupied with the fossils.

Stephen sat on a patch of grass and lay back against a boulder. He let his thoughts drift, watching Hugo at the quarry face and hearing the chink-chink of his hammer and the sound of the horses champing the sparse grass. He remembered the previous evening and Nancy. He had been more enraptured by her than he would care to admit to anyone. He recalled her soft flat voice, her seriousness over the feminist issue, and the contrast of mood in her when she was dancing with his sister. Edith had pronounced her a 'good sort' afterwards, but 'perhaps not quite the thing for Midwinter' and 'not very mature'. Mature. Who wanted a woman to be mature? His mama was mature. Old Mrs Farringdon was mature. Nancy was too lively for Aubrey Farringdon, he decided, and too natural and lovely to be buried in Dorset.

Stephen returned with Hugo along the road, passing through the village of Winchborne. He had grown up here, and the village seemed hardly to have changed in all those years. And yet the world was changing: class distinctions were less rigid, so that men like his father, who had risen in industry, mingled more easily in society. As a child Stephen had believed that his papa's views on everything were right. The tile company was their way to prosperity. They must look to the solid, respectable men of the past — like his papa and Joe Chamberlain, and Aubrey Farringdon and Asquith — for their models of morality, solid performance, the proper order of things. Childlike, he had believed in Empire and England's supremacy as top nation. Now, although he would fight for his country with a patriotism which burned no less strongly, Stephen was not so convinced about the old notions of order and morality. He thought again of Nancy. She belonged to the same uncertain generation as himself, and to a class which had less of a foothold on the social hierarchy, yet she had aligned herself to Farringdon. For security, to better herself — or could she really be in love with him?

The sun warmed the yellow-brown stone of the cottages. Horses and carts stirred up the dust as they had done when he was a boy. Some things had changed. A motor cycle roaring towards them made the horses shy suddenly.

"Was that Powers?" Stephen said when the cycle had passed and the horses were calm again. "Doesn't he work at Midwinter?"

"Grandmama keeps him on as a woodman," Hugo said. "He used to work in the stables years back, when my mama was alive."

"He should have stuck with horses," Stephen said feelingly.

They rode on. "I can hardly remember my mama," Hugo said.

Stephen could remember Hugo's mother clearly: a beautiful woman who smelled of flowers. He recalled the glamour and colour of being taken to Midwinter as a child. "It was all very much grander when we were children. Your mama was always having parties and inviting lots of people." They had reached the wood. The trees were light with fresh spring growth at the roadside. Stephen peered into the trees. "Have you *never* been near the other quarry?"

Hugo flushed. "You know it's always been out of bounds to us."

"But haven't you even been tempted? Think of the fossils, just waiting to be discovered."

"Yes, but — oh, you know what's supposed to have happened." Hugo flushed. "My mama was discovered with a man there."

"*Inflagrante delicto*," Stephen grinned. "Strange, how it's never a crime until one is found out."

"It's not funny."

"No, I suppose not." Stephen had been a small boy, but he remembered it all the same, the adults' whispered gossip, the initial pity for Farringdon. And then the almost greater scandal when, instead of divorcing his wife, Farringdon had lived quietly with her at Midwinter until she died, just as if nothing had happened, though the parties and entertaining had come to an end. "Doesn't it seem rather ridiculous, to treat the place as if it's plague-infested all these years afterwards?"

"I suppose so."

Stephen laughed, teasing, yet without much malice. "Where's your curiosity, Hugo? Call yourself a scientist?" And then, more thoughtfully, "You're very well-behaved, dear boy, aren't you?"

They rode on in silence, and Hugo felt himself diminished in Stephen's estimation. His friend's criticism had cut deeply.

He spread out the fossils in his room when he reached Midwinter. They were the sort of specimens he might have found in any spot which had already been picked over by earlier geologists. They looked very dull and commonplace. Call yourself a scientist? Hugo tipped the fossils into a cardboard box. He had been looking forward to cataloguing them, but now the afternoon was ruined.

8

NANCY had the impression that Aubrey had been looking at Augusta's portrait. He turned with a slightly guilty expression. "I have been considering whether I should go away for a while."

Nancy stared. "But why?"

"I think a small space apart . . . " He glanced uneasily towards the door. His mother and the children had gone upstairs to change.

"Because of what happened the other night?" Nancy felt her anger and hurt boil up inside her. "Is it?"

"Nancy! Please."

"Why? I don't understand."

"If you would only stay calm, you might see that a small separation is the best thing."

Nancy's voice rose shrilly as she fought to control her feelings. "Because I asked you to make love to me! What if I don't want you to go?"

"Your wants, Nancy, are rarely based on rational judgement."

"And this is?" She shook her head in disbelief. "When I married you, Aubrey, I thought I would always be able to respect your judgements. I believed in your superiority. Marriage means just that, doesn't it, a woman must give way to her husband's decisions?"

"It is the way things are."

"Because, for you, society demands it. But that wasn't my reasoning. I fell in love with you. I truly believed that you were a finer person. You had raised me from what I was, you gave of your time to help me with my studies."

"A great deal of time."

"And I'm grateful. But I want more of you than that. I feel as if I've surrendered my whole nature and all of my independence to you, yet your life hasn't changed at all. You can decide to live at Midwinter or go to London or even to Africa again if you took it into your head, but how many decisions may I make? Not even that we might make love?"

He spoke very calmly and reasonably.

"I think a brief separation would do us both good. It will give us time to forget this small unpleasantness between us."

"Aubrey! I love you. I wanted you. Is that really so unpleasant?"

He lowered his voice. "My darling, why do you always have to shout?"

"Because I feel angry! People shout when they are angry."

"Your kind of people, perhaps."

"Yes! Real people. People with passions and emotions."

"That's just it," he said quietly, "I can't bear such a loss of dignity, such a surrender to one's emotions."

"Because of her." Nancy looked up at the portrait. Why, since finding her diaries, did it seem as if Augusta's eyes were mocking her? "So, I'm always to be sweet and docile because of Augusta. Why? Because if you find out I'm not perfect, I might just let you down like she did? Well, I'm sorry, but there are other sides to me as well, and if you love me, Aubrey, you must take them all. If I can love you with all your faults — and, believe me, I'm beginning to see that you have a few — why can't you accept me as I am?"

They heard his mother and the children come downstairs. Aubrey waited until the hall fell silent again. "I have decided," he said, and it was as if he had not even been listening to her. "I shall stay in London for a few weeks and visit a few old colleagues." He turned from her and left the drawing room.

* * *

Aubrey left the house and strode across the fields. He was troubled by the change in Nancy. She had been so innocent and loving in her acceptance of him in the early days of their marriage. How could he bring himself to approach her again, when she might repeat the sexual vulgarity of her performance in the drawing room? It was best he should go away. When he came back they could forget it had ever happened.

His thoughts turned to the women with whom he had appeased his carnal appetite. He went through this catalogue guiltily, out of a delicate sense of disloyalty to Nancy, and because having thoughts about the sexual act in broad daylight, where God might observe every corner of his brain, seemed offensive. Augusta had always wriggled and strained and made brutish noises, which had disturbed him and inhibited his own pleasure. He had never accustomed himself to the idea that she had enjoyed the act of sexual union. It was distasteful to him that a woman should take rather than give. The native women knew about giving, but one could not really count the blacks.

A Speckled Wood butterfly danced near the hedge and settled for a moment on the path. He paused to let it fly away before he walked on and remembered: Augusta in the small drawing room, very still and pale, a Cabbage White butterfly fluttering against the window. "I am leaving you. He and I are going away together." The only sound had been the beating of the insect's wings against the glass.

He had told his mama, "I shall have to let her go."

"Don't be a fool. Imagine the scandal.

We'll think of something. We must tackle this another way."

Augusta had refused to believe that Viner had abandoned her. "He hasn't. He loves me!" She had screamed and torn at her clothes and breast. Aubrey shivered at the memory of the obscene savagery, the raw agony on her face.

Didn't I love you more, Augusta? he wondered. For I had pitied you and taken you back. He remembered Augusta in her prime, her long, swan-like neck and white breasts, the cascade of auburn hair on her shoulders and her deceptive air of being unattainable, and he felt afresh the sharp pain of losing her, as if time and Nancy had never intervened.

* * *

"You should make a friend of Edith Lennox while I'm away," Aubrey told Nancy at lunch. "You seemed to get on well the other day."

Mrs Farringdon glanced up sharply. "You're going away, Aubrey?"

He blushed. "I thought so. Only for a few weeks."

Nancy met Mrs Farringdon's gaze head on. She knew his mother was aware that Aubrey had not slept with her since the children had come home. Little escaped her in this household; her hawk eyes were alert to any nuance of disagreement between them, ready to pounce on it and rejoice. Nancy would not give her anything to feed on. She held her gaze steadily until Mrs Farringdon looked away.

"You mean you're going to leave us alone with *her*?" Connie glared at Nancy.

Aubrey frowned. "I shan't warn you again, Connie. I really don't know why you are behaving so unpleasantly."

Nancy knew, but she was losing patience with Connie's jealousy.

"I suppose Edith is a suitable companion for Nancy," said Mrs Farringdon. "They are pleasant enough people, the Lennoxes, though they are not our sort of people. Not that they are not cordial, but they don't have our background."

"They are twentieth-century people. I find them refreshing and lively," said Nancy, realising that Augusta had said almost the same thing in her diary.

"*We* are nineteenth-century people," declared Mrs Farringdon with satisfaction. She had included Aubrey in this Victorian legacy and instantly Nancy saw that it was true: Aubrey *was* a Victorian. Why had she not seen it before — his belief in self-control and conformity, his sadness over her own lack of either, his assumptions that she should merge her existence with his own? Aubrey clung to the moral order in which he had been raised. Augusta had felt the changes coming and had been ill-at-ease with the old stuffiness. How much harder it was to conform, thought Nancy, when the gap was widening so quickly between the past and the present.

"Will you be lonely on your own?" Aubrey said later.

"I shall have your mama for company." He was not aware of the irony in Nancy's tone.

"Will you type up the notes?"

"Of course," she said coldly. "That's what I'm here for."

When it came to the moment of parting, Nancy weakened and kissed him. He looked so serious and, at the last minute, as he climbed into the Wolseley, reluctant to go. For a whole hour she walked about the kitchen garden, feeling disoriented and restless.

* * *

Nancy had decided to open up Augusta's sitting room and make it her own while Aubrey was away. It would be a project which, when he returned, would prove to them both that Augusta's influence was dead and gone. She locked up the diaries in her writing desk in her bedroom and ordered the servants to turn out Augusta's sitting room; they cleaned and polished, vases and ornaments were brought out from the cupboards, the curtains were washed and rehung. Mrs Farringdon watched the changes with suspicion at first, then decided to approve of the plan. "Here. You may have these. I have never liked them." She gave Nancy the Tiffany lamps from the drawing room. Nancy added them to the others in the sitting room, and knew at once it was where they should be.

Nancy spent the mornings typing Aubrey's manuscript notes on the

Egyptians for his book on primitive religions. She took a small pleasure in altering his syntax and, by way of improvement, changing a word here and there: *Death was an opportunity for the pharaohs to demonstrate their power. Their self-assertion* — she changed the word to 'arrogance' — *Their arrogance accompanied them into the next world, and was sealed up with them in the darkness of the tombs.* The claustrophobic nature of the subject made her restless with the stuffy atmosphere of Aubrey's study, and she flung the windows wide and went outside to the kitchen gardens.

The greenhouses were too humid to stay in for long; she watched Mortimer pot up geraniums, then wandered the gravel paths of the vegetable garden. How orderly it all was, and yet there was no sense of strain in the neat rows of beans and peas, nor anything claustrophobic about the high brick walls with their espalier-trained fruit trees. The butterflies which flickered around the garden could flutter at will up and over the wall.

Nancy walked through an archway in

the wall into the dappled shade of the orchard. The summer-house was at the far end, made of rough-hewn timber, with a pointed, rustic-work roof and narrow leaded windows on all four sides, each of which opened to a different aspect of the orchard. The little wooden hideaway had an abandoned air; it smelled of damp and wood-mould and filled Nancy in an indefinable way with nostalgia for her childhood. She opened the doors wide and took a deckchair from the pile of chairs stacked against the wall; brushing off the cobwebs with her hand she opened the chair under the shade of an apple tree, where she lay, letting the light play on her closed eyelids, feeling self-indulgent and indolent, until the faint clang of the lunchtime gong reminded her that she was hungry.

She met Roberts in the hall. "The mistress has asked for lunch to be sent to her room, ma'am. Will you be wanting the same?"

Nancy hesitated. "No, Roberts. Out of doors. On the terrace."

Hugo and Connie were away for the day, and Nancy ate in isolation near the open french doors of the small drawing room, missing Aubrey a little. Mrs Farringdon walked into the drawing room and advanced towards her as far as the doors. "This afternoon I shall be visiting Colonel Gregory." The statement might as easily have been delivered to one of the servants; it anticipated no response. Nancy nodded coldly and watched her mother-in-law's dignified departure. The state of war between them was as unspoken and as savage in intent as it had always been. It occurred to Nancy that Mrs Farringdon had so far won most of the skirmishes, and that she had from the very beginning been put in her place at Midwinter, ranking perhaps with Hugo and Connie rather than with the domestics, for servants were biddable and she was not. She heard the Wolseley brought to the front door and Mrs Farringdon leave with Browne. Only then did she go indoors.

The house was dark after the hot sunlight of the garden. The dogs slept on the hall floor, lying with their chins flat to the tiles; the servants were buried deep in the kitchen quarters. No one stirred in the main part of the building as Nancy went to her bedroom. She unlocked her writing desk and pulled Augusta's diaries from their hiding place. Hugging them to her breast, she made her way to the orchard.

She had been reading for almost an hour. Accounts of Goodwood and Henley and the season spent in London. Augusta's writing was hard to decipher and she was tempted to abandon whole pages, but references to Viner lured her on. There was the occasional letter conveyed by Charlotte, the trusted lady's maid; a chance meeting at a dinner party, when no more had been exchanged than glances. The passion had not died. Sometimes Augusta wrote about the pool, how she would go there on hot afternoons and lie alone on its bank, 'and remember how we lay, he and I, gazing into the water, or staring at the trees and the sky, silent, with no need for talk'.

Nancy closed the diary and folded it inside the deckchair, which she propped in its place in the summer-house. She crossed the meadow behind the stables and outbuildings, feeling the grass spring beneath her feet. This was the way Augusta would have come, knowing that her lover waited for her. She glanced towards Midwinter and saw that she was hidden from it by the mass of the stable block. She paused briefly by the fence of rusting barbed wire, then stepped between the rotting posts and plunged into the wood. She halted after a few yards and drew in her breath in a sharp gasp of pleasure, for before her lay a sea of blue flowers reaching under the trees. The birdsong at the lighter edges of the wood grew fainter and finally silent as she walked on further among the bluebells, and the canopy of tree branches deepened overhead. It was as mysterious as she remembered, but green and damp in the summer heat. The bluebells had an airy beauty. Their scent was strong. The silence as she neared the wood's centre grew more intense. And then she was on the edge of the pool.

She crouched by the water and brushed her hands against the heads of the flowers. This was where they had lain. Here John Viner had poised like a naked god, had taken Augusta in his arms and fused his body with hers. Nancy sank to the ground and, faint with the scent of bluebells, she curled up among them, absorbing their scent with slow breaths. The wood was full of magic. A man could become Pan, and a woman lie with him and know that she was loved. She let her body unfold, rolling on to her back and stretching her arms behind her head, and her fingers grasped the long stems of the bluebells. The sky was laced with leaves and tree branches; when she closed her eyes she could see their pattern in reverse, gold on black behind her eyelids. The bluebells filled her senses; their perfume was in her nose and in her mouth, exquisitely delicate, their stems voluptuous between her fingers. Their rustling silence beat in her head when she turned her face among them, and she was drowning in their beauty as she lay without sense of time.

Sweet delirium of love, wrote Augusta. How had Viner come to her? Like this? Nancy parted her legs and felt his weight upon her, his breath against her neck, his flesh against her breast. She let her left hand move languidly from the flowers and rested it against her thigh, then drew it down between her legs. Smooth like an olive fish . . .

Nancy felt the vibration of the earth, heard the thud of footsteps. She sat up quickly with a gasp of fear. A man stood on the path, his figure in shadow. He stood very still, then he came on towards her, and she recognised Ted Powers.

"Sorry. Did I give you a turn?"

Nancy scrambled to her feet. "You again . . . !" She could feel her face on fire as she brushed the skirt of her flowered frock; there were green stains on the white background and the bluebells were crushed and flattened. He held her gaze without smiling, and she remembered Augusta's description of John Viner and the look in his eyes, as if he could see what one was thinking, though Ted Powers was nothing like Nancy's imagined picture of Viner.

He came to stand beside her at the edge of the pool, scanning the surface of the water, then turned to her. "This isn't a very safe place, ma'am. I should have warned you."

"I think I can be the judge of that."

He nodded and looked away. "Just a word of advice."

"Well, I don't want it," Nancy said crossly. What she wanted was to tell him to go away, she told herself. Instead she was silent, and neither of them made a move. After a while Nancy said, "Why *do* you creep about so much in this part of the wood?"

He hesitated, then said as he had before, "I patrol all of the woodland, ma'am. It's my job."

She did not reply. She knew that, for whatever reason, he was drawn to the pool as she was. "Do you like your job, Powers?" she said with an attempt at sarcasm.

He answered pleasantly, as if she had asked the question out of curiosity. "It's not so bad for a man with an eye to nature. There's always something to see, and it's quiet and out of the way." He looked at her. "No one ever bothered with the wood before you came."

"Which is precisely why I like to walk here," Nancy said. "I should prefer it, Powers, if from now on you would confine your patrols to the part of the estate near Keeper's Cottage."

He spoke quietly. "I'm sorry, ma'am. I take my orders from your husband's mother."

Nancy sensed a confrontation in which she could not win. She reddened with frustration. "Don't you ever get bored with your job, Powers? You don't have much to do with the rest of the staff."

"I'm best on my own."

"Don't you have any family?"

"I've an uncle who farms over Melcombe way. My mother, his sister, died of consumption a long while back."

"I was alone in the world when my mother died," Nancy volunteered.

He put down his gun against a tree. "Ah, but you boxed clever. You joined the idle rich."

She did not answer, feeling the remark should have been insolent, yet it had been spoken without hostility.

He turned to her. "How do you like being married into the Farringdons?"

She was taken aback and did not answer.

"Marriage." He shook his head. "The

upper classes recommend it as a way of keeping down the workers; the feminists see it as a way of repressing women."

"You've got an awful lot to say for yourself," Nancy said stiffly. "And not all of it very respectful."

"So they tell me. It's a fact though. Time's running out for the old ways of thinking." He looked at her. "You're not like the Farringdons. You can't pretend you are. What were you — a secretary before the master married you?"

"It's people like me who are breaking down the barriers of class," she said defensively. She told him about the secretarial school and working for Aubrey in London. "Haven't I taken a step towards a future where class doesn't matter?"

"There's plenty wouldn't forgive you for that," he said.

"My mother-in-law hasn't forgiven me." With a sudden impatience with her fading attempt at authority, Nancy decided to discard it entirely and sat down on the bank at the edge of the pool, tucking her skirts round her knees. She said, looking at the water,

"Do you think there will be a war one day? Everyone seems to say it's bound to happen."

"A war, a revolution, women in Parliament. Who knows? An end of some sort, anyhow. The only thing of any permanence is the land."

"Do you mean we should only trust nature?"

He sat on the bank with his back against the tree. "I said 'the land'. You can't trust nature. She's fickle and a deceiver and there's evil in her too. You tell a countryman he can trust her and he'll laugh in your face."

Nancy was silent. She did not believe him entirely, for the wood, with its carpet of flowers and the stillness of the bluebell pool, was beautiful, in spite of Augusta's faithlessness all those years ago.

He looked at her. "You're not a country woman, are you?"

"My parents were provincial working class, struggling to better themselves. A roast joint on Sundays, washing day over the copper Mondays — sometimes a Bank Holiday at Scarborough."

"And have you really bettered yourself, would you say?"

"Not in the way you mean, by marrying into money, but I thought if I could only *know* as much as Aubrey . . . When I was a child I wanted more than anything to learn things. I used to go to art galleries and concerts back home. I read and read everything I could lay my hands on."

"My dad used to thrash me for reading, unless it was the Bible."

Nancy looked at him in horror and felt a flood of sympathy towards him. "Didn't you go to school?"

"I never learned anything at school. I couldn't wait to get away so that I could get on with life. I knew that learning came from books, not from what they could teach me at school, but there's so much to catch up on." He paused reflectively. "The rich take their education for granted. They read all the best literature, see great works of art, listen to music, and don't know how lucky they are."

"Oh, yes," said Nancy. "That's just how I feel."

"When things change, it will be the

educated working man this country takes notice of."

"And woman," Nancy prompted.

He did not contradict her. He rested the back of his head against the bark of the tree and closed his eyes. I feel almost at ease with this man, thought Nancy, and yet to remain here with him, chatting about revolution and the idle rich, and on the very spot where Augusta took a lover, is really very odd. There was an energy in him, a suggestion of danger which had a powerful attraction.

"When we met once before, you spoke about my husband's first wife. You said you should be surprised if I knew what had happened." She watched as his eyes snapped open. "Do other people know what happened? Did you think I should know as well?"

"Like you said, sometimes I've got too much to say for myself."

"I could always ask someone else."

"People round here don't like raking up old business, and you wouldn't like what you heard. It wasn't very pleasant." He stood and picked up his gun.

Nancy scrambled to her feet. "Well

then, I wish you joy with your shooting." He did not answer. "Doesn't it bother you — killing things?"

"Why should it? None of the vermin show mercy to my birds."

"You seem to take the matter of death rather lightly."

He looked at her, and again she sensed an anger in him which made her pulse quicken. "You're wrong. I don't take life and death lightly. Far from it."

Nancy watched him walk away into the wood, then she wandered through the trees towards the brighter sunlight of the meadow. She returned to the summer-house with the scent of the bluebells still in her hair, and searched the diaries for the answer to her question about when Augusta and Viner were discovered, but she could not find a satisfactory account of what had happened. In any case, she had vowed to herself that she would not become obsessed by Augusta's story, and that she would follow the diary entries, when she read them at all, in sequence.

Nancy sat before her mirror that night. How pleasant it was to be quite, quite alone. She curled her bare toes on the carved foot of the dressing table, shaped like an animal's clawed foot. She raised her arms above her head and arched her body. "Augusta beware. You may think you still have Aubrey, but you no longer have the wood all to yourself."

* * *

"Midwinter really is like a museum," Edith Lennox said one day when she came to visit, as they walked along the upstairs corridors. "All those dead things in glass boxes."

"I hate Midwinter," Nancy said vehemently. "I feel more and more trapped in the showcase of this horrible house, as if I were just another specimen."

"But Aubrey loves you, Nancy."

Nancy felt herself rebel against Edith's gentle disapproval. Why should Aubrey escape censure? Didn't she love him just as much? For she had given up so much freedom by marrying him. She was beginning to find Edith priggish. "Is that all a woman ought to ask from her husband? And I thought you were a feminist!" She remembered Powers's views on marriage, that the feminists saw it as a means of repression, and she thought how exhilarating it would be to hear him offer the same opinion now, in front of Edith.

Edith looked at her steadily; her eyes had a concerned, observant quality. "Why *did* you marry Aubrey?"

Nancy shrugged. "I wanted a man I could respect. My father was feckless. I hardly remember him, but I know my mother, though she loved him, looked down on him in the end. And I had been in love with Aubrey from reading his travel books ever since I can remember." She paused. "I wanted so much to absorb his intellect. He stood for everything I could only dream about — fame, research fellowships, exotic travel. I suppose I fell in love with his glamour."

"My education has been patchy too."

"But you don't mind that."

"Helping Mama do the garden? Paying calls at the vicarage? Exercising the dogs and the horses? Who says I don't mind?"

"But you don't have to do it," said Nancy, sure that Edith could have pursued an academic life, like Stephen, if she had wanted; for the Lennoxes must have been wealthy enough. "I used to make up stories about these wonderful rich people who lived in big houses."

"And now you know how it really is."

"Dreary," Nancy laughed.

"Unutterably boring," added Edith.

"Unutterably."

"Except for being married to Aubrey, of course."

Nancy said distantly, "Oh yes. Except for that."

They entered the downstairs sitting room with its light colours and blue china and Morris settees and the Tiffany lamps. "It was Augusta's room." Nancy was pleased at Edith's surprise.

"No stuffed eagles? No dried butterflies?" Edith sat on the sofa.

"No, thank goodness. When I first came in here I almost *liked* Augusta." Nancy fell silent, remembering the diaries. She sat beside Edith. "Aubrey can't bear me to mention the wood."

"It's supposed to be dangerous because of the pool."

"I wish you would tell me about

Augusta. You must remember something."

"I always thought she was very glamorous," Edith said. "Very beautiful. Very gay. She had wonderful taste in fashion. Mama quite liked her, I think. She felt sorry for her later, when she was so ill. Sometimes we children were invited to tea. We always felt we had to behave terribly well, or we might incur Augusta's wrath or that of Aubrey's mama. I don't know which was the most frightening. Augusta, I think. I once spied on her room when she and Aubrey came to stay with my parents. All her gorgeous Paris dresses were spread out on the bed ready for her to choose from. She caught me there and I was terrified, but she wasn't a bit cross. She let me try on her necklaces. She was not so daunting afterwards, when her lover had left the country. Of course, I didn't know what it was had made her so ill at the time, but people said it was the separation that broke her."

"Did she really just waste away? It's terribly romantic. Do you think she *wanted* to die?"

"I would. Wouldn't you, if your lover exchanged you for cash?"

"I don't have a lover," Nancy said wryly.

Edith sighed. "Nor have I. I'm to stay with a stuffy aunt in London when Stephen goes back to Oxford because my parents are going abroad. No lovers in sight."

"You won't be coming to see me again?" said Nancy in dismay.

"Not for weeks." Edith jumped up and went to the window. "Where is everyone? Where's Connie?"

"Gone off somewhere. She avoids me most of the time. So does Aubrey's mother. They are two of a kind. Hugo is off hunting for fossils."

"Dear Hugo. I think he will make a name for himself, like Aubrey, don't you?"

"Hugo has his future all mapped out. A geologist. Founder of a museum."

"And then there's Connie," said Edith. "Poor silly, mixed-up Connie." She paused. "You know, she's not in league with Mrs Farringdon at all. Her grandmama can be quite horrid to her."

"I've not so much sympathy for Connie myself these days."

"Do you know she's in love with my brother?"

"I'm not surprised. He is very endearing." Nancy frowned. "I shall miss you both next month."

* * *

Connie had wandered to the edge of the meadow. She kicked her foot against the fence post. Edith was with Nancy. They would be chatting together and laughing about her. She felt sullen and hard inside. She hated them and she hated herself, yet she could not understand what made her so furious with Papa and Nancy. Was her grandmama right to believe that wicked behaviour was inherited? Grandmama thought that criminals and the mentally insane should not be allowed to breed. Connie suspected her grandmama did not like her because she reminded her of her mama; when Hugo was there, she talked to him all the time and ignored her, asking him about school and the museum which he was one day going to build.

Connie looked beyond the fence into the wood. They had been forbidden to enter it ever since they were small. No one ever went there except Powers the gamekeeper, who was probably paid just to keep everyone out. The old habit of obedience lingered, and she felt no desire to brave the deep mystery of the trees. The shadows made her uneasy. The thought of the bottomless pit was worse. That was where they had done it, at the edge of the pool, her mama and the man who had gone away to Malaysia: and her papa had not been able to bear anyone talking about the pool ever since. Fornication, Grandmama called it. Connie knew what that meant. It was what the school guinea-pigs did, and the animals on the Midwinter farm, but she could not imagine people behaving in that way. And then her mama had died. Perhaps God had punished her and made her sick enough to die because of her wickedness. Connie thought of the Bible and the sins of the fathers. Would God punish her too one day? Were the sins of mothers visited on daughters, the same as the sins of the fathers on sons? She thought of the bottomless pit and shuddered.

A figure was coming towards her through the trees. She drew back in fright and then saw that it was Hugo.

"I shall tell Papa. You're not allowed," she cried in her thin high voice.

"No you won't, because he's in London, and if you tell Grandmama, I shall say you were in the wood too and that's why you saw me." He climbed the fence easily and slung his leather specimens bag over his shoulder. Connie hurried after him as he crossed the field.

"What were you doing?"

"I wanted to take a look at the quarry, to see if there are any fossils." Hugo was excited. He had defied his papa's authority, had braved the shadows of the wood, and had found there was nothing to fear. He had found no fossils either, for the quarry faces were overgrown, and he had been wary of climbing very far. But that seemed to Hugo to be irrelevant; he wanted to tell Stephen about his defiance so that he would be forced to admire him.

"The wood's a bad place. The devil lives there," said Connie.

Hugo laughed. "That's just an old nursery story."

"Grandmama said so."

"Grandmama was trying to frighten off silly girls like you, so you didn't go and fall in the pool when you were little."

"All the same — you'd be punished if she knew."

Hugo sighed, knowing it was true. His elation left him and they were silent.

"I think it's disgusting," said Connie after a while.

"What is?"

"Him and her. Doing that."

Hugo looked superior. "You're not supposed to know about such things."

* * *

How pleasant it was in London, and to lead a bachelor existence again, thought Aubrey. Mrs Mason clucked round him like a mother hen. The ambience of the British Museum was very agreeable and, at his club and the offices of the Royal Geographical, old friends hailed him as if he had just returned from darkest Africa. It was like putting on a pair of favourite old slippers which lie waiting after a long day's work. He could almost forget the problems he had left behind at Midwinter. How much nicer it was to recall the early days of marriage to Nancy, when she had been the compliant student, eager to learn, and he the mature teacher, telling his traveller's tales and elaborating on his ideas. The relationship had been perfect. He did not understand what had altered it.

He wanted to tell someone about the change in Nancy. He felt in need of sympathy. His club offered male solace of a kind, a quiet smoke and fine port and inconsequential gossip with Lang and Singer with no intrusive feminine influence; but however comforting this might be, he perceived that something was lacking.

"What a pleasure it is, Lang, to hand on one's learning to others. And yet how quickly they begin to take things for granted."

"Your son Hugo?"

Aubrey murmured a noncommittal reply, for he had meant Nancy, not

Hugo, and Lang's assumption reinforced the discomforting picture of himself as an old man and Nancy as a child-bride.

"This interest of your son's in geology seems just the thing," said Lang.

"Yes. I think he will stick at it. Hugo *is* a sticker."

"So, your son is interested in fossils?" Frank Singer lowered his newspaper. "Funnily enough, my interest in archaeology began in your part of the world. I was taken to see a mosaic pavement near Dorchester and it whetted my appetite for digging. You must let me have a scrabble around at Midwinter sometime, Farringdon. See if there's anything in Lang's Roman villa story."

It isn't Lang's story, thought Aubrey, it was Viner's.

"The Romans," declared Lang, made melancholy with port and in a philosophical mood, "spent decades laying down the foundations for British society — and look at it now. All in decline."

"It was the monarchy that started the rot," said Singer. "Edward's rule was absolute vulgarity. His mama would have turned in her grave."

"The old lady knew very well what was coming," said Lang. "Which is why she kept him from the throne for so long."

"At least our present monarch is respectable," remarked Aubrey.

"So do a lot of men appear to be, though they are not," said Singer. "Lang here, for example."

"Who said Lang gives any impression of being respectable?" laughed Aubrey.

"Yourself then," said Singer. "Who could be more of a pillar of society? Any tasty stories tucked away, Farringdon?"

Aubrey drew on his cigar. "Do I look like a man who is hiding 'tasty stories'?"

"But that's precisely my point." Singer stabbed the air with his cigar. "For all Lang and I know, you could have half a dozen sensational mistresses tucked away somewhere."

"Why do I need half a dozen mistresses, when I have a very nice young wife?"

* * *

Aubrey had invited Singer and Lang to dine. He wished now that he had not asked Singer, afraid that he might resurrect the business about the Roman villa. Was there anything in the theory? At the time he had seen it as a cynical move on Viner's part; a close personal interest in an archaeological dig would have given him ample opportunity for visiting Midwinter.

Why had he let Viner come to Midwinter again? Because of the butterflies, his own greed for acquisition? Greed — it was a word Nancy had used. Was it greedy to want to preserve beautiful things? Viner had brought him the Javan species, beautiful samples. Some collectors shot the larger species down from the trees and they ended up riddled with holes, but not these, they were perfect. He still admired them. His mama had wanted him to get rid of them all afterwards, but one could not jettison such exquisite creatures.

Had it been because of the butterflies, or had he wanted to throw Augusta and Viner together? Had he hoped the affair would burn itself out? The memories began again, though he had thought them buried with Augusta, and a wave of self-pity engulfed him. If only she had lived, he would have shown her that he had forgiven her. They might have grown old together and put the memory of Viner behind them.

Singer was in an unusually nostalgic frame of mind at dinner, saying how much stronger British Imperialism had been in his youth. "We were swept along into the South African war, as if it were some great colonial adventure."

"Everyone talked a lot of cant and humbug in those days," said Aubrey.

Lang said, "Remember the Mafeking celebrations? By Jingo!"

"Jingoism too has become an ugly word," said Aubrey.

"Patriotism is a worthy ideal," said Singer. "They were good times. I won't have you adopt this modern cynicism, Farringdon."

"They were good times in principle," conceded Aubrey. "In practice they hid a lot of cruelty and corruption. I am proud of my country, but I detest the attitude which supposes us to have some racial or religious superiority."

"Ever thought of taking up politics,

Farringdon?" said Lang.

"I'm a traveller. I have no time for politics."

"You are a writer," corrected Lang. "You have not travelled for years."

"Where was your last trip?" inquired Singer.

"West Africa," Aubrey said tersely. "The mouth of the Niger, 1900."

"Ah — the year I was with Arthur Evans in Crete."

"Your last bid for glory too?" said Lang maliciously.

A bid for glory? wondered Aubrey. Perhaps the expedition to Crete had been a simple quest for fame in Singer's case, but not in his own. He remembered that final expedition: not a day had gone by when he was not haunted by suspicions about Augusta.

"That was some time before Viner got his theory about the Romans," recalled Lang. He was watching Aubrey closely.

Singer rose to the bait. "What was it led him to his conclusion?"

Aubrey answered reluctantly. "He had come across some shards of pottery."

"On a credible site?"

"He found them embedded in the bank of an old quarry while spending a weekend at Midwinter. We looked. But no more came to light and, since he was walking alone when he found them, we only had his word for the story."

"Why doubt it? There have been excavations in your area. It could be an exciting find."

"The man was a cad. He could not be trusted."

"But Lang says he even told *him* about it. You saw the pottery, Lang. You said he brought it to London."

"It was Samian," said Lang. "And quite a good sample."

"You let him keep it, Farringdon?"

"It was very flimsy evidence." Aubrey remembered Viner's excitement, the maps unearthed from the library, theoretical converging lines drawn from the Fosse Way and known encampments to illustrate his point that the wood grew on the site of a settlement. "And the area would be hard to dig. As I said, it lies among trees."

* * *

Singer left early at the end of the evening, saying the ties of domesticity called him away. Lang settled himself more comfortably into Aubrey's chair. "You fellows with wives . . . " he said pleasantly.

Aubrey poured him another brandy. "When are you going to marry Marjorie and make an honest woman of her?"

"Never mind that. I'm concerned about you, Farringdon, You say you have no use for mistresses because you are in love with your wife, and here you are skulking in London with a face as long as a fiddle."

"I feel old, Lang. That's what it is."

"You're older than I am, certainly. But you're far from being eligible yet for Mr Lloyd George's old-age pension."

"I'm afraid of Lloyd George's radicalism. I'm afraid of feminism, afraid of socialism, afraid of war. Worse, I'm terrified of my own decline into old age."

"Is this what comes of taking a young wife?"

"She's not the girl I married. You wouldn't believe the degree to which I believed in her sweetness and innocence.

Either she has changed, or else I was blind to the truth. Nancy is neither discreet nor reasonable. I'm half afraid I shall not hold on to her. She shows more than a trace of wilfulness."

"You're a romantic, Farringdon, Marriage is very hard on romantics."

"The Arab potentates manage these matters so much better than we do. They lock up their wives and feed them sugared almonds and it all works very splendidly."

"I'm reluctant to say I told you so, but you should have known where you were heading. You'd been married before. Augusta was strong-willed too — and clever."

"Augusta was no fool and she was wilful, but she was one of us. Her father was a Fellow at Oxford. She had been educated to become the mistress of Midwinter." Aubrey paused. It had all been so perfect. Why had it gone wrong?

"She was very beautiful."

Aubrey lowered his gaze and swirled the brandy in his glass. "Yes. She was beautiful."

"Lots of us thought so."

Aubrey looked at Lang and saw in that moment that he knew the truth, "She couldn't help herself, Lang. It was as if she were bewitched."

"Was it Viner?"

Aubrey nodded. He drank the dregs of brandy and stood up shakily to pour himself another glass. "He trumped up that story about the Roman remains, you know. He just wanted an excuse to spend time with my wife."

Lang let out a slow "Ah," of acknowledgement.

"I knew right from the beginning, even after the Mafeking party. I watched them, the glances they exchanged." Aubrey was silent, remembering. He had not slept well the night after the party, and the following morning had risen early. He had gone outside, meaning to ask Powers the stable-hand, always the first up, to saddle him a horse. He had seen them from the stable yard: they were standing close together by the remains of the bonfire. "I had to come up to London soon afterwards. I heard that Viner had stayed on in Dorset while I was away.

There was nothing conclusive."

"Perhaps you were wrong."

"I wasn't wrong."

"And still you went to Africa all the next autumn?" Lang raised his eyebrows. "Nothing like cannibals and mangrove swamps to take one's mind off things."

"I thought, if anything was happening, I knew Augusta, it might have been over by the time I came back."

They were silent. Aubrey said, "People once thought the mangroves lifeless, you know. There's something very unnatural about the way they rear up from the black slime on their long white roots. There's a species of fly in the mangroves which is large and quite silent. It looks harmless enough, but after it has laid its egg in its human victim, the egg becomes a maggot. It lives just under the skin, biding its time, until it is fat and ugly and is ready to eat its way out to the light of day." He looked up. "They went to Paris. Augusta paid her annual visit to Worth, the Paris dressmaker. She always was as vain as a parrot."

"Did the affair eventually wear itself out?"

"Don't you know?" Aubrey said, looking at Lang keenly, wondering whether he had always known more than he had revealed.

Lang's glance flicked away. "I lost touch. I was abroad the year she died."

Aubrey recalled the dreadful year with Augusta after Viner had gone away. He sighed. "No. The affair didn't wear itself out."

9

Paris
Sunday, 12 August, 1900

AUBREY is in Africa, and I in Paris with my loyal maid, Charlotte. Aubrey's mama believes I have come to Paris for the fashion houses and is fearful for Aubrey's money, though he gave me *carte blanche* to spend as I please while he is away. I shall, of course, find time to purchase a few gowns, to convince everyone that my journey has not been in vain. Poor Aubrey. I know he does not deserve such treatment. I do so hate lying and cheating when I see it in others and I am dripping with guilt tonight. But I have detached myself from all that, and for the next weeks I swear to live only for my love.

Charlotte and I arrived off the boat-train last night, but John was not there to meet me. I sent a message to his apartment and have not heard a word in reply. What if he has travelled straight through? The thought that he may even now have gone south chills me to the marrow.

Has he found someone new to amuse him? Has the passion all been on my side and I have been deluding myself? Oh, how love has changed me into a frightened, nervous creature. I shall go mad if he does not come.

Paris
Tuesday 14 August, 1900

Two whole days, and at last!

He said he had been detained: friends make such demands; one simply has to see everyone while one is in Paris. I said that I had seen no one at all and that he was very cruel to keep me in such suspense. He has promised I shall visit the most entertaining of them.

Paris
Wednesday 15 August, 1900

We have seen the electrical illuminations in the Chateau d'Eau and the Hall of Illusions and all the splendours of the Exhibition. John says that Paris is too beautiful for lovers. Her attractions threaten our absorption with one another. And yet, how could this be possible when we are so enraptured by one another? His tenderness and passion have moved me.

Paris
Thursday 16 August, 1900

We are becoming regular tourists and have scaled the *Tour Eiffel* and sailed the Seine by *bâteau mouche*. He has even accompanied me to the dressmaker's, saying he felt like a husband as he waited and held my parcels. How I wish he were my husband, and we could stay here for ever and ever and never go back to Midwinter.

Paris
Friday 17 August, 1900

We went to his apartment and the afternoon was delightful and leisurely and full of passion. He brought me to ecstasy again and again, merely smiling when I begged him to stop until I thought I would die of love.

He says he believes copulation, with all its varieties, is an act of spiritual union.

Paris
Saturday 18 August, 1900

John took me to an apartment in the Rue Descartes, where some of his friends live, who, he says, are very stylish and witty. The men are certainly elegant, but some of the women I thought extremely ugly. I cannot say I was attracted by a single one of them. They talked a great deal about the theatre and the fabulous Isadora Duncan who dances barefooted. They all adore Sarah Bernhardt, yet pull her to bits with their criticism: she gives only the impression of being a great actress, both her mother and her aunt were whores, and so on. Some of the remarks were very near the knuckle.

They talk in exhausted, sardonic voices and think a great deal of themselves. Two poets were dressed exactly alike: they wore a high collar, black suit and patent shoes, with black hair, parted very precisely and apparently of the same patent leather. Each had a monocle. It was a full hour before I learned that these strange phenomena were not men but women.

Paris
Sunday 19 August, 1900

To St Germain once more, and John talked very animatedly with a woman with a very noble nose and a handsome gown of Lyons silk. She is Lally Durand, and he thinks her hawkish features very beautiful, though I could not see anything very remarkable in them. She has a reputation for risqué jokes and told a perfectly disgusting story about an Englishwoman she knew, who kept a pet frog about her person everywhere she went.

They talk very freely about love, and joke about homoeroticism and contraception until, after a while, it seemed pointless to appear to be shocked.

John says that France suffered a great deal during the last century, and it is not surprising the French should turn to pleasure for solace. Many people can still remember the German invasion and the débâcle of the Paris Commune, and everyone I met today lived through the anarchist bombs a few years ago, when the president himself was murdered.

Paris
Monday 20 August, 1900

At the Exhibition, I was marvelling at the Lalique designs and John had promised me a bracelet, when two of those beastly poets spotted us and followed us about with their fatuous talk. The worst of it was, John seemed to welcome them. Then they began to drop hints, as if to say there was some sexual intrigue between John and Lally Durand.

We said nothing as we took a fiacre to my hotel, but I was furious with him. I sent out Charlotte to buy souvenirs, and when we were alone I grew even more angry with John. I begged him to tell me there was nothing in my suspicions. He played with the flowers in the hotel room and toyed with the dresses I had bought and feigned indifference to my misery.

I begged him to say how much he still loved me, but he was very cold with me, even when I fell upon the bed in a fit of weeping.

I told him he was cruel. I recovered a little and said, "How could you let me humiliate myself so?" He was upon me then, his mouth on mine, his hand at my throat, pressing his thumb hard into the collar bone so that I almost expected to hear it splinter.

When I screamed and asked again why he wanted to humiliate me, he said that it was because I am 'small-minded' and because of the way I once made him stand on the very edge of the bluebell pool to prove how much he loved me. He shouted at me. Did I think I cared for him? I cared only for myself. I could never love him as he loves me. Would I risk life and soul for him? Would I risk hell itself? Would I even risk this much — snatching up one of the dresses from Worth and flinging it to the floor? What if he were to ask me to confess to Aubrey that we were lovers? Would I give up Midwinter or the children, or one penny of Aubrey's money? He laughed at my plea that I would go anywhere with him if only I could be sure he meant to stay with me. "You see?" he said. "You will always need promises, Augusta."

Paris
Tuesday 21 August, 1900

We went to his apartment and made love in the afternoon. How sweet he was to me after yesterday. How tender after frightening me so. He said he was jealous of Aubrey. He could not bear to think of him having me. His jealousy made him despise his own frailties, but he would conquer it in time, as I must conquer mine.

He kissed the bruise at my neck and bathed it with his tears. The sun shone on our naked bodies through the open shutters, and there was no sound except for the clatter of hooves and rumble of wheels in the street. We lay together until the light began to fade, and there was a harmony between us. It transcends everything that has gone before or can possibly come after.

We promised always to be true and that, even when we are parted by circumstance, we shall find a way to be together again, for he loves me as he has never loved a woman before, nor shall do again, he promises. In the evening we strolled along the river and sat until late drinking wine. I could believe that he was mine and I his and there was and never had been Aubrey.

Paris
Wednesday 22 August, 1900

Only two more days.

Midwinter
Sunday 26 August, 1900

How desolate is Midwinter in August.

Nancy put away the diaries and, going to the stables, asked Radley to saddle Nelson for her. She rode along the south drive past the farm.

Midwinter was sleepy, the air heavy

as if with thunder. Edith had gone to London, Stephen was up at Oxford, and Hugo and Connie had returned to school. In the fields the workers were haymaking: a horse, attached to an iron bar, plodded in endless circles to power an elevator which transported hay up to a rick. Nelson fell into a leisurely pace, and Nancy let her thoughts drift to the long afternoons she had spent by the pool while Aubrey was away, when she had taken the diaries or Whitman poems, reading them over and over. The wood had become more secretive as the summer wore on, the canopy of leaves drawing in more thickly. When the wind blew, when the branches creaked gently and small sounds rustled in the undergrowth, she would lift her head, half expecting to see Ted Powers, hopeful even, for she had wanted to question him more closely about what he knew about Augusta and Viner. She had not met him once since that afternoon among the bluebells, and she wondered whether he had, after all, respected her wish that he should not patrol the pool. She was aware of a disappointment, for she had sensed a level of understanding between herself and Powers, which she had found nowhere else at Midwinter. *You're not like the Farringdons,* he had said. *You can't pretend you are.*

She slowed Nelson to a halt as they approached the track which led to Keeper's Cottage. Nancy had never seen the cottage, for it was hidden by a bend in the track. There was a strong air of mystery about it. She resolved to ride a little way among the trees; just to see, she told herself — just to dispel the enigma. Once she had satisfied her curiosity, she would retreat.

She had not expected to come upon the house so quickly. She reined Nelson to a halt, staring at the large and pretty whitewashed cottage ahead of her with its borders full of summer flowers. It was obvious that the owner took a pride in his garden: the hedge by the gate was clipped neatly, rose bushes lined the path and sweetpeas climbed a rustic-work trellis which formed an arch over the front porch. Powers himself, in shirt-sleeves and waistcoat, leaned on a garden hoe as he watched a bird flit from branch to branch in one of the trees. He had heard the horse at the same time as Nancy saw him, and he turned and came to the gate as she urged Nelson on towards him.

"Did you want something, ma'am?" His manner was correct and civil, with none of the familiarity of their last meeting.

"Not really. I . . . " Nancy sought for words. "What were you looking at? Did we frighten it away?"

"A goldfinch. They come for the rose-hips later in the year."

"How pretty."

"Yes, they're a sight."

She hesitated. "I was being curious."

"About the goldfinches?"

"About your house. It occurred to me that I knew all the other estate houses but I hadn't seen where you live. Nelson and I were out for a ride, so . . . "

He looked down at the blade of his hoe. "I expect you get a lot of time on your hands. It must be a bit grim for you, alone with the old lady." He moved closer to the gate and reached out to pat the horse. He knew all about what she did when she was alone, for her visits to the wood all through June had not gone unnoticed. He had watched her, his back against a tree, blending into the woodland until he was a part of it, a trick he had learned from his father. He had asked himself why she persisted in going to the pool with her books, instead of sitting on Midwinter's well-tended lawns.

"Your garden is beautiful," Nancy said. "You must like flowers."

"Does that surprise you?"

"A little." She paused. "I find it — reassuring."

"Have a closer look." He saw her hesitation. "Unless you think you should tell me to mind my place."

She smiled and shook her head, leaning down to the gate catch, but he reached it first and, opening it, helped her to dismount. She secured Nelson to the fence and walked up the path with Powers, while he pointed out the roses, naming each in turn, until at last they had reached the porch. Nancy touched the delicate head of a sweetpea flower by her shoulder, and bent her face towards it, breathing its strong scent.

"Take some with you. I'll cut you a bunch before you go. They'll be a sight prettier than those hot-house things they rear at Midwinter." The offer was touching. He seemed to want to please her. She thanked him and flicked him a tentative smile.

The door of the cottage was propped open with a metal boot-scraper. The passage was cool and inviting. Through an open door at the back of the house she caught a glimpse of a cobbled yard and brick outhouses.

"I've got the kettle on the hob," he said. "I was just going to make a mug of tea."

She stepped back and he led the way, ducking his head to avoid the low ceiling. His boots scraped the stone flags and his body blocked the light as she followed him into his kitchen.

The walls were whitewashed, the stove and kettle clean, but the room bore the austere influence of a man who lived alone. The pictures on the walls were of game-birds. There were no stitched samplers or pretty china plates and bowls. The only superfluity — and to Nancy a surprising one — was a piano which stood against the opposite wall with its lid closed, its top draped with a wine-red runner fringed with wool tassels. She accepted his invitation to sit on the black, cloth-covered sofa which stood against one wall. A faded red plush and mahogany armchair, its seat cushions comfortably hollowed and worn, stood in one corner near a lighted stove. Rugs covered the stone floor around the plain wooden table. Adjacent to the sofa was a dresser, stacked — another surprise — with books instead of crockery.

Nancy watched Powers open the doors of a high cupboard built into the wall by the chimney breast and take out two china cups and saucers. He wiped them carefully with a cloth and set them on the table, then lifted the steaming kettle from the hob and poured the water into an enamel teapot. His arms were hard and tanned, his fingernails short and broken and his forearms lightly covered with dark hairs. Nancy found herself staring, noticing details, the impression of tension in his hands as he stood by the stove, one arm resting against the mantel, waiting for the tea to brew. Then, as he eased his body away from the chimney, she fixed her attention on the piano. "Do you play?" she said at the same time as he, following her glance, said, "Do you play the piano?"

She laughed. "Very badly."

"My mother used to play. She was a bit of a lady, my ma. She brought the piano with her when she got married. Dad could never bring himself to turn it out after she died, and I've got used to seeing it sitting there."

"I wonder if it's in tune."

"You'll have to try it out." He poured the tea and handed her a cup.

"I might just do that."

She glanced at the titles of the books on the dresser as she sipped her tea, intrigued by the mix of Darwin, Freud's *Interpretation of Dreams*, and H. G. Wells and Rider Haggard; faintly excited as well to discover the poets Masefield and Housman.

"I told you," he said, following her gaze, "I got on with educating myself after I escaped school." Suddenly he looked at her, and his smile was direct.

"How about you trying out that piano then?"

Nancy set down her cup and saucer on the table and, walking to the piano, lifted the lid. The keys were yellowed and some of the ivory was cracked. Powers left the kitchen and returned, carrying a high-backed chair. She played a phrase from 'When Irish Eyes Are Smiling'. The notes were shrill and jangling, the piano strings badly out of tune, and she laughed as he winced. He placed the chair for her to sit on, and she settled herself comfortably, pushing up the sleeves of her blouse at the wrists, then began again to play. After a few bars he stood behind her and sang, and the mellow sound of his voice combined with the haunting words of the song brought a lump to Nancy's throat.

"That took me back," Powers said when she had finished playing.

"Me too. It reminds me of when I was a child." Nancy dabbed at her eyes with a handkerchief, half crying, half laughing. "Why are our happiest memories always of when we were children? My mother used to play and Father would dance with me." She pushed the handkerchief up her sleeve and fell silent.

"It's only looking back they seem happy. It's more the strength of the memories that's so moving, not what's in them. I don't think anyone's touched that piano since it was shut with the lid of my mum's coffin."

"You sing well," Nancy said.

"I sing to myself sometimes. It would sound silly if anyone came by of an evening — not that anyone ever does. It's a bit out of the way up here."

The observation reminded Nancy that she was alone with him. She could not interpret the expression in his eyes as the silence lengthened, but there was danger there, and she felt a mixture of excitement and fear. She should not have accepted his invitation to enter his house. She wanted to ask him, What secrets do you know about Augusta and her lover? Why are you employed by Mrs Farringdon to do nothing? Instead she closed the piano lid and stood up. "I ought to go. Nelson will be getting restless. Thank you for the tea."

He went with her to the front door,

and the heat of the garden met them like a wave of warm water. "You'll take some sweetpeas?" He drew a penknife from his pocket and cut flower stems, one by one, from the trellis by the door, handing them to her a few at a time until she had a large bunch. "Sweetpeas were all the thing with ladies when I was a boy."

She buried her face in them. "They're very lovely. I so much like flowers with a strong scent."

"I know. I seem to remember that you like bluebells."

She looked up and saw the amusement in his expression. She thanked him once more for the flowers, turned and walked away down the path to the gate.

* * *

Ted felt a twinge of tenderness towards her as he watched her go. He had embarrassed her with that last shot, remembering the time he had come across her, lying among the bluebells in the wood. She had moved him with her playing, though. He turned away.

Nostalgia. That was all that was. Was he getting too soft? He turned back to the house. He had lied when he said no one had played the piano since his mother died, for Mary Bond had played, she had played like an angel — Chopin and Tchaikovsky. He had been just turned twenty and had thought himself in love, convinced that, because she could play Chopin, he had found the only girl within ten miles of Winchborne with any soul. She had complained about the piano being out of tune, and she had been right; you needed a good instrument when you could make music like that.

Ted returned to the kitchen and raised the lid of the piano again, gently stroking the keys. Mary Bond had long since left Winchborne for better prospects than marrying a gamekeeper. His mother had been the one for song tunes, he remembered. And his dad a one for singing. Not just hymn tunes in those days, either. He recalled him belting out 'Ta-ra-ra-boom-de-ay' and 'My Old Dutch'. They had had some fun in the past. He closed the lid, and his eyes became shuttered and impassive.

Oh, but his dad had changed towards the end.

* * *

Nancy had decided she would ride over to the Lennoxes; Edith had returned after staying with her aunt, and Stephen had come down from Oxford for the weekend. In a few days Aubrey would be home. She resolved as she rode through Winchborne that she and Aubrey would start afresh with the summer all before them. She felt she had begun to triumph over Midwinter. She had taken possession of the orchard and of Augusta's sitting room, and she had made the wood her own.

Nelson's hooves scuffed the gravelled drive and came to a halt outside the Lennoxes' house and, as Nancy dismounted, it began to rain.

The Lennoxes' home was very different from Midwinter. It had modern furniture and central heating which worked efficiently and there were innovations like a portable gramophone with proper discs, not cylinders. The Lennoxes also had electric lighting in all the rooms, with pearlised globes, and delicate prints on the walls.

The downstairs sitting room was comfortably furnished and light and welcoming. Nancy sat in the cushioned window seat. She leaned her arms on the broad sill and pressed her forehead against the diamond-leaded glass where the rain now streamed in torrents outside. She listened to the scratchy polka which Edith played on the gramophone, remembering the piano at Keeper's Cottage, and she hummed the tune lightly until it ended.

She turned from the window, "Who was it found Augusta and Viner in the wood?"

Edith stood up to remove the record from the gramophone. "Don't you think you should forget all about it?"

"Was it Aubrey — or someone else?"

"Oh, Nancy!" Edith gave a cry of exasperation.

Nancy turned to face her. "I shan't give up until you tell me everything. You weren't *that* young you can't remember, and I should think people must have talked about it afterwards."

Edith sighed. "I think it was the gamekeeper. He was patrolling the wood with his son."

Nancy released an exclamation of satisfaction. "I should have guessed as much. So, Ted Powers and his father caught them at it."

"Nancy! How can you? Poor Aubrey."

"But it's just like a jigsaw, don't you think?"

"What is like a jigsaw?" Stephen came into the room. He had been riding in the rain and his hair was damp. He looked very pink and healthy and brought an air of eager vitality with him.

Nancy turned to Stephen with barely constrained excitement. "I was saying how the story of Aubrey's first wife is so much like a puzzle."

"There's no puzzle, Nancy," Edith said gently. "At least, not for Aubrey. I'm sure he remembers it all too well."

"How much do you remember, Stephen?" Nancy quizzed him.

"I'm sure we were both too much concerned with our own childish interests," said Stephen. "We always were self-centred little beasts."

Nancy tried to picture him as a child. It was not difficult. He still looked ridiculously boyish.

"Nancy, don't you think you should let it rest?" Edith said piously.

Nancy sighed. It was, after all, a sordid story. "I suppose you're right. Which is why I'm going to occupy myself with planning a house party next month."

Edith smiled with relief. "Splendid. It's just what you need. Oh, it will be great fun."

"We'll invite Aubrey's London friends and all the local swells, and your family of course, and anyone *young* you can find. Stephen, you must have some lively friends at Oxford."

Stephen looked at her. Did she have any idea that he was in love with her, that his joking infatuation hid an adoration which hurt, that he had looked forward to coming down from Oxford this term purely because of her? The whole summer stretched before him, with Nancy shining golden in its midst. Of course, he knew that he was playing with fire, yet one felt that people everywhere were behaving dangerously these days. Some lunatic had shot the Austrian Archduke in Servia, and two chums from his college had fought a duel over a woman. Women were all drinking too much and throwing their reputations to the winds. He had been to see a review in the West End which was called 'The Passing Show of 1914': everyone had the same feeling that nothing was going to last. One ought to take risks and live recklessly, grasp the present while one could.

"I could bring a couple of poets."

Nancy thought of Augusta's stay in Paris and the poets of ambiguous sex, with patent-leather hair. What had the woman with the pet frog done which was so disgusting? Did Stephen know people like that? "Respectable poets?" she asked.

He grinned. "Tolerably so. We wouldn't want to shock Aubrey's mama."

"Then you may bring them."

"Who is your favourite poet?" He knelt on the settee and hung over the back of it. "Yeats?"

"Whitman," she said quickly.

"Good Lord! Do you mean it?"

"I know there are some pretty shocking parts, but he is so spontaneous and real."

It was telepathy, thought Stephen. Whitman. She was *so* honest. She was wonderful. Why the hell had she gone and married an old fogey like Aubrey Farringdon?

* * *

"Why did I tell Stephen that Whitman was my favourite poet?" Nancy wrote in her diary that evening. She lifted her head and looked out of the window. The sky was darkening over to the east. Whitman was Augusta's poet — a secret, like Augusta's diaries. And yet, Stephen had been so ridiculously joyful to discover they had something in common. She smiled a little and bent her head again to write. "Compared with Aubrey he is such a child."

* * *

Aubrey had returned from London. Nancy showed him the heap of manuscript she had typed, and then linked her arm in his as they walked through the gardens. He had been right, the separation had given them time to reassess one another, and it was good to see him again.

"Edith is home from London too," she told him. "It won't be long before Hugo and Connie are here. I've decided we shall have a house party."

He paused by the flower border, its hot orange lilies framed against the hedge. "Do you really want to go through all that rigmarole?"

"It will be fun. Midwinter needs people, and there almost always used to be parties here in Augusta's day."

He frowned at the mention of Augusta and, in spite of her happiness, Nancy felt a familiar surge of exasperation. They walked on through the clipped arch of the hedge towards the tennis court, under sycamore trees whose roots grew through the closely mown path. "I don't know," Aubrey said at last. "It's a lot of work for Mama."

"Your mother need not lift a finger. I shall arrange it all, down to the last detail. It's high time I acted like the wife of the great Aubrey Farringdon, whose book on primitive religions is going to be a runaway bestseller when it comes out."

He laughed and they came to a halt by the tennis court. "Do I really deserve such faith?"

"We should use the tennis court," Nancy said, looking at the deserted court behind the mesh fence. "It's such a waste. If we had a party, people would play tennis and walk in the gardens and say what a wonderful display Mortimer has achieved in the herbaceous borders. Midwinter would come to life again."

Aubrey tilted her face towards him. "I missed you, Nancy. I missed your enthusiasm for everything."

"We'll make it a celebration for when you finish off the manuscript."

He frowned again, letting his hand caress her shoulder. "But, Nancy — a house party."

She reached up and kissed him, smiling with her eyes. "Please? Just for me."

She thought that everything would be fine, and then, in the afternoon, he discovered that she had opened up

Augusta's sitting room.

"Why? Of all the rooms in the house?" His tone was deeply injured.

"But I wanted *that* room. It's pleasant and inviting and it gets the afternoon sun. And it's the only square inch of the house which is not full of stuffed birds and insects."

"It was Augusta's sitting room."

"And Augusta is dead. She has been dead for years. If you didn't want to be reminded of her, why in the world did we come to live at Midwinter?"

Aubrey shook his head. "I don't know. I thought — "

"You thought you could ignore the past. But to do that you have to let it go, which means I have to be allowed to change things, and we have to stop treating Augusta and what she did as if we are forever treading on glass. Forget her. Forget what she did. You married me because we love each other and that should be all that matters."

He did not come to her room that night. She knew that she had offered a dangerous challenge; it was as clear as if she had said, you must choose between

Augusta and me. Aubrey had withdrawn from the conflict: in his own way he had given his answer.

Nancy lay, watching the long shadows cast by the oil-lamp, until her eyes drifted shut; and in the morning the lamp still burned, though the daylight streamed in at the window. He did not come to her room all week and, after that, Nancy no longer expected him.

The warmth of their reunion had chilled. But, as July wore on, arrangements for the house party became more exciting and more pressing. Aubrey had detached himself from her plans. Her own involvement in them meant she was becoming careless about his work, and he complained frequently about her neglect of his manuscript, now and while he had been away, saying with an air of forbearance that she had ruined his arguments by her corrections of his style. "Why have you been so cavalier about it? I was in London over a month. There was ample time to do it properly. What did you do with yourself all day apart from organising your sitting room?" He had begun to treat her appropriation of

Augusta's sitting room with faint, ironic amusement, as if he had allowed her to take it over, as an indulgence to her.

"I walked," Nancy said defensively, and with an irrational fear that he would find out about Augusta's diaries. "I rode, I visited Edith. You said I ought to go to see her."

"Not at the expense of primitive religions!"

Nancy began to laugh, which made him crosser than ever, and she thought, I have almost exhausted my childhood infatuation. She realised that she was no longer dazzled by him. Was this what people meant when they said the bloom of marriage wore off?

"Very well then," she said. "I shall swelter indoors and type up your horrid manuscript."

"Nancy." He was patient again. How she detested his being tolerant and forbearing. "You know it has to be finished by August."

"I know. I know." She sat down at her typewriter. "Or what shall we have to celebrate at the house party?"

* * *

"Why is love so difficult?" Nancy wrote in her diary. She recalled the heady pleasure of being in love. It seemed so dreary now, to be little more than a secretary for Aubrey, and even that with a host of irritations.

"He has a theory that I've spoiled his manuscript by my interference," she said to Edith, when she arrived one day to see her. It was not strictly true, but the exaggeration helped to dispel her suspicion that Aubrey was justified in his complaints. "I've lived and breathed primitive religions for months and he's not the least bit grateful."

"He must have the final word," said Edith gently.

"He's not infallible." Nancy saw how much her opinion of Aubrey had changed since she had first met him. "Sometimes I think he should have married someone who had no thoughts or opinions except those which echo his own. How can men be so arrogant?"

"Poor Nancy."

Nancy accepted Edith's ready commiseration, but guessed that her sympathies really lay with Aubrey. The more she saw of Edith the less she liked her, she decided, and confided to her diary that evening, "Edith really is very simple-minded if she professes to be an admirer of Mrs Pankhurst yet thinks a husband should have the last word. And what does Edith know about love?"

Nancy, hearing Aubrey go down to dinner, put away her diary and went downstairs to the drawing room. Aubrey waited for her, standing impassively beneath the portrait of Augusta. What did anyone know about love? thought Nancy. At least Augusta had understood passion. Nancy stared at the eyes in the beautiful, mocking face and felt no jealousy, no resentment, but a sneaking admiration for the person behind them.

* * *

Hugo and Connie had returned to Midwinter for the summer and Nancy no longer went to the wood. Ted Powers stood at the edge of the pool one day soon after the Farringdon children had arrived at Midwinter. He had learned as a child how to enter a wood, like a fox, with the wind in his face so as to smell anyone smoking and be able to hear if anyone was about. He scanned the milky surface of the water, remembering the afternoons when he had watched Nancy Farringdon reading by the pool. The trees were very silent now, no birdsong in July and August. He retreated from the pool to a place where the sun dappled the moss with light and shade, and watched, silent as the wood itself, while a figure came with clumsy stealth, rustling and cracking among the trees, from the direction of Midwinter; it moved to the quarry face, searching among the bushes and ragged edges of the old workings.

Ted chewed his lip in thought. Now what was young Hugo Farringdon doing there? Should he report it? He had said nothing about Farringdon's wife, but that was different, and she had done no ferreting and digging around.

The figure at last turned away. Ted released his breath slowly. The boy was harmless. He decided to say nothing.

10

NANCY'S lists were growing longer and more confusing. The summer party must extend over a whole weekend, from Saturday to Monday, with no flagging of amusement until the last guest had left Midwinter. Lunch and dinner must consist of several courses, with appropriate wines for each, all of which required grave discussions with Roberts and Mrs Cassell. There were so many things to remember: napkins were not used at tea but were to be used at dinner, though they should not on any account inadvertently be called serviettes. Careful arrangements must be made to house the visiting servants, which meant turning out attic rooms long disused. Even more painstaking thought must go into the sleeping arrangements for guests: should Gilbert Lang be in close proximity to Marjorie Benson, or just close enough to cover all eventualities without being obvious? Nancy could get no help on this point from Aubrey and, on principle, she would not ask his mother.

"Augusta and I always discussed details endlessly," Mrs Farringdon told her one day with her twisted smile. "One has to have been brought up to country house parties to do the thing properly. I'll say this much for Augusta," she added as she watched Nancy compile a guest list, "she may have been extravagant and her morals may have been those of an alley-cat, but as a hostess, she excelled."

The heat had made Nancy short-tempered. Underlying the knowledge that she had brought all the harassment of the party arrangements on herself, was a certainty that Augusta would indeed have taken the details of the party in her stride. She was tired suddenly of the indirect warfare with her mother-in-law, and longed for an open spat. She laid down her pen. "What a disagreeable old woman you are."

Mrs Farringdon's mouth gaped.

"I don't know why I've put up with it for so long," Nancy continued, "except perhaps for Aubrey's sake. And I expect Augusta did the same, *when* she wasn't being the perfect hostess."

Mrs Farringdon gripped the rim of her embroidery frame so that her knuckles were white. "How dare you talk to me in that way, you — you common little girl!"

"I might be common, but I'm Aubrey's wife."

"He should never have married you. He should never have dragged the Farringdons down like that."

"But he did. And, Lord knows, I've done my best to make him happy."

"Happy!" Mrs Farringdon said bitterly. "What about his duty — to the family name, to Midwinter?"

"Your family name isn't worth tuppence where I come from. Aubrey's reputation was built on his intellectual efforts, and Midwinter is an ugly old heap of stones with a way of life which is stuck fast in the last century." Nancy picked up her pen and continued with her list. A feeling of intense satisfaction expanded to fill the void of her mother-in-law's indignant silence.

Nancy's sense of victory was short-lived. July was too hot for turning out rooms and cleaning. The servants were resentful of the extra work, and Nancy knew that her informal way with them was inadequate. The truth was, she had no idea about handling the Midwinter servants; there was a vast difference between giving Mrs Mason instructions for a dinner party in Bloomsbury, and directing the Midwinter machine. Nancy's easy manner merely puzzled the staff: she sensed their contempt, yet she was incapable of assuming the air of command they were accustomed to from Aubrey's mother. Mrs Cassell advised her with menus and Roberts steered her with his reserved tact, but they seemed wary of prompting her too closely. There were conflicts of loyalties, guessed Nancy. She even began to suspect they had been given orders not to help her.

On the morning when she ordered all the pictures in the main drawing room to be taken down and cleaned before the house party, the women servants stood around looking sullen.

"We'm afraid to touch that 'un, ma'am," said Doris, the boldest of the housemaids; she jerked her head at

Augusta's portrait. "The master wouldn't like it."

Nancy looked up at the portrait and laughed in disbelief, feeling a surge of frustration. What would Augusta have done? she wondered. Ordered the girl to do as she was told and be damned? She turned to her. "Doris, are you questioning my instructions?"

The girl hesitated. "No, ma'am, I just thought — "

"You weren't asked to give your opinions," Nancy snapped. "Take all the pictures off the wall and clean them like I told you."

Nancy went to the small drawing room as the work of removing the pictures began. She should have been reading through Aubrey's proofs of *Primitive Religions*, but felt no inclination to begin. Mrs Farringdon sat outside on the terrace. Nancy went to the grand piano and lifted its lid and, without warning, a mental picture of Ted Powers's cottage flooded her thoughts. She pressed the keys lightly and played a few bars of 'Irish Eyes', sensing a self-indulgence in the memory, a touch of sentimentality.

Mrs Farringdon ignored her, though the doors stood open between them.

One of the housemaids from the drawing room came hurrying along the terrace and halted with her hands clutching her apron. "Ma'am. Oh ma'am!" She addressed Mrs Farringdon, not Nancy. "Doris went to take one of the pictures off the wall to clean it, like we was instructed, ma'am, and the whole lot did come down on her head."

Nancy felt a lurch of superstitious fear. She went outside to the terrace. "Which picture?"

The girl looked at her with a trace of righteous satisfaction. "'Tis the one of the master's first wife, ma'am."

Mrs Farringdon did not stir but turned to Nancy with an inquiring, challenging expression.

Nancy followed the maid along the terrace and into the house to the main drawing room. A moment of wild paranoia swept through her as she saw the portrait lying on the hearth, and she wondered whether the women had somehow manufactured the accident. Then she saw that Doris was in tears.

"Are you hurt?" she asked her coldly.

"No, ma'am."

"Go to the kitchen. Tell them to get you a cup of tea. And stop grizzling, it doesn't look as if much harm's been done."

"'Tis the frame, ma'am." Doris dried her eyes. She added with a stroke of defiance, at the same time incongruously bobbing a curtsey, "I told 'ee we should never have touched 'n." The maid turned to the doorway but, confronted by Mrs Farringdon, she stood as if rooted to the spot.

"Don't just stand there, girl," murmured Mrs Farringdon. "Help the other servants to take down the rest of the pictures." Doris, with a frightened glance in Nancy's direction, joined the maids who had begun lifting the remaining pictures from the walls.

"We shall have to have it reframed," said Mrs Farringdon, bending to examine the gilding where the frame had split along the bottom edge. "I shall tell the restorers it is urgent." She lowered her voice and said through clenched teeth, "Though really, I feel bound to say it was a foolish thing to do. That portrait has not been moved since — ”

“Since she died,” Nancy finished for her. She looked down at Augusta. The imperious, slightly mocking expression was less striking from its position on the hearth. The painting looked exposed: Augusta seemed suddenly vulnerable, spread in a symbolic gesture at her feet. She turned to her mother-in-law. “Why do we have to be so awe-struck about it? As far as I can tell, there was never any love lost between you and Augusta.”

“It was Aubrey’s wish that it should always hang there.”

“Why, when she did what she did?”

“He has his reasons.”

“For goodness’ sake. It’s only a picture.” Nancy turned and left the room and went outside into the garden, where Connie was sprawled on a wicker *chaise-longue* on the lawn, a straw sunhat resting on her carroty fair hair. Connie seemed to have grown that summer: her legs were long and slim under her cotton skirt, her skinny figure was rounding out under her blouse. She pushed her spectacles higher on the bridge of her freckled nose.

"You're wishing you'd never started all this, aren't you?"

Nancy flopped on the grass beside her and hugged her arms round her knees. "And I suppose, like your grandmother, you're just over the moon when anything goes wrong."

Connie shrugged. "I leave that to Grandmama. Anyway, what does it matter to me? I shan't be allowed to join in. At least, not for the formal entertaining. Grandmama thinks fifteen is too young for dinner parties."

"But that's awful. What about Hugo?"

"Oh, he's a *male* and turned sixteen, so that's all right."

"But it's not fair, Connie. You're almost grown up. Why should you miss out on the fun? I shall do something about it."

"I suppose you mean you'll get round Papa for me."

"I could make him see it's not fair."

"And then I suppose I shall have to be eternally grateful to you."

Nancy sighed, losing patience. "For goodness' sake, it wouldn't be a favour. And I shouldn't want any back. I just don't think it's right that you should be left out."

Connie's green eyes were calculating behind her spectacles. "How about a bargain? Then I shouldn't feel obliged to be grateful."

"A bargain?"

"You get Papa to let me join the grown-ups for the formal dinner, and I shall tell you what still needs doing. I do know what needs doing. There are a thousand things you haven't even thought of. Preparing the rooms is only the half of it."

* * *

"Oh no," said Aubrey. "Absolutely not. Connie is still a child."

"But how can you ever expect her to have the graces and manners of an adult if you treat her as if she's still in the nursery?"

"Nancy, I am sure that one day, God willing, Connie will become human. At present she is unreliable in adult company."

"She's just not sure of herself, that's

all. Having to adjust to a stepmother made her angry and she reacted badly. If we had been more careful about it, maybe she would have known how to handle her feelings."

Aubrey sighed loudly.

"Let me take the responsibility for Connie," Nancy coaxed. "I swear you'll see a change in her." He hesitated. She had won him over. She could see that he would take the easier option and give in. At last he said testily, "You know I never wanted all this fuss anyway."

"I know, Aubrey. All you want is a quiet life."

"The cost is going to be phenomenal. All that food. Heaven knows why you want to do it. Hours and hours of being sociable, the women gabbling on and on and the men playing billiards until all hours and proposing facetious theories all about nothing."

"When all you want is a quiet corner somewhere, and I shall be longing to kick off my shoes and let down my hair."

He did not smile. Nancy foresaw the

years ahead of them, filled with similar small irritations and petty conflicts. "So may I tell Connie she's to join the dinner party?"

He sighed. "I suppose you may."

⋆ ⋆ ⋆

"I think we should practise arranging your hair."

Nancy laughed as Connie's jaw dropped. "Naturally your maid will do it on the day, but it would be nice, don't you think, to see how it should look for the dinner?"

They went to Connie's bedroom, a sparsely furnished room near the top of the house, overlooking the stables. Nancy guessed it had once been the nursery: the furniture was painted white and the boards were stained with varnish and scattered with Indian rugs.

"Whilst I dress your hair, you can tell me all about becoming a great hostess. How is it you know so much?"

Connie sat at the dressing table. She swung her thick mane of hair over her shoulders. "Grandmama has taught me.

She used to give me long lectures about how I would have to be the mistress of Midwinter for Papa until Hugo got married."

Nancy drew in her breath sharply. "And then I came along."

"Oh, I'm not jealous about that. I don't want to be the mistress of Midwinter anyway. I shouldn't enjoy it."

"I'm beginning to understand why. I so much wanted to fill Midwinter with life and people, but there's such an awesome quantity of things to organise." Nancy began brushing out Connie's hair.

"My mama liked parties. She liked dressing in pretty clothes and looking beautiful."

"I want this party to be as good as your mother could have done it," Nancy said, and felt a sudden fierce determination to succeed. She coiled a strand of Connie's hair experimentally round her fingers. "You know," she said, "you have lovely hair. It will look very becoming piled up high."

"Like yours?"

Nancy, accustomed to Connie's spite, was surprised by a note of wistfulness in her voice. "If you like." Connie was silent, and Nancy sensed she was being studied in the mirror. "Shall we try? Just for fun?" Connie did not resist and she began coiling and twisting the heavy hair and pushing in pins. "Well, I've kept my side of the bargain. Now it's your turn."

In the process of putting up Connie's hair, Nancy learned the fine details of becoming a society hostess: the importance of table plans and place cards, menu cards in little silver holders, of sprays and buttonholes from the greenhouse for the dinner guests to choose from, brioches and jam and cakes for tea, and sandwiches and devilled chicken for the gentlemen with their brandy and soda after late-night bridge or billiards. She learned about the petty hierarchies of visiting servants, the precise timing of meals, who should accompany whom into dinner, all of which she should plan with the cunning of a military strategist beforehand.

"I feel sort of panicky," confessed Nancy.

Connie looked at her with none of

her usual hatred. "I think you'll be all right."

"Do you?"

"Some of them like you already. If you do anything wrong they'll forgive you and say it's because you're from the impoverished classes and that you don't know any better."

Nancy laughed. "You really are an atrocious child."

Connie frowned and turned to the mirror. She pushed her glasses more firmly on her nose. "I like what you've done to my hair."

They both looked at Connie's reflection. With the weight of hair drawn back from her face, attention was drawn to her delicate bone structure. A resemblance to Augusta was striking, but in Connie the resulting effect was winsome, slightly waif-like. Her spectacles emphasised the impression of vulnerability.

Nancy drew in her breath slowly, feeling pity for her. "I think it would look nice cut short."

"Why? Because you say so?" said Connie with her old animosity.

"Because I think it would suit you.

It would make you look modern and lively."

Connie wrinkled her nose. "Perhaps." She had turned from the mirror, for something had caught her eye from the window. Nancy followed her gaze and saw Hugo leave the stable yard and turn the corner of the building. After a few seconds he came into view again, walking quickly across the meadow.

"I know where he is going," Connie remained watching, sitting upright and very still.

Nancy held her breath as she saw that Hugo was making his way towards the wood. "But why?" she said softly as she watched him enter the trees.

Connie let her body relax. She turned again to the mirror and tipped her head from side to side, admiring her reflection. "He'll be going to the quarry. He's hoping to dig out some fossils."

* * *

Hugo felt a tension take hold of him as he neared the centre of the wood. He carried his empty specimens bag over his shoulder. The ground beneath his feet, even here, where it was cool under the trees, was hard and cracking in places where there was a worn path. The weeks without rain had lowered the water level in the pool; more than a foot of the steep sides of the pit were revealed, green with algae and stinking slightly in the heat. He peered over the edge, wondering whether its reputation of great depth really had been just another of their grandmama's tales to frighten them. The water was thick and cloudy. Hugo threw in a stone, which with a 'flop' of sound sank quickly from sight.

Flies buzzed round his face as he pushed his way through elder bushes which grew at the base of the quarry face. He searched the area for a sign of fossils embedded in the banks of earth, pushing his hair from his eyes. The heat made his face itch and his jacket felt too tight. He removed it and retreated from the quarry workings to lay it carefully on top of his satchel at the foot of a tree. As he did so, he noticed a ridge of moss-covered ground running from tree to tree. He knelt and began making excavations here and there, digging out and chipping at stones with his hammer. As the moss came away, his attention was caught by a discolouration of the soil, a reddish, uneven layer. He pulled away more of the moss and could see the feature clearly, a broken patch of small red tiles, perhaps once laid edge to edge, but crushed together and distorted. Hugo's heart beat painfully with excitement as he gouged out the bank and collected up some of the tiles. They were cuboid and regular, about half an inch across, and he was almost certain they were Roman tesserae. Hugo put them carefully in his jacket pocket. He glanced at the pool with its sinful reputation. It would be marvellous to do a proper investigation, but he knew his papa would never allow it.

* * *

Nancy sat in the shade of the marquee, reading 'A Lady's Book of Etiquette'. She looked up and saw Aubrey come down the steps of the terrace and cross the lawn. He was wearing flannels and a blazer, and he seemed to walk in a haze of light which had somehow slowed his body; as if, though he moved constantly towards her, he would never in fact reach her. How beautiful he is, she thought with detachment. Is that why I once loved him, just because he looked like a god? She realised that she had used the past tense. So it's true, she thought, I have fallen out of love. At the same time she had a strong sense of premonition, that something was going to happen which would make the severance final.

"So there you are." Aubrey was sweating in the heat. He wiped his forehead but did not enter the patch of shade cast by the marquee. "I thought this would be a last chance to go over the proofs together."

Augusta's portrait had been part of it, thought Nancy, remembering that Aubrey had been strangely subdued about the damaged portrait; he had looked at it long and solemnly, then said, without anger or passion, "Poor Augusta." He still loves her, she had realised, and had felt neither jealousy nor pain. The picture was back in its place for the party, housed in a brand-new frame, but for Nancy it no longer dominated the drawing room.

They walked back to the house. "Have you read the newspapers yet?" Aubrey asked gravely.

She shook her head. "What was it — in the newspaper?"

"Austria-Hungary has declared war on Serbia."

* * *

Nancy had thought the gathering momentum of the European situation would overshadow the party, but it received no more than perfunctory comment, on the lines of, 'Let Serbia take care of itself,' since after the murder of the Archduke at Sarajevo the Serbians deserved little support. "If anyone ought to do anything, it's up to the Russians and French to sort it out," said Colonel Gregory genially. Even Mrs Farringdon agreed that if Russia and France were drawn into a war, Britain would certainly have more sense than to go in as well.

And in any case, it would all soon be over. The talk digressed to rival weekend parties, holiday resorts, the delights of Cannes and Aix-les-Bains and attending a cure in the Pyrenees. Frank Singer's wife disclosed her 'infallible' diet at luncheon while devouring *mille feuilles*, and struck up a firm rapport with Daisy Lennox.

By the afternoon, more of the guests had arrived and milled about on the terrace and the lawns. A further dozen would join them for the formal evening dinner. Nancy relaxed at last. It was glorious summer weather; the borders were bright and scented; the servants in the blue and white marquee dispensed tea and sherry and claret cup efficiently. The lawns were immaculate and dotted with figures, strolling, lounging, getting along it seemed without her, though she moved among them dutifully and chatted and smiled and looked cool and gracious in a cream chiffon gown and a straw hat trimmed with pink roses. It was all very amiable and harmonious. She was sure that Augusta's parties had never been so pleasant nor, frankly, as dull.

She confessed as much to Stephen when he arrived with Edith and his friends from Oxford. "Something is missing. There's no excitement, no vitality."

"I could do you a song and dance turn — Burlington Bertie, Gilbert the Filbert," suggested Stephen.

Edith said, "It's because it's so hot. Nobody has any energy," She shielded her eyes with her hand and her gaze rested on Gilbert Lang. "I'm sure he has been here before."

"Yes. Last spring. Soon after we came here," said Nancy.

"Before that. I know I've seen him somewhere."

"He's an old friend of Aubrey's. So is the man with him, Frank Singer. Gilbert came here when Augusta was alive, but I don't think Mr Singer has stayed at Midwinter before."

"And the woman with her hooks into Mr Lang, is she an old friend?" Edith regarded Marjorie Benson critically.

Nancy lowered her voice. "I think Marjorie and Gilbert are lovers. He ought to marry her. She would be very good for him."

Edith pulled a disparaging face. She

continued to watch Gilbert Lang, ignoring the students who had come with her brother. Connie, however, did not ignore them. She was flirting with a dark-eyed young man, hoping Stephen would notice. She looked bright and pretty, her hair fastened for the afternoon into a long pigtail, which Stephen had pulled, calling her a 'flapper'.

Stephen had eyes only for Nancy. "I don't think the day is lacking in anything," he told her. "You look wonderful. Aubrey must be proud of you."

"You mean I've managed to prove myself a fit helpmate?"

"That is a woman's sphere — to look wonderful and bolster her husband in front of his friends."

"And nothing else?" Nancy bridled quickly, though she knew that he was teasing her. "Has she nothing to prove on her own account?"

"Why should she? Men prove themselves. Women smooth their path."

"What rot. That's too bad of you, Stephen. Oh, you men think you are so clever!"

"But of course," he laughed. "Come and play tennis with me later, Nancy. I'll let you win if it will make you feel better."

Edith wandered away. She felt lazy, unwilling to fall in with the superficial chit-chat of the afternoon. She felt the constrictions of her upbringing and saw how dull was her parents' existence, how unworthy their attempt to ape the manners of aristocratic society. She had thought once that she envied Nancy, with her more earthy working-class background, but Nancy was becoming absorbed by the genteel tedium of respectable middle-class life. Edith longed for an instant to break out, to have some sort of a fling which would shock her family and everyone else here. She glanced at Gilbert Lang who stood on the steps of the terrace and lounged against the balustrade, talking in a desultory way to the people on the lawn below him. If she were to decide to break out romantically, she did not think she could choose better: he looked very much 'travelled' in a worldly way. It was tempting to let her eyes meet his and linger there for a second or two.

Lang left his group of companions and was coming across the lawn to speak to her. "You look bored," he said in a low voice.

"Not at all," she replied quickly.

"Don't I remember you when you were a little girl? You and your brother came to Midwinter for tea and ran circles round poor Augusta. She never really liked children, not even her own."

"She was very kind to me once and let me try on her necklaces."

He smiled, flirting with his eyes. "What a charming picture that evokes."

Edith blushed and gripped her parasol tightly. "I remember you too. You seemed to have come straight out of the Naughty Nineties."

"I escaped the Nineties. I was still growing up towards the end of all that decadence."

"Aubrey must have been a young man all through the Oscar Wilde business."

Gilbert laughed, "Farringdon did not escape the Naughty Nineties. He just ignored them."

"Yes. That is his way. Aubrey is terribly proper, but very heroic as well, don't you think?"

Gilbert shrugged carelessly. "Anyone who has travelled acquires a touch of heroism."

Marjorie passed close by them and overheard the last remark. "Gilbert was fed on the accounts of Burton and Speke," she said. "Has he told you yet how he was given a copy of Speke's journey to the source of the Nile and kept it on him all the time, after he had fallen in love with the notion of travel?" She looked at Edith and added over her shoulder as she walked away, "He falls in love rather easily."

"Are you going to marry her?" said Edith, when she had gone.

"Who, Marjorie? Good Lord, no."

"Nancy thinks she would be very good for you."

"Nancy would. Marjorie is a good woman. But she's not sensual. Her sensuality is subordinate to her goodness."

Edith began to giggle. "Did you really carry Speke's journey to the Nile with you everywhere you went?"

"Everywhere. I tore off the covers to reduce the weight."

Edith laughed again and he was smiling too. "How fiendishly romantic."

* * *

Connie and Stephen played tennis with Nancy and Stephen's friend, Gus Wyatt. Gus was a poet, Stephen said, and lived in Sherborne. They had been at school together. "He writes extremely stirring stuff," and then, with a disarming grin, "Nancy likes Walt Whitman."

The game was lighthearted but fast, and after the first few minutes Stephen had begun playing to win. Connie played well, eager to impress, though Nancy noted that Connie's allegiance had changed: her eyes were all for Gus with hardly a glance at Stephen. How lean and supple the men looked in their white flannels. Nancy was aware of the muscled grace of their bodies, the ripple of white cotton and the flick of their hair, damp with perspiration, from shining, reddened faces. She flung herself into the game with boisterous abandon, and realised that she was enjoying herself for the first time in weeks.

"You play a hard game," said Stephen when the match was over and he and Connie had won.

"All thanks to Gus," laughed Nancy.

"Nonsense," said Gus. "You were a poem of movement, a Diana."

"But *we* won," said Connie.

"Ah," said Gus. "That is because you, Connie, are a goddess of even more superior virtuosity."

They walked slowly up to the house, Gus and Connie going ahead. The lawns glared in the sun; the shrubbery was a jigsaw of pattern, of yellow-green leaves and deep, dark areas of shade.

"Do you think young love is blossoming?" Stephen said, indicating the figures ahead.

"I guess it could well be. You know, of course, that Connie was madly in love with you right up until today."

"Well, I'm dashed."

"You can't pretend you had no idea."

"Not a scrap."

They passed under a sycamore tree and paused in its luxuriant shade. He pulled a handful of leaves and fanned Nancy's face with them and she leaned against the trunk of the tree. "How insensitive you are, dear boy." She smiled at him affectionately and closed her eyes, feeling the cool, scented breath of the bunched leaves.

"And there was I, all this time madly in love with her step-mama."

Nancy opened her eyes wide and saw a strange look, a burning earnestness in his expression. Her heart skipped a beat, for he was very close and for a moment she had thought that he was going to kiss her. And then he laughed and swung away. "Madly, passionately worshipping the ground she walks on."

She released her breath in a sigh of relief. "Oh, Stephen. You are a fool."

* * *

Nancy surveyed her dinner table, the blue and gold Coalport china, the cut glass, the candlesticks and the flowers from the greenhouse forming a centrepiece of blue and silver. The lobster sauce, the quails and fish had been perfect, the beef was tender, the wines free-flowing, the desserts and fruit exquisitely presented. The servants stood in the shadows around the walls, sensitive to Roberts's directions. Nancy felt a little smug, convinced that Augusta could not have done better.

Connie, her hair swept up into a coil, was deeply engaged in conversation with Gus beside her. Nancy had helped her to choose the square-necked gown, prettily draped across her breasts and covered with embroidered knots and flowers; she felt a glow of satisfaction, for Connie looked animated and absorbed and no longer glanced at Stephen to see if he was looking at her.

Edith seemed peculiarly fascinated by Gilbert Lang. Nancy wondered whether he would sleep with Marjorie at Midwinter. She looked at Aubrey, who was talking to his publisher, and she felt lonely. Mrs Lennox had been dropping hints that afternoon about the 'patter of tiny feet', and Nancy had attempted an enigmatic 'wait and see', though, Lord, she did not want children yet. But where was the chance of children if Aubrey never even shared her bed?

Stephen was very appealing this evening. He was flirting with one of Frank Singer's daughters, probably declaring himself madly in love with her. He was impossible. He had such high spirits and a self-confidence which amounted to a kind of arrogance. Stephen was full of the bumptiousness of youth, Nancy decided. Had he been going to kiss her? And if he had, what would she have done about it? She knew she might have been tempted to kiss him back. She hoped he would find himself a nice, pretty girl and settle down. Nancy smiled at herself. Youth. Had she outgrown it already at nearly nineteen? When she looked at Connie and Hugo she certainly felt old.

* * *

"I hear you want to be a geologist," said Frank Singer to Hugo. "Have you found any interesting deposits around Winchborne?"

"Very little on the estate, sir. Some ammonite sections and whorls. A few plant stems and brachiopods."

Singer dabbed his podgy mouth with his napkin. "Lang has an interesting story that a guest at your house once discovered Roman pottery on the estate."

Hugo was startled. So he had not been the first to find Roman deposits. But why had no one ever said anything? "Roman?" he echoed casually, and saw that Connie had begun to listen, her goggle eyes growing rounder. He held his breath, knowing what she was going to say and praying that she would not. He wished fervently that he had never shown her the tesserae.

"I have been a digger from childhood," Singer was saying. "When Lang told me there might be a villa, actually here, on the estate, naturally I — "

"It's true! Hugo found some floor tiles." Connie's voice, shrill, excited, sounded loud in Hugo's ears; the dinner table seemed to fall silent in response to her revelation, though he knew it could not have done so. When he looked up he saw that no more than a few people had heard her. The staccato of gossip continued. But his grandmama and his papa had been listening.

"Where did you find these floor tiles?" asked his papa in a low voice, and now others were looking too.

Aubrey's face became hard and angry as Hugo said as quietly as he dared. "In the wood, sir, Near the old quarry."

* * *

Nancy was aware of something going on at the far end of the table. Mrs Farringdon looked very peculiar: her sharp face was white and pulpy. Aubrey, with a furious expression, was saying something to Hugo, while Connie looked at the same time excited and anguished. In a second or two the incident was over, yet Frank Singer seemed acutely embarrassed and Hugo looked as if he were going to cry. Nancy gave the signal for the women to gather up their belongings and leave the men alone in the dining room. At a word from his father, Hugo left too and, before Nancy could question her, Connie slipped through the hall and ran upstairs.

"What in the world has got into everyone?" Nancy caught up with Mrs

Farringdon and drew her aside, out of hearing of the other women.

"Hugo has been very wicked." Mrs Farringdon's face was set in a grim mask and she was trembling.

Nancy was puzzled. "The dear child hasn't a wicked bone in his body."

"He disobeyed his papa's orders."

"But all boys rebel a little. It's a part of growing up."

Mrs Farringdon interrupted her, fixing her with a fierce expression. "He has been near the pool in the wood." Nancy's heart lurched. "You see? Even you are astounded that he could so entirely disregard Aubrey's feelings."

"But I know Hugo could not have meant any harm." Guilt piled up in Nancy's chest, making her breath feel tight and her face flush with heat.

"Hugo has become a vessel of sin. To promote such curiosity — in front of all these strangers." Mrs Farringdon turned away. "We should never have ignored the fact that he is Augusta's child."

* * *

Somehow Nancy got through the evening of music and cards and conversation until the guests began to depart or retire to bed. She left Aubrey to his billiards with Gilbert Lang, Frank Singer, and a handful of others, and went upstairs to her room.

She awoke with a start at 3 a.m. Aubrey had lit the lamp on her table and stood close beside the bed.

"Did you know that Hugo had been in the wood?"

Her instinct was to lie. "No. And I don't think — "

He began to pace the carpet. "Mama says I should beat him."

Nancy, still dazed with sleep, struggled to sit up. "For goodness' sake! It was only a small act of defiance."

"Nevertheless, he should be punished. I have to assert my authority."

"Leave it be, Aubrey. He was only exploring."

He stopped pacing, close to the bed. "You don't seem to understand what it means — that Hugo, my child — her child — should be drawn to the place where she — " he passed a hand across his brow — "where she perpetrated such wickedness."

"I expect he was looking for fossils at the quarry. The Winchborne Hill quarry must be almost worked out by now."

"He disobeyed my orders." Aubrey turned away.

Nancy felt sick. "What are you going to do?" He did not answer. "Aubrey, you mustn't beat him. You'll despise yourself if you do such a thing. Hugo was only following his instincts as a scientist. It would be wrong to punish him for that." She knew she must prevent him and that there was only one way. "I have been to the quarry as well, after you asked me not to. Am I wicked and disobedient? Would you care to beat me too?"

"You have been near the pool?"

"It's such a pretty place."

"But you know that it's abhorrent to me."

"Aubrey, it's only a pool of water amongst the trees. I find it incredible that someone who has faced cannibals and crocodiles cannot face up to this incident from the past."

He was looking at her in a way which

made her skin crawl. She had no idea that he could be so angry. "You have lied to me," he said at last.

"No. Not exactly. I should have lied to you if it meant we could have avoided all this fuss; but, to be honest, I'd rather have had it all out long ago in a row."

He passed a hand across his brow. "After all I have done for you, Nancy. How could you! How many times?"

"What times?"

"How often!" he shouted. "How often to that place!"

She could not lie now and did not feel inclined to do so. It was all too ridiculous. The resentments of the past months filled her mind. "I go there whenever I can get away from this ghastly museum of a house, because it's the only place I feel I can truly be at peace." She gasped as he raised his arm and she steeled herself not to flinch from him if he should hit her.

But he lowered his hand and said heavily, "I'm very disappointed in you, Nancy. You seem to enjoy hurting others. You are not evil, but you are susceptible to evil influences, just as she was."

After he had left her, Nancy sat for a long time, staring at the globe of soft light of the oil-lamp. She remembered the blue haze of the bluebells by the pool, the light filtering through the trees: there was evil in nature, Ted Powers had told her, but she had not believed him and she knew that there had been no evil intent behind her visits to the pool. Nor did she believe that Augusta had been evil, she told herself fiercely as her fingers gripped the bedcover. The past scene with Aubrey now had the unreality of a nightmare: there seemed to be nothing at all left of their marriage.

* * *

Nancy could not face breakfast the next morning. She forced herself to dress and to attend the ritual of morning service at the village church with their guests. The vicar devoted his sermon to the worsening situation in Europe. Germany had declared war with Russia, and France was asking for assistance from Britain. Would they all be drawn into the madness? Nancy prayed half-heartedly for some means of reconciliation between the countries and between herself and Aubrey, but she could not think that God would know the answer to either situation. She had started out with such high hopes of marriage, she thought, remembering the blissful period in London. Perhaps she and Aubrey had always been doomed and it had nothing to do with Augusta: the differences between them — of age, of education and class — were too great, and he had preserved too closely his image of her as a child.

The weekend continued according to Nancy's plans, with a relentless succession of walks in the grounds, tennis, lunch and tea and music on the lawn, just as if nothing were wrong. The sun still blazed. It all seemed very unreal.

On August Bank Holiday Monday, the sun shone, as if time stood still, but the mood of the party had become one of suppressed excitement. England was being drawn inexorably closer to war. Everyone was agreed that if Germany were to invade Belgium, Britain would be honour-bound to go to Belgium's aid. News was that the fleet had already been mobilised, and reservists were being called up everywhere. There would be a run on the banks, said Frank Singer. People began to talk anxiously of getting back home.

The last guest drove away before lunch and, in the afternoon, Aubrey shut himself in his study as if to deny that anything had happened. He had not beaten Hugo. He had set the children holiday tasks and confined them both to their rooms. Nancy felt no desire to see any of them. A strong weariness had come over her. She did not want to think about Aubrey, nor about the possibility of war. She went to the drawing room and stood before the portrait of Augusta. It was strange how the expression in the eyes had changed, for they no longer mocked her, and Nancy was aware of a strange affinity with the woman who gazed out from the portrait. Had Augusta discovered the emptiness of marriage? Who could blame her then for taking Viner as a lover? Nancy went to the window and stared out at the grounds. The dogs lay on the floor near the empty fire-grate. An occasional bird scooted across the slab of blue sky.

She heard lowered voices and glanced towards the drawing-room doors through which she could see, in the shadows beyond the stairs, the corridor with the green baize door which led to the servants' offices. One of the dogs lifted its head and gave a low growl, and Nancy froze against the curtain, startled to see for a brief moment the figure of Ted Powers cross the hall in the wake of Mrs Farringdon. The voices fell silent and a door along the corridor closed with quiet stealth.

Nancy turned again to the window, her heart beating painfully against her ribs. She had not seen Ted Powers since the afternoon when she had played the piano at his cottage. Why, after the row over Hugo going to the pool, should Mrs Farringdon have summoned him to the house?

11

AUBREY had known that the European situation would not go away, all of his generation had known. For years people had been saying there would be a war, there had to be a war some day. And yet, however much they had expected it, he did not think they had really envisaged it happening.

He crossed the sheep meadow, carrying a butterfly net and a large wooden box with a handle. He had lived in a private limbo since the house party, avoiding his children, avoiding Nancy in particular. He kept his gaze on the horizon as he walked, not looking at the wood: he would not think about it. He could forgive Hugo's disobedience, had forgiven him immediately in the face of Nancy's greater treachery. She and he did not understand one another and would never do so. They came from separate worlds. He saw clearly now what he should have seen from the start: that she would never be able to measure up to his standards. More than this, he saw now that he did not love her, perhaps had never loved her. He had been beguiled by her youth and her naïvety and by the idea of raising her from her modest origins.

He reached the far side of the meadow and came to the village road from where he cut across farmland to the Winchborne Hill quarry workings. He pictured the Midwinter quarry, its overhanging trees and the dark pool which it sheltered. It was as vivid in his mind as if he had seen it only yesterday, though he had not been near the place for years. Frank Singer was not going to let Hugo's discovery alone. Aubrey knew he could not put him off for ever. Singer had written, pressing to let him dig. Aubrey considered telling him the story of Augusta's infidelity, but the prospect of dragging it all up again was abhorrent. Singer was a gossip. He did not have Lang's sense of loyalty, for Lang, even when he was drunk, could be relied on to keep his counsel.

A mental picture of Hugo, chipping earnestly at fossils, produced in Aubrey a sudden wave of paternal sentimentality.

Nancy had been right, he conceded, he would have despised himself if he had beaten the boy: Hugo knew nothing of the dark memories stirred by the pool. Had he wanted to beat Nancy? Aubrey remembered the rush of violence through him, like a sexual impulse. But he had conquered the instinct to strike her, as man must conquer all his most base instincts if he was to call himself a civilised being.

And now, the most evil of all instincts was to be unleashed: Britain had declared war, and men would tear like dogs at one another's throats. He remembered that his first thought had been: Thank God, Hugo is not yet old enough to fight. "Well, Aubrey," his mama had said, "if only you were twenty years younger." Aubrey had privately thanked God that he was forty-five. His mama would see such reluctance to smash the Hun as cowardice. Was he a coward? It was an odd notion after all those years of travel. But it had been easy to be a hero when one was a civilising agent in a primitive land.

Nancy had accused him of not being

able to face the past. Well, it was true, but did his real cowardice lie in the fact that he no longer felt able to face up to the future? He felt a strong nostalgia for Arabia and the uncompromising codes of the desert. There had been a seductive simplicity about life when he was young.

The quarry baked in the afternoon sun. Light bounced off the rocks and he could smell the heat of the stones. The only sound was the intense chirruping of grasshoppers; no breeze stirred the scrubby undergrowth. He set down his box of jars and bottles on a rock and stood perfectly still. Lizards scurried near his feet, the air was flecked with small bright butterflies; he surveyed the flickering Skippers, Blues and moths, searching for a Marbled White. Colonel Gregory had told him that an almost completely black specimen had been spotted near the quarry.

Aubrey picked out a good Clouded Yellow as second best and waited for it to settle. He approached the resting insect and brought the opening of the net down hard over it. The butterfly fluttered up to the top of the net where he trapped it and transferred it to the waiting killing bottle. The desperate fluttering of wings ceased instantly. He placed the limp insect in a paper envelope and turned to select one of the Blues.

After about an hour, he had collected more than a dozen specimens. The outing had, after all, been rewarding, and it had led him to a decision: he would compile a fresh reference collection of the local species, something he had not done for more than a decade. Aubrey returned across the fields, recalling his more exotic collections, thinking again of Viner, remembering the man's insistence that he had come upon the site of a Roman settlement. Damn Lang for being there all those years ago and telling Singer. Damn Hugo for digging up the tiles. Damn Connie for her impetuous, "Hugo found some floor tiles." She should never have been allowed to join them at dinner. Damn Nancy for that. Damn Nancy for everything, for deceiving him with her sweet, lovely air of innocence. Damn all women. He felt sick, remembering. Damn Augusta? But he could not, in retrospect, condemn her, for poor Augusta had already been damned. He had begun to cry. The sun dried the tears on his cheeks and made his skin feel dry and old.

⋆ ⋆ ⋆

The summer-house had been creosoted, its windows, the floor and furnishings cleaned of cobwebs, but Nancy knew that now, weeks after the party, no one would come to look for her here. The little rustic house would fall again into neglect. Perhaps she preferred it that way.

Aubrey had been saying that the Army might want to take over Midwinter and turn it into a hospital, but for now it remained as it had always been: ugly, peaceful and isolated. Connie and Hugo had already returned to their schools. Except for Mrs Farringdon, alternately pronouncing death to the Kaiser and cheering Asquith and Kitchener, and the fact that one of the under-gardeners had volunteered, it was hard to believe that the country was at war.

Aubrey had barely spoken to her since the house party, except with a cold hostility. She had not seen Edith or

Stephen, but she had heard that Stephen had gone back to Oxford, no doubt to discuss the ever-fascinating topic of the war with his friends before the start of the new term. She remembered his fooling, pretending he was in love with her, his face in the shade of the sycamore tree and the fact that he had nearly kissed her. She was sure now that, if he had, she would have kissed him back; but how irrelevant the house party seemed, how far away that sun-filled atmosphere, so harshly shattered by Hugo's admission and then the declaration of war.

The early apples had already begun to fall. They made splashes of colour, red and white in the grass. Nancy took a deckchair from inside the summer-house and set it under one of the apple trees. Sitting down, she opened Augusta's diary on her lap.

* * *

The autumn of 1900 had been a continual round of house parties, of secret meetings between Augusta and John Viner at friends' country residences while

Aubrey was in Africa. There was golf and tennis and walks, word games and flirting and charades and creeping along corridors to steal a few hours of passion. And then, in November, Aubrey had come home.

Nancy read more intently, aware again of a feeling of affinity with Augusta:

Midwinter
Monday 19 November, 1900

Why did I marry Aubrey? He was, of course, the handsomest man in England, charming and manly, decent and candid. He was wealthy, so my life was assured of being comfortable and pleasant. I was of an age to marry and, if I must marry someone, why not him?

But Aubrey no longer has any romance in his soul. Life is not an adventure to him, and all experience must be judged beforehand by weighing up the advantages or drawbacks. When I asked him, what of Africa? he said that his experiences there might make a worthwhile book.

Does he suspect anything? Has someone told him? His mama gave a long account of my activities while he was away, saying I scarcely spent one weekend in two at home. You know how the autumn round is, I said. Was I to refuse invitations? Of course not, he told me. You thrive on company. You must enjoy yourself.

I told him we shall have a Saturday-to-Monday as soon as I can arrange it, to celebrate his return. We shall have a fancy-dress ball. I insisted on it, though he smiled so sadly and said, "Augusta, you know how I dislike parties." Sometimes, when he looks at me, I tremble and am sure he must know. Yet he says nothing. And so we go on.

Midwinter
Tuesday 20 November, 1900

When Aubrey first married me he treated me with the utmost respect, yet I knew that he loved me to the point of obsession. It was this indication that he could be ruled by dangerous impulses which made me love him so well in return. But they are impulses which he has tried so hard to eradicate that I fear he has finally succeeded.

Midwinter

Tuesday 18 December, 1900

The past days and weeks have been such a stream of activity I have scarcely had time to breathe. But how agreeable was the end result.

My idea of a fancy-dress ball was a spectacular success. Aubrey's mama was dressed as Queen Elizabeth and had kept her costume a secret. Colonel Gregory came as the Laughing Cavalier and they made a splendid couple. The hall was thronged with Caesars and Napoleons, Boadiceas and Josephines. The Lennoxes, costumed as Mr and Mrs Punch, lowered the tone somewhat, said Aubrey's mama, though I thought them colourful and rather delightful. Even Aubrey, dressed in his favourite Arab burnous, was bewitched by the magic of the evening and I could almost have fallen in love with him again.

Almost. For John, who had come as Bacchus, outshone them all, in a costume of vine leaves and with a heavy garland of grapes on his naked shoulders. He said in my ear that he thought I was dressed as a Bacchante, which vexed me more than a little, since I had followed Millais' portrait of Ophelia, in a gown appliquéd with flowers, and having let down my hair, I whispered that he flattered himself if he thought that I would act the part of his handmaiden in public and risk making an open scandal of our relationship. I told the servants to prepare a bath of tepid water and, without being observed, slipped upstairs and immersed myself entirely, until my hair was in rats' tails, like poor Lizzie Siddall when posing for Millais' portrait. My reappearance caused a sensation, for the gown, weighted almost beyond endurance, flooded bath-water all down the stair and across the hall tiles; the water soaked into the drawing-room carpet, so that the servants have, since the party, been constantly employed in drying it out. But I had my reward when John's eyes met mine and I saw how my defiance had excited him.

He came to my room that night. He placed his garland of grapes round my naked breast and said, "Now, a Bacchante you shall be." His teeth shone white in the candlelight and I was full of terror and delight all in one.

Afterwards, though he had hurt me, I forgave him as we lay together and talked and loved one another almost until morning. He says that danger in love is for him an added stimulus, and that the risks should be physical as well as moral. He knows that my own passion is never so strong as when I tremble for fear of being found out. His own is never greater than when he is conscious of his lust driving him to the edge of depravity.

I did not go with the men to the shoot, though John had expressed a desire for me to watch him bag more than any of the rest. In this I share Aubrey's aversion to bloodshed. Aubrey is not what one would think, given his mama's enthusiasm for the sport and his late papa's passion for hunting and shooting. We tend more to the aesthetic life, I once told him, long ago when we were in love. Certainly he dislikes the whole business and maintains a shoot, he says, purely for the pleasure of his guests — and for his mama, who takes immense delight in the butchery, discussing score cards and surveying the corpses laid out on the terrace for everyone to admire, and even, this weekend, taking part. One would think she was shooting for England, declares Colonel Gregory, full of his own success and taking pride in hers and saying she would make a 'damn fine soldier'. Colonel Gregory is a Philistine of the first order, more so than the Lennoxes, who at least took no part in the slaughter.

John told me a story before he left. He said that, when the shoot was over, he came upon the gamekeeper's son, Ted, a lad of thirteen or fourteen, who had been performing the duties of one of the beaters. John gave him a sixpence and said, "Well, boy, have we had a good day of it?" The boy spoke up quite charmingly, saying, "No, sir, I don't much care for it when the birds get shot, for my dad has looked after them from them being chicks." The colonel, overhearing this conversation, said that the boy did well to carry out his duty so proficiently in view of his dislike of the killing, and that he was sure that he would one day make a fine soldier. He had not seen John give him a tip and gave the lad another sixpence.

Midwinter
Thursday 27 December, 1900

How dull Christmas has been after the house party. I learned, when relaying the story of the keeper's boy to my maid Charlotte, that Powers had boxed his son's ears for speaking up to his betters and made him hand over his sixpences. Roberts says that, in chapel, Powers fancies himself as a lay-preacher. Powers, though a religious man, is less sentimental than his unfortunate son and has little enough affection to spare on his birds. I find him a brutal creature, but Aubrey's mama thinks the world of him because he is 'dependable' and would, she says, give his life for Midwinter.

Midwinter

Thursday 3 January, 1901

What if Nature should turn personally against me for my wickedness? What devastation the elements can wreak when they are roused. Yesterday I stood at the edge of the pool in the wood, and the wind soughed and groaned among the trees. I imagined to myself how the water might swallow me up, like the Deluge in the Bible, or the great tidal wave which swept the American coast last September. I read this week in the newspaper that one of the upright stones at Stonehenge has blown down in the gales. Another omen? How superstitious I have become. I stared at the water for a long time, almost wishing it would rise in a water spout and take me down with it to its depths.

I have not seen him since the house party. I hear from various sources that he is in Paris. I remember the Rue Descartes and Lally Durand, her mellow laughter and the musical sound of French conversation. I see again all those women with their loud mouths, extravagant gestures and crude stories of love, and am sure I shall die of misery.

Midwinter
Wednesday 23 January, 1901

So, that tired, ugly little woman in black is no more. With its Queen gone, the last century is well and truly over. I felt a strange sense of release when I heard. Aubrey, rather self-consciously, sports an armlet, and his mama has gone into full mourning. They affected to be very scandalised when I refused to wear a trace of black. To them it is the death of everything they hold sacred. I said, "The Queen is dead. Long live the King. And may a much jollier time be in store."

I shall be punished for my wickedness, says his mama — and perhaps I shall.

Midwinter
Friday 25 January, 1901

John has sent word by Charlotte with a book of Whitman poems, several passages marked. "I believe in the flesh and the appetites," he says.

"I love you, Augusta, and with us all lusts are transfigured. We are indifferent to virtue and vice. One day, you will believe me when I say that I love no other woman but you. But true lovers do not own one another and I am a man with many appetites. Does that make my love for you any less?"

I am not forgotten. He loves me. He will be going to Paris again in March, can I get away? I have written in reply, "Yes. Yes. Yes."

Midwinter
Thursday 31 January, 1901

Connie has begun talking. She said 'Mama', and I was inordinately pleased. Nanny says this is the first word she has spoken. Can there be a maternal spark in me after all?

Midwinter
Friday 1 February, 1901

I am keeping a separate account of the children's progress. I have resolved to be a good mother and have asked Nanny to give me constant reports of every sound that Connie utters which might possibly be construed as belonging to the English language.

Midwinter
Monday 4 February, 1901

How fascinating small children are. Such innocence in those cherub features and winning eyes! What tender sympathies their beauty calls up from the depths of one's soul. I have never felt such natural affection and devotion in my life.

Midwinter
Tuesday 5 February, 1901

The children are a perpetual delight and the days pass quickly.

Midwinter
Wednesday 6 February, 1901

Connie today displayed a fit of temper which seemed frightening in one so young. She flailed at me with her little fists and screamed so that her innocent face was quite red and ugly. Nanny calls it a tantrum and shrugs it off, but I saw a new side to my usually winsome daughter and found her, I confess, most unlovable.

Midwinter
Thursday 7 February, 1901

Hugo has a sweet and loving disposition. He of course takes after Aubrey, while Connie, Nanny tells me, is 'so much like her mama'. She says this after Connie has displayed the least angelic side to her nature.

Midwinter
Monday 11 February, 1901

Preparations have begun for Hugo's third birthday next month. I have been engaged with Aubrey's mama in drawing up a list of children who might attend. I bought Hugo the sweetest sailor suit. He is a dear and so willing. Connie, I fear, has an obstinate nature.

I feel a mounting impatience for the weeks to pass until Paris.

Midwinter
Monday 25 February, 1901

Connie today said, 'Pa-pa', and I rushed to tell Aubrey the news. I was shocked to learn that he had discovered Hugo in his study this morning, crushing the entire content of Aubrey's egg collection between his fingers.

He must of course be punished, though I felt a little sorry, and Nanny wept when she learned that he had been beaten.

Midwinter
Monday 4 March, 1901

Hugo's birthday. Twelve 'little angels' to nursery tea. I do not have an affinity with children.

Escape to Paris in two weeks. Thank the Lord.

Paris
Sunday 17 March, 1901

John says that if I do not get a grip on my jealousy I will ruin everything. This *affaire* with Lally Durand means nothing to him. Is he supposed to behave like a monk when we cannot meet for months at a time? He is a man with unusually strong needs. He wanted to know whether I make love to Aubrey still, and when I said that of course I must let him come to my bed, we are husband and wife, he grew very angry and says I am a hypocrite and a whore.

We went, tonight, to the apartment in the Rue Descartes. The evening was extremely tiresome. These people make me ill-at-ease with their desperate hedonism, and when we are with them John is very unkind. Tonight he said, "Women play up to men's lascivious natures with their frou-frou and padding and tight-lacing. It is an elaborate imposture. Take it from me, Augusta is not half so impressive naked as she is clothed." A gallant came to my defence, saying, "Is it possible, Augusta, that you are in love with this uncouth fellow? I should treat you like a princess if you would care to defect to me."

Lally Durand rattles on in her harsh voice, completely absorbing John, so that he rarely addresses himself to me when she is present — which, thank goodness, has so far been infrequent. They none of them listen to a word I say, interrupting any observation I might make with a stream of incomprehensible comment in quite the most appalling French manner. I am so miserable and John so disagreeable that I wish I had never come.

Paris

Tuesday 19 March, 1901

Last night, the fabulous woman with the pet frog was at the Rue Descartes. She has an overbearing attitude and I felt nothing but pity for the frog, a large, yellow-skinned, glistening creature, which she removed from a silver-beaded purse and placed on the palm of her hand. She wore a low-cut gown of silk and, at a signal — a weird, high-pitched whistling sound — the frog shifted itself around and leaped with one bound into her bosom, slithering with its legs into the gown and out of sight. Its movements were accompanied by the woman's fierce grimaces and most offensive body contortions, as if she was in sexual ecstasy. John says that for a select audience she will perform a more intimate party trick. This he described to me afterwards, as if telling the most splendid joke. When I expressed disgust he merely laughed at me and said, who could have thought I would be such a puritan. He told me to undress, his own polliwog was feeling restless.

Paris
Wednesday 20 March, 1901

He has engaged a very extravagant suite at his hotel. Last night there was a dreadful scene. John got very drunk and yelled and flung himself about like a wild animal. He had invited several of the Lally Durand set, ugly, talkative women, and a couple of English writers, skilful rather than significant, and all of them very vulgar. Even his friends were furious with him, though at first they laughed and said, "Poor Augusta. Why do you put up with this fellow?"

"Poor Augusta?" he screamed. "Poor Augusta pretends to be put upon, but she always gets what she wants. She has me dying of love for her, but she is coldhearted, for she will not leave her husband for my sake." He upset all the wine and smashed the leg of a small table, which he says I must pay for, since I was the cause of his anger. I have done so discreetly, having to bribe the hotel servant an exorbitant number of francs to keep the thing quiet.

Am I weary of all this? When I think how cruel he can be and how he neglects me for weeks at a time, when I think of Lally Durand and the other women he has had since he met me, yes, I am weary. And yet, when I am alone and remember him in his tender moods, when I imagine his olive flesh and the beauty of his manhood, I could go mad with craving.

Paris

Saturday 23 March, 1901

Sometimes I am sure that he hates me. He tells me I am a whore, that I have no real feeling. Women always disappoint him.

I asked him if we should part and he cried, saying I must forgive him and that he did not know what he was doing when these angry moods are on him. He fears there may be nothing at the centre of him, or even that he might be perilously close to madness. Only I can fill the emptiness of his soul, for it is I alone who give his life purpose. And it is true, for I know that if we were to part he would follow a path to ruin. He says he can see himself ending his days in some Parisian hovel or whorehouse if I were ever to desert him. We wept together and promised eternal love to one another.

Paris
Sunday 24 March, 1901

He was angry when I asked how he could afford to stay at his hotel. I know he has written next to nothing for a year and cannot make enough by his sales of butterflies to justify such expense. He suggested I should contribute to his upkeep, since Aubrey has made me rich enough.

I said that I would leave Aubrey tomorrow if I could be sure that he loved me, though he certainly had not shown it these past few days. "Why must you always want proof?" he asked. "Still you whine: love me, please, love me. You know nothing at all about love. You are like a spoilt child."

I said again that perhaps our affair should end and he smashed a wine glass and threatened that if I leave him he will tell Aubrey everything, so that he will divorce me and I shall lose the children. He repeated that I have no true conception of love, which is not patient and kind, as the Church would have it, but violent and terrible and free of all limitations, He took me then in his special way, saying I will learn through pain that I should not doubt him. Do we not castigate those we love? He says the thing I have come to dread is not wrong or indecent and pain is merely another form of ecstasy. All things are permissible between lovers. Obedience and trust are fundamental.

All this I can bear, because I know it is very arousing to him, and because I have grown accustomed to it now. Was not Aphrodite herself cruelly treated by Vulcan her husband? He says, as I raise my nightdress and bend over the bathtub, as I feel him inch his way inside me, where the discomfort is intense, he says as he rams and shudders with pleasure that I shall have my reward afterwards. He keeps his promise, and I feel only love, then mounting paroxysms of delight as, his agitation over, he consoles and pleasures me as always.

Midwinter
Thursday 4 April, 1901

How strange, always, to take up the reins of Midwinter again. Connie has been sick while I was in Paris. She looks pale and thin and I spent almost all day in the nursery to Hugo's delight and Nanny's annoyance. I have pledged myself once more to being a good mother, dressing them and playing with them entirely by myself. I shall do my duty as Aubrey's wife so that he cannot fault me.

Aubrey seems very peculiar and distant. His face looked grey, his eyes weary when I returned from Paris. I declared he had been spending far too many night hours on his sequel to *Across Widest Africa* while I have been spending his money at the fashion houses. Now and then I have the recurring feeling that he knows everything. Has John told him? Is it only a matter of time before all is lost and he will say he wants to divorce me? Then what? Could I bear it if the scandal were out; to be shunned by society and have nothing in the world but John?

Midwinter
Wednesday 17 April, 1901

Aubrey has agreed to another house party next month. He will leave it to me to draw up the guest list, but I am to include Gilbert Lang and Gilbert's current obsession, Ottalie Cay, also the Lennoxes, the Moretons, the Allinghams and John Viner. He was very particular to mention the latter, which makes me ever more fearful.

Midwinter
Tuesday 7 May, 1901

The usual anxieties about getting everything arranged with less than two weeks to go. Menus: discuss with kitchen — red meat, red cabbage, beets, and so on; the desserts ditto — redcurrants, jellies, blancmange. The table decorations, flowers, etc, all to be crimson. John to have the Red Room.

It will be almost a year to the day since we met. I have been to the wood to see, and the bluebells are in flower.

Midwinter
Sunday 19 May, 1901

Last night I went to him when Aubrey was sleeping. He had lighted the candles, one on either side of the bed as if it were an altar. The curtains and hangings glowed like fire in the darkness. I asked, why did he think I had chosen the Red Room for him? He said because it was the room most conveniently at the end of the corridor. And I answered, red is for desire. I placed his hand on my heart and asked, could he not feel it pulse for him with passion? I allowed him to bind me, as he has always wanted. I had two beautiful chiffon scarves ready, but he discarded these in favour of a pair of laces from his riding boots, by which he wanted to fasten my hands above my head by the wall and attach them to the lamp brackets. I said he might use the laces on condition that he was loving and did not humiliate me this weekend.

He kept his word. At the height of my pleasure I pulled too hard on one of the brackets and caused it to jerk out from the wall. My terror was intense, for the noise of the bracket crashing to the ground should have awakened the whole household.

Great ingenuity was required by John satisfactorily to explain the broken lamp bracket. Aubrey has been fussing about getting it mended on a Sunday, with all the upheaval of the handyman traipsing up and down the stairs in the midst of all the guests.

I had to prevent myself from catching

John's eye and bursting out with laughter during the conversation over lunch. But John had other fish to fry. He came back from a walk, quite reckless with excitement because he had found a piece of Samian pot and has formed a notion that there is a Roman villa in the wood.

Midwinter
Monday 20 May, 1901

Poor Aubrey was made to drag out all the old maps from the library this morning to support John's theory about a villa. John plans to stay on in Dorchester this week and is quite obsessed with this fancy of his about the Romans settling at Midwinter. Aubrey has given him the freedom of the library. He looks at us with such a sad intensity that I tell myself he must know, and yet I cannot pity him. It is true that love is like a madness.

Midwinter
Tuesday 21 May, 1901

John has visited the museum and is chasing up all the local sites. He asked if I have read all the poems he gave me. He says, above all, one must be true to oneself. Other men might call him wicked and say that his desires erupt from a core of depravity. I too might think him cruel at times, but I am wrong to think him inconstant because his appetite encompasses other women. I must never doubt his love for me, which is fierce and abiding and stronger, far stronger, than Aubrey's, who knows only the love taught by honourable men, which signifies nothing except to uphold the institutions of marriage and family. Whatever happens, I am to remember always that he truly loves me.

Tomorrow, I promise myself. Tomorrow afternoon, among the bluebells, we will recapture all the pleasure of our love as it once was.

Midwinter
Wednesday 22 May, 1901

All is lost.

Nancy read again the bleak sentence. Nothing more. The next entry was dated four days later, with no explanation, no indication of what had happened. She searched the succeeding pages, deciphering the words, for the writing had deteriorated to a scrawl, but she found no record of what had taken place that afternoon among the bluebells.

She watched a Red Admiral feed on one of the fallen apples, its dark velvety wings flexing. She could see its long tongue probing for the juice. Flies buzzed in the fallen apples on the grass. They crawled over the red and white flesh and she had a swift impression of half-eaten skulls with the flesh still adhering. The heat of the day seemed all at once filled with corruption.

Nancy closed the diary in her lap. She no longer claimed to understand the nature of love. Had she ever loved Aubrey, except in the way a child idolises a hero figure? Had Viner loved Augusta, in spite of his perverted appetites and his womanising, and had Augusta's love for Viner been so strong that it had transcended all his cruelty? Nancy considered Viner's claim that Aubrey's love for Augusta had been limited by the conventions of his class and family. She did not believe it, for Aubrey had forgiven Augusta the greatest of middle-class society's crimes, that of creating a scandal.

Nancy looked up again. A figure was coming towards her through the orchard. She saw that it was Stephen, and she slipped the diaries behind the cushion of her chair.

⋆ ⋆ ⋆

Aubrey had been setting more of his butterfly specimens. It was a task which required great patience, handling the butterflies with forceps. He lifted a Large Blue, a female, with very beautiful, heavy black spots marking the upper wings. The late summer sun shone through the study window and made the colours of the wings seem translucent. He squeezed the forceps against the insect's body and paused for a second to admire the wing-spread before pinning the butterfly vertically through the thorax. He positioned the specimen on the setting board, flattening the wings on either side of the groove in the board, adjusting the right upper wing by pushing it forward with a needle against one of the veins, then pinning it with setting strips to hold it firmly while it dried. He extended the hind wing in the same way, adjusting it until he was satisfied that its position showed the creature to the best advantage. The setting of the wings and the antennae required intense concentration and he was irritated by a knock at the door of the study. Roberts, apologetic, announced that Stephen Lennox was in the drawing room and had come especially to see him.

* * *

"Stephen, my dear fellow," Aubrey, masking his annoyance at the interruption, strode into the drawing room and stopped short at the sight of the khaki uniform. It had not occurred to him that the Lennox boy would be affected by the recent frenzied weeks of recruiting; enlistment fever seemed to pertain to the mob rather than members of his own circle.

"My God, Stephen! So soon?" The boy looked very handsome and ridiculously young.

Mrs Farringdon was looking at Stephen with unreserved admiration, "What a pity the children are back at school and cannot see you. Hugo will be so envious when he hears."

"Yes," said Aubrey grimly. "I'm afraid he will."

Stephen's expression was sheepish. He felt awkward in his uniform and the boots and puttees were tight and hot. "It seemed the right thing to do, sir, after the Officer Training Corps."

"But did you have to go the whole hog?"

"I had to serve, sir. We have to make a stand for the neutrality of Belgium, don't you agree? Britain is fighting for freedom and democracy all over the world."

Mrs Farringdon said, "Well spoken, my boy."

Did he believe it? Stephen asked himself. He had been pretty certain of where his duty lay when he and the others in his set had decided to apply for commissions. It had seemed a magnificent gesture, to take up arms for King and Country against the brutality of the Hun; it summed up everything for which, it seemed, he had been waiting.

Aubrey managed to muster an appropriate enthusiasm, "Well, now. I'm sure this must call for a drink." He poured a glass of sherry and handed it to Mrs Farringdon, then gave Stephen and himself a good measure of whisky.

Stephen watched him, aware of a feeling of superiority. He was heading for adventure, while Aubrey Farringdon would stay safely at Midwinter, reading the newspaper despatches about how the young men of England were putting the Hun to rout and discussing the battles academically with his papa and other men of the same generation.

"A toast," said Aubrey, with what seemed like false bravado.

"To our brave soldiers and to victory. Death to the Hun!" said Mrs Farringdon with rather more conviction.

They stood for a while, sipping their drinks and making awkward conversation, as if they had all at once become strangers.

"Your parents must be very proud of you," said Aubrey at last.

"Yes, sir."

He had come to the end of the measure of whisky and Aubrey shook him gravely by the hand. "Well. Good luck, my boy." He did not seem to know what else to say and looked far too serious. Stephen wished he would make a joke, as his papa might have done, to speed him on his way. He wondered where Nancy was, for he had come especially to let her see him in his uniform. He cleared his throat.

"I wonder if I might say goodbye to *Mrs* Farringdon."

"My wife?" Aubrey looked embarrassed. "Well then. Yes, dear boy. Go pay your respects, by all means."

Stephen was nervous as the maidservant led him along the terrace and, pointing the way, left him to cross the lawn towards the kitchen gardens. He rounded the corner of the wall and saw her, sprawled in a deckchair close by a summer-house at the far end of the orchard. How wonderful she looked, in a cream-coloured dress and with the sun lighting her figure. He pulled his baggy uniform jacket straight and his heart began to race.

"Stephen! You haven't! Oh, you haven't joined up?" Nancy scrambled from the deckchair and hurried towards him.

Her dismay was gratifying, delicious, Stephen repeated his piece about duty and fighting for justice and democracy, which had begun to sound pretty ridiculous in his ears. "So," he ended jokingly, "I've come to bid you a fond farewell."

"But how will your poor parents and Edith get along without you? And what about your studies at Oxford? Oh, Stephen. Are you sure?"

"It's too late now, if I'm not." He laughed to show that this heroic business of becoming a soldier for King and Country was something one did regardless of personal feelings.

She stood, looking at him, smiling sadly, and reached out a slim hand to touch the rough khaki material of his sleeve as if to smooth it. The pressure of her hand was barely perceptible, but it sent a fire shooting through him. "I shall really miss you." Nancy's voice was low, its north country accent still discernible despite Farringdon's attempts to coach it out of her. "Oh, Stephen. What's going to happen to us all?" She gathered her emotions and pulled herself together. "Oh well, at least Hugo can't go following your example."

"He would if he could."

"I know. And he's going to be ever so jealous. He hero-worships you, you know."

"I can't think why."

"I can." She was looking at him tenderly. He could smell the perfume she wore and the warmth of her body. Her dress was close-fitting and her hair was soft, as if newly washed, fastened in heavy billows back from her face.

It had begun to spot a little with rain, Nancy swung on his arm and steered them towards the summer-house, where she made him sit on the bench inside. The doors were open and looked out over the orchard. The house had been cleaned and painted and was furnished with rush mats, deckchairs and cushions from the recent house party. It smelled of creosote and mown grass. "Now." She plumped up the deckchair cushions and tucked them behind him, settling herself on the bench next to him. "Tell me when and where you are being posted."

He told her that he and Gus Wyatt were to leave the next day for a training camp near Wareham. He felt too hot and wanted to touch her, to rest his head against her breast and feel the cream muslin of her dress against his face.

"Will they let you come home to see us?"

"I expect things will have changed at Midwinter by the time I get my first leave," he joked.

"Nothing ever changes at Midwinter. Though there's been talk of turning it into a hospital."

"I heard Aubrey's archaeologist friend say he hopes to persuade him to let him dig in the wood."

"I don't suppose Aubrey will let him." Nancy lowered her eyes and plucked at the chain which she wore at her neck. "He was angry with Hugo for stirring things up. He was angry with me as well." She looked at him with an air of betraying a confidence. "I've been to the wood too, you see. It's so beautiful and mysterious. I thought it would not do any harm, but Aubrey saw it as a kind of treachery." She paused, then smiled again. "How trivial it all seems next to the news that you are to be a soldier."

"A second lieutenant."

"An officer. My goodness."

"Nothing that concerns you is trivial to me," Stephen said suddenly.

She raised her eyebrows with an amused look, and he saw that she thought he was pretending to flirt with her.

"No — don't mock me. The truth is . . . " He felt his face go crimson. "I really have fallen in love with you, Nancy." He tried to laugh, as if, after all, there was still a chance it was a bit of a lark.

Nancy stared. She half hoped he was still ribbing, then she saw that he was not. She put her hand to his lips to silence him, and he bent his head and feverishly kissed her fingers, catching her wrist and pressing her hand against his mouth. "Stephen, dear." His mouth was hot and tender, too tender for a soldier. She stroked his hair and moved her head to kiss his cheek. She had intended a sisterly peck, a reassuring gesture to show that they could ignore his confession and still be friends. As she turned her face to him he turned his own and, perhaps by accident, perhaps not, their lips met.

The shock of contact was devastating. Nancy felt a sexual heat sweep through her. She did not draw away, but sat, waiting for him, as he took her gently in his arms.

She felt the touch of his mouth and hands, the silky brush of his hair against her face as he bent his head to kiss her throat. She closed her eyes and, for an instant, saw an image of Augusta and Viner. She opened them, banishing it, and a tremor of desire ran through her. "Oh, Stephen — we ought not," she whispered as their hands entwined, parted, sought buttons and fastenings and tenderly unclothed one another. Feelings, long submerged, flowered within her: she had been denied the healthy fulfilment of her young body for so long.

He spread his uniform jacket and the cushions on the floor of the summer-house for her to lie on, and she watched him, smiling as he straightened the corners of the cushions. He held her as they sank to the floor and she drew him down to lie beside her. She told herself that he was going away, perhaps to die. And they made love.

She had not known that the act of union could be such a joyous thing. Nancy was in awe of her own sensuality, half afraid of his tender exploration and the sweet sensations he drew from her. They lay together, finding and giving gratification, and at last, crying out his own pleasure, he filled her up with a quivering, intense delight. She clung to him and lay back in his arms.

They lay, looking at the rafters, giggling now and then at the thought of what they had done, a suppressed hysteria, until at last they were sober.

They dressed swiftly, sure that someone would come searching and at any moment discover them, and Stephen said, "Now what do we do?"

"We pretend it never happened." Nancy looked down at her dress and tried to press out the creases. "Can you tell?"

"Yes. You look even more beautiful."

"Oh, Stephen." They kissed again and she felt a wave of tenderness for him, but she knew it was not love. She hoped he was not going to be difficult. At last she pushed him away. "I mean it. We pretend nothing happened. This was for once only. It won't ever happen again." She felt years older than he was.

He opened the door. "If I die now, I shall have something wonderful to remember with my last breath."

"You silly boy," she said. "You're not going to die."

She picked up the diaries when he had gone. She would not read them again. She took them to her room and locked them in her writing desk, and refused to listen to the voice of her conscience which said, You are no better than Augusta. Worse. At least Augusta was in love.

12

IT was October, and the trees were a mass of brown and gold. Nancy cycled slowly along the rear drive, away from the house. She enjoyed cycling, it reminded her of her childhood and of riding with her mother on a fixed wheel machine. She felt the breeze lift the brim of her straw hat and cool her legs under her cotton skirt. She considered visiting Edith, but rejected the idea. Edith had changed since the outbreak of war, associating herself with the handing of white feathers to able-bodied men who had not yet succumbed to the recruiting campaign; she had become even more keen on the Pankhursts and had taken to attending feminist rallies. Aubrey's mother approved of the white feathers but condemned Edith for her alliance with the suffragettes. Nancy felt uneasy on all these counts and more: friendship with Edith had grown more awkward since that afternoon in the summerhouse with

Stephen. She had not heard from him since. Relief that she was not pregnant had been brief; more recently she had been aware of a subtle disappointment, less with Stephen than with herself, for it would have been very pleasant to have been in love.

She heard the sound of a motor-cycle engine and stopped pedalling, waiting for the rider to come into sight along the track from Keeper's Cottage. Ted Powers brought his machine to a halt and swung it round alongside her before turning off the engine. She remembered seeing him with Mrs Farringdon after Hugo had admitted to Aubrey that he had been to the pool, and asked herself again, why? Why on *that* day had he come to the house?

"So. You've not let anyone persuade you to enlist yet?" she said.

"Not me, ma'am. But I heard Browne's gone off."

"There'll soon be no one left at Midwinter. As well as the chauffeur, the Army have taken nearly all the horses." So many things were changing because of the war, thought Nancy. A small band of local women had replaced those male servants who had been patriotically inspired or bullied by Mrs Farringdon into joining up. There remained only a handful of staff — among them Roberts — too old for military service: Mortimer in charge of the gardens, Radley over the stables, and Powers, whom Mrs Farringdon, to Nancy's astonishment, had said they could not spare. She looked at him and wondered again why Midwinter could not spare its keeper.

"It'll take more than a recruiting sergeant to make me put on a soldier's uniform," he said, as if interpreting her thoughts.

She looked down at the handles of her bicycle. "So many young men are going to die."

"It's what happens. Pity no one thought about that before they began it."

"It seems rather naïve to hope to defeat the Kaiser in only a matter of months."

"Is that what they say?"

"Mrs Farringdon believes it. She's become very war-conscious since she decided Midwinter should be helping the war effort." She smiled, remembering the zeal with which her mother-in-law had begun on the conversion of Midwinter into a private convalescent hospital. It was as if her years of committee work and charity fund-raising, of being a director of useful effort in the community, had been in preparation for the national crisis. The Army had rejected the house for use as a hospital but, undismayed, she had brought all her managerial skills to the fore and secured private subscriptions and the financial blessing of the Red Cross, had hired equipment, a matron, and the services of the local doctor. Nancy looked at Ted. "I'm surprised she has left you alone. She's been bullying the farm-hands to enlist."

"I expect I'm too old for her to bother with." He glanced at her bicycle and said, as if wanting to change the subject, "That's a good machine."

"My husband bought it for me. He has responded in his own way to the emergencies; he handed the Wolseley over to the Red Cross, ordered the pony-trap to be brought out of storage for his mother, and bought the bicycle for me. Times are changing." She met Ted's gaze, remembering that he had said as much when she had first known him.

His glance travelled from her eyes and mouth, down the line of her body to her exposed ankle. "Times might be on the move, but your husband wouldn't be too pleased if he knew you talked so freely with your servants."

"I don't think of you as a servant. You're not like the rest," In any case, Nancy thought, Aubrey scarcely noticed what she did these days. Now that his book had gone to the publishers he said he no longer needed her to act as his secretary. She had tried to discuss her role at Midwinter when it became a hospital and Aubrey had answered with no apparent interest, "You must arrange all that with Mama. You know, Nancy, that you may do as you please." Sometimes she thought to herself that, if she had never found Augusta's diaries, or, if she had not told him she had been to the pool, Aubrey and she might still believe themselves in love with one another. If they had not come to live at Midwinter, perhaps everything would have been different.

"Midwinter pays my wage and board like all the rest," Ted said in reply to her claim that he was not like the other servants. He began to walk along the track wheeling the motor cycle between them, and Nancy, who had been cycling slowly, dismounted and walked as well.

"I feel as if I've almost become one of the staff as well, in a way," Nancy said, and she told him how she had been drawn into the conversion scheme, had attended Home Nursing and First Aid classes in the village and passed the examinations. "It was wonderful, to strip the house of its museum atmosphere and pack all the glass showcases in the attics." She recalled how the main hall and corridors and drawing rooms had been cleared of their trophies, each tasselled spear and stuffed mongoose transported with reverence along the emptying corridors under Aubrey's anxious supervision. She laughed. "You should have seen me in an apron, with a handkerchief wrapped round my hair and sleeves rolled up to the elbows. You would not have been able to tell me from the skivvy."

"A bit of a come-down, after all your aspirations," he said without humour.

"No." She halted. "I feel I can at last channel my energies into something practical."

He smiled. "You're hankering after your life before you married."

She was startled by the truth of what he had said. "Not the drudgery of the life my mother led," she said, analysing it, "but the freedom from formality, yes, I still miss all that."

They walked on, the bicycle rattling over the rutted track, an air of companionship between them.

"You *are* different from the other staff," she insisted after a while. "You don't mix with them. You don't behave like them." She hesitated. "And you know the story about Augusta and her lover."

He was silent.

"I know it was you who found them together."

"You're wrong. It was my dad found them."

"You're a bad liar, Edith Lennox told me you were there as well. Why can't you say what happened?"

"Oh, now come on. You can't expect me to tell you that."

She halted. "Why not, if they were making love — if that's all there is to it?"

He looked at her, dropping his gaze as he said, "I should forget all about her. She's been gone a long time and so has he."

"You're right. But I'm curious."

"Curiosity killed the cat."

Let it go, thought Nancy. There's no point in it. Augusta's story is dangerous: it does more than kill cats, it destroys marriages. She walked on, the turning of the bicycle wheels the only sound between them. "My stepson found some tesserae near the pool," she said after a while. "He thinks there could have been a Roman villa here. One of my husband's friends wants to set up a dig."

Powers continued walking but there was a change, a sudden constraint in his manner; he seemed to be about to say something, then changed his mind and continued in silence. They had reached the road. Ted swung his leg over the seat of his cycle and looked at her. His eyes had taken on a blank, cold expression. "I should do your best to stop anyone nosing about in the wood."

"Is that your job?" she said quickly. "I've seen you come to the house. Is that why Mrs Farringdon employs you: to report to her and deter the curious from stirring up memories for my husband? Is it a mother's duty to protect her son and a servant's duty to obey the wishes of his mistress, however peculiar?" She hesitated, then said in a rush, "Or is Mrs Farringdon afraid you might tell?"

He seemed to relax a little. "I'd never let anyone know how we found them at the pool that day. It wasn't fit for a lad to see, never mind for me to tell it to you — a young lady — years afterwards. But, I promise you, no good can come from stirring it all up again."

She shrugged and mounted her bicycle. "Then I shall have to leave it to my imagination."

* * *

Ted watched her go, seeing her figure in the checked coat, the skirt with its suggestion of shapely legs and hips, and her slim ankles pushing on the pedals. He started up the motor cycle and rode to Dorchester.

The town was full of men in khaki and brass bands and recruiting posters. He could ignore them, he felt immune to the war fervour, but he could not so easily dismiss his recent encounter with Nancy, for she disturbed him in more ways than one.

He went into a pub. Men in khaki were here too. Women were all over them. The men expected admiration and got it; they were doing the decent thing for King and Country. Ted thought about the women he had known. About Mary Bond, whom he had loved. Mary had heavy ankles and long yellow hair, which he had been privileged to see fall over her shoulders. But she had set her sights on better things than marrying a gamekeeper. She had gone off to Bath and given herself to a schoolteacher.

The memory of Mary's tumbling hair brought back other memories. Some you could blot out for a while, but they never went very far away.

Ted thought about his father as he drank his beer. A cruel man? He had loved his pheasant chicks, crooning over them like a mother hen, but he had never minded when it came to the shoot and he had shown no mercy towards vermin. The slaughter had been regular: foxes, squirrels, rooks, crows, hedgehogs, weasels; they had all hung on the keeper's gibbets, as a warning to others to keep away from the wood. His father had been cold-blooded too about chapel; he had believed in all of it — hell-fire, the just retribution on the sinner, rewards in heaven for the righteous.

Ted remembered the afternoon when they had found Augusta Farringdon and her lover. There had been a big party at the house that weekend, but no shoot, for it was mid-May. He had gone with his father to check on the birds or the traps — or perhaps they were only out for a stroll: those sort of details were harder to remember.

It was important to be quiet when working in the wood and they were not spotted that afternoon. The ground was a sea of bluebells; he remembered their scent and the moment when his dad placed a hand on his arm to steady him. "Careful now, Ted. I reckon there's something going on over by the pool." Ted had fallen into the silence of the wood, freezing, like a hare when it melts into the field. He had heard nothing at all at first, then a sound like the shriek of a pheasant, but human.

They had moved forward and into a clearing. His father said, "Almighty Christ!" and Ted saw a sight which made the hairs on the back of his neck bristle and his cock stiffen in his shorts.

The man wore nothing but a wreath of leaves on his head. The woman was completely naked. Her fair hair was loose to her shoulders; her arms were bound in front of her at the wrists, wrapped round the trunk of a tree; she had fallen on her breasts against it. It was she who had given out the shriek. She cried out now, in a sobbing monotone, as if she knew the words would be ignored. "No, John. Enough now. Please. Enough."

The man was intent on his objective. He pumped in and out, grunting a little, but otherwise in silence. His hands gripped the fronts of her thighs to prevent her falling to her knees. The woman's weeping only made him go at it harder. "No. Enough. Please John . . ." she began again with her pleading.

His father had not waited on protocol: he ran at the man, roaring and plunging through the bluebells like a maddened bull. They had rolled on the ground at the edge of the pool, his dad in his keeper's clothes and the struggling naked figure, and it had looked, to Ted's impressionable imagination, as if his father were wrestling with a demon.

Only when the woman shrieked again, "Stop it! Stop it! My God — you'll kill him!" had Ted recognised her. Then he saw that the man taking a beating from his dad was one of Farringdon's guests.

He had not dared untie her. He did not dare go near her. He had never in his fourteen years seen a naked woman, and his experience of sex had been crude, solitary and innocent compared with that scene of immorality. 'Depraved', his dad had called them. He said it in a voice like thunder, with impressive dignity and right to Farringdon's wife's face. He had untied her and made her put her clothes on, saying they were pagans and sinners and an abomination in the sight of the Lord. She begged him all the while not to tell her husband, saying it was not Mr Viner's fault, it had been her idea to come to the pool.

"I know where my duty lies." His dad had looked very stern and trembled with anger, and Ted had seen at once who was the figure of authority in the situation. It had seemed strange, his father taking charge, when people like Viner and the mistress were always ordering his own kind around. When she was dressed, Mrs Farringdon clung to his keeper's coat and said, "I'll pay you. Anything. And the boy. I'll give you anything you want. It's yours for the asking. But don't tell my husband."

His father had said, putting on a voice like the preacher in chapel, "Just you fall down on your knees tonight, my lady, and pray to the Lord to forgive you for your pagan wickedness."

All this while, Viner, who had put on his clothes fastidiously, as if dressing in front of his mirror, was standing dabbing at his face with a handkerchief and staring at the pool. "For God's sake be quiet, Augusta," he said at last. "Can't you see it's no use whining?"

Ted had watched them walk away, Viner strolling up through the trees in the direction of the road, as if he had not a care in the world, his father helping the mistress along the path towards Midwinter. His father had called over his shoulder, "Get on home, boy. And not a word about this to anyone. Not a word, mind, or you'll wish you'd never been born."

He had kept his silence for fear of his father's wrath, and, in a superstitious way, because he was afraid to describe what he had seen. His dad had not kept silent to Farringdon though. Oh, he doubted he had told him exactly — there were things you could not say to a man about his own wife — but enough to cause an uproar, and Farringdon would know Harry Powers was not a man to make up a story like that. Some of it got out round the village: perhaps his dad had let something slip somewhere; or one of the maids at the house, in the know about what had been going on. But Ted had kept his own silence, and the village did not know the whole story, nor ever would know what had happened after. Ted finished his beer, still remembering. He wiped the back of his hand across his mouth and saw that his fingers trembled.

* * *

Nancy went to her room that afternoon. Though she had vowed not to touch them, she took out Augusta's diaries from her desk and locked the door. She stroked the leather binding of the book and, opening it, stared down at the now familiar, oddly comforting scribble. She began with the scrawled entry after Augusta and Viner were discovered, reading patiently through every page to the final volume.

Midwinter
Sunday 26 May, 1901

Aubrey said today, he did not think I had any notion of the torment I put him through. He cannot hate me, but my wickedness has made his existence constant hell. When I admit I have wronged him, he says I have no compunction about what I have done, that I am totally without conscience or morals. He will not contemplate divorce and, in any case, so long as Powers and the boy can be persuaded to keep quiet, no one will know that anything has happened.

Perhaps this is his only concern — that respectability and the unity of the family should be preserved? He looks at me with such disgust. I have a feeling of being reduced to the lowest I have ever been in his estimation. I have promised not to see John, but my poor body aches and longs for him.

Midwinter
Monday 27 May, 1901

Aubrey said today that John has agreed to leave the country. That he has accepted a payment of five hundred pounds not to set eyes on me again. This I will not, will not believe.

Midwinter
Thursday 30 May, 1901

A letter. The last to be delivered by poor Charlotte, whom Aubrey says I must dismiss because of her complicity. Aubrey's mama has taken it upon herself to interview for a new maid. She watches me like a cat over a mousehole, but she does not have his letter. How sad I feel about Charlotte and the end of our long association. She wept bitter tears to leave and swears she bears me no ill-will over her dismissal. I have said I shall find her a good position in Dorchester or Blandford.

John says in his letter I am to pay no regard to anything I am told. He has been obliged to agree not to see me again, but was he ever a man of his word, except to me? If I can only be patient, he will find a way for us to be together again, but Aubrey will not settle for less than that he should leave England.

Midwinter

Sunday 2 June, 1901

Aubrey said to me today, "That bounder tried to threaten us. He swears he will tell the whole story if I don't pay him another five hundred." Powers the keeper has pledged himself and his son to secrecy for no more than five pounds, that at Aubrey's own suggestion. "What is the world coming to," says Aubrey, "when one can trust the servant class to behave more honourably than one's own kind?"

Certainly Aubrey has paid John money, and his mama supports this latest story, but that woman would say anything for her darling son, and for the sake of saving face. John's letter asserts that Aubrey, for his part, has threatened to have John blackballed from every club in London if he does not comply with his terms. John says he does not care for his own reputation, and knows Aubrey is bluffing, for the Farringdons would suffer more damage from any revelations anyone cared to make public. As for going abroad, the idea of going to Malaysia until the fuss dies down appeals to him, for it has always been his second home. Men are making fortunes all the time. He says he will take ship and send for me. He has given me a poste-restante address to write to him. If all else fails, he will come in person. But I must keep faith.

Midwinter
Monday 3 June, 1901

They are sending me away to 'recover'. I suppose they will make up some story about my having had a convenient attack of neurasthenia, like Ottalie Cay who has had so many 'cures' for nervous collapse that she is known at every hydropathic hotel in Europe.

I am at a pitch of agitation in case John tries to write to me while I am away and I miss his letters, or they fall into the wrong hands, but there is no arguing against it; I must go along with their little charade.

Harrogate
Saturday 8 June, 1901

I have written to let John know where they have sent me.

There is a woman here who has suffered from nervous debility for thirteen years. She has such 'flurries', she says in a persecuted, affected tone, and her body feels constantly oppressed.

I find this whole business very tiresome. To be woken at six a.m. by the bath lady, who administers a cold bath and a rubdown, is far from agreeable. It is supposed to produce a sense of well-being. At eight o'clock a bell summons everyone to a breakfast which consists of little more than dry toast. At nine a.m. I am given an appointment to see Dr Peters the hydropathist, who prescribes my medicines and routine for the day. The medicines I can endure, the purges are merely disagreeable, the nerve tonic — an interesting green liquid — is not altogether unpleasant. But the baths! My poor flesh is by turns being boiled, frozen and scrubbed away. The first bath is taken, very hot, in a vast marble tub in a room like a Greek temple. This is followed by a cold shower. In the afternoon, just when

I am beginning to enjoy the ambience of the gardens, I am summoned by the bath lady to yet another going over. The evening dinner at least is ample and really rather congenial.

Harrogate
Monday 10 June, 1901

The evenings here are taken up with party-pieces and recitations, a torture even more excruciating than the constant bathing. I absent myself from the proceedings as much as possible and retire to my room where I can in secrecy write to John.

Harrogate
Wednesday 12 June, 1901

Dr Peters says, if he can treat me with water from Bohemia for the duration of my stay he will have me cured of my 'sex lunacy'. I said, 'Am I to drink it or be washed in it?' and he was very much put out.

Harrogate
Saturday 15 June, 1901

My birthday. I am thirty. Nothing from John.

Aubrey came today to visit me. He brought me a brooch shaped like a dragonfly. It so reminded me of the brooches I had coveted when John and I were at the Paris exhibition that I at once began to cry and Aubrey took it for signs of remorse and said, in his stiff way, "When all this is over we can perhaps be as we once were to one another again."

I dried my eyes and challenged him as to what I am being cured of. He said, his expression very sorrowful, "You know, Augusta, that you have always been sorely afflicted with a sexual temperament."

Harrogate
Monday 17 June, 1901

A new patient was brought in today. We talked briefly during dinner. She has taken to a feminist way of thinking and her husband, much frightened, hopes that by sending her here she might be cured of it.

Harrogate
Tuesday 18 June, 1901

Grace Hammond, for that is the young

lady's name, is a member of various women's organisations at her home in North London, all in secret, so as not to alarm her husband. She is very much in favour of women one day having the vote. She says that because she attended a public meeting for women's suffrage against her husband's wishes he has threatened to cut off her allowance. We talked for a long time in the garden about the despotism of marriage and the tyranny of respectability. We have exchanged addresses and promised to meet when I am next in town.

Harrogate
Thursday 20 June, 1901

This afternoon Grace smuggled in some whisky, the perfect cure for hysteria, she said. Certainly it improved our sense of well-being. We sat in the summer-house, out of sight of the attendants, smoking cigarettes and drinking the whisky from washstand glasses sneaked down from our rooms. We felt ourselves to be perfect rebels.

Harrogate
Friday 21 June, 1901

We finished the whisky this afternoon. I hid from the bath lady whom I could hear calling for me. I told Grace about John while we skulked in the summer-house. She thinks I must follow my heart and not let Aubrey wear me down. "He will send for you," she said of John, with such certainty in her clear, understanding blue eyes that I knew it must be true.

Harrogate
Sunday 23 June, 1901

Dr Peters says I am cured. I have a healthy colour and seem so much more cheerful; he says the hydropathic treatment must have been very effective. I pretended to be very reserved and solemn, and said his hotel had done me the world of good and I would recommend it to all my friends.

Midwinter
Thursday 18 July, 1901

Went up to London yesterday to see Grace Hammond, who has written to say that she is newly released from the wilds of Harrogate. We met in a teashop in Piccadilly. Afterwards she took me to a lecture on 'The Political Stance of Women'.

I cannot say I felt myself part of the sisterhood, though Grace sat on the edge of her seat and applauded every other word, her eyes shining with all the conviction of a zealot. I cannot see them achieving their ends, nor should I like to see women in Parliament. No woman has the political experience for making national decisions. Imagine Aubrey's mama or Ottalie Cay given the power of the vote! And yet to see so many women, all of one mind, was very impressive. I shall join the campaign for a while, if only to help spite Grace's husband and his niggardly ruling over her allowance and to fill in the dreadful time until John sends word from Singapore.

Midwinter
Friday 19 July, 1901

Aubrey has discovered some books, lent me by Grace, and was at first displeased with my befriending her and the idea that I have espoused the suffragist cause. "You have your children's physical and moral welfare to think of," he says. Campaigning and attending public meetings only diminishes women. But he has not forbidden it outright, believing, no doubt, that while I am occupied with Grace my mind will be diverted from John. He could not be more wrong, for Grace has become a willing conspirator. We have devised a plan whereby John writes to me, care of her address in London, and she will pass the correspondence on, concealed under cover of her own letters.

Midwinter
Friday 26 July, 1901

No word yet from John.

Midwinter
Monday 19 August, 1901

A shoot at Midwinter. Aubrey's mama was in her element. To London tomorrow to see Grace, but still no word from John.

Midwinter
Monday 30 September, 1901

A letter! He says he has found a house with a wonderful garden, profuse with flowers and luxuriant vegetation. There are butterflies everywhere. He is going to turn it into a pleasure palace for me and we are going to be so happy. He has bought an interest in a tin mine where, since the ore is at no great depth and Coolie labour cheap, there is a fortune to be made. He wants me to sail early next year and go to him; he will arrange everything.

Grace says if I love him, I must go to him. But I tell her this is not the same as merely tripping off to Paris. How can I leave my children, my home, my country and travel alone half-way across the world, knowing I shall never return? I have written to him, pleaded with him: he must come for me. I am so afraid. I cannot do it alone.

Midwinter
Wednesday 2 October, 1901

I went to a meeting with Grace and was proud to hear her address the audience on women's rights. She said again, I must up and leave Aubrey. It is the only thing to do. I am killing myself by staying, when my heart is with John. "You do not understand," I told her. "You are strong. I do not have your temperament."

But it is true that the affair is destroying me. I suffer the most terrible attacks when I contemplate the future. My body begins to tremble and my heart bangs about under my ribs. I cannot stay. Grace is right when she says the heartache is killing me. And yet, neither can I go, for how can I throw over everything for him?

Midwinter
Monday 11 November, 1901

What is there for me at Midwinter? Nothing at all. Then why does my poor heart tremble so when I contemplate the alternative?

Midwinter
Monday 23 December, 1901

An angry letter from John, accusing me of inconstancy and moral cowardice.

"If you love me as I love you," he says, "you would not hesitate to come." I have written back, pleading with him, telling him of the persistent physical weakness since last he saw me, which threatens to become chronic. I cannot do it alone. I should falter at the first obstacle. Besides, Aubrey would come chasing after me, and his mama lock me up. They will send me away again to that ghastly place in Yorkshire and never let me out. I am like a helpless creature, paralysed in mind and body. He must come to fetch me. If he truly loves me he will prove it and come for me.

Midwinter
January, 1902

The South African war is going badly, How long it seems since that innocent joy of hearing Mafeking was relieved and John first declared himself to me. I weep for hours when I remember. No word since Christmas. I wake in the night in a sweat of dread and fear that he has abandoned me altogether. I fear the agony of all this is killing me slowly. Can one die of love? I believe it. And truly, if John came for me now, he would have to carry me away, like a medieval knight, my spirit has grown so faint.

Midwinter
March 1902

John very angry, complaining again about my frail willpower, how he must always prove himself to me while I prove nothing in return. But — oh, he means to come to fetch me. I am to wait until I hear from him again.

Midwinter
Tuesday 6 May, 1902

He is here. My love is here! He has written through Grace. She telephoned me. "Seize your happiness while you can, my dear."

John's note is brief: "Be ready next week. I will let you know where and when."

No words of love or comfort. But how like him.

Midwinter

Monday 12 May, 1902

Today I sat all day in the small drawing room. No further word has come. The hours pass slowly, and my heart beats out the words, another day or another and then he will be with me. Aubrey came into the room and sat beside me. He pointed out a butterfly trapped in the window. I had been watching it for an hour. "It wants to be free," I said. Aubrey looked so sad that I thought, he knows, he must know. How can I go away and not give him one word of comfort? I said, "You have been more than generous with me, Aubrey. And there was a time when we made one another happy." He said that we could be happy again if only I would be patient, and I told him, no, my happiness lies elsewhere. "Oh, yes?" he said heavily. "With your lover in Malaysia?"

I told him then that John is coming for me, and he expressed no surprise. Perhaps he did not believe me. I said more firmly, "I am leaving you, Aubrey. When he comes for me, he and I are going away together." Still he said nothing. The room was very quiet — just the sound of the butterfly fluttering against the glass.

He watched its struggle and I asked, was he going to free it or should I? He seemed so strange. He looked very sad and after a while he went to the window and cupped the butterfly in his hands. "I could crush it," he said. I replied, "Some men would crush it." He looked at me with such misery in his eyes, saying, didn't I know that John was that sort of man? Then he went to the doors. He opened his hands wide, like a priest bestowing a blessing on the garden, and let the butterfly go free.

Midwinter
Tuesday 13 May, 1902

Aubrey has gone to London. He did not say goodbye. It occurred to me that perhaps I should never see him again and, in spite of my impatience to be with John, the thought made me cry.

His mama is avoiding me. She has been all day interviewing the outdoor servants about their duties.

I am so restless and anxious because there has been no further word from John. Having dared so much and come thus far, could he even now have abandoned me? No. He will come for me. He will find a way. I suffer such strange sensations, as if another blow might have the power to destroy me.

Midwinter
Wednesday 14 May, 1902

Mrs Farringdon came to me today and said that she knows all about John being in England. I said and what did she hope to do about it? She said it was common knowledge that his chief weakness is greed; I can rest assured he will succumb to a bribe again if the price is high enough, and this time he must stay away from me for good.

I am in an agony of suspense. He could not. He would not. He loves me. Why did I tell Aubrey I was leaving him? His mama will watch me now and prevent my going to him, Why does John take so long? I have written to Grace for help — but no reply.

Midwinter
Sunday 18 May, 1902

Misery is eating my heart from my body. Aubrey's mama told me, when she and I were alone together, that John has gone away for ever. She said, did I believe he would come, like a fox in the night, for my poor sick body? Yet last night I dreamed he had come, and I thought that Aubrey spoke to me: he said that I must follow my heart. Was it a dream? I have so many dreams and visions. I have written one last time to Grace. No longer trusting the servants, I consigned it, when no one was looking, to the care of Daisy Lennox, who came today to see me. Grace will tell me whether the tale is true. If I should die? Shall our two poor souls drift desolately about, to unite at last with one another? I daresay I shall not be missed much. Aubrey will pretend to grieve for a while, perhaps sincerely, for he has proved his love for me and I so little in return. I have brought him much misery. It is for the best.

Midwinter
Tuesday 27 May, 1902

I can scarcely write I am so weak. Aubrey returned today, much moved to see me so low. His mama repeated her invidious story about John taking money never to darken Midwinter's doors again. He has not. She's lying. He loved me! I cried, and it was all Aubrey could do to restrain me. If John is gone for ever, then I have no reason left to live. I am a weak, broken creature and my only comfort from pain is sleep, which too often eludes me. The children tire me. I have no patience for the living.

Midwinter
Wednesday 28 May, 1902

I am so melancholy today and have swallowed none of the medicine they give me. I dreamed that he came to my room last night. I cried out in my ecstasy, and he placed his hand on my mouth to stifle it, saying Aubrey would hear. I awoke and I was drenched with tears and sobs broke from me in utter desolation. There is nothing for me now. I await the sure-enwinding arms of death. I know he loved me. If only I had loved him just a little more.

13

NANCY closed the final volume of the diaries, tense with the effort of reading. It was hard to believe that any love could have survived such bitter disillusionment as Viner had inflicted on Augusta, let alone abase itself with that final sentence. There was something odd about the final diary entries. They pecked away at her mind. If Viner had taken another bribe, what had Mrs Farringdon meant about his coming 'like a fox in the night', and why did Augusta write to Grace Hammond to ask her if what she had dreamed was true?

Nancy put away the diaries in her desk and went downstairs, her head throbbing with unanswered questions and with that incredible assertion, "I know he loved me." Mrs Farringdon, dressed as always in black and wearing a large hat with a veil which shrouded her face, was coming across the hall from the front entrance; she had not noticed Nancy on the stair and her expression was blank as she lifted the veil and unpinned her hat. Her silver-white hair was flattened to her skull, giving emphasis to the shape of her head and long neck. Like a vulture, thought Nancy, aware that behind the grim mask, Mrs Farringdon knew the whole story about Augusta and Viner. Mrs Farringdon and one other, she reminded herself as, watching her mother-in-law cross the hall, she heard a voice and, immediately alert, was conscious of the familiar accent of Ted Powers. She saw him come forward from the rear passageway near the servants' quarters. How long had he been waiting there? He moved from the shadows of the corridor and followed Mrs Farringdon into her room. As before there was something secretive about the lowered voices and the soft closing of the door. Nancy gripped the banister rail; this time she would not dismiss what she had seen: she would demand an answer from Ted about his secret interviews with Mrs Farringdon.

She cycled out again along the farm lane the next day, hoping to confront

Powers on his way to or from the cottage, but though she hung around the lane and the wood she did not see him, and when she went to Keeper's Cottage she found a dismal, autumn mood over the garden and there was no answer to her knock.

She did not see the keeper all that week. "Has Powers joined up?" she asked Radley, who set his mouth and said firmly, "Not as far as I know," in a disapproving voice, for Radley would have willingly followed Browne and the others into the Army. At last Nancy was forced to conclude, like Radley, that Powers was keeping a low profile while the fervour of recruitment was on. After a while, the mystery of his meetings with Mrs Farringdon seemed less significant, for the hospital had thrown open its doors to the first patched-up casualties of the war.

* * *

Nancy pinned up holly and streamers towards the end of December. The main drawing room, scrubbed and painted, had been transformed into a hospital ward and held a dozen men — commissioned officers only, since it was understood that Midwinter could not be expected to let ordinary 'Tommies' lounge on its sofas and make free with the inexperienced Voluntary Aid Detachment nurses and other helpers. The guest bedrooms between them housed a further dozen officers who merely needed a brief period of rest before going back to the Front.

Nancy began to fear for Stephen. He had completed three months of training; it was only a matter of time before he too would be sent to France. He had written in November to say the weather had been mild, the country near his training camp very picturesque; he had been drilling and learning about manoeuvres. It all sounded very pleasant and reassuring and bore no relation to the devastating reports of the war; he said he was looking forward to having a go at the Hun now that the French had sent them packing on the Marne and the Aisne. That was all. No veiled messages for Nancy's eyes only. Had he decided to forget what had happened between them in the summer-house? And had she dismissed it too?

Nancy wondered. She had labelled it and set it alongside Augusta's 'Foul Deed'. A 'Moment of Madness'. More forgivable like that.

Nancy moved to the patient in the bed nearest the fireplace. The portrait of Augusta hung above the mantel and gazed down with its cool smile on the patients, who lay on or under the blankets and talked in low voices to one another or were silent with their own thoughts. A log fire blazed in the hearth and a wrought-iron oil stove stood at the other end of the room: Mrs Farringdon had embraced the administrative side of the hospital, hiring and firing, raising funds and talking on the telephone to the Red Cross; Nancy had been responsible for significant innovations — such as the comfort of adequately heated rooms and sustaining meals — to suit Midwinter's new role. She made out diet sheets for the kitchen staff to follow, read to soldiers, talked to them, and kept them supplied with books, cigarettes and skeins of knitting wool. It was she who joined the other helpers in washing the men, changing their dressings, making beds and carrying bed-pans. The soldier in the bed by the fireplace followed her gaze to Augusta's portrait. "She's very lovely, Who is she?"

"She was my husband's first wife."

"I like to lie and look at her when it's quiet in here. It helps me to remember there's still some beauty left in the world."

"Yes. She was very beautiful in her day." Nancy stared into Augusta's eyes, wanting to understand the woman of the diaries, who had believed Viner's flawed love to be greater than her own.

"You are lovely as well . . . " The officer in the bed watched Nancy, admiring the line of her figure in a blue and white pin-striped frock, and the tilt of her head towards the portrait, with a stiff white kerchief pinned to her hair. "You cheer us up no end. But it seemed such a golden time, don't you think, all those years ago, before anyone could have guessed there would be a war?"

"I think the past must always seem more golden, looking back." Nancy let her glance fall from the portrait. "Perhaps more than it really was."

A photograph of a smiling, fresh-faced girl was propped on the table beside the man's bed. "She keeps me sane too," he said. "It was pretty awful out there, you know. I lay in a shell-hole for hours after I got it in the leg. There was nowhere to go and I thought they'd never find me. But I could picture her here in England and I kept on telling her I was coming back." He glanced at the photograph and looked again at the portrait of Augusta. "What happened to your husband's first wife?"

"She died." Nancy entered the man's pulse rate on the chart at the end of his bed. She hesitated. "She died of love." She tucked the sheets round him briskly. "Unlike you, who are going to get fit and well for that fiancée of yours."

Nancy walked between the double row of beds to the further end of the room, past men with missing limbs, cleaned of Flanders's mud and blood, and others in that strange state of spirits labelled 'exhaustion', which affected so many of the admissions.

It had all been an adventure at first,

setting up the hospital, before the fighting in Flanders had brought living casualties from the war to Midwinter's wards. Most of the patients had abandoned the concept of adventure. There were some who managed to preserve a gung-ho attitude, who chafed at their confinement and gladdened Mrs Farringdon's heart by their impatience to return to the action, but others clearly dreaded going back to the lines.

Mrs Farringdon had begun to nag Aubrey over his lack of conspicuous effort in the war. "Hugo has written to say he has joined his school's Cadet Corps," she told Nancy, in Aubrey's hearing, during lunch later that day. Relations between Nancy and her mother-in-law had become, on the surface at least, almost amicable since their joint administration of Midwinter: in the evenings they invited the officers who were not bed-bound to join them in Midwinter's dining room for formal dinner; at lunchtime Nancy, Aubrey and Mrs Farringdon ate together without any extra company. "Aren't you pleased about Hugo?" Mrs Farringdon turned to

Aubrey. "Aren't you proud to call him your son?"

"Just so long as this business is over before he is old enough to enlist," murmured Aubrey.

Mrs Farringdon clicked her tongue. "You should rejoice that Hugo wants to be in the thick of it. It's only natural for a boy to want to fight for his country. He says he wants us to let Nelson be taken with the other horses for the Army."

"I would sooner they both stayed at home, Mama, and lived to see their country enjoy victory," Aubrey said dryly.

"I should be proud of a son who would give up his horse and die for his country. If only, Aubrey. If only . . ." Mrs Farringdon did not enlarge on this line of wistful thinking, though it was understood that nothing would give her greater pleasure than to see Aubrey don khaki and sacrifice himself.

Nancy threw Aubrey a look of commiseration. Mrs Farringdon had discovered a mission in the running of the convalescent hospital. Nancy too had found fulfilment of a sort; but Aubrey seemed unable to adapt to a country at war. It occurred to her that she felt more genuine sympathy for him now than she had ever done when she was in love.

Aubrey cleared his throat and dabbed his lips with his napkin, "I have something to tell you both. A short while ago I offered my services should a vacancy come up in the interpreterships. Well, it seems they can use me, I shall start at the War Office after Christmas."

"I am so glad," said Nancy quickly, knowing how much he had hated feeling useless.

He gave her a tight smile, misinterpreting the remark. "Well, no doubt I shall be out from under everyone's feet for while."

"But, my darling," said Mrs Farringdon, "how shall I manage Midwinter without you?"

"Mama. You know you will manage perfectly well. You have Nancy to help you run the hospital, and Colonel Gregory, as always, to offer splendid advice in the unlikely event that you should need any."

Mrs Farringdon was silent for a while, digesting Aubrey's news about the War Office; she decided to approve of it.

"Well, it is something. And it should not be for long. The colonel is of the opinion that we shall have pushed back the Boche by Easter."

Nancy recalled that Colonel Gregory had said with equal confidence the previous August that the British would 'roll them up by Christmas'. She was struck by an image of the colonel and Mrs Farringdon plotting the progress of the war between them. They had established a kind of authority locally, to which others deferred when it came to discussing what to do about spies and doing one's bit on the Home Front. Mrs Farringdon organised knitting circles, Colonel Gregory was on the local War Committee, lending his voice at recruitment meetings and distributing intermittent rashes of posters; and he sat on the magistrate's bench, signing warrants on behalf of the War Office to seize local horses and cars, vans and carts for ambulances and army transport vehicles. Nancy sometimes suspected that the two of them were thoroughly enjoying the war.

She noted the colonel's sphere of

influence as she rode her bicycle into the village that afternoon: on every telegraph post Kitchener's weather-tattered but stern image pointed its imperious finger; the Post Office window bore its usual cluster of exhortations to 'Rally Round the Flag' and 'Join Your Country's Army' alongside the message 'Merry Xmas' strung in red letters behind the glass. A band of the Dorsetshire Regiment was playing in the schoolyard, drawing a crowd to a recruitment meeting in the school building. A faded Union Jack flapped in the wind over the door above which 'BOYS' was chiselled into the stone lintel. Nancy cycled on towards the village square. She could hear strident voices and the occasional sound of cheering borne behind her on the wind.

She gave her order in at the butcher's, knowing that she could easily have done so by telephone or could have asked Mrs Cassell to do it, but she was glad of the short break from Midwinter's wards. She slowed as she approached the school again. The group of military bandsmen were reassembling in the square, waiting for the recruitment meeting to break up, when they would play the lads who had volunteered on their heroic way. They stamped their feet and swung their arms to keep warm.

Nancy, pulled by curiosity towards the sound of the meeting, propped her bicycle against the railings and slipped inside the school hall.

Colonel Gregory was on the platform with other members of the War Committee. "We have a great duty to perform," he shouted. "We must continue to come forward, to rid the world of those bullies, those dirty crooks, the Boche. We shall smash them in, every mother's son of them. Remember what they did in Belgium? Remember your pals who have already taken the King's shilling? Aren't you going to do your bit and make your pals and your mothers proud of you? Come on, you fine young fellows. That's the stuff."

Nancy glanced at the faces round her as a few youths bunched together and pushed towards the front of the room, eager to be seen to give their names at the recruitment desk. As the crowd thinned and she turned to go she was startled to see Ted Powers move from where he leaned against the wall at the back of the room. She remembered her determination, weeks earlier, to confront him about his furtive visits to the house: she had said nothing and had not approached him, though she had seen him come and go recently around the estate.

"Have you got a reason or only an excuse?" a woman shouted as Ted passed her. He turned and said something to her and Nancy looked away. It was time she let Augusta's story rest; if Ted Powers was hiding something about the lovers, now was not the time to pursue it. She left the hall with the crowd of people jostling in the corridor and walked away from the school.

Ted caught up with her as she wheeled her bicycle out of the yard.

Nancy said without looking at him, "Still not ready yet to put on that soldier's uniform?"

"Are you going to have a go at me? It's your duty, lad, and all that?"

"Don't worry. I'm not handing out any white feathers," she said, though she knew she felt a perverse disappointment in him because he had refused to get involved with the war.

They moved away from the gates as the band struck up and the new recruits emerged from the building, marching in uneven file.

"Out to France we go for Flag and Country," Ted murmured above the clash of drums and cymbals and the weighted tread of boots on cobbles. "Stirs in your gut, that sound, doesn't it? You can't help feeling the excitement, a joy even." Nancy nodded, feeling it too. It was primitive, a rush of blood. "But it's all wrong," Ted said. "People are only joining up because it's getting too uncomfortable to stay out of it these days."

"Not so uncomfortable as when they get to the Front." Nancy watched the dozen or so recruits, mostly farm-workers, shuffle into a semblance of drill order in the square. "There are some awful things happening in France. You should see some of our cases at the hospital."

"I've seen them." He pitied them, too, the poor buggers, walking about the grounds; those that could walk, if a shell hadn't taken off a foot or a leg. Nancy Farringdon was doing a grand job, contributing, making those who were doing nothing at all feel small. Ted looked at her. She did not know that he had watched her during the past weeks and that he knew she had been to his cottage to look for him. Why? To ask more of her awkward questions? She had been like a terrier with a rat, spying on him when he was summoned by the old lady, lying in wait for him, like some damned devil forever on his shoulder. He looked at her and immediately regretted the analogy: she was too innocent to have been after him with any sinister intent. Ted knew that his perception of her was more than of a pretty face and figure — though there was plenty to appreciate about that: she wore a closefitting black coat over her striped nurse's uniform, and a soft black velvet hat framed her thick brown hair. He observed how her grey eyes sloped up at the corners under neat brows: a man could lose himself and his judgement, looking too long into eyes like that. Cutting off his train of thought quickly, he shifted his glance from hers to one of the posters on the school wall. "We should have stayed neutral. Ramsay MacDonald did the right thing when he resigned from the party because Labour backed the war. They've come to a stalemate in France. If they're digging in, getting ready to slog it out from trenches from now on, it could go on for years. I'm all for the peace party. I'm for anyone who sees through the high-ups and says what he thinks."

"But you're not a pacifist at heart."

"And you're not really a nurse," he countered.

"I do my bit," she said and smiled. Ted returned the smile and, though he regretted this sudden admission of warmth, he felt his heart inexplicably contract. The moment of weakness was fatal for, still smiling, she said, with an assuredness which struck like a knife. "What's the mystery about you, Ted Powers? What's the secret you share with Mrs Farringdon?"

"No secret," he said easily.

"I've seen you, skulking in corridors when you go to her office. Why do you merit a special interview?"

"If you've seen me round the house, it's because the mistress asked me to take on more duties. The estate has few enough able-bodied men around, and you can't run it with old men. She kept it all a bit quiet. She didn't want to tread on any toes."

Nancy watched him, her eyes narrowing as she decided whether to believe him, and Ted looked away, impatient with her renewed pestering. His glance fell on a poster pasted to the school wall. "It won't be recruitment meetings before long. They'll be yelling, 'You get out there and fight, mate.' Like it or not." He read the words of the poster out loud. "'Do your duty! Join now!' No one thinks about what it really means, how dirty and bloody killing really is."

"And how would you know? How many men have you seen die?" Nancy said. Her voice tailed off, for she immediately regretted the jibe, telling herself it was more worthy of Edith and the rest of the white feather brigade.

Ted jerked his head round, hating her briefly. "You ask too many questions. Has nobody ever told you that?"

* * *

Stephen came home on Christmas leave to find that Edith was in London, helping with the campaign to extend women's war work; Mrs Lennox told Stephen that she would be home on the afternoon train. "Why, my darling, you've grown a moustache. It suits you."

"Makes you look older," said his father.

Stephen smoothed the growth on his top lip self-consciously.

There was a marked absence of servants in the household. "The men have enlisted," said his mother. "It seems wrong to be fussing about where to find good servants when there are far more important things to worry about, but it does seem a shame, the way everyone has had to let go of standards."

"It's an emergency, Mama," Stephen said with a complacent smile. "We're relying on you ladies to keep your end up at home."

He hung around the house for a while, then said he would walk to the village to meet Edith off the train. It seemed strange to slip back into the old ways after all the camaraderie and routine of officer training camp. Winchborne had nothing at all in common with his new life there, and he felt like a stranger in his own home. He whistled to himself as he walked. "It's a long way to Tipperary . . . " The tune was reassuring, reminiscent of route marches, and the parades and the bullying roar of the NCOs. Good too was to be told he was fine officer material. It was all like a huge game, an adventure to surpass all previous adventures, but at the heart of it he knew that he was doing something terribly important and for real. "We are going to change the tide of history," Gus Wyatt had said, and that was how it felt.

A band was playing in the village. He could hear the steady 'oompah-oompah' of the music as he drew near. A crowd had gathered at the fringes of the square; people craned their necks and laughed and chattered, excited by the throbbing of brass and drums. He sauntered among them in his uniform, conscious of the women's slightly predatory glances.

He reached the drinking fountain and saw Nancy. She had not noticed him, but was standing with a bicycle, talking to Midwinter's keeper, Ted Powers. It was time men like that joined up. What was he? Not yet thirty? He was tough, fit, unmarried. Just what the Army needed. Why hadn't Farringdon released him? He watched as the man turned away and disappeared among the crowd. Nancy had spotted him. She was wheeling her bicycle across the street.

"Someone ought to shame Powers into enlisting," Stephen said piously. "You should talk to Aubrey about it. We need every able-bodied man in the country if we're to secure the defeat of Germany."

Nancy thought of the summer-house. It was as if she were remembering some distant dream: she recalled her own voice telling Stephen they must pretend nothing had happened. He seemed to be doing it rather well. He looked different. Brash, and the moustache gave him an air of self-importance. "How are you, Stephen? You look every bit the gallant young officer."

"Still only a second-lieutenant," he

said self-consciously.

"Only." She laughed. "My goodness."

He blushed, remembering the summer-house too, seeing that she was teasing him. He remembered how he had once adored her. It all seemed rather childish now. He had continued to adore her for a while, until the crude stories told by the men in camp had made him see Nancy in a different light. Frustrated married women were all too ready, it seemed, to throw themselves at junior officers in uniform. Nancy smiled at him, and he felt a twinge of compunction. "I'm on my way to meet Edith off the London train," he said stiffly. "I used to mock the suffragists rather, but I must say they've turned up trumps now, with the war on."

"I'll come with you. I haven't seen Edith for ages. She spends nearly all the time in London with her friends." They walked along the street, away from the sound of the band, towards the railway station. Stephen said how the war would bring about a changed world. "It's like the clean cutting of a surgeon's knife. We are defending the way of life we know for the sake of the next generation." He was acutely aware of the awkwardness between them, and said as they reached the station yard, "Nancy, you're not by any chance — I mean, after we — "

"Pregnant?"

He flushed, wishing she was not always so direct, and then remembered that it was what he had once found fascinating about her.

She smiled. "No, Stephen. I'm not."

He blew out his cheeks, "That's all right then," and immediately despised himself for being so crass.

They stood side by side as they watched the train pull alongside the station platform. Nancy was aware that strangers might possibly regard them as a couple: they were of an age, good-looking, well-matched; but she found it almost impossible now to believe that, only a few months before, they had made love.

"There she is." Nancy caught sight of Edith, leaning and waving from the carriage window. Her dark hair was tucked fashionably under a large velvet hat. As she stepped down from the train, her manner was energetic and animated.

Edith looked vibrant. Nancy, recognising the symptoms, thought to herself that she looked like a woman in love.

"Nancy! How kind of you to come with Stephen."

Nancy sensed the condescension in Edith's remark, the contempt for her own lack of interest in the suffragists, and the fact that she was doing nothing more stirring for the war effort than nursing a handful of officers back to health. "I was in the village. We bumped into one another." She realised it sounded as if she was excusing herself.

"You look very blooming, Sis," said Stephen.

Edith did not reply, but fiddled with her gloves and purse, hunting for her ticket.

Nancy fetched her bicycle from where it was leaning against the station fence. Who? Who could Edith have fallen in love with? she wondered, briefly indulging her old habit of inventing little histories for people. A soldier? One of her recruited officers? We don't want to lose you, but we think you ought to go . . . ? Their relationship of shared confidences was a thing of the past and she knew she would not be able to ask. They walked side by side through the village. The parade and the crowd had almost dispersed. Nancy hoped, for Edith's sake, that she had not fallen for an officer. Stephen was talking about going to France. He was afraid that the war would be over before he completed his training. She glanced at him. Wasn't he at all frightened about going into action? Was learning how to 'biff the Boche', the importance of 'strong points' and 'offensive postures' really all that absorbed him? She had thought him sensitive, that his imagination would make him fearful of dying, but, she supposed, if one was going to fight a war it was necessary to become part of the machinery of it all. She remembered Ted Powers's conviction that the Army would eventually introduce conscription. What would he do then? Join the peace party or fight? Either way, she did not think he was a coward. She remembered the cold way in which he had looked at her when she had asked him so stupidly if he had seen men die. Of course he would have witnessed death: there would have been his own father, for one. Why had she not been more sensitive to the possibility that there might be elements of tragedy as well as intrigue in his past?

Edith and Stephen were chatting lightly, repeating the clichés that one heard everywhere now: the great thing was to win this war; everyone must do their bit. Nancy did not feel as if she were part of it.

She left Edith and Stephen, kissing Stephen lightly and wishing him God speed. "Come to visit us while you are on leave. Connie and Hugo will be home soon and would love to see you. And Edith, you must come to Midwinter more often."

She rode along the drive which passed the track to Keeper's Cottage. She slowed, for she would have liked to have spoken to Ted again and apologised, but there was no sign of him and she cycled on. It was then that she realised that, if she aligned herself with anyone in her attitude to the war, it was with people who thought like Ted Powers, who had distanced themselves enough from what was happening to see it clearly.

14

MRS FARRINGDON, dressed in her usual black silk alleviated only by a white Red Cross cap, was talking to a newly admitted soldier. His right hand had been amputated after the Battle of Le Cateau and the man was weeping.

Nancy, instructing Connie about making up the spare beds near to the door, paused as she heard Mrs Farringdon's voice carry down the ward, telling the man to pull himself together and that he should thank God he had not lost the whole arm. Instinctively she and Connie turned away.

"How can she be so *awful*?" hissed Connie under her breath. She bent to tuck in the blanket of one of the unoccupied beds, and Nancy saw that her eyes had filled with tears.

Connie, home for the Christmas holidays, had thrown herself with unexpected intensity into the work of the convalescent hospital, voluntarily taking on the worst tasks as well as the easy fetching and carrying. Nancy's relationship with her had altered since the previous summer's house party. Hugo came and went between his school and Midwinter, yet his energies were concentrated on the progress of the war and on wishing the next year to pass quickly so that he might enlist. As Connie grew more detached from her brother, she seemed to draw closer to Nancy. Now she brushed the top blanket of the bed with her hand to smooth it and, looking at Nancy, said passionately, "Sometimes I'm really ashamed of my family. And I don't mean because of what my mother did."

When Mrs Farringdon had left the ward, Nancy moved to the side of the bed of the officer who had been weeping. She pulled a chair close by the bed and, taking the man's good hand, held it in both her own.

After a while he said, "It wasn't for myself." His eyes filled up again with tears. "I wasn't blubbing over the hand. I had a letter this morning. My brother's been killed at Ypres." Nancy looked at him. He was very young, yet word was that he had distinguished himself well at Le Cateau.

"I'm sorry," she said, knowing that nothing she could offer would make amends for his loss, nor for the more subtle wounding inflicted by Mrs Farringdon.

It was later the same day when Connie announced that she wanted to leave school and become a nurse.

"I'm afraid you have allowed her too much freedom on the Midwinter wards during the holiday, Nancy," said Mrs Farringdon, "We must not forget that Connie is a young girl, protected neither by age and experience nor by marriage."

Nancy released a groan of incredulity, and Connie threw her a conspiratorial smile.

Mrs Farringdon turned to her. "Your enthusiasm seems to confirm my recent fears, Connie. You are deriving an unsuitably romantic exhilaration from being in proximity to these young men."

"Surely not, Mama," protested Aubrey.

"Oh, yes. We must take care. First-rate British officers they may be, but men are men. They have been starved of female company abroad. And I'm afraid we must always be conscious of the fact that Connie is her mama's daughter."

"Oh, really! Don't be so ridiculous!" said Nancy, aware that her response was as much in defence of Augusta as it was of Connie. "What about the fact that Connie has worked extremely hard?"

Connie, who had flushed to the roots of her hair, threw her a look of gratitude.

"The fact is, though, that she has been doing very unsuitable work for a young girl," said Aubrey, for he had been shocked to discover on his return from the War Office for Christmas that his daughter was not confining her holiday ministrations to reading to the men from *A Christmas Carol* and plumping up pillows.

"I don't mind," protested Connie. "I love it. All of it. And they are so grateful."

"You must at least wait until you are sixteen."

"But that isn't until June!" wailed Connie. "And even then the Red Cross won't have me."

"Of course not. You're still a child!" said Aubrey in exasperation. "I must say, Nancy, I'm very surprised at you for encouraging her."

"I grew up quickly," Nancy reminded him. "I was living on my own at sixteen."

"The war will be over by June," Mrs Farringdon reassured Aubrey. "The Allies are only waiting for the new Armies to finish their training and then we shall be in a position to smash the Hun once and for all."

Nancy knew that the war would not be over by June. She knew too that Connie was not 'romantically exhilarated' by the officers at Midwinter, for Connie was receiving letters from Gus.

She had taken her a mug of cocoa one night, and had discovered her, sitting on her bed in her nightdress with her hair in a thick braid over one shoulder and surrounded by Gus's letters.

"You're not to tell anyone!" Connie hugged a bundle of letters fiercely against her nightdress.

"But how have you managed to keep it hidden?"

"Gus and Stephen are in the same battalion. He sends his letters with Stephen's to avoid a fuss."

"It's not very honourable of him. Nor of Stephen."

"I don't care. Can you imagine what would happen if Papa, or Grandmama, knew?"

Nancy was silent, nursing the mug of cocoa, surveying the sea of correspondence on the counterpane.

"Are you going to tell them?" Connie challenged.

Nancy handed her the mug. "Of course not. Drink your cocoa."

Connie had confided in Nancy, pouring out her fears for Gus, making her sit on the bed and reading out parts of his letters; how the route marches in the cold and muddy Dorset terrain were miserable, how they were learning about night operations, that it didn't do to wonder if the Germans were just as good at shooting, and how it was hard not to imagine what it must be like to be hit by a bullet.

"That's the poet in him talking," Connie said, tears shining in her eyes. "He says it's hard not to be afraid of dying."

Nancy took her hand, feeling a mixture of pity and envy to see Connie, at fifteen, embark on the painful adventure of love. "It must be very comforting for him to know that he can write how he feels about it all to you."

"We're going to get engaged when I'm sixteen."

Nancy nodded.

"You're not shocked?"

"What's shocking about being in love?"

"Papa and Grandmama would be shocked."

"Only because they still think of you as a little girl."

"When he goes to France I shall train properly as a nurse. If I have to I shall lie about my age."

"Perhaps I can persuade Aubrey to let you consider the idea of nursing."

Connie began to gather up her letters, sorting them into a heap. "Do you remember when you fell in love with Papa?"

"Not the exact moment."

"Are you in love with him now?"

Nancy saw that Connie wanted the truth. "No. I'm afraid I'm not."

Connie looked at her. "Do you remember when you persuaded Papa to let me join the house party guests at dinner?"

Nancy frowned, remembering the disastrous nature of that weekend.

"He was so angry when I put my foot in it about Hugo nosing around in the wood." Connie sat back on her heels. "He's always been like that about the wood. It's as if there's a curse on the place for him."

"He would wipe it from the face of the earth if he could," Nancy said. "But, since he can't, I suppose it helps if he pretends it's not there."

"He can't forget her. Can he?"

"No. I don't think he can. It's as if she died with something between them left unresolved."

"But that isn't fair on you, Nancy. I shall tell him so one day."

Nancy smiled. "That's very loyal. But it doesn't really matter any more."

* * *

The year moved on.

In France, the British Expeditionary Force broke through the German line at Neuve Chapelle and then were beaten back; there were reports of shortages of ammunition.

Midwinter took in the Neuve Chapelle casualties and opened its doors to Saturday 'communal song evenings', when Winchborne residents and patients alike were invited to raise their voices to such rousing tunes as 'Pack Up Your Troubles', 'Onward Christian Soldiers', and 'Are We Downhearted?— No!'.

In Belgium, the Germans released clouds of poison gas on the Ypres Salient. The infantry on both sides dug more deeply into the system of trenches and dug-outs in the increasingly desolate landscape of the Western Front. And at home, people's certainty that they were not downhearted wavered, the Liberal government fell and Asquith was forced into a coalition with the Tories.

The shortage of shells had shocked the country. The new government responded by setting up a Ministry of Munitions, with the result that Edith went to live permanently in London that summer, helping in one of the campaigns to recruit women to train for war work. Hugo was spending the summer months at a cadet camp and Stephen and Gus had at last been posted to France.

Nancy and Mrs Farringdon remained in uneasy partnership at Midwinter. Nancy felt increasingly isolated, for Connie, instead of coming home at the end of her school term, was in London too: after much soul-searching on Aubrey's part, she had been accepted to train at a private hospital and had gone to live with him in Bloomsbury.

It was a hot afternoon in August. The leaves of the hollyhocks in the estate workers' cottage borders were crisp and yellowing, the track from Midwinter hard and rutted. The summer was going to be as dry as it had been the previous year, thought Nancy, realising at the same time how much Midwinter had altered after a year of war.

The air was close and flies buzzed round her head. She wondered whether, if she had been in London, enrolling women for war work or serving tea on station platforms to heroes in khaki bound for the Front, she would be more convinced that she was doing something worthwhile. If she had a husband or lover or son or brother at the Front, would she feel less detached from what was happening across the Channel? She paused at the track to Keeper's Cottage, remembering that she was not the only one who was less than enthusiastic about the war. She had seen little of Ted that spring and summer: it seemed his claim that Mrs Farringdon had wanted him to take on more duties at Midwinter was true, for these days he divided his time between the estate and the farm. On the rare occasions when Nancy came upon him they were cordial with one another, a little distant, keeping to the accepted terms of mistress and servant; and if Nancy ever thought about the time they had played and sung together in his kitchen, it seemed as if she were remembering a sentimental scene which had happened a long time ago.

He was in his garden. It was filled

with dahlias of all colours, fastened to stakes, with flowerpots on top to catch the earwigs. He looked up, and she caught an expression of pleasure in his eyes before he said, "Good afternoon, ma'am. Not looking after your soldiers today?"

"Like you, I get time off for myself sometimes."

He resumed digging the border by the gate, and Nancy watched him, unable to believe that he was indispensable to Midwinter, for Mrs Farringdon was so proud of the men who had gone from Midwinter to serve in the Army and Navy; of Browne, out in Gallipoli, who wrote to them regularly, with stilted letters full of references to the 'old days', and cheery news about the men being 'in good heart'. When Nancy had broached the subject of Powers to Aubrey, he had agreed it was a little eccentric of his mama to insist that the keeper was necessary to the smooth running of the estate, though he was glad enough to have men doing honest toil, he said, rather than joining the business of war. He had shifted responsibility, saying the hiring of staff was not his concern, and Powers's reluctance to volunteer was a matter between himself and his conscience.

"The Sixth Dorsets went out a while back," Ted said after a while.

"I know. Stephen Lennox was with them, and a friend of Connie's."

"There's a few I know too. Lads from round about. Don't expect they'll get the treatment your lads get though, if they come back missing an arm or a leg."

"They all need nursing. Even senior ranks."

"They don't all have it so cushy."

"I suppose that life on the Midwinter wards is cushy, compared with the heavy task of a working man watching a few pheasants and tending his garden."

He looked at her sideways. "Did you come here just to have a go at me?"

"No. And I'm sorry." She did not understand why he brought out such a contradictory reaction in her. Would she rather he was gung-ho like Stephen? "If you only knew how much I really loathe the war. It's becoming more and more difficult to believe that it's being fought for a just cause, or that all the excitement at the beginning was justified, when we see the men they send back from the front lines."

He jerked his head towards the house. "I've got the kettle on. Like to share a pot of tea?"

She laughed. "You've always got the kettle on."

"You never know when a lady might drop by." He stuck his spade into the border and picked up his coat, and Nancy followed him up the path.

"Go in then," he said, pulling on his coat and running a hand through his hair with an oddly self-conscious gesture as she hesitated by the porch.

* * *

The kitchen was as Nancy remembered it: the red plush chair, the hard black sofa, and the piano with its red fringed runner. Her glance rested on the piano, and she told Ted, while he made tea, how Mrs Farringdon had instructed one of the Midwinter maidservants to paste black tape over the name Bechstein on her piano at Midwinter in a patriotic gesture against all things German. Nancy sat down on the shiny sofa while he poured water from the kettle into a pot. She took off her straw hat, placing it neatly on the seat beside her. "I suppose it's necessary to believe the worst of the Germans — that they rape nuns and kill babies — or we couldn't hate them; but I don't know what is being gained by it all."

"I doubt anyone knows that." Ted sat in the red plush chair which had, after years of wear, moulded itself to the contours of his body, and Nancy remembered Mrs Farringdon once telling Hugo that a gentleman should always detain a lady in conversation after offering her his seat, should keep her standing for a few minutes, so that she would not be embarrassed by the chair cushions 'retaining the heat of his person'. She smiled, recalling how Hugo had turned a fiery red.

Ted looked at her inquiringly. "What's amusing you?"

"I was just thinking what a silly old trout my mother-in-law is."

"That sounds to me like anarchy."

"Oh, I admire her, in a way. At least I do since the war, for the way she has sacrificed Midwinter to the cause. Did you know, she's afraid Winchborne might have become a centre of Hun infiltration? She lectured the Music Society because they had been playing Strauss waltzes, and all of them have gone about, suspected of being spies ever since."

"That's the daft sort of thing you'd expect," Ted said. "That's what this war means to most people. It's easy to hate an enemy when it's at a nice distance." He stood and poured the tea into white china cups.

"Is that why you haven't joined up?" she said gently. "Because you can't bring yourself to kill an unknown enemy?"

"Oh, I'll kill Germans. I'll kill Englishmen, if there's good reason. But only if. And for this show I'll put it off as long as I can."

She did not really understand. He seemed very intense about it.

"It's beginning to get to me," he said as he handed her a cup and sat again in the chair. "Doing nothing. Seeing other men in khaki. Seeing boys of eighteen go off — " He drank his tea. "Did you know the blacksmith's lad was killed first day out?"

She nodded.

"That's the sort of thing makes you feel bad."

"I'm sorry I said what I did earlier, about having nothing to do but watch pheasants," Nancy said. "You've every right to decide not to join up. But I feel strongly about the officers who end up at Midwinter. Some of them are no older than the blacksmith's boy."

"I know that." He fell silent.

"And I'm so afraid for Hugo. He will be eighteen next year. What if the war isn't over by then?"

"It would be a blow for your husband if he went. One he would take hard."

Nancy was surprised by the compassion in his voice. "Mrs Farringdon would see it as a triumph for the family name," she said. "A Farringdon in the front line would buck her up no end."

"Yes," he said quietly. "I can see that."

Nancy leaned forward. "You don't like

her, do you? I mean you *really* don't like her."

"No."

"Then why do you go on working here? Just because your father did? It doesn't make sense."

"It would make sense if you knew the whole story."

Nancy drew in her breath. "I know more than you think. I've read Augusta Farringdon's diaries."

He stared at her with a frightened, frozen expression, then set his cup and saucer on the floor beside him carefully, but not carefully enough to prevent the base of the cup rattling briefly in the saucer. "You mean, she wrote everything down?"

"Nearly everything. Except the day they were found . . ."

"What about afterwards — after Viner went away?"

"She seemed to get sadder and sadder. She was preoccupied with the idea of dying towards the end. And she still thought Viner loved her. She refused to believe Mrs Farringdon when she said that he had accepted money to go back again to Malaysia. She thought he would come for her and take her with him."

"What do you think?"

"About whether he let her down? I'm sure he was capable of it. But there are things she wrote towards the end, when she was so confused by her sickness. She dreamed that he came back to her." Nancy, watching Ted's expression closely, saw his eyes flicker. "You know something, don't you? Why won't you tell me about it?"

He hesitated, then shook his head, and she felt a surge of disappointment. "It's best forgotten, especially nowadays, and if you and me are to stay friends, it's best we keep it that way." He stood up and she saw that he meant her to go. She felt that a shutter had come between them as, gathering her hat, she followed him into the brilliant sunlight of the garden.

"We *will* stay friends," she said. "Sometimes I think you are the only real friend I have made since I came to Midwinter."

* * *

He watched her until she had turned the bend in the track. Ted looked up at the sun burning in the sky. She had frightened him with her talk about diaries, and he had frightened himself by how much he had wanted to confide in her. But he had lied when he talked about killing Germans. Would he? He still didn't know and he hoped he would not have to find out.

How that sun burned everything up. The water levels were low, streams were drying up; it was only a matter of time before the old lady would be on at him again: "Are you keeping watch, Powers? I rely on you."

The anticipated summons to Midwinter came the next day. He stood in the shadows of the rear entrance with his cap under his arm, waiting for the servant girl to give the all-clear to go to Mrs Farringdon's office. It was all 'wards' and 'offices' now, and the place smelled strongly of disinfectant. Wounded officers, in the regulation blue shirts and red ties, hobbled in and out from the old drawing room. He looked for Nancy, craning his neck a little, surprising himself by how much he hoped to see her trim figure, but she was not on the ward.

At last the girl called to him, and he followed her to the room where the mistress, like a carrion bird, all in black except for a nurse's cap, sat behind a desk. She was writing and did not look at him until the girl had gone. He stood, staring with a feeling of loathing at her bowed head with its starched white crest.

She glanced up and set down her pen. "Well, Powers. You will know, after all this dry weather, why I have asked to see you."

"The pool level is low, ma'am, but not much worse than last year."

"We must be vigilant. We must keep up the vigilance, Powers."

"Yes, ma'am."

He wondered if the old lady was a bit touched after all these years, and he remembered Nancy's story about her pasting over the name on her piano. But no, she was as sharp as she had always been as she told him calmly what he must do, should it be necessary, and perhaps she was right to keep on about it; nobody really knew how deep the pool was.

"If anything comes to light . . . " How often he had heard that phrase and heard this woman repeat the same instructions. It would be his task and his alone to dispose of it. They always spoke of 'It'. They never referred directly to what had happened. He wondered what it would look like after all this time, and closed his mind to the images which threatened to fill his head.

Mrs Farringdon smiled. Her face was like a mask, as if it were cracking open. "I rely on you, Powers. You know that. You must never think of leaving us."

"Ma'am."

"I've always paid you well and I shall continue to do so, but you must keep a close watch. If you need anything — "

"No, ma'am."

"Well, then." She paused, and Ted thought the interview was at an end, except that she seemed still to have something on her mind. "I hear one or two of the young women in the village have been harassing you."

"Ma'am?"

"The war, Powers. I hope you have not been thinking of enlisting."

He allowed himself a little sarcasm. "You don't think it's my patriotic duty to go?"

"Your duty is to the people who employ you," she said sharply. "Nevertheless, I realise that you may be tempted. You're a little confused perhaps in your conscience."

"No, ma'am. My conscience is clear." He was gratified to see her expression falter and her glance flick away. "Of course, if they make us go . . . " He left the sentence unfinished, taking an obscure pleasure in taunting her.

"There'll be no enforced enrolment," she said. "The Liberals worry too much about losing popular opinion." But she was more worried than a bunch of politicians, thought Ted. And conscription would come, he was sure of it.

Mrs Farringdon stood up. An idea had suddenly occurred to her. "Perhaps you could marry. They will only conscript single men." She looked him up and down. "How old are you? Thirty? It's time you married. You must know some suitable young women."

Ted was so taken aback that he laughed out loud. But this was a mistake. Her face set again in its mask. "Do you think I find all this amusing, Powers? Do you perhaps think that what happened was easy for me?" She leaned across the desk. "I had God on my side. I had faith. Was I to blame because your father lost his?"

"Faith!" said Ted. "My dad was blinded by religion. It was too late when he knew right from wrong."

Mrs Farringdon regarded him critically. "Under any other circumstances I would dismiss you without question. Do you think I don't know the Army needs fit men?"

"Then sack me. I've had enough anyhow."

For a moment she looked alarmed. "I dare say you don't like me much. And I certainly don't like your insolence. But we are stuck with one another, you and I." She paused, "You were there, remember. You had a hand in it."

"I was fifteen. No more than a boy." Anger welled inside him. He wanted to tell the evil old bitch what he really thought of her. If it weren't for his father he would have told the whole world years ago.

* * *

Edith sometimes wondered what she would have done if the war had never happened. She enjoyed her work for the Active Suffragists, liaising with the Ministry of Munitions and the various departments of the Civil Service, finding training places, organising hostels for women who had moved to work in London. She enjoyed living in London and the sense it gave her of being at the heart of everything important, instead of stuck out in the wilds of Dorset. She even enjoyed it at its blackest, when cones of searchlights raked the sky and she had to scurry to shelter from air-raids. The danger and excitement were part of the city's attraction, that and Gilbert — long, long evenings drinking wine at his flat, going to the theatre, hearing Phyllis Dare sing, 'We Don't Want To Lose You' at the London Opera Theatre, and cheering,

cheering until she was hoarse, or going to the Café Royal with Gilbert's friends. She had scarcely seen Aubrey Farringdon since coming to London. She did not think he knew that she and Gilbert were lovers. Gilbert said that Aubrey was 'translating German paybooks' for the War Office. Gilbert had a job in the Code and Cipher Department. He said the work was all very secret.

In July Edith had played her part in rallying women for a meeting in Trafalgar Square and had distributed leaflets and posters. She had stood in the rain and heard Lloyd George and Mrs Pankhurst address the crowds. Thousands of women had come together and marched, shoulder to shoulder, to demand the right to work in factories, on the land, in the Civil Service, wherever they were needed. The bands had played, and they all sang and chanted, and it had been very stirring and wonderful. Gilbert had come with her. He supported the suffragists. He said she was doing sterling work.

Poor Gilbert had been declared unfit for military service because of a malarial illness due to his years in West Africa, though Marjorie Benson had said unkindly that Gilbert's occasional deliriums owed more to the whisky bottle than they did to mosquitoes. Marjorie, who had discovered that Gilbert and Edith were lovers by arriving at his flat unannounced one afternoon, had met Edith at a women's conference a few days later and told her that she bore her no ill-will. "None whatsoever. Good luck, my dear," she said heavily, as if she were handing over responsibility for a difficult child. Edith had been amiable towards her; she resolved that she owed her that much for not being jealous. But London was like that, people were not absorbed by petty jealousies. Life was too short. The war might be over before one had time to prove oneself.

She had taken the precaution of asking Marjorie to say nothing to anyone about her relationship with Gilbert — for the sake of 'discretion', she said, and in fear that an unfavourable report should get back to her mother. Not that she cared what her mama thought, Edith told herself. One could almost disregard parental opinion. How could anyone in Dorset understand that everything was different because of the war? She thought a little disparagingly of Nancy at Midwinter, reading and serving tea to convalescents.

Edith did not worry about Stephen, though she saw evidence of the war daily, trainloads of wounded men in khaki, and others, trench-stained, on leave, subdued by their experiences in France. She was too busy of course. But it was more than that: she had a strong belief that her brother would come to no harm; and anyway, there was not much happening at the Front, according to his letters to her that summer. He had written from Base Camp at Étaples and then again, when his company moved up the lines, to say that he was 'browned off'. He did not know why the 'brass hats' were waiting so long for the next push.

But in London spirits were high. When people talked about the Front it all seemed rather remote. Her own 'Front' was here, working to get women's efforts recognised, so that when the war was all over the government would see how much they owed to the women of

England, who were helping to keep the life-blood of the country flowing; they would see that women could do things as well as men.

At the end of September, Edith went home for a holiday. Her mama was fussing about the war, nervous about Stephen; her papa was worrying about the collapse of the Russian Front. No one seemed interested in what she had been doing, and her mama annoyed her by singing Nancy's praises, saying what a marvellous job she was doing at the Midwinter hospital. Edith visited Midwinter; she took parcels of chocolates and cigarettes and distributed them on the wards. Nancy looked like all the Voluntary Aid Detachment nurses: calm and efficient and immune to anything which might have shocked a woman of genteel birth a year earlier. But then, Edith reminded herself, Nancy was not from genteel stock. They went into one of the upstairs rooms, previously given over to cases well on the road to recovery. Edith was puzzled, for the men sat or lay in strange attitudes of withdrawal, as if unaware of their surroundings, some with truncated limbs, others with no apparent injuries at all. "What is wrong with them?" she asked after she had distributed her parcels.

"They've got the wind up," said Mrs Farringdon, who had joined them. She closed the door firmly on the patients. "Did you see that one sitting there with a silly grin on his face? Not a scratch on him. 'Nervous exhaustion', according to his medical report."

"He says he doesn't remember who he is," said Nancy, watching Edith's reaction, glad that she was shocked by what she had seen and that Edith, so much at the centre of things in London, could learn a little about the realities of war from Midwinter.

Mrs Farringdon snorted scornfully. "I tell them they won't get out of doing their duty that way."

"Their minds are exhausted," said Nancy.

"Do you mean they've gone mad?" said Edith, her eyes widening.

"In a few cases," conceded Mrs Farringdon. "Of course, if they're too difficult — shouting and upsetting the other patients — they have to go to a hospital which deals with that sort of thing. Though I still say most of them are shirking."

"I won't have it," said Nancy, with a steely quietness. "They've all seen terrible things. Is it their fault they've broken under the strain?"

Edith caught her alone before she left. "What do you mean — they've seen terrible things?"

"Well, it's not a picnic out there. We seem to have so little imagination about it here at home." Nancy regarded her calmly, feeling years older, realising that the inadequacy she had always felt in Edith's company had entirely gone.

"I know it can't be so jolly, being shelled, killing Germans — but a soldier is trained to kill," protested Edith.

"Oh, we say that so glibly. I don't think any of us has any idea what it's like."

* * *

Edith shook off the image of the man with the silly grin as she walked home.

If he had seen such terrible things as Nancy supposed, why did he sit there smiling at them? And why did others make light of it all, saying it was hell, but one just had to see it through? One of the men in the main ward had had his leg smashed by a piece of shell, but he said he wouldn't have missed Neuve Chapelle for anything; there was nothing more exhilarating than being under fire and he was longing to get back at Fritz. He had said that his men were always cheerful and they made one proud to be British.

She called a greeting to her mother and went upstairs. She took off her coat and hat and paused on the landing and, as she glanced through the long window, she saw the telegraph boy turn the corner of the house, swing his leg over the bicycle saddle and dismount. Edith's heart began to pound. Stephen! She flung her coat across the banisters and sped downstairs, but she was too late to intercept the telegram before the maid handed it to her mama. She heard the howl of distress, saw the yellow envelope flutter from her mother's hand as Mrs

Lennox fell back into her chair like a large, limp doll, moaning, "My boy. Oh, my poor boy."

Edith took the telegram, scanning it swiftly:

> *. . . regret to inform you . . . 2nd-Lieutenant Lennox S. . . .*

Relief hit her hard under the ribs, "Wounded. It's all right, Mama. He is only wounded."

15

CONNIE was in London when she heard the news about Stephen. Nancy wrote to her from Midwinter: "My dear Connie, I know how this will make you fear for Gus . . ." Gus, like Stephen, had been involved in the Loos offensive. Casualties had been coming home in vast numbers since the end of September.

Yes, she was afraid for him, thought Connie. More afraid than she had ever been of anything. She knew that she would shrivel up inside and die if Gus were killed. He wrote in his letters, more and more, about the prospect of dying, and with a resignation which Connie could not copy. And now Stephen had been injured — a 'Blighty'; but he was out of the firing line at least for the time being. She had once planned to marry him, she remembered as she caught a tram from the hospital. She had been madly in love, or so she had thought, and jealous of Nancy because Stephen had seemed to take such a shine to her. What a spoiled little beast she had been in those days, and how she missed Nancy now: she so badly needed someone to talk to about Gus. Edith was too pragmatic; the war had made her unsympathetic about things which she called 'trivial'. Edith would have thought Connie's feelings for Gus were trivial. Connie knew that Nancy was the only person she could trust. She smiled at the irony of it and wondered how she could once have hated her stepmother so much.

A man offered her his seat and, although she had seen the empty sleeve pinned across his chest, Connie took it, because there was always a look of humiliation in a man's eyes if one refused. What if Gus were wounded? It was the lack of news which was so awful. She looked at her navy gloved hands, folded neatly in the lap of her navy-blue coat. Hardly the smartest of outfits for the West End. Hugo was up in London and Papa had invited them both to lunch with him. She felt a surge of guilt, for even at this moment, as she headed towards a pleasant lunch with her papa and brother, Gus might be lying in a trench, injured — or worse. She would have no way of knowing whether her life had been taken over by a great tragedy. She regarded the action at Loos as a kind of watershed. Superstitiously she had decided that, if Gus survived this, then everything would be all right. There were times when she had prayed that he might come home maimed or even blinded — for a Gus disabled was better than no Gus at all. She could look after him. She would nurse him for always.

The sister at the hospital had allowed her some time off to meet her papa and brother. Sister Greenfield was not one of those dragons who, according to the other nurses, ruled in some of the Red Cross and military hospitals. She should not really have allowed Connie to work in a hospital at all, but had said she would bend the rules a little. Connie was allowed to 'assist' with the VAD trainees, running errands for the sisters and acting as a general dogsbody. Since she was not on the official hospital staff, she was not supposed to venture on to the surgical wards, and was allowed a degree of freedom with regard to her hours of duty. “That will be nice, dear,” Sister had said when she heard that Connie’s brother was in town, and with a vague impression that he was a soldier on leave. “You run along and enjoy yourself for the afternoon.”

Connie did not know if it would be nice or not. The family seemed to have floated apart in the last year. Papa, never jolly like other girls’ fathers, seemed more serious than ever these days. Her grandmama was totally absorbed by her war work in Dorset, and Hugo was obsessed by the war and his own inactivity.

She saw her papa’s tall, slightly stooped figure as she entered the restaurant. And Hugo, very handsome, very much like Papa in a way, though his sandy hair was short and smooth and he was attempting to grow a moustache.

“Hello, Papa, darling.” She kissed his cheek. “Hello, Hugo.” Hugo grinned at her. He talked at once about Stephen’s ‘Blighty’, saying how marvellous it must be to have been in action and then to come home and be treated like a hero. Their father tried to steer him away from the subject of the war, and suggested they should choose something to eat. But it was not out of respect for her feelings, thought Connie, for what would Papa say if he knew about Gus and that he might ask her to marry him on his next leave? If there *were* a next leave. Her heart raced with renewed anxiety as she waited for her papa to order.

The restaurant was observing a meatless day in response to rumours about coming food shortages. "Just our luck," said Hugo, tucking into braised salmon and then jam roly-poly pudding.

"We must all do our bit," Aubrey commented. "And yours is to do well at school this year before you go up to Oxford."

"Oxford! What does all that matter?" Hugo said scathingly. He did not try to hide his disappointment in his father.

"It will matter when this bad business is over." Aubrey turned to Connie and asked her about her morning at the hospital, but not because he really wanted to know, thought Connie, only to change the subject. He asked her the same thing each evening, "How was your day?" preoccupied with his own work, hating the whole business of the war, which he called a gigantic crime.

Hugo was not interested in the hospital either. "I shall be eighteen next March," he reminded them, "And then I shall really be able to do my bit."

Their father sighed and grew more and more morose. He did not like to think that Hugo was becoming a man, thought Connie. It was not just the war. It made him feel past it. She was no longer a child either: she caught a glimpse of herself in the mirror on the opposite wall of the restaurant and saw a fair-haired, bespectacled young woman with sharp features, dressed in a serviceable navy tailor-made and neat-brimmed hat. She did not consider herself pretty, and would have been surprised to learn that some people regarded her fine bone structure as beautiful. She glanced round the restaurant. "Oh, look, Papa. There's your friend Mr Singer. I think he means to come over to our table."

Emboldened by the knowledge that in

six months he would be old enough to fight for his country, Hugo said with a show of bravado, "Do you remember that awful row, Papa, when you made us stay in our rooms all day because Connie told Mr Singer I had found some Roman tesserae?"

Connie looked at him in admiration. She would never have dared to say it. Their papa did not have time to do more than throw Hugo an angry look before he stood up and Mr Singer was upon them, and then they were all greeting one another like old friends.

No one mentioned the tesserae again. They talked about air-raids and Mr Asquith spending all his time playing golf and how the war was no nearer a conclusion than it had been the year before. Papa seemed relieved when Singer left. Connie said boldly, not to be outdone by Hugo, "Well, at least he didn't nag you about letting him bring a load of archaeologists to Midwinter. I expect the war has driven all that out of his mind."

"A good thing too," murmured Aubrey.

"I think you should let Mr Singer dig

in the wood after the war is over, Papa," Connie said that evening when they were alone.

Aubrey laid down his book carefully. "Well then, I should rather you kept your opinions to yourself. I was very angry with Hugo when I realised that he felt he might treat the matter so lightly."

"Don't you think it's just a bit silly? All that fuss, because of Mama. You can't still *feel* about her, or you wouldn't have married Nancy."

"You know nothing at all about it." Aubrey's heart pounded as he tried to keep his voice moderate.

"But I do. I do know. She misbehaved with a man and got found out. It was all such ages ago."

"I repeat, Connie. You know nothing."

Connie was silent for a while, then the subject began to nag at her again. "If you were to let Mr Singer have his way and allow him to chop down trees and dig it all up, you might start to feel differently about the wood. It would be an act of purification," she said dramatically.

Aubrey flinched at the word, and yet there was a seed of truth in what Connie had said. Purification? Death in itself was an act of cleansing. Was that how Augusta had seen it? He sighed. "It's more complicated than you think."

"It must be, if it still bothers you after all this time. Lots of women have a fling like that. You forgave her. You married again. Why is it all so tragic still? Because she died?"

Aubrey's voice shook as he said, "Don't meddle in things you don't understand."

"But that's warped! And it isn't fair on Nancy to keep the wood like a shrine, when Mama did such a wicked thing there."

"Go to your room, child!" Aubrey's control broke at last. "You have no sense of propriety."

Connie stood and with dignity said, "I am not a child."

* * *

A letter. Gus was coming home on leave. Connie counted the days and then the hours. And then he was here.

He said he wanted to forget, to have fun. They went to the theatre, but he did not seem to be enjoying himself. It's all wrong. We should be deliriously happy, thought Connie miserably. We were going to become engaged. But, when she reminded Gus, he said in a cold, queer way that he did not suppose they should think about the future too closely. After the theatre they walked in the dark through the streets near the British Museum. Connie felt very sophisticated, all alone with him. She had told her papa she was going to a meeting with Edith. He would have called Gus a bounder for taking her to a theatre unchaperoned, but Gus was not a bounder and the old restrictions did not seem to matter any more. She could not have borne it if anyone else had been with them.

Gus talked feverishly about the war as they walked along, their feet echoing on the almost empty pavements. "There's a kind of brilliance about being there," he said. "In spite of all the filth, the lice, the corpses, there *is* a magnificence about war. I'm sure of it now. One longs all the time for Blighty, but then when one comes back and sees how small and petty everything is — people chasing pleasure, chasing money, the old music hall jokes — all one longs for is to be back there, doing something worthwhile. I know I would not have missed it for anything."

"You would rather be there than here with me?" said Connie rather piteously.

"No of course not, you ass."

But she was not sure he meant it, and his mood became impassioned again as he said, "One begins almost to hate the people at home — old school chums, who pat you on the back and say, 'Well done!' and 'We're proud of you, old chap', and have no idea, absolutely no idea, what it's like out there."

Connie thought, I have no idea either. Her only impressions of the war were from the heroic accounts in the newspapers and the casualties she saw at the hospital, who were uncommunicative. Gus had been reluctant to talk at first: there had been an aching silence between them, but now he seemed to want to talk and talk, as if he had not spoken to anyone properly for months. He said that the men in the trenches spoke all the time about Blighty and speculated about getting a 'Blighty' wound and how wonderful it must be. "Everyone is terrified of being killed, but we have to pretend we are not. The men sing coarse songs and make jokes which I can't tell you about, for they would turn you up, Connie darling. The newspapers and everyone bang on about us being heroes because we volunteered, but we are only doing what the French have had to do without being asked. 'Take heart you brave Frenchman,' they sing. 'Victory will be ours'."

There was a kind of sob in his voice and Connie squeezed his arm, and suddenly he pulled her into the shelter of a doorway and kissed her fiercely. Yet he still seemed distant and strangely hostile, and he only ceased talking while he kissed her.

"The worst of all is going over the parapet, saying to oneself, 'We've got to go over the top once the guns ease off', and then actually doing it. It's like being in the grip of an ice-cold hand and propelled forward, and then — shells, screaming and bursting, everywhere swarming with men, yelling, running, falling." At last he was silent.

He did not speak again until they reached her papa's house.

"Is it sensible for the Armies to carry on?" said Connie with the insight of the very naïve.

Gus's strange mood had left him. He said soberly, "The ordinary soldier doesn't have to make decisions about what's sensible and what isn't. Thank God we don't." He kissed her again. "Look here. I'm sorry if I've been a bit of a bore this evening. I promise you we shall have fun tomorrow."

He was true to his promise. They went to a restaurant with Edith and Gilbert, and Gilbert made everyone laugh by getting tipsy and performing party tricks. Gus pretended to singe his hair on the candles and showed them how to balance a matchbox on his nose. It was his last evening, and he cried before he left her. Connie was horrified; she had never seen a man's tears.

She missed him more than ever after that. She wrote to Nancy saying she did not care for being in love: it was not pleasant to feel so intensely. It made her confused, and she wanted to lash out at someone because he had gone away and she could not reach him and because, when he had been with her, she had not been able to reach him either.

* * *

Stephen was looking at the portrait of Augusta. "I've never really had time to study her before. Would you say Connie is like her?"

"More so as Connie grows older." Nancy pretended a preoccupation with the chart at the end of his bed. She had known that they would send Stephen to Midwinter after the London hospital. All the same, it had been a shock to see him arrive in the main ward downstairs.

"Connie came to see me," Stephen said. "I was surprised at the change in her. She seems so grown-up all of a sudden. I suppose it's because of Gus."

"She worries about him terribly."

"She wanted to know about him, but I couldn't tell her much; she's seen him more recently than I have. The last time he and I spoke there was a bit of a show going on. Seems he came out of it pretty topping after Loos. In line for an MC and all that, while there I was stuck in a French hospital. Strange. He's been home on leave, but he never told Connie about coming up for the medal."

"He's obviously too modest. And, from what I've heard, you didn't do so badly either," smiled Nancy.

"No ribbons though."

"You can count your bandages as ribbons as far as I'm concerned." Nancy made herself look at him. How thin and white he was, and there was a touch of that expression in his eyes which she had dreaded seeing, which all the men at Midwinter shared, of having witnessed horrors which those who had not been there found it hard to comprehend.

"Soon have these off." He looked down at his bandaged shoulder. "Piece of cake. And what's a medal after all? The position we were attacking was respectably crumped, so that's a glorious enough feeling."

Nancy suspected that a medal would have made it more glorious. She hung his chart back on the end of the bed and tucked her pencil into her pocket. "You have to rest now. Get yourself fit again." A rush of tenderness, a memory of the brief passion they had shared, brought a sudden lump to her throat.

"I'm in the pink. Truly. Soon be wobbling back to have another go at the Boche."

* * *

He was sitting alone on the terrace, wrapped in a travelling rug. It was mild for November and the leaves were still on the trees; a weak afternoon sun touched them and lit them with shades of brown and gold. A few patients walked about on the lawns.

He had been crying. Nancy saw him scrub at his eyes as she came outside. She pretended not to notice, and set down a tray with a glass of hot milk on it, then pulled up a chair and sat beside him.

"I was never really frightened," he said after a while.

"There's no shame in admitting you're afraid."

"Most of the men would rather be dead than be thought a coward. And one is either going to get crumped or not."

"Drink your milk."

He took it from her. "It's got a skin on it."

Nancy laughed and, leaning forward, fished out the layer of cream with her forefinger and flicked it on to the paving.

Stephen stared into the milk, nursing the glass with both hands. "There was a fair amount of death around."

Nancy looked at him. "One of the officers who came here last year was at Le Cateau early on. He had lost a hand and his brother was killed shortly afterwards, but he struck me as being very brave. He told me once that anyone who says he isn't scared is either a liar or a madman."

Stephen looked up. "The rest is true. The elation when you've carried out an attack. It *is* a glorious feeling, to know that you've taken part and come out of it alive. Smacked in the shoulder but alive. I just wish the Boche hadn't done for me quite so effectively." He looked down at his injury, which was proving slow to heal.

"Do you remember much about it?"

said Nancy, searching his face for the boy she had known and had once almost loved.

"Just a lot of noise. Going over the top. Then an almighty thump in the chest and looking down to see my uniform soaked in blood." He laughed. "I thought, Crikey, I've been shot through the heart, like they always tell the nearest and dearest when a chap's bought it, only this time it's true. Then I realised I was still alive, but I couldn't feel my arm. It didn't seem to belong to me. Just hung there." He grinned, but the humour did not reach his eyes. "A splendid Blighty. Didn't hurt a scrap at the time."

The pain had come later. He was ashamed of it now, remembering how he had screamed out, not for his mother as did most of those who were badly injured, but for his sister. He remembered hearing a weird, keening voice, crying 'Edith' over and over, and eventually recognising it as his own.

"Edith came to see me in London," he said. "She and Connie seem to have become pals." Nancy stood up and took the empty glass from him. How nice she looked in her nurse's uniform, and how very sensible and practical she seemed. Strange to remember that one time in the summer-house. Almost as if he had dreamed it. Had it really happened? "Thank you, Nancy," he said, meaning the drink, and for looking nice and sensible, and perhaps for the summer-house as well.

* * *

Nancy watched over him with care, coaxing back the Stephen of old with reminiscences of their lives before the war. "Do you remember when I confessed to you that I liked Whitman?" she said one day. "You were so excited, I thought you were going to turn a somersault over the back of the settee."

"I remember everything you did and said," Stephen told her gravely. "Right from when I first saw you and Pa called you a bonny lass."

"There's not much of the lass left these days."

"Not much of the lad in me either."

She looked at him and linked her arm

in his. "Oh, we shall find him again, I think."

They were walking in the grounds towards the meadow: Nancy often walked with him now that he could get about more easily; the shoulder was healing at last and his arm responding well to the doctor's prescribed exercises. It was his last afternoon before he went home for Christmas into Mrs Lennox's tender care. "I shall miss you," Nancy admitted when he reminded her of that fact.

"And I shall miss being at Midwinter. But I miss the war as well. Strange, but I miss the companionship of it all. I know it's been another disastrous year and that the war is no nearer an end, but I can't help a feeling that, if only I could get back there and do my bit, even my little contribution might help tip the scales the right way. One begins to despise the people at home a little," he acknowledged. "One resents fellows like that." He jerked his head towards the trees and Nancy saw smoke rising from the chimney of Keeper's Cottage. "Still. What's the use of grumbling about the shirkers? There are enough good lads out there to fly the flag." Stephen paused. Did he really want to go back? He recalled the smell of the hospital train full of wounded men, the nervous, haunted look of most of them.

Nancy shivered. "It seems odd to be celebrating another Christmas."

"Will Aubrey and Connie be coming home to Midwinter?"

"Oh, I expect so. Hugo will be back from school tomorrow. It will almost be like old times."

"Except for the lame ducks filling the drawing room."

"A lot of them, like you, are going to their families for Christmas. It will be pretty quiet."

They had reached the wood. Stephen stood with one hand in his pocket, staring into the trees. "Do you remember all that business when Aubrey was furious with Hugo because he found some Roman deposits in the wood?"

"I remember," Nancy said, recalling that the house party had spelled the end of her marriage to Aubrey.

"In a way it was my fault, you know. I goaded Hugo a bit about the wood, said he was scared of going there, of doing the wrong thing."

"It couldn't really have been anyone's fault. It seems very silly now."

"What has Aubrey got against the wood? Oh, I know Augusta was caught there with that fellow and all that, but it looks very innocuous these days."

It was true, thought Nancy. The wood looked crisp and rather beautiful, stripped of its leaf cover. "Shall we walk a little further?" she said. "It's so long since I visited the pool."

They entered the trees, picking their way slowly and in single file, Nancy leading the way. Now and then a pheasant crashed its way through the undergrowth. The only other sound was the rustle of their feet on the path and, in the distance, sheep calling to one another across the meadow. At last they reached the pool, lying cold and flat under the sky. Nancy remembered the first time she had thrilled to the mystery of the place, the trees rising on all sides, drifts of leaves blanketing the roots and melting into the water as they did now. Dark, spidery reflections of the tree branches intersected the pool's surface. There was no hint of what had once happened there. For a moment Nancy allowed herself to speculate on what exactly Ted could have seen as a boy. If it had been indecent, she could understand Aubrey's distaste and even anger, but she could think of nothing which explained why he should treat the place with an almost religious kind of respect.

Stephen was examining the rough ground around the old quarry workings; he stepped into a dip between two banks of moss-covered stones. "There could be something in this Roman theory, don't you think?"

"Perhaps." Nancy followed him. "But, in a way, I should hate it as much as Aubrey if Frank Singer and his friends were to come here busy-bodying all over the wood and digging around."

She sat on a mound of rock, the earth bank behind her.

"It would make a good defence trench," Stephen said suddenly. "Not really muddy enough, of course. No rats. But a good fire-step to sit on." He walked away, plucking at his sleeve and she saw that, though he had been joking, the wood had begun to oppress him. He turned. "I fell into a trench after I was hit. There were bodies everywhere. I was more frightened of being trampled on and left for dead than anything. I remember I kept trying to get out and slipping back in the mud. I was surprised that I was too weak to do more than flounder around. Then, after a while, this gunner, who must have seen me go down, came and patched me up with my field dressing; he filched some iodine off one of the corpses and gave me brandy from his flask. Then he went away again. I don't know what happened to him after that." Stephen fell silent. He had lain in the trench all that day, his chest and back exposed, flies settling and crawling on his neck and sweating face. He had smelled the awful stench of his own blood and the dead bodies near him. He could smell it now, here under the trees, that awful rotten smell which clung in one's nostrils. The man in the trench beside him had been dead, though there had not been much left of him: "Well, *his* mother wouldn't recognise him, poor sod," the stretcher-bearers had joked when, hours later, they arrived to take him to the dressing station.

Nancy stood and went to him. His face was very white under the trees. "Perhaps we have walked too far. We'll go back." She touched his hand gently, then took his arm and they returned the way they had come.

Stephen did not linger as Nancy did when they neared the edge of the wood; he waited for her by the fence, breathing the sharp, cold air of the open field, glad to be out from under the trees, which smelled of death.

"I want to get back to the Front," he said. "I feel I've joined the shirkers here at home. I'm almost one hundred per cent fit again." He turned to her, "I just want to get back there. You know?"

"You could take home service. No one will expect any more of you."

"I should miss the sound of the guns. I want to go again, to hit the Boche bloody hard. It's a game we have to win."

"Oh, Stephen. You make it sound like cricket." She kissed him, and he pulled her close, remembering, as Nancy was remembering, the afternoon in the summer-house, knowing that neither of them regretted what had happened that day. He kissed her mouth with restrained hunger. "Aubrey should pay you more attention than he does."

"Aubrey doesn't need me any more." They turned away from the fence.

Nancy gave an exclamation of astonishment, for Aubrey himself was half-way across the meadow and was striding downhill towards Midwinter.

"Do you think he saw?" said Stephen.

Nancy's look was troubled. "Oh dear. I'm almost sure he did." She released Stephen's arm and they made their way across the slope of the meadow. Neither of them noticed another figure, half hidden by the trees, who slipped away and merged into the shadows of the wood.

16

"ARE you sure?"

"I'm telling you, they were together. And they were coming out from the wood." Aubrey ground the palm of his hand into his forehead as if he could push out the memory. "How could she, Mama? How could she be so heartless as to do this to me?"

Mrs Farringdon stood by the window of her office, hardly regarding the hunched figure in the chair at her desk, but staring out across Midwinter's lawns. She turned to him. "You're certain about this?"

Aubrey groaned. "I saw them kiss."

His mother tapped her fingers against the black silk of her sleeve. "You must send her away. The Lennox boy will go back to the Army soon, but she cannot continue to live here, I cannot have her living here after this. How can we be sure she will not throw herself at any one of the other officers?"

Aubrey raised his head. His face was

grey as he said self-pityingly, "Who would have thought history could repeat itself so cruelly? She and Augusta have ruined my life between them, Mama."

Mrs Farringdon frowned impatiently. "You brought it on yourself. But Nancy has certainly ruined Christmas."

⋆ ⋆ ⋆

When Christmas Eve came and went, and then Christmas Day, and still Aubrey had said nothing, Nancy began to hope that his silence meant that he had seen nothing. The strain she had detected in him, the shifting of his eyes from hers, was because of the coldness which already existed between them, or because of his living in London: London was a strain on the nerves, what with the bombing and being so much nearer to the news of how badly the war was going.

Christmas passed quietly. For the sake of the remaining patients, Nancy tried to instil it with the atmosphere of a small house party but, even at Midwinter, everyone's nerves seemed stretched.

"How gloomy everyone is," complained Hugo.

Connie snapped, "What is there to be cheerful about?" for Connie was missing Gus.

On Boxing Day there was the usual ceremony of bestowing gifts on the servants: handkerchiefs for the female staff, handkerchiefs or cigarettes for the men. The reduced house staff was joined by the nurses who had not gone home for Christmas; they stood awkwardly to receive their gifts. Aubrey passed slowly among them, exchanging a 'Merry Christmas' with each in turn, and presenting a small parcel, handed to him by Roberts from a basket over his arm.

How positively prehistoric it all is, thought Nancy, wondering what thoughts lay behind Ted Powers's expressionless, "Thank you. The season's greetings to you all, sir." His face was red, as if he had been out for a long time in the wind, which whipped and howled round the house and made the generator flicker.

The servants dispersed. Ted Powers nodded to her as he passed on his way out through the servants' quarters.

"A happy Christmas, ma'am." "A happy Christmas, Powers," she responded, and pictured him returning to his cottage. He would light the oil-lamp in the comfortable kitchen and settle in his chair to smoke one of his cigarettes, brew a pot of tea, or perhaps sit and read as the last of the afternoon light deepened to winter darkness. She was startled by the vividness of the picture, and by the realisation that she would have liked to go with him. She imagined playing Christmas carols on the jingly piano and his pleasant tenor voice singing 'The Holly and the Ivy' and 'God Rest You Merry Gentlemen'. She pictured him standing close behind her right shoulder; it would have been very companionable and pleasant.

She turned to go upstairs, where a few of the patients were already gathering, seduced by Mrs Farringdon's promise of 'jollifications', which would be nothing more than a game of charades and lavish supplies of the mint humbugs which she purchased for the relief parcels which they sent to the Front.

Nancy had begun to climb the stairs

when Aubrey, dismissing Roberts, called to her in a harsh tone, "Nancy, might I speak to you for a moment? Perhaps we should go into the study." His face was grim as stone, and Nancy knew at once that her fears had been well-founded. He had seen her with Stephen by the wood.

"Why did you wait until now?" she said, when he had closed the door and indicated that she should sit down. "And for goodness' sake, Aubrey, why so civilised?"

"Do you think I feel civilised?" He sat at his desk and lit a cigarette and she saw then that his hands were shaking.

"You're always civilised. It's what once made me fall in love with you."

He gave a short, ironic laugh.

She sighed. "Oh, Aubrey. What do you want me to say?"

"You could try to give an account of yourself, explain your behaviour, You were kissing. Are you and he in love with one another?"

"No. Not at all. I promise you, you've read far too much into it."

"I think not."

"If you could just try to believe

me. It meant nothing. He has been very depressed in spirits. All the men who come here need some degree of comforting."

"So you propose to provide this kind of personal comfort for them all?" Aubrey said with an attempt at bitter humour, which failed when his voice broke with anger.

"No, of course not. Stephen is very close to us — "

"To you at least. That much is obvious. And yet you still say he means nothing to you."

"I'm fond of him, but not in the way you are implying."

He flicked his head impatiently and drew hard on the cigarette before saying, "Don't prove to me that you're a liar, Nancy. *She* was a liar. Don't forget, I've been through all this before. I lived with Augusta's lies and her deceit."

Yes, Augusta would have been lying if she had said her affair with Viner had been nothing, Nancy thought, remembering the agony of the diary. "It's not important," she said, and it was true, for she was weary of the whole business. What did it matter whether he thought she was lying or not? They had ceased being honest with one another a long time ago.

"Our marriage is over." Aubrey echoed her thoughts.

"Do you want a divorce?"

He drew again on his cigarette. The only sound in the room was the sharp intake of his breath. Outside, the rising storm rattled the doors and windows. "No," he said heavily. "I won't divorce you. But when Christmas is over I shall not want to see you at Midwinter again."

The shock of his words hit her. He was going to rid himself of her. Her mother would have said she had received her marching orders. And all because of a misunderstanding. It was all too ridiculous. A gust of wind slammed against the window and made her jump.

"I'll leave as soon as I can," she said quietly, "I should have gone away before."

He weakened a little then, as if her submission made it all seem too easy and now he regretted his decision. "Give yourself time to find somewhere . . . "

"Marjorie Benson has offered more than once to put me up. I shall stay with her until I can find somewhere to live."

"Well — you know, time to get your things together then."

She smiled ruefully and stood up. "That won't take long, Aubrey. Nearly everything I have is yours."

* * *

She packed the next day, throwing a few clothes into a suitcase, some things the children had given her and, with a slight soul-searching, her jewellery, presents from Aubrey — one never knew when one might need money. Last of all, she unlocked the writing desk and pulled out Augusta's diaries. She had never considered they belonged to the Farringdons. She tucked them into the suitcase under her clothes.

Two hours to go before she could catch the London train. She stood by the window. Her coat lay over a chair, her hat on the seat beside it. She had decided she would say goodbye to no one. There was no point in seeing Stephen and stirring him up with guilt. She would write to Connie and Hugo once she had settled in London, but she had no doubt that Aubrey's mother would get to them first with Aubrey's side of the story. Mrs Farringdon had been triumphant: Nancy's departure marked the conclusion of a warfare as intractable as the one across the Channel. Had she been able openly to acknowledge victory, she would have marched about, clashing cymbals and beating a celebratory drum.

Nancy stared at the Midwinter gardens. The storm had hardly abated since the previous evening: twigs and leaves scudded across the lawn and the sky was dark with the threat of rain. She thought of Ted Powers's kitchen and recalled her whimsical picture of the two of them singing carols, and it occurred to her in that moment that he was the one person at Midwinter to whom she wanted to say goodbye.

* * *

The wind snatched at her breath and Nancy pulled her collar round her ears and held on to her hat with one hand as she battled her way towards the cottage.

She thought he was out at first, for the house was closed up tightly against the storm and there was no immediate response to her knock. Then came the sound of footsteps along the stone-flagged corridor.

He was dressed in faded cord trousers and a knitted fisherman's jersey and looked different, less brutal than in his keeper's jacket and waistcoat. He seemed taken aback. "Have you come all across here in this dirty weather just to see me?"

"I had to get out. I couldn't bear waiting in that house."

He stepped to one side, and she slipped into the cottage as a gust of wind caught the door and tore it from his hand. It slammed shut with a crash. He jerked his head. "Go on down into the kitchen and get yourself warm."

The kitchen was dark, though it was not yet three in the afternoon. He lit the oil-lamp and set it on the table, and their shadows leaped against the white walls. Nancy stood close to the stove and rubbed her hands together to warm them. She had been right in thinking she would feel at ease here: it was almost as if she were coming home. The idea was fanciful, yet his house made her think of her childhood, of coming in from the cold and sitting on the hearthrug to toast her feet at her mother's black-leaded stove, making them itch and tingle.

"Waiting for what?" he said, shifting the kettle on to the hob. "You said you couldn't bear waiting."

"I'm leaving for London today. I'm going away for a while."

He did not comment or ask her why, but she sensed a sudden tension in him. Had he guessed that something had happened?

She said brightly, "A friend asked me to stay with her. I've decided to take her up on the invitation." She saw that he was not deceived.

"What will you do?"

"I'm sure I can find something useful. The only thing I regret is leaving the hospital. I feel as if I'm walking out on the men."

"I expect you'll be back," It was a question. This time he was probing.

She did not reply.

Ted poured water from the kettle into a waiting teapot. He remembered the figures at the edge of the wood and the kiss which had jarred all his preconceptions about her, for he had thought he understood her a little. More, he had thought he knew everything that went on. And yet, seeing her here, soft and strangely innocent, Ted found it hard to make sense of his feelings, for he could not instantly condemn her. He hid his confusion, saying calmly, "Do you want to tell me why you're going?"

She shook her head. "I just felt I had to come over to say goodbye."

He nodded. "That's good. I'm glad you did that." He glanced at her and their eyes met for a moment without expression, before he said, "Well, sit down then. The London train doesn't leave for more than an hour yet."

Nancy took off her hat and put it on the table and sat in the red plush chair. She stretched out her feet to the stove and, for the first time since Aubrey had asked her to leave Midwinter, she understood what a relief it would be to go. She flung back her head, releasing her breath in a sigh as Ted handed her a mug of tea. "This is very good of you. I'm sure you weren't expecting visitors."

"To tell the truth, I'd dozed off. There's not much to do when the weather's against you. Not much to do at all these days." He leaned his back against the chimney wall and sipped his tea. After a moment he said, "I've been thinking — it's time I joined up, before I'm fetched. Mrs Farringdon says she needs me here with the other men gone. But I've had enough of it: doing nothing while younger men than me are getting themselves killed."

Nancy thought of Stephen's injury and those of the other men she had nursed. She said quickly, "No, Ted. Stick to your principles." She realised that she had used his first name instead of the more formal Powers.

He too had noted it, for again his glance held hers momentarily. "Do you think I've got principles then?"

"I know it. I don't think you're a coward either."

"Well now, that's because you don't know me very well."

"Perhaps not. But I think you're right in the way you feel." She smiled suddenly. "You were right, too, to be sceptical about my fitting in at Midwinter."

"Was I?"

"I thought I detected it?"

A wry smile flickered around his mouth. They drank the hot tea in silence.

"You should marry," Nancy said. "You shouldn't be all on your own like this." She did not know why he laughed.

"So I've been told." He looked at her. "I nearly did marry once."

"What happened?"

"She went off and married somebody else before I got round to asking her."

"I'm sorry."

"So was I." He put his empty mug on the table and leaned back against the wall with his hands in his pockets. "So, this is it then?"

"Yes. The end of it. A complete failure."

"You'll be better off out of it," he said quietly, and there was something more to his words which she did not understand.

She stood and felt reluctant to leave the warmth of his cottage. She handed him the empty mug. "Thank you. The tea was very comforting."

He walked with her to the gate and the wind snatched at their voices as she said, "Come and see me, won't you, if you're ever in London?"

He smiled. "If ever."

"Goodbye, Ted."

He took her hand. "Goodbye, Mrs Farringdon." She went with reluctance and was left with a sensation of the solid strength of his fingers.

* * *

Nancy departed the estate as she had first arrived, on a dark afternoon in winter, with an impression of empty acres, of sightless windows and bleak pillared columns fronting a hostile grey façade. She did not glance back as she walked away with the wind tugging at her clothes and her suitcase banging against her legs. She did not think of Aubrey. She heard her feet crunch on the track and the wind howl in the trees and remembered the warmth of a handshake and a kitchen stove which had reminded her of her childhood. She sat on the draughty station platform at Winchborne, freezing in the wind, until a wisp of smoke in the distance heralded the arrival of the train, and the roar and clatter of the great steam locomotive obliterated everything else.

* * *

Colonel Gregory waited outside the school-house after the afternoon's Winchborne War Committee meeting, ready to waylay Mrs Farringdon. He had suspected she had been avoiding him ever since Farringdon's wife had gone off to London. Rumours were rife about some irregularity or other. It was something similar to the last bad business, he supposed, when Farringdon's first wife kicked over the traces. Some men seemed to attract that sort of bother. The colonel was not interested in gossip, and he felt irritated by Mrs Farringdon's embarrassment. She ought to know that he had too much respect for her to let a thing like that affect their friendship. He would tell her so, but first there was something else on his mind.

He saw her come along the path from the schoolhouse. "My dear Mrs Farringdon — Alicia."

Mrs Farringdon halted and her face stiffened defensively. She knew what the colonel was going to say. He had been saying the same thing repeatedly for weeks, and now that conscription had become a reality . . .

"Alicia. I know how you rely on the fellow, but I'm going to have to call him out."

"You promised me," she said coldly.

"I did. It's true. But I only promised we wouldn't harass Powers while voluntary enlistment was the order of the day. You must see how, as chairman of the War Committee, my hands are tied."

"You can make exemptions. You made

an exemption for the Warren boy."

"He's a semi-idiot. The country's desperate, but not that desperate. But your man Powers is tough, intelligent, just the sort of man the Army needs." His look was pained. "I can't understand your lack of patriotism in this respect, Alicia."

"I need him here," said Mrs Farringdon obstinately. She turned away as if to show that the subject was closed.

The colonel hurried along beside her. "Why this obsession with keeping the fellow? He seems to do nothing but roar around on his motor bicycle and take a few potshots at the local crows."

"He's a good woodsman. He is invaluable to me."

"Alicia. You know I have always supported you. Under normal circumstances I would go on supporting you. But not this time." He halted, struck by the magnitude of what he was about to say. "This time the needs of the Allied cause must come first."

She halted. "Our long friendship . . ."

He was adamant. "In spite of our friendship."

Mrs Farringdon hardened her heart. "Then I want nothing more to do with you."

She left the colonel standing. He called after her: "The fellow's a blackguard — a coward and a cad. You must see I'm right." She did not look back and he turned away, aware that he had done his duty, but looking as miserable as responsibilities of office could ever make a man.

* * *

Ted did not know whether it was because of Nancy leaving Midwinter or something in himself which had finally made him volunteer. He told himself that nothing Farringdon's wife did could affect him and, in more cynical moments, that it had been the threat of conscription which had made him join up. And yet, when he searched his heart, he knew that it had been seeing Nancy with Stephen Lennox which had finally decided him. He wanted to get out. And if 'out' meant going to France and getting himself killed, well, thousands of others were doing the same, for various reasons, not all of them noble.

He stared down at the letter in his hand. He had been accepted. The motor service of the Machine-Gun Corps. Logical. He knew all about motor-cycle engines. The old lady had fought hard against his enlistment: she had wanted him to wait and go before a military tribunal. She could get him an exemption, she had promised; just give her time and she would talk Colonel Gregory into helping them. Oh, she was frightened to lose him and no mistake. She was frightened of another dry summer and what someone might find without him there to keep a look-out. He supposed it gave him a kind of hold over her; though if that were all there was to it he would have gone long ago. What had changed things? The war? Meeting Nancy? Whatever it was, he saw now that he was best out of it — like Nancy Farringdon.

So this was it then. Report for training. He folded the piece of paper, carefully, closing his mind to all that the word 'training' could mean. He could have picked on something else — Medical Corps, Engineers. Why go for the worst of all? Machine-guns. A test — or a final purging?

* * *

"I have been thinking about the wood," said Aubrey on one of his infrequent visits from London. It seemed strange to come home and know that Nancy was in London instead of here at Midwinter. He had not seen her since Christmas and, in a ridiculous way, he missed her.

Mrs Farringdon hesitated only briefly and did not glance up from the papers on her desk. "Thinking about the wood in what way?"

"That now that Powers is leaving, there will be no one here to manage it. I think we should have it cleared." He had said it. Did she know how much it had cost him to make that decision, how much more distress it would cause him when the work began?

Mrs Farringdon's head had snapped up and her eyes were less angry than frightened as she fixed him with a look.

"We shall do nothing of the sort."

"My mind is made up, Mama. The War Office needs the timber. And I have no use for a pheasant shoot."

"How can you contemplate such a terrible idea, after all you have suffered, knowing what memories are buried in that place?"

"Exactly. They would all be wiped out in one go." He wondered whether his decision owed anything to Connie. It had been tempting in the end to see it as an act of cleansing, of wiping out the past.

"And the latest?" said his mother, "Nancy and the Lennox boy?"

"It is largely irrelevant. But that too." He sat down on the opposite side of the desk. "If this war has taught me anything, Mama, it's that the past no longer has much relevance. I've spent too long brooding about things that happened years ago. With the wood gone — "

Mrs Farringdon was trembling. "With the wood gone and Powers gone, the pool would come to light. You do remember the pool?"

He flinched from the cruelty of her

words. "You know I remember."

"Then you must not do it. For your own sake. I couldn't bear the way it would upset you." Her voice had a note of panic in it.

Aubrey sighed and promised not to do anything in a hurry. He left her and went into the small drawing room, where two of the officers from the hospital wards sat in the thin warmth of the winter sunshine. Aubrey sat near them and asked the usual questions. How long had they been at the hospital? Were the nursing staff looking after them? How were their injuries healing? The answer to the latter was always 'very well', regardless of the extent of the destruction to the man's person. After a while Aubrey's stock of banalities dried up and they sat staring out at the terrace. They were only boys, he thought. Not much older than Hugo. Hugo. Another month and he would not be able to hold him back.

He thought of the recent scene in his mama's office. Her reaction to his decision about the wood had puzzled him. Why did she oppose it so violently?

The wood held no emotional pain for her in the way that it did for him. For the first time, he wondered about her role in the affair. For the first time? Perhaps not. But now, as then, he would not allow himself to think the unthinkable.

A moth was caught in a spider's web in the corner of the window; there had been a time when one of the servants would have attended to such things. There had been a time too when his mama would have noticed and someone would have been reprimanded or even dismissed for the oversight. But now no one bothered. Short of house-staff, Midwinter was falling into neglect. The moth's dried up body must have hung there since the previous summer. Aubrey stared at it. Sometimes it was as if it had been yesterday. Augusta in this very drawing room: "I am leaving you. He and I are going away together"; a cabbage white flickering against the glass. Then, when he came back from London, the change in her, as if she were demented. "He can't have gone. He wouldn't. He loves me." And then, when at last he had thought that she might be his again —

"Mr Farringdon?" Aubrey looked up. One of the young men had spoken — he had lost an arm, the sleeve was pinned loosely across his tunic. "Sir — are you all right?" Only then did Aubrey realise that he had groaned aloud.

* * *

Stephen went to see Nancy before he returned to France. She was alone when he arrived at the house in Chelsea where she was living with Marjorie Benson. She showed him into the comfortable sitting room, with chintz covers and dried flowers and Marjorie's botanical studies of lilies and orchids on every wall.

"Edith let slip where you were," he said.

Nancy nodded, saddened to see him in uniform, though she had been half expecting his embarkation for France. "I didn't think Edith knew where I was."

"I expect word gets around." He hesitated. "She's not been to see you?"

"Perhaps I've embarrassed her. I've

embarrassed everyone else."

"No. I don't think she knows why you left Midwinter."

She sat on the sofa and could not look at him, for she had hoped he would not guess at the truth. She could do without complications, she thought, feeling again the exhaustion which so often came over her since she had left Aubrey; it was as if the final rift between them had drained her of energy. She smiled. "So the stories haven't been too lurid."

Stephen sat down close to her. He took her hand. "*Was* it because of me?"

She drew away her hand and fiddled with a notepad on the table beside her. "You mustn't start on self-recriminations. There's no point in it. Aubrey and I should have parted months ago. I can see it now."

"Have you spoken to him? Perhaps if you explain."

"Oh no, Stephen. I don't even know whether he is in London. And I really haven't wanted to see him."

"So it's really over?"

She nodded. She did not resist when he took her hand again; she took comfort from it: she had not realised how lonely she had been since coming to London. "I suppose Aubrey will make sure Connie stays away from me," she said bitterly. "I wrote to her. I wrote to Hugo too. I don't know what they think about it all." She smiled suddenly, regretting the distress in his expression. "Don't worry, I shall snap out of it, as Marjorie would say. She's been very kind. Too kind. I must get on and find a place of my own; I've been here quite long enough for anyone's hospitality, and besides, she has her own problems." Nancy lowered her voice with a mock confidentiality and with a glimmer of her old sense of mischief. "Gilbert Lang has abandoned her for a younger woman."

"I should think she's better off without him. From what I've heard, Lang's a bit of a shirker and a philanderer."

"Maybe. But Marjorie was awfully fond of him." She paused. "I was awfully fond of Aubrey once."

Stephen got up and went to the window, looking down on the shrub-filled garden below. She glanced at him, remembering the summer-house and their weeks together when he was recovering from his injury. Was he still in love with her — and what was love anyway? She knew that she cared for him more deeply than she had when they were innocent about the war, yet she knew too that it was hardly different from the love she felt for Hugo and Connie.

He turned to face her. "Did you know, Aubrey's having the wood cut down?"

Nancy gasped. "He can't!"

"It's true. My papa heard. He will make some money out of it, I suppose — "

"But he can't! The wood is special." She pictured the bluebells, the little paths, like streams of dappled light, and the pool lying secretly under the overgrown quarry face.

"He can do what he likes. It's his timber, And the War Office will be glad of it."

"It was never his wood," said Nancy vehemently. "It was Augusta's and then it was mine. All he could ever think about was Augusta and Viner. That's why he's doing it, you know. Because of her. It's got nothing to do with the war."

Stephen did not understand her. He

wondered rather miserably whether leaving Aubrey had unbalanced her. He felt a certain responsibility, but the more pragmatic side of his nature questioned whether he should be shouldering all the blame. Hadn't Farringdon himself got a lot to do with it? "Well . . . " He turned his uniform cap in his hands.

Nancy recovered herself. "I'm sorry, Stephen. When do you go back to France?"

"This evening." She did not miss the effort with which he kept his voice steady, keeping up the show of being relaxed about going back to the Front. "Mama and Edith are coming to Victoria. I asked them not to but — " he shrugged — "you know how it is."

She nodded, her indignation about the wood forgotten, "Thank you for coming to see me."

"I couldn't leave without saying goodbye." This time his voice broke a little. She kissed him and he held her self-consciously before he stepped away.

Nancy went downstairs with him to the pavement. "London has changed in the past two years and none of it for the better. Everything is so drab and depressing."

"Everything is changing. I meant to tell you. Your keeper is joining up at last."

Nancy stared at him and a sudden and inexplicable distress ran through her.

"Well, with the wood gone . . . "

"Of course." It had not occurred to her. She had not even considered what would happen to Ted if the wood were felled. She wondered whether Mrs Farringdon had put up a fight to keep him. Why *had* Aubrey decided to fell the wood? Hadn't the war caused enough devastation? One name ran through her head as she returned upstairs. Augusta. Everything always came back to Augusta.

* * *

It was the following day when Nancy received a card asking her to meet Edith and her mother while Mrs Lennox was still in London. She was invited to tea at Mrs Lennox's hotel. Feeling apprehensive, for she still did not know what conclusions people might have drawn from her swift departure from

Midwinter, she dressed in a plain suit and hat, in order not to look like a 'scarlet woman', and made her way to Knightsbridge.

"Nancy!" Mrs Lennox sailed across the soft-carpeted lounge to greet her on a wave of furs and scent. "Nancy, dear — what dreadful times we live in. My poor boy, gone off again to France, and who knows — who knows what might not happen this time!"

Edith put her arm round her mother with a commanding air. "Come on now, Mama. Stephen thinks it won't be long before he can get some leave."

Mrs Lennox dabbed at her eyes and her mouth quivered into a smile. "Edith is such a comfort. I do miss her, you know. I've tried to persuade her to come back to Winchborne with me and take a holiday. Don't you think she needs a holiday, Nancy? They work her so hard. Everyone has had to work so hard lately." She bit her lip. "Times have changed so dreadfully."

Mrs Lennox had recovered by the time tea was brought to them and she presided over the tea table with an air of enthusiastic gaiety.

Edith, who seemed to have caught her mother's mood of exuberance, laughed and chatted about the women at the Recruitment and Training Bureau where she worked.

"Edith practically runs the office singlehanded," Mrs Lennox said proudly to Nancy. She laughed fondly. "Edith was always so very impatient with idleness."

Nancy felt a renewed sense of her inferiority, for she had done nothing since coming to London. Edith was becoming a 'suffragette-type' she thought as she watched her beside Mrs Lennox. Her dark hair was cut very short and she wore a baggy two-piece costume, emphatically belted in the middle.

"Now tell us, Nancy," said Mrs Lennox. "How long are you staying with your friend in London?"

Nancy toyed with her teacup. "I don't know exactly. I'm thinking of looking for a flat."

Edith looked puzzled. "But won't you be going back soon to Dorset?"

Nancy looked her in the eyes, wondering how long it would take for the story to spread. She decided to forestall the gossip. "Aubrey and I have parted. I should think it's permanent."

Mrs Lennox's hand flew to her mouthful of seed cake.

Edith flushed. "Oh dear, Nancy. I'm sorry."

"But you would like to say, 'I told you so', I can tell." Nancy turned to Mrs Lennox. "I'm sorry. I didn't mean to shock you, but it's as well you hear it from me. It's true. I shan't be going back."

"We understood you were taking a holiday, visiting an old friend . . . " Mrs Lennox tailed off. So, Mrs Farringdon had not thought up a story yet, thought Nancy, grateful for once for Midwinter protocol, which dictated that one must avoid scandal at all cost.

"I always felt you went into the marriage too lightly," said Edith, which, Nancy supposed, was another way of saying 'I told you so'.

"How different you girls are from the girls in my day," said Mrs Lennox. "We would no more have dreamed of leaving our husbands, or running offices and managing people, than we would of flying, though I expect young girls will be doing that too before long."

"You managed Papa instead," teased Edith.

"Ah, now that's something your generation could learn a thing or two about," agreed Mrs Lennox, with a glance at Nancy which, though sympathetic, was tinged with an element of disappointment in her.

"It's true that I didn't manage Aubrey very well," Nancy agreed with disarming candour.

"I can't understand what went wrong, dear. You both seemed so happy at first."

"Oh, I'm sure Edith is right, we should never have married in the first place."

Mrs Lennox sighed. "Perhaps the fault lies with Aubrey."

"Oh, no. Poor Aubrey," protested Edith, with a vigour which suggested that she would have known precisely how to manage him.

"One can't help thinking of Augusta — I always rather liked Augusta, you know," mused Mrs Lennox, "She had her faults of course. It was all very shocking and one knew what was going on, but somehow, before John Viner came on the scene, her little affairs seemed rather innocent."

"You mean there were other affairs?" Nancy said in astonishment.

"Well, yes. Everyone knew about them. Aubrey, I suspect, most of all. But he adored her. Everyone adored her."

"Did she have many lovers?"

"My goodness — yes. She was very discreet about it, of course. Women *were* more discreet ten or twenty years ago."

Nancy felt cheated. She had thought Viner the great love of Augusta's life; and now, to discover that he was one in a line of many — her conceptions about Augusta and about the diary seemed suddenly to have been turned upside down. "Do you remember much about the affair with Viner?"

Edith groaned. "Not that old chestnut again, Nancy."

Her mother ignored her. "I remember it rather well. You see, in a way, I became involved."

"You, Mama?" laughed Edith. She

turned to Nancy. "Forgive my mama. She has a vivid imagination. I'm sure she was in no way involved in Augusta's affair."

"Not directly," agreed Mrs Lennox. "Good heavens, child! No. But there was a woman who used to write to Augusta from London. The correspondence seemed to bring her some comfort when she was so ill towards the end."

"Grace Hammond," said Nancy with a flicker of the excitement she had felt when she first came upon Augusta's diaries.

Mrs Lennox looked at her curiously. "Now however did you know that?"

"Aubrey must have spoken about her," Nancy said quickly.

"I'm surprised, knowing how much Aubrey disapproved of the friendship. More seed cake?"

Nancy concentrated on the cake and said casually, "Tell me about this correspondence."

"Well, for a while Augusta's friend had neglected to write, and Augusta got the idea into her head that her letters were being interfered with. She was very strange towards the end." She lowered her voice. "It was the medicine, you know. The doctor gave it to her." She mouthed the word 'morphine'.

"Did you believe her?"

"Not at first. And, if Augusta's letters *were* controlled, perhaps it was for the best in the end. I went to see her shortly before she died. She gripped my hand as if she would never let it go. 'I've done a terrible thing,' she kept saying."

"I expect she was feeling guilty because of the way she had treated poor Aubrey," said Edith.

"I suppose so. The poor thing was in great distress. She said she must get a letter to her friend, Grace Hammond, and would I post it for her without telling her mama-in-law? Well, what could I do?"

"Did you send it?" Nancy asked, trying to hide her impatience.

"I'm afraid I did. Although, at the time, I didn't really think Mrs Farringdon had done anything with her letters. Then afterwards I began to wonder. Perhaps Aubrey thought the correspondence would excite her too much and he had asked his mama to intervene — as I said, he disapproved very much of the friendship. Anyway, I heard later that Grace Hammond had come looking for Augusta, round about the time of the funeral."

"Why did Aubrey disapprove of the friendship?" asked Edith.

"Because Grace Hammond was a suffragist," said Nancy. "A bad influence, you see."

Edith laughed. "Augusta embraced feminism? I don't believe it."

"Augusta was always having fads and fancies," said Mrs Lennox. She sat back in her seat with a look of satisfaction, "A strange tale, though, don't you think?"

* * *

"I have decided to get myself a flat," Nancy said to Marjorie that evening.

"Oh dear, I shall miss you."

Nancy suspected that Marjorie would in fact be rather glad to see her go. "I thought I might ask Edith Lennox to find me some war work through one of her societies."

Marjorie looked up from her painting, a delicate water-colour illustration of a tiger lily. She tried to look self-composed, but her expression was odd, her complexion slightly more pink than usual. "Do you have to do that through Edith? I could put you in touch with people."

Nancy laughed. "Why not Edith? Don't worry, she knows about me and Aubrey."

"I don't mean because of Aubrey."

"Well, what then?"

Marjorie coloured more deeply and flung down her paintbrush. "I suppose you would have found out sooner or later."

Nancy stared at her in amazement. "You're being very dramatic and secretive. Found out what?"

Marjorie said with a sudden and extraordinary sob, "Found out about Edith and Gilbert!" She stood and, with a crash of her chair against the wall and an agitation totally unsuited to her, ran from the room.

⋆ ⋆ ⋆

"Why didn't she tell me before? Why didn't you say anything?"

Edith stirred her coffee. The café was quiet. The customers were mainly women, with a scattering of servicemen on leave. "Perhaps she thought you would have divided loyalties. As for me, I felt embarrassed about it, and I didn't want Mama to know about Gilbert."

"But I have hardly seen you in the past twelve months." Nancy looked out of the window at the people passing on the street. It was a dark, cold afternoon; spring was going to be late this year. She turned back to Edith. "She's rather upset, poor thing."

"I thought she was being terribly decent about it."

"She always is terribly decent, but I saw a very different side of her the other day."

"Oh, dear. It makes me feel such a beast."

"I don't know why I didn't guess," said Nancy. "After you met him at the house party — and then, when I saw you the Christmas before last, I had an idea you had fallen in love with someone."

"Do I stand condemned?"

"What to? A lifetime with Gilbert? I knew him when I first met Aubrey, remember. He's fascinating and clever but he's a supreme egotist. I like him enormously, but you won't find him easy."

"I know that. I love him."

"Ah." Nancy dropped her gaze and sipped her tea. Why did women always fall for such unsuitable men? Herself and Aubrey. Augusta and John Viner, who, it seemed, had been only one of Augusta's lovers. Had the others been equally unsuitable? She thought about the diary; since Augusta fell in love with such apparent frequency, did the final diary entry now make any more sense? Certainly the words, *if only I had loved him just a little more*, showed a degree of self-awareness. But why such grief and a longing for death? Guilt because of Aubrey — but, according to Mrs Lennox, Aubrey had known about Augusta's other affairs. Besides, it was clear from the diary that it was Viner's desertion which had caused Augusta such anguish. If only Nancy knew what had been in the letter to Grace Hammond. She looked at Edith. Would her love affair with Gilbert last? Edith was energetic, resilient, but men like Gilbert tended to get bored, and Edith did not possess that tolerance which was Marjorie's chief strength. Gilbert did not need a lover, he needed a prop. She looked up. Edith would have to take her chance, as she had with Aubrey, as anyone did when they fell in love. "Did you know that Aubrey is cutting down the wood at Midwinter? I can't bear to think of it being destroyed."

Edith was unmoved. "Gilbert and Frank Singer have been plotting to tackle Aubrey again about digging there. That should hold them up for a while. I don't think it's good for Gilbert to get these whims." She looked at Nancy. "At least the timber will go to a good cause."

"That's more or less what Stephen said."

"You've seen Stephen?"

"He came to see me before he went back to France."

"He never said."

Nancy changed the subject. She smiled.

"I'm so glad you agreed to have lunch with me."

"So that you could make me feel a beast about Marjorie?"

"No, silly. I want you to help me find some work to do."

"Nursing?"

"I was always better at talking to the patients than I was at changing their bandages." Nancy paused. "Look — I really want to do something useful. I can type. I was a secretary for Aubrey. Can't your own organisation use me somewhere?"

Edith smiled suddenly and relaxed. "And I thought you just wanted to disapprove of me."

"Then why did you agree to meet me?"

"Perhaps I felt I deserved to be disapproved of."

Nancy wondered how much Edith would disapprove if she were to tell her about Stephen. A thought struck her. "Does Connie know about your pash for Gilbert?"

"Yes, but she has been sworn to secrecy. My mama would have a fit.

I had an awful job keeping it from her when she was in London."

"Of course you know all about Connie and Gus?"

Edith laughed. "Yes. It's a great mutual conspiracy."

* * *

Connie lived only for Gus's letters and news of his next leave. She felt as if nothing else could move her; not pity for her papa now that Nancy had rocked the boat too far at Midwinter and cast herself adrift in London; not anxiety over Hugo, who was in training for the Front; not even the casualties of the war. Two of the estate workers at Midwinter had been killed in France, and there had been a letter to say that Browne had died of injuries in Gallipoli. Her grandmama was grieving, but Connie, who had never felt much affection for the Midwinter servants, had received the news about Browne without emotion.

She knew she should go to visit Nancy, who had written to her, explaining how she and Aubrey could 'no longer live together in all honesty as man and wife'. When Connie asked her papa about it, he refused to say what had caused them to part. Edith said she thought the separation had something to do with her papa's plans to cut down the wood. Connie was glad he was going to cut it down. She hoped that she had been responsible for his decision by telling him he should let Frank Singer dig. She would let Singer dig there, let him turn it all upside down and stir it up. When she was a child her grandmama had frightened her with stories about the place being visited by the devil, and sometimes, to punish her if she had been really bad, she would say that ghosts would come out of the wood to haunt her. Connie was no longer afraid of ghosts, but she was glad about the War Office timber, for she was sure the wood and its pool had been the cause of all the trouble there had ever been at Midwinter.

Connie was glad she was in London, far away from all the fuss. She knew that if she concentrated on her hospital work, on writing letters to Gus and praying to

God to keep him safe, nothing would go wrong and she could get through until his next leave. The French had the worst of the fighting that spring: Verdun seemed remote, it was not Gus's battle; but she could imagine how terrible it must be for everyone in the wet and the cold. He could die of pneumonia and she would not know. He had written to her from rest camp, and again after being involved in an action north of the Ypres-Comines Canal. He seemed distant and miserable. Connie hated the war. It had drained all the joy out of living. She hated the constant hoping, the constant worrying, and living from one letter to the next.

Edith had said that Nancy was going to join her in helping to organise war work at the Women's Recruitment and Training Bureau. "You should make an effort to see her, Connie. She is very much on your side about Gus." But Connie was wary of disturbing the routine she had invented for herself. It was not that she felt as if Nancy had betrayed her by leaving Papa: not even that Connie believed she had betrayed him — she refused to accept her grandmama's hints that Nancy had been sent packing because she had taken a lover. Connie did not want to see Nancy because she could no longer talk about Gus without breaking down.

He had not written for more than two weeks. The worst thing of all was knowing that, if anything had happened to him, no one would think it necessary to tell her.

As a third week went by with no news, Connie could bear the uncertainty no longer. She left London and went to see Gus's parents in Dorset.

17

THE searchlights scanned the sky in the darkness. Nancy heard people shout to one another that the Zeps were about as she left the Training Bureau late one evening. She heard the distant buzzing sound of an air-ship and gave an exclamation of irritation: it was a good walk to her flat. A thin tide of people were making for the nearest cellar shelter and she turned on her heel and went with them.

It was cold and crowded in the cellar and she wished now that she had not stayed on so late at the Bureau. She had been working through the files on the various London women's suffrage organisations, hoping to come across the name Grace Hammond, for it had occurred to her that if Grace still worked for the suffrage movement, she might be involved in war work. She had drawn a blank, and, confined in the cellar, she told herself that the exercise had been silly and obsessive. Why was it that even now, miles from Midwinter, she could not let Augusta's story go?

People began to sing to pass the time, 'Annie Laurie' and 'Oh, You Beautiful Doll'. Someone struck up on a harmonica. Nancy joined in when they sang 'When Irish Eyes Are Smiling', remembering the piano at Keeper's Cottage. The haunting sound of the harmonica and circle of strangers united in the semidarkness made her throat constrict so that suddenly she could not sing. She thought of Ted. How reassuring it would have been to hear his pleasant tenor voice again. She wondered whether he would already have left for a training camp, and it struck her, with a heavy sadness, that she might never see or hear him again.

The man next to her ignored the singers. He was reading a newspaper by the light from the hurricane lamp which stood between them on the cellar floor. He folded the paper and handed it to her, "I always look. See if I recognise anyone." Nancy took it and, almost at once, she read Gus Wyatt's name in the

Roll of Honour column: "Fallen Officers . . . Wyatt, Lieut. G., M.C., Dorsetshire Regiment." She gave a cry of despair.

The singers fell silent.

"Someone you know?" the man said sympathetically.

She nodded. "A friend." Did Connie know? And if she did, who would comfort her? Certainly not Aubrey.

Nancy went to the house in Bloomsbury as soon as the raid was over, swallowing her distaste at the idea of confronting Aubrey again.

He was clearly appalled to see her.

She said briskly, "I'm not going to make a fuss. I've only come to see Connie."

"She's not here. That is, she's gone to Midwinter for a while." He hesitated, then his natural sense of correctness prevailed and he showed her into his study.

The house had not changed at all, Nancy noted. A little more shabby perhaps. She remembered the first time they had faced one another across his desk. How bewitched she had been by his brilliance and fame. Now, though he was no less handsome and urbane, he seemed faded, his glory diminished.

She felt the need to make her purpose clear. "I've just read in the newspaper that a friend of Connie's has been killed. Gus Wyatt. He once visited us at Midwinter."

He nodded. "She telephoned me from Dorset. I'm afraid she was rather incoherent."

"Poor Connie."

"Why she should have taken it so badly I can't imagine."

"Oh, really, Aubrey!" Nancy said in exasperation. "Can't you work it out?"

"An attachment?"

"She was in love with him. Don't you ever see anything beyond your own nose?"

"Don't be ridiculous," Aubrey said coldly. "Connie's too young to be in love. And the accusation isn't fair. I've been aware of many things in my lifetime — things about which others may well have believed I had no conception."

"And dwelled on them so long you've neglected your own daughter," Nancy said angrily.

"Because I didn't notice an adolescent infatuation?"

"She'll be seventeen this summer. I was no more than seventeen when I fell in love with you. You noticed that infatuation well enough."

He blinked and she saw that she had wounded him.

"That was love. At least, Nancy — I loved you."

"Did you? Or were you flattered? Certainly you seemed to want to keep me for ever in a state of childish innocence." Nancy saw how far she had come since those early days of her marriage.

"You can be very harsh, Nancy. And blinkered, if you can't see that it's your own selfishness which spoiled everything. That and your fickle behaviour — "

"Did you have to destroy my wood?" she said angrily.

"*Your* wood?" He frowned. "The War Office — "

"Oh, for goodness' sake. It's got nothing to do with the war." She turned away. "There's no point in prolonging this. I only came because of Connie. I'll see myself out."

Aubrey said as she moved towards the door, "Hugo goes out to France next month."

She hesitated. "I'll pray for him."

"Thank you."

Nancy halted. "Do you mind if I go down to Midwinter? I'm sure I could help Connie over this a little."

To her surprise he nodded and she wondered whether she had stirred his conscience, or perhaps he had at last decided to forget the business about Stephen. "I'll let Mama know you are going."

A thought occurred to her. "Have you cut down the trees yet?"

He could not meet her eyes. "I believe the workmen have started."

* * *

Nancy walked from the station, for no one came from Midwinter to meet her. The air was sharp, the hedges dotted with light green leaf buds; clumps of pale primroses clustered on the banks. She took the lower road, not wanting to witness the destruction of the wood at close hand, but she could hear the noise of the steam engines as she drew near to Midwinter. She passed the end of the track to Keeper's Cottage. No smoke rose from among the trees. She did not venture along the track, for she did not want to see the house standing empty.

Roberts met her in the entrance hall of Midwinter. He had lost his usual imperturbability and his eyes were suspiciously moist. "It's very good to see you here again, ma'am."

Nancy was touched, not expecting that the servants would have missed her. She handed him her suitcase. "Thank you, Roberts. It's good to be back." What a strange thing to have said, she thought as she followed him up the stairs. And yet, it really was good to be there. She felt none of the leaden depressing of her spirits which the house had once exerted over her.

Two Army officers passed her on the staircase. She did not recognise them, nor any of the other men she saw. They stared at her and she thought, they don't know that I belong here, and the fact is that I *don't* belong to the Farringdons any more. I can come and go as I want. How liberating that feels.

She caught up with Roberts. "Is Mrs Farringdon at home?"

He did not look at her. "The mistress says she expects to be engaged in hospital work this afternoon, ma'am. She will see you at dinner."

Nancy set her mouth. So the petty warfare was not over. Her suspicions were confirmed when Roberts led her to the guest wing instead of to her old bedroom, "And where is Miss Connie?" she said as Roberts threw open the door to the Yellow Room. The air smelled musty. The room — too small to be used as a convalescent ward — had been shut up since the beginning of the war. Nancy remembered that Marjorie had occupied it at the house party. How important it had seemed then to do things properly, to prove that she was as good as Augusta. She checked herself, for she had vowed that nothing at Midwinter would beguile her into thinking about Augusta.

"Miss Connie will be in the small drawing room, ma'am," said Roberts. "She will be gossiping with the patients."

Did she imagine it, or was there a hint of disapproval in the old man's expression. Nancy considered the significance of Roberts's last remark as she unpacked her clothes and hung them in the wardrobe. Gossiping? Well, at least it did not seem as if Connie had withdrawn into herself.

* * *

Connie was in the drawing room, as Roberts had predicted; she was talking loudly with a group of young officers and they were laughing. One of the men glanced at Nancy, and she heard him say, "Who is this — a friend of yours?" Connie turned. Her bright smile faltered for a second, then she jumped up from her chair. "Nancy! Nancy, how marvellous!"

Nancy had been prepared for a change in her, but not for this. Connie's dress was modern and clung to her figure; it almost exposed one knee when she was seated and, when she stood, revealed her silk-stockinged calves. Her hair was short, bobbed round her ears, and her lips were sticky with colour. She looked pretty in a racy, vulgar kind of way, but it was Connie's eyes which disturbed Nancy most of all: they were bright with a feverish animation and set in deep hollows behind her spectacles.

Connie hugged Nancy very tightly and, taking her by the arm, dragged her to a chair. "This is my step-mama. Isn't she delightful? But why didn't anyone say you were coming?"

Nancy smiled. "I can only suppose your grandmother thought it wasn't worthy of a mention."

"That's just like her." Connie flung herself down again, "Nancy — guess what the men call Grandmama."

One of the officers began to protest, but Connie laughed and pushed his arm. "Don't be a chump. Nancy is friend, not foe." She turned to Nancy. "Go on. Guess."

"Oh, I don't know. You'll have to tell me." Nancy felt desperately that something was wrong, that if only she could talk to Connie alone she would shed this awful brittle performance.

"They call her the *Kaiser*." Connie

squealed with laughter.

Nancy smiled in spite of her unease.

"Isn't it rich?"

"It does seem appropriate."

The men relaxed. "She *is* on our side," said a young lieutenant whose sleeve was pinned across his chest.

"Of course she is!" Connie cast her brilliant smile on Nancy. "Oh, we're going to have such fun now you're here!"

* * *

Mrs Farringdon took her seat at the dinner table and proceeded to behave as if Nancy were not there. Connie was vivacious and talkative throughout dinner; the four young men who had been invited to join them were clearly fascinated by her. Mrs Farringdon turned her back on Nancy and spoke earnestly to the captain on her right.

"Grandmama, you haven't said a word to Nancy all evening," Connie said reproachfully when the three women had retired to the small drawing room.

Mrs Farringdon swung round and

regarded Nancy coldly. "I told Aubrey he was a fool to let you come back here. If I had my way you would never again have set foot over Midwinter's threshold."

Nancy met her gaze levelly. "I take as little pleasure from your company as you do from mine. I came back to Midwinter for Connie's sake."

"You thought she would be grieving! If Connie is depressed she has a very strange way of showing it."

Connie lifted her head and tossed back her hair. "People don't talk about grief these days, Grandmama. It's pointless."

"You see?"

"I see very well," said Nancy.

"I *told* Aubrey not to let you come. After the way you had behaved . . . " Mrs Farringdon's mouth twitched with suppressed fury.

"I want Nancy here," snapped Connie. "You should have told me she was coming back, not kept it a secret."

There was an uncomfortable silence. Connie went to the door, and her manner was again effervescent. "Come and make up a four for bridge, Nancy."

Nancy hesitated. "You go along. I

should like to talk to your grandmother for a moment."

Mrs Farringdon sat by the fire. When Connie had gone she picked up a half-worked knitted cap. "I have tried to get Connie interested in the war parcels, but she won't knit a thing. The time that girl wastes! Well, I have given up with her. I've better things to do than worry about the reputation she is making for herself."

"You're wrong about Connie," Nancy said. "This act of hers wouldn't fool anyone."

Mrs Farringdon began counting stitches. "She's just like Augusta. I warned Aubrey that he was always too lenient with the children. Connie grows more like Augusta every day."

"Did Augusta mask her real feelings too?"

Mrs Farringdon finished counting to the end of the row. "Feelings? What feelings?"

"I think she was very unhappy when she died."

Mrs Farringdon looked up and her eyes were cold. "What has Aubrey been saying?"

"Very little. But I don't think he blamed Augusta entirely."

Mrs Farringdon made a noise somewhere between a snort and a laugh. "He felt sorry for her. Did you know that? In the end he pitied her. She behaved like a whore, threatened to destroy the family name, and still he maintained that he loved her." She returned her attention to her knitting. "It's a tragedy. He could have been as big a man as his papa, but when he married Augusta she ruined him."

"I'm not here to talk about Aubrey and Augusta."

Mrs Farringdon looked up. "And I didn't ask you to come here. I don't want you near me. You and Augusta between you have made it your business to destroy my poor son. So, I've decided you shall keep to your room while you remain at Midwinter. You may talk to Connie, since Aubrey has allowed it, but I don't want to see you on the wards, nor at mealtimes. One of the servants will bring your meals to your room."

Nancy swallowed the exclamation of disbelief which rose inside her. "I suppose

I might walk in the grounds and go to the village? I'm not a prisoner?"

"Do as you please," snapped Mrs Farringdon. "And when you've satisfied yourself that Connie's heart is as shallow as her mama's, you can go back where you came from."

* * *

There was an oil-lamp burning in the Yellow Room. One of the servants had also set light to the fire and drawn the curtains while Nancy was at dinner. The bed-clothes were turned down and her night clothes arranged on the coverlet. Nancy suspected that it was Roberts rather than Mrs Farringdon who had given the instructions.

She decided to write to Edith: she would tell her about Connie. Perhaps Edith, with her distinction of being so well-balanced, would be able to offer some advice. "I am," she admitted in her letter, "completely out of my depth. I came to offer a shoulder of sympathy to a grief-stricken young girl, but this brittle side to Connie is going to be difficult to deal with . . ." She had been sitting at the writing table for half an hour when there was a light knock at the door.

"I thought you were going to play bridge with us. The others have been asking where you were. I think you scored a hit with them."

Nancy closed her writing case. "I'm sorry. I was tired."

Connie went to the fire and warmed her arms. She was shivering. She looked at Nancy, met her eyes and looked away, then laughed suddenly. "Midwinter is always so damn cold."

Nancy went to her suitcase and pulled out a cardigan. "Here." She handed it to her.

"I'm all right."

"Don't be silly. Put it on." She handed it to her and sat on the bed.

Connie pulled on the cardigan and wrapped it round her. "I always liked this room. Do you remember the house party? You put Marjorie Benson in here." She paused. "I wonder if Gilbert Lang slept with her. You know of course about Gilbert and Edith."

"Yes. Poor Marjorie."

Connie sat down on the bed, pulling the cardigan more tightly round her shoulders. "Poor Marjorie? At least she can still see him. At least he's not *dead.*" She flashed Nancy a smile, her mouth trembled and she bit her lower lip. "No — don't start feeling sorry for me." She stood up and moved away from the bed. "I don't want to think about him. I'm glad he's dead, if you really want to know. It means I don't have to go on hoping and feeling any more."

"You can't stop feeling, Connie."

"Yes, I can." She swung round to look at herself in the dressing-table mirror. "What do you think of my hair? It was you who said I should cut it short. Do you remember? It was when you put up my hair for the house party."

"You can't just block him out. Do you think that's what Gus would have wanted?"

"Did he think what I wanted when he went and got himself killed?"

"Gus was a fine young man."

Connie swung round to face her, "I hate him!"

Nancy felt an ache in her throat. "You

know that isn't true. Do you remember when you first met him and we all played tennis? You were so happy to have found one another."

Connie stood with her arms by her sides. She fought for a while with a defiant stare and then her face puckered. "Oh, Nancy. What am I going to do?" She walked to the bed and, sitting down, fell into Nancy's arms. "How could he leave me if he loved me? He wouldn't do that to me, would he?"

Nancy hushed her as if she were a child again, saying, "He didn't want to. I know he didn't want to."

"He wouldn't even get engaged. If he'd done that I could have put up with it. But now I've got nothing."

* * *

Nancy stayed on at Midwinter into April. The work of tree-felling continued steadily, the band of trees beyond the meadow growing shorter, those on the skyline thinner. Almost daily there was the throb of steam engines and the crash of timber. Aubrey did not come to see the work of the contractors. Nancy wondered if he had stayed away because she was at Midwinter, or whether it was because he could not bear to see the devastation.

Connie complained about the noise of the tree-felling and turned up the gramophone to drown out the sound. There were days when she seemed bright and shallow, and others when she came to Nancy's room. Then she would talk about when she and Hugo were children and about Gus, and she would weep for a while.

"He was the first person I had really loved," she said once. "I really think he changed me. I always wanted people to love me when I was little; I longed for them to say I was pretty or clever. No one ever told me I was pretty, but sometimes Grandmama would praise me for something and I would be so happy. But with Gus, I didn't really need him to say anything. We talked about everything; I could tell him about when I was little, and he understood. He always felt that no one wanted him either. That surprised me, because he seemed so steady and popular, and his family were so nice when I went to see them and when they told me he was dead. He has a lot of brothers and sisters." She told Nancy how strange he had been on his last leave. "It was almost as if he knew what was going to happen. Do you think people know when they're going to die?"

Nancy remembered Augusta's certainty of it at the end of her diary and said that perhaps one did.

* * *

April crept on to May. When Nancy talked about going back to London Connie would say, "No. Wait a while, and I'll come with you. I'm not ready to face London yet and it's so good to know you're here when I need you."

One day Nancy cycled to the Post Office in the village. She no longer tried to avoid the evidence of the tree-felling: the trees near the top road lay smashed and broken and the timber wagons had gouged deep channels in the mud; a crane was lifting tree trunks on to a wagon; the men shouted instructions to one another above the rattle and bellow of the engine. Nancy pedalled on past the margins of the wood, where trees, as yet undisturbed, put out fresh leaves for another season's growth, past the hedgerows and fields to the garage and the school until she came to the centre of the village.

She posted a letter to Edith, explaining that she would not be returning to London and the Training Bureau for a few more weeks. She mounted her bicycle and set out from the pavement and wobbled suddenly to a halt, for a figure was coming towards her. She waited as he came nearer and her heart beat quickly with pleasure. It's only Ted Powers, she told herself. Looking rather handsome in khaki. But the feeling of elation persisted.

"I didn't expect to see you," she said. "You're still in England then."

"Training. It's all very secret and hush-hush. I've got a thirty-six-hour pass."

"The Army is so generous."

He smiled briefly, then looked down at her bicycle. "Are you back for good?"

She explained about Connie. "I shall

go back to London soon." She paused, feeling the colour rise to her cheeks. "I don't know what was said here after I left Midwinter."

He too hesitated, and the silence was strained before he said, "There was gossip, but that's Winchborne for you."

She nodded. "Look, we can't talk here. Can we meet? It's so nice to see you again. Tomorrow somewhere?"

He seemed reluctant. "I'm staying with my uncle over Melcombe way. We can't really meet at the farm."

"At your cottage then — oh, I forgot. It's not really yours any more."

"Mrs Farringdon took back the key. The worst of it is, my books are still there."

"And your piano?" she said in dismay. "I didn't know."

"It doesn't really matter. I shan't be going back to it."

"I expect my husband will find a position for you — after the war, I mean."

He shook his head. "I'm finished here. Besides, the wood's gone. Midwinter won't ever keep a shoot again."

"You've seen it?"

He nodded. It was because of the wood that Ted had returned to Winchborne. It had been a shock to see the timber wagons and jumble of felled trees, but the area near the pool had not been touched. Was that the old lady's orders? He glanced up the road. "It's not all bad. There's still a few of your bluebells." He turned to look at her, absorbing this second shock in one day, for he had not expected to meet her here in Winchborne; he had imagined her in London, banished, disgraced like her predecessor for taking a lover. He heard a warning voice in his head: steer well clear, remember what happened to Viner. She met his eyes and her expression was warm: it hovered on intimacy and stirred long-buried feelings in him. He drew in his breath. "We'll try the cottage. See what the place looks like. Eleven o'clock?"

Nancy nodded and mounted the bicycle. There was a sudden tension between them, an unspoken acknowledgement that to meet at Keeper's Cottage was a peculiar sort of an arrangement. Ted steadied the handlebars for a moment and felt a strong desire to place his hand on hers and close it tightly over her slim fingers. Nancy's eyes flicked down in confusion, and he released the handlebar and watched her cycle away.

The men had stopped felling for the day; the machinery stood silent among the ruins of the wood. Nancy cycled along the road to Midwinter's gates and free-wheeled down the drive towards the house. The evening sun struck across the grass, throwing long shadows; the air was sweet, the sun warm on her back; her body felt as if it had floated free and become the silhouette on the tarmac which bowled down the drive before her. She came to a halt on the gravel and wheeled the bicycle round the side of the house to the stables. Only then did she pause to wonder why she should feel so extraordinarily happy.

* * *

It was raining lightly when Nancy arrived at the cottage. She was shocked to see that someone had boarded over the windows.

Ted had found a fork and was digging out the weeds around the front step. She watched him for a moment before she spoke. "I'm so glad you've changed out of khaki."

He turned and tipped back his cap, his foot on the fork. "Only for a few hours." He bent and turned a forkful of soil. "Don't know why I'm doing this."

She surveyed the garden: it was very overgrown. She remembered when it had been bright with flowers. "It's so sad to see your house boarded-up and empty." She sat on the step and leaned against the door-post, watching him continue to fork the ground. She watched him closely: he looked fit, if anything leaner than before. "Things have changed since we first met."

"Haven't they just?"

"I want you to know that I didn't leave Midwinter of my own accord. My husband sent me away." He did not stop forking the ground, but she sensed that he was listening more intently. "He thought I was having a love affair with someone. He was wrong, but it meant the end of my marriage."

He looked at her, then looked away, and there was a hostility in his voice when he said, "Makes no difference to me. I never take any notice of gossip."

"I just wanted to get that straight. I didn't want you to think I had misled you." She did not ask herself why it mattered to her. "I came back because Connie was grieving over a young man and I thought she needed me."

"I told you. It makes no difference what you do or why you do it." He seemed angry.

It had begun to rain more heavily. There was a murmur of thunder, a threatening rumble, like a distant explosion. He said, "You'll get wet sitting there." He went to the window and tugged experimentally at one of the boards nailed across it. He pushed the prongs of the garden fork into a crack between the planks and levered until one came loose, then worked on the others. "Do you mind an act of vandalism on your property, Mrs Farringdon?"

"I always thought of the house as yours, not mine." She went to help him pull the boards clear. "And I've never thought of myself as a Farringdon." The rain was hard and vicious now, stabbing with long needles against her shoulders. She stepped back as the final board came away and she began to shiver.

"This catch was always a bit loose," he said. She watched as he slipped his pen-knife blade into a gap in the frame and forced the window open. He hesitated. "It's a bit of a step up. Easier if I lift you."

Nancy stood, silent and rigid, with her back to the window, and allowed him to place his hands round her waist. He gripped her firmly; she felt the strength of his hands, and her skirt brushed his face as he lifted her on to the sill. For a moment he paused, and she had an impulse to pull him against her, to hold his head in her lap. Then he released her, turning away with a constrained modesty as she swung her legs over the sill and into the room. She stood, her heart beating painfully, while he followed.

"Just in time." Ted closed the window and the rain drummed against it; he went to the hearth and picked up a fire iron and wedged the window shut with it. "I never thought I'd be breaking into my own parlour."

The house was in pitch darkness beyond the room they had entered. Nancy watched him go before her and followed him, feeling her way along the corridor to the kitchen; she reached out her hand for the kitchen furniture and her fingers closed on the corner of the dresser. She heard him moving about. After a moment the oil-lamp flared and the details of the room came to life. He placed the lamp on the table and came to the dresser, searching along the row of books to check that nothing had been disturbed in the time that he had been away. A crack of thunder split the silence between them; the only other sound was the heavy drumming of the rain against the boarded window and water running in the gutters and in the yard outside.

Nancy was shivering violently.

He turned to her. "Are you all right?"

She nodded. "Just cold."

"I'll light a fire."

"Someone will see the smoke."

"In this storm?" He went to the stove and began to lay a fire in the grate. "Strange. It's as if I walked out only yesterday."

She went to help him. She knelt on the rug and crumpled up newspaper and handed it to him to tuck among the sticks and coal from the scuttle. "I like this room. I liked it the first time I saw it."

He looked at her sceptically. "After living in those grand rooms at the big house?"

"Midwinter never felt like home. Here — well, I know it's silly, but it's the sort of house where I really belong. My mother had a stove like this and a dresser — only it was full of china plates and cups hanging on hooks." She laughed. "And there was a ghastly black horsehair sofa next to a piano in the parlour. I can still see it all so clearly."

He was kneeling on the rug beside her. He watched the flames catch the paper and lick around the coals. "I don't think that's silly." He turned to look at her and, lifting his hand, pushed a lock of wet hair from her face.

"Why were you so angry when you said it didn't matter to you what I did or why I did it?"

"Because I'd still feel the same about you, even knowing what I know." He turned and pushed lumps of coal into the flames, unable to confront her with her lie about Stephen Lennox and the evidence of his own eyes. "I wish you'd never got mixed up with that lot and neither had I."

"I've escaped. I'm only mixed up with them in name. I've left them, and so have you."

He looked at her. "Have you? Have you finished with them all?"

"I'm only Aubrey's wife in name. I fell out of love with him a long time ago."

"I want to kiss you," he said harshly.

She stared at him. "Then why don't you?"

He took her awkwardly in his arms, then as their mouths met he pulled her hungrily to him. "Nancy. Nancy," he murmured, kissing her neck and throat. Abruptly he let her go. "This isn't right."

"Do I have some say about it?"

"I don't know. I only know I've dreamed nonsense about you ever since I set eyes on you."

She smiled. "I don't believe you. You thought I was after the Farringdons' money when we first met."

"I still wanted you." He stroked the back of her neck, their lips touched. "Like I want you now." They kissed again. He held the back of her head in his hand and she felt the strength of his fingers. She was locked by the touch of his hand and the mounting strength of her own senses. He held her, and they clung in an embrace which neither was willing to break. Then Ted's grip on the back of her neck slackened. "It isn't right," he repeated. "You of all people must know it isn't right."

She sat back on her heels, and he stood and moved restlessly away. She watched him walk to the piano and lift the lid. "Don't you want to know what I think about you?" she said.

He did not answer, but stroked the piano keys with a slow tension, depressing them without making a noise.

"All right then, I'll tell you. I think you're brave because you're fighting for your country even though you hate violence. I think you're honest and gentle — "

He jerked his hand across the keys making a crash of discordant sound.

"Now you're angry again. Why?" Nancy felt close to tears.

"Because I know if I were straight with you, and if you were honest with me, you couldn't say those things."

She said softly, "I've fallen in love with you, but I wish you hadn't quite so many scruples about my being married to Aubrey."

He looked at her, wanting to tell her, I saw you, I saw you with him. You're no better than she was. "We both know about your husband's first wife," he said. "What we feel just now doesn't make it right."

She stared at him. "Augusta? What has this got to do with Augusta?"

"You can't ignore things like that."

"Like what? Things like what? Just because you saw them?"

"Oh, I saw more than you can imagine.

I saw all the consequences of what she did. I saw an old man driven to his grave because of it. My dad wasn't a bad man. Harsh maybe, but not wicked. The whole vile, stinking business broke him in the end."

Nancy shook her head. "I don't understand. I've read her diaries and still I don't understand."

Ted let the piano lid fall with a bang. "I wish to God you'd never come here and married into the Farringdons!"

Nancy said tentatively, "What is it, Ted? If it's about when you found them — well, the diaries show that Viner could be pretty obnoxious."

He shook his head. After a moment he said coldly, "I saw you. I saw you with Lennox in the wood."

Nancy took a slow breath. "And you thought — "

"What should I think? I saw you with him." He gave a short laugh. "And now you tell me you've fallen in love with me. You fall in and out of love pretty bloody easily, don't you? Farringdon must have a jinx on him. You're turning out just like her."

She interrupted him. "Something *did* happen with Stephen, but it was a long time ago."

He gave a laugh of disbelief. "It was all of last Christmas."

Nancy repeated, "It was a long time ago. We had a brief, very brief affair at the start of the war. I was . . . lonely. He was a friend. He's still a friend, but I'm not in love with him and I wasn't when you saw us together." She looked at him, searching his face, disappointed when he looked away. "This is my fault," she said. "I should never have asked for us to meet."

"No. It's better we did."

"I'll go as soon as the rain stops." She half hoped that he would try to dissuade her; she knew that if he showed just a hint of weakening she could make him understand about Stephen, but he was inflexible. He knew what he had seen, and it was not in his nature to reason things out or view a situation in shades of grey.

She watched him cross to the dresser and pull out some of the books. He did not look at her again but said, "I'll take these. I've missed reading while I've been in camp."

* * *

They walked together in silence to the junction of tracks, then separated, Ted going towards the road, Nancy to Midwinter. Ted did not look back. He felt shaken up by what had happened and he was frightened by how much he had told her. He remembered his boyhood nightmares, his father's drunken mumblings and terror of hell-fire at the very end. Could he believe her about Lennox? He thought of Farringdon's first wife and knew that his first instinct had been right. He should have steered clear: Nancy and Augusta Farringdon were of a kind.

* * *

Nancy crossed the meadow from Midwinter later that day. She had felt a sense of emptiness — almost a hopelessness — since leaving Ted's cottage. What if he were killed in

France? She had imagined often enough the deaths of Stephen and Hugo; she had felt for Connie and had mourned the loss of Gus Wyatt and all those other men who had died since 1914. She did not want to imagine the death of Ted Powers.

She walked to the point where the boundary of the wood had been. He would be on his way back to his camp by now. She looked at the wrecked woodland before her: the wire fence was gone; ridges of earth and broken saplings marked where the timber wagons had ploughed through the mud; the ruts were deep in water from the morning's heavy rain. Nancy, surveying the wasteland before her, remembered the intensity with which she and Ted had held one another, and knew in her heart that it had felt right. What would Augusta have thought of it all? Would she have been amused by the devastation of the wood or would she have grieved over it? "Oh, Augusta," she murmured. "You have a lot to answer for."

She picked her way round the fringes of mud, where grass and saplings grew thinly. Ted had said there were still bluebells. She came to an untouched section of the wood, where some of the trees had been marked for felling, but the ground was firm where the carts and tree-fellers had not yet advanced. Nancy walked among the trees until she reached the old quarry workings and the pool. The sun struck through the branches on to the path and illuminated patches of bluebells with a dusky light. The blue drifts made her sad; their scent, the damp earthy smell after rain and the faint wafts of wild garlic were mingled with the sour smell of mud and the pungency of sawn timber.

What had Ted meant before he told her he had seen her with Stephen, when he said his father had been driven to his grave by Augusta's affair? Had it really shocked the old man so deeply — a gamekeeper, a countryman? And had a boy in his teens been so scarred by seeing the lovers that he thought of it as a 'vile, stinking business' years later? She thought of Viner's moods, his predilection for humiliating Augusta, his 'desires which erupted from a core of depravity'. Distasteful, yes; shocking to her own imagination when she had first read the diary — and perhaps Ted had seen some perverted behaviour which had disturbed him as a boy — but surely a man like Ted would not still be scarred by such a memory? Her own imagination could not devise any unnatural behaviour sufficiently appalling to account for his veiled hints that some great evil had occurred.

Nancy stared at the water and allowed herself to wonder again why Mrs Farringdon had employed Ted to patrol the wood and forgone all notions of duty to Country because she wanted to keep him at Midwinter. The dark surface of the water seemed turbid rather than mysterious; the landscape of broken tree stumps and mud was too near at hand: in a few weeks the devastation might encroach on the pool itself. The romance was gone; the air of secrecy which had once hung over it threatened to dissolve and to reveal something crude and unpalatable. Ted's words kept running through her thoughts — 'the consequences of their wickedness' — and his assertion that his father had not been a bad man. She remembered his frightened reaction when he had first learned that Augusta had kept a diary. What was it he had asked her? "What about afterwards after Viner went away?" What could Ted know about Viner after he had gone away? Nancy tried to recall the exact words of Augusta's final diary entries. A preoccupation with death. A certainty that Viner had not abandoned her. Nancy stared at the flat, sinister surface of the water. People don't think, Ted had once told her, how dirty and bloody killing is.

A jolt of understanding ran through her. Mrs Farringdon telling Augusta that Viner had gone away for ever, paying Ted to keep people away from the pool; Ted's father driven to his grave by the whole 'vile, stinking business'. She stepped back from the water's edge. Not the discovery of the lovers. Not that. Ted had been hinting at something more terrible.

Nancy turned from the pool with a murmur of horror and hurried back through the bluebells until she came to the edge of the trees. Her breath hurt in her throat, her mind reeled and then steadied. Before her lay Midwinter, its flat façade, its colonnade lit by the afternoon sun and, in front of it, between her and the meadow, nothing but a wasteland of mud and broken trees.

18

"IT'S good to be back in London. Aren't you glad to be back?" Connie said.

Nancy laid a fire and put a match to it in the sitting room. It was a cold afternoon for August and the air in the flat smelled stale after months of lying empty. "I shall be glad to get on with some work at the Training Bureau again."

Connie hugged her. "You were so good to stay with me like you did. You don't know how grateful I am. And for letting me come here instead of living with Papa. I think it was frightfully decent of him to let me: Don't you?"

"Yes. Very decent," said Nancy. "But then, your papa always does do the decent thing." She wished Connie would stop talking. She was thinking about Ted and really wanted to worry about him in peace; she was afraid his battalion had been posted to France. She refused to think about the pool, could no longer bear to follow the avenues of speculation which had been laid open that afternoon when she had stared into its surface. She had rung the Training Bureau that day and had asked one of the girls to try to trace Grace Hammond, convinced that if she could only discover what Augusta had written in her letter to Grace, she would know the truth about Viner. Had he been murdered? Was it possible this time that reality had exceeded her own, melodramatic inventions? She had avoided Mrs Farringdon at Midwinter, afraid for once of her own imagination, yet aware that, if Ted's father had been involved in Viner's murder, Mrs Farringdon would know more about it than anyone.

Since she was barred from the convalescent wards, Nancy had given her attentions to the estate farm: a further call-out of men in May had rendered it desperately short of labouring men. Nancy had joined the force of women Land Army workers; had worn breeches, boots and leggings and a coarse holland overall and grown brown and hard at the haymaking, too busy all day to think, too exhausted at night to do anything but sleep. But she had made inquiries about Ted in Winchborne and had written to him at his training camp; not about their meeting at the cottage, nor with questions about the wood and the pool, but telling him about her work on the farm, asking him not to turn his back altogether on their friendship. She had not heard from him and knew that she had made a fool of herself.

Nancy shivered and began tidying the sitting room of the flat. She told herself that if she could know that he was safe it would be enough. The trouble was, the Somme had put the fear of God into everyone. She had been with one of the other land-girls to a picture house in Dorchester and seen film of the battle; a landscape of appalling bleakness, of mud and tangles of barbed wire, men marching, scrambling from trenches, going 'over the top', being taken away on stretchers. Nobody knew where the war was going. It was like being in a long nightmare in which events got worse and worse and one began to realise that the awfulness of it might just possibly go on for ever.

Connie, watching her, said, "I don't know whether I want to go back to nursing."

Nancy nodded. "Perhaps you're not ready."

"I thought I might go to see Edith."

Nancy held a cushion to her ribs, regarding Connie sympathetically. "Yes. That's a good idea. There's plenty to do besides nursing. Tell her I'll come into the office tomorrow."

Nancy began to unpack her things when she was alone. She opened drawers and tucked away stockings and underwear and blouses. The flat was large and comfortable. Aubrey had insisted on paying for it. He had insisted too on a further allowance when he agreed that Connie could live with her in London. He was too accommodating, too decent, too much of a gentleman, thought Nancy, and remembered that she had once thought the description desirable. She opened a drawer and saw the black leather binding of Augusta's diaries. Reluctantly she picked one up and turned the pages. Augusta before the Mafeking party, making love to Aubrey. It no longer had the authority to shock her. But by the pool, among the bluebells — that was shocking in its potency and the force with which it now stirred feelings akin to jealousy in her. *To have lain among the bluebells and know that I am loved . . . sweet delirium of love . . . we drowned in the scent of the bluebells.*

Nancy took the diaries into her sitting room and sat in an armchair by the fire. She remembered the stillness of the pool and the beauty of the bluebells in spring. She felt none of the horror of the last time she had looked into its depths, but a sweeping sadness because the wood had been destroyed. She read the Paris entries. How could anyone believe Viner had loved Augusta at all when he had treated her so callously? Yet, who could define the nature of love or separate it from passion, or say it must be gentle, accommodating, reasonable, or kind? Augusta had believed Viner loved her. She had believed his love was stronger than her own. Nancy turned to the final diary entry. *I know he loved me. If only I had loved him just a little more.* She stared at the words. Did Augusta mean that if she had truly loved Viner she would have gone to him in Malaysia — or was there a certainty in her words that something terrible had happened to her lover? Augusta wrote that she dreamed he had come. Dreamed? A morphine-induced delusion, or a pragmatic piece of self-deception?

Nancy closed the book; she supposed she might never find out the whole truth and, with hindsight, she was less certain now that she wanted to. The diary had stirred up thoughts and further anxieties about Ted. She went to the window and looked down on the empty street. She would be glad to get back to the office: she needed to be busy, to keep her mind occupied. She crossed to the fireplace and stared into the yellow flames, remembering the storm at the cottage, kneeling on the hearthrug and Ted saying that he wanted her. She turned restlessly from the fire. She could not go on like this: she was becoming as nervy as Connie. She sat at the desk and took a sheet of notepaper.

Dear Ted . . .

She crumpled the paper and began again.

* * *

Ted's first experience of driving a land-ship had been terrifying. The monster had blocked the road at the camp, awesome in its size and in its potential to strike terror into its keepers as well as into the enemy. Ted had been selected from the Machine-Gun Corps, transferred from motor cycles to the armoured car section; he was selected for driver training, absolved from becoming a gunner, though part of the training had involved guns. He had been relieved to find he could cope with it. The target and bayonet practice was impersonal. The enemy was faceless, inanimate.

The secrecy which surrounded the land-ship gave it an added element of menace; it had been code-named 'tank', to confuse, with vague and harmless images of water-carriers, all but those in the know. Ted concentrated on learning to handle the machine; it was his task to operate the primary gearbox and the clutch and throttle while the commander, seated beside him, steered and gave directions and the secondary gearsmen struggled to co-ordinate their efforts in the rear. Even a small change in direction, with its combination of braking and gear-changing, needed all their strength. The creature lurched about the countryside under the inexperienced hands of its crew, its engine red-hot and roaring, the cabin filling up with the stink of petrol. They sweated in the semidarkness, and the tank reared and bucked and ploughed on with a will of its own as they practised manoeuvres which demolished bushes and banks, crashed over trenches and flattened trees.

Some of the crew had already been in action; they talked with a bleak humour about the Front. "Oh my, I don't want to die," said Smithy, one of the gunners, when, in August, the news came that they were to leave for France.

After Le Havre, there was the long slow train journey to the front line, and more tank manoeuvres, route marches and days of inactivity. They were encamped south of Ypres, in a wood stripped of its greenery and branches and a landscape scarred with ruined farms and villages. The camp was within sound of the guns: one night the whole sky was ignited with a brilliant white light. A raid, someone said. Nothing to worry about. They would soon get used to the sound of shelling.

Harder to get used to was the mud and their first sight of Ypres, a ghost town, and the Salient with its grim associations. Was it really as gruesome as its reputation? Ted saw the ruins of the town, its crumbling walls, a church tower pointing a skeletal finger at the sky and, all around, as far as the eye could see, a desert of stagnant mud, ochre-coloured, pocked with shell-holes. There were no landmarks except stumps of trees; here and there a duckboard track broke the monotony of the landscape and patches of red brick stained the ground where once a building had stood.

And then there were the wounded . . . but one did not dwell on that side of things. Ted knew if he was going to keep his sanity he must keep his mind off the wounded. He could not joke about them with the bitter humour of his companions.

Ted rarely joined in the tank crew's easy banter, and they had soon learned to leave him alone. His silences were interpreted variously as surliness by his superiors, and aloofness by his fellow soldiers. They did not dislike him, but he had gained a reputation for being a bit of a 'dark one', tough. He would not go into a funk or let the team down, but he was also a tough nut to crack.

Ted had not adapted easily to the Army. He had been a loner all his life, lived alone, worked alone, and preferred birds and animals to people. He had been used to working without interference, had taken orders from above, as did most working men, but with the luxury at Midwinter of interpreting most of those orders to suit himself. In the Army there was no room for interpretation: instructions had to be carried out to the letter. There were too many orders which were harsh or stupid or issued for the sole purpose of saving some brass hat's own skin.

Too many senior officers sat on their arses in cushy bunkers, travelled in cushy staff trains, knew nothing at all about tanks. Too many junior officers were overgrown school prefects who talked down to their men with plums in their mouths, whose men swore under their breath that they would shoot them if the Boche did not get to them first.

Ted returned to camp one evening in time for the distribution of the day's post: there was a letter from his uncle in Dorset and — his heart skipped a beat — one from Nancy. He tucked the envelopes in his pocket and, walking across to the tank for greater privacy, leaned against the bulk of one of the gun sponsons, feeling the rivets dig hard into his back. He read the letter from his uncle quickly, skimming the lines about a strike of harvest workers, who wanted more than the previous year's harvest money. The letter from Nancy was only a few days old. He held it for a long while, just staring at the opening words, 'Dearest Ted . . . '

Dearest Ted,
I only ask that if you have any feeling for me at all, you will let me know from time to time that you are alive. You see, I cannot just dismiss what happened between us that day at Keeper's Cottage. I am sure, if we were face to face, you would remind me again of what you saw — a kiss, nothing more.

I was a silly impressionable girl when I met Aubrey. I was blinded by his superior manners and his education, but I soon stopped being a wife to him in any sense of the word. This was his decision, not mine. Aubrey expected me to be grateful for him taking me up. I was expected to immerse my personality in his and forget all notions of self. He talked of my selfish desire for independence. I felt like one of his butterflies, pinned under glass. I think this is how Augusta saw herself too. I have read her diary and I have sometimes hated her and also pitied her for the havoc she caused. But I felt for her, Ted. I know why she broke out like she did.

I don't offer this as an excuse. I am only telling you how it was. If you cannot bring yourself to write, I shall have to accept that our friendship is over, but I hope you won't so easily dismiss it. As for what you saw in the wood long ago. Augusta and Viner in some type of indecency, I can only guess. But Ted, I don't believe that is all that troubles you when you remember them. If I am right, and there is more, and if you ever want to tell me, I shall be there to listen . . .

Ted folded the letter carefully and put it back in his pocket. It had begun to rain again. It pattered on to the tank and through the thin trees as he made his way back through the mud. He thought of the devastation of the wood at Midwinter, the steam engines ploughing up the ground, the sawyers getting nearer to the pool.

He lay in the tent that night with the letter tucked in his breast pocket and the rain drumming on the canvas. Should he reply this time? He believed her about the Lennox boy, but he knew there were too many other obstacles; Midwinter with all its evils would always come between them. He thought of Nancy's firm waist under his hands, lifting her on to the window sill of the cottage, her breasts close to his face. He thought of her kiss and the torment of wanting her soft body, and the sound of the rain on the roof of the tent became that of the rain drumming against the boarded window of his cottage.

* * *

Connie had joined Edith and Nancy on the staff at the women's recruitment office. "Edith didn't come back to the office at all this afternoon," she said as she came into Nancy's sitting room. "Not even after you'd gone home. The other girls were complaining that she's never there." She flopped on to the settee. "How's your headache?"

Nancy folded her letter from Ted and slipped it inside her writing case. "About the same," Her head throbbed with the fact that, after all this time, he had written. He said that he had been in action but his company had been withdrawn because of technical trouble; he was safe; she was not to worry about him. He did not mention Midwinter. The information was meagre, but Nancy was jubilant. "I expect Edith's been campaigning about the Franchise Bill," she said in response to Connie's complaint. "The suffragists are still determined to wear down the government over the vote."

"I expect she was with *Gilbert*," Connie said dryly. "People kept turning up from all over the place to say they'd been sent to the wrong factory and some of them had nowhere to stay, and it's all because she's not there to tell people what to do. We found a hostel with beds to spare for one night, but I'm to beg you to go in early tomorrow and sort things out."

"I doubt they rely on *me*," smiled Nancy, but she was pleased by the idea that she was becoming indispensable to them. She put away her writing case. At least she knew that he was alive. She could immerse herself in work and forget all about him. But, as she lay in bed that night, she knew she could not forget, nor would she stop worrying about him, and in the morning she wrote again: a carefully lighthearted, sisterly sort of letter.

She posted it on her way to the Training Bureau. "Who are you writing to in France?" said Connie, peering over her shoulder curiously.

"One of the Midwinter staff," Nancy said. "They appreciate letters from home." She walked on stiffly and hoped Connie would not ask any more questions.

She found the office crowded with women who milled around in confusion. The lobby was piled with suitcases and bags and smelled of wet clothes, for it was raining. Nancy set Connie and the other assistants to making lists, and began to sort the women according to their skills and needs: those who sought work in munitions factories; those from outside London who needed accommodation as well as work.

"By the way," said one of the assistants as Nancy passed her desk. "I've ferreted out some information on the woman you wanted to find out about."

"Woman?" repeated Nancy blankly, distracted briefly from the hubbub in the room.

The girl searched through the papers on her desk and pulled out a pamphlet. "Grace Hammond. She's a long-standing heroine of the suffragette movement: hunger strikes, the cat-and-mouse act —" she handed the pamphlet to Nancy — "it's all in here. She had to retire from committee work because of poor health. Like the Pankhursts, she saw it all."

Nancy read the leaflet swiftly: it advertised a talk at a North London suffrage group headquarters later that month at which Grace Hammond would be the principal speaker. She stared at the name on the paper with a sense of having suddenly turned another page of Augusta's diary.

At that moment Edith arrived. She was rain-soaked and suspiciously red-eyed as she looked around the office, taking in the accusing stares of the assistants and the women who stood by the wall with suitcases at their feet.

"Oh, no. Is something wrong?"

"There were *fifteen* girls yesterday evening," said one of the other women pointedly. "They came back this morning, all totally confused as to what they were supposed to be doing."

"I'll deal with it." Edith took off her hat and coat and hung them on the stand.

"Nancy already has."

Edith glanced guiltily again at the women by the wall.

"Don't worry. They're the last," said Nancy. "And they know where they are going. I told them they might wait here until it stops raining."

Edith threw her a look of desperation, "Thank you. I don't know what I'd — " She broke off and hurried into her room and closed the door.

Connie said sotto voce, "I told you. It isn't votes for women which occupies her these days."

Nancy sat at her typewriter, tucking the information about Grace Hammond into her skirt pocket. The knowledge that Grace could supply the key to what had happened to Viner filled her with a peculiar apprehension.

It was Gilbert who solved the mystery about Edith: Nancy bumped into him near the War Office a few days later. She had been thinking about the coming North London meeting and did not see him at first.

"Nancy! How charming you look. Are you going my way? Come and talk to me." They headed towards St James's Park. "Have you been to see Aubrey?"

"Aubrey and I rarely communicate these days, Gilbert," she said. "I've been to the War Office on women's business."

"Of course — you work for Edith's organisation." He looked away, lifting and tapping his rolled umbrella against his shoulder. "Marvellous job you are doing. Just the thing. You ladies have worked dashed hard these past two years."

Nancy looked at him. Gilbert had changed; he was as dapper as ever, more respectable these days in a city suit and bowler, but the war had hardened him, as it had hardened everyone. "Gilbert, has something happened? Edith seems terribly low," A thought struck her. "It's not Stephen?"

"Stephen?"

"Her brother. He's in France."

"Of course. No. He's fighting fit apparently."

"You see, she's been crying rather a lot lately . . . " Nancy said.

He halted by the lake. He looked at her and attempted a light laugh. "The truth is, old girl, Edith and I have sort of reached an impasse and, now the time's come, she's finding it hard to let go."

"Oh, Gilbert. You are a wretch."

"No, I'm not. Truly I'm not. I think the world of her. But I can't take much more of this feminist business."

"You hypocrite! And I thought you were sincere about the vote."

"I know. Beastly, isn't it? But, I mean, a person doesn't like to play second fiddle."

"I suppose not," said Nancy, wondering what it was about Gilbert that prevented her from disliking him, when he was so patently shallow.

"Now you despise me. And I thought you, of all people, might understand."

She stared at him. "Why ever should I?"

"Isn't that why you and Aubrey parted — because he was too set in his ways, too wrapped up in his work?"

"Oh, I'm sure it was more complicated than that." Nancy turned to look at the lake.

"Well, at least *you've* never been a feminist."

Nancy laughed. "Is that supposed to be a compliment?"

"I mean you've got your head screwed on firmly. We all thought old Aubrey was insane when he married you — no offence, old girl — but I soon saw you were sound. Strong-willed, but sound. I told Singer: that young lady will never get carried away by any nonsense."

Did you indeed? thought Nancy. And what does one mean by nonsense? Was Augusta carried away by nonsense? What about Stephen and the Moment of Madness in the summer-house? Is what I feel for Ted foolish nonsense? She looked at him as they walked on. "Gilbert — you remember Augusta. Did she love Aubrey once?"

He considered the question. "I think she did in her way. But Aubrey was far too dull for her. Augusta needed to glitter."

"Do you think she loved John Viner?"

"You know about that? Oh, I suppose she thought she did. Augusta needed romantic interruptions. That's what Viner was — a dark interlude."

"Did you know there had been several such interludes, that Viner wasn't the first?"

"Good Lord, yes," he said breezily. "Dear Augusta was undoubtedly a whore. Aubrey was away so much, and Augusta was so — what shall we say — energetic? What did he expect?"

"Poor Aubrey."

Gilbert looked away, and Nancy wondered with a swift insight whether he had a more direct experience of Augusta's need for romantic diversions than he was ever likely to tell her. They walked on until they came to the Mall, "Oh, Gilbert. Why is it that, just when we think we have things clear, something comes along to turn everything on its head?"

"Are we talking about love?"

"I suppose that's got something to do with it." She smiled wryly. They had reached the point of parting and she held out her hand.

"You're abandoning me," Gilbert said. "And you haven't told me what to do about *my* love life yet."

She regarded him for a second. "Marry Marjorie. She's the only woman, besides me, who can see through you and yet still loves you." She released his hand. "Is Frank Singer going to dig at Midwinter? You heard that Aubrey has had my lovely wood flattened?"

"I have heard. It was where Aubrey's keeper and his boy tripped over Augusta and Viner *in flagrante*. Did you know?"

Nancy nodded. "Oh, yes. I know."

★ ★ ★

Nancy entered the hall, which buzzed with female voices. The meeting was already opening and she took a seat at the end of one of the rows of chairs, searching the faces of the women on the platform for some mark of recognition, something from Augusta's diary which would immediately distinguish Grace Hammond from the others. She fixed all her attention on the woman who rose to her feet after the chairwoman's introduction: a frail, undistinguished creature with a mouse-like face and mouse hair and dressed in a mouse-brown coat and hat. Was this the bold rebel who had defied her husband, shared bottles of whisky with Augusta, become a heroine of the suffragette movement? Yet, as Grace Hammond began to speak, a shock ran through Nancy: she sat on the edge of her seat, wondering how so much energy could emanate from such a fragile source.

When the speakers had finished and people were getting up from their seats to gossip, Nancy made her way towards the platform. She turned to a woman who had been sitting next to Grace. "I wonder if I might speak to Mrs Hammond."

The woman smiled. "Tell me your name and I'll introduce you."

Nancy followed her through the crush of people and waited until Grace held out her hand and, with a puzzled frown, said, "Do I know you? Where are you from?"

Nancy told her, watching for a reaction

as she said the name 'Winchborne'. Grace Hammond's eyes were a steely blue in her thin face; she stared at Nancy keenly. "You say you're called Farringdon?"

Nancy nodded. "I married Aubrey Farringdon. I think you knew his first wife."

"You mean Augusta?" Grace said softly, with a peculiar catch in her voice.

"I wonder, Mrs Hammond, if we might talk?"

They went into an ante-room. Grace was alert, slightly suspicious, as she closed the door and leaned against it. The room was bare except for a table and a stack of chairs against the wall. Nancy perched on the corner of the table. "It feels very strange finally to meet you."

"I must tell you that Augusta was my friend," Grace said sharply, "I don't know what your husband has told you, but I will not let you speak ill of her."

"Then perhaps I should tell you that I'm estranged from my husband. Augusta played a large part in that estrangement."

"Augusta is dead."

"Her spirit is very much alive."

Mrs Hammond smiled and relaxed a little. "Yes, Augusta once had a great deal of spirit."

"I feel I've come to know her well." Nancy paused. "I've learned that you went to Winchborne to look for her."

"I didn't know she had been so ill. I went to the house, but the family were taken up with the business of the funeral, and by then they had closed ranks."

"That sounds very typical."

Grace's expression was still watchful. "My dear, what exactly do you want from me?"

Nancy took a deep breath. "I want to know the truth about what happened when John Viner came back for Augusta. I want to know what Augusta wrote in her last letter to you about a terrible thing she thought she had done."

The other woman gasped. "You know about that?"

"Augusta left a diary. I found it among her books." Nancy drew the volumes of the diaries from a bag by her feet. "By a miracle, no one else knows anything about them or I'm sure they would have been destroyed."

Grace stared at the diaries as Nancy placed them on the table. "She wrote about the love affair?"

"She set down the whole story. But towards the end her account disintegrates. She was very confused."

Grace looked up. "Do you know why she died?"

"A broken heart?"

"A peculiarly romantic idea, but I think so too. At least, it may have been instrumental in her illness. I believe Viner had become the most important person in her life, and she fell mortally sick and died when she could not or would not have him."

"Would not? You mean because she would not go to him in Malaysia?"

"Perhaps." Grace looked away.

Nancy leaned forward earnestly, "Mrs Hammond, will you take the diaries and read them? And, when you have read them, perhaps you would talk to me again?"

The other woman picked up the books reverentially, "You would entrust them to me, a complete stranger?"

Nancy smiled. "You're no stranger to

me. I've read the diaries, remember. And I know that you were Augusta's friend."

* * *

Grace phoned Nancy some days later. She arranged to return the diaries one afternoon at Nancy's flat. She came into the sitting room solemnly and sat in the window seat. Nancy occupied herself with the business of arranging teacups and pouring tea, recognising in her own preoccupation with minutiae that she was more nervous than she had been for a long time.

Grace placed the diaries on the table between them. "Thank you," she said at last. "Thank you for letting me read them." They both stared at the books as if they had some mystical quality. "I begged her to go with him, you know. It was only afterwards that I saw my advice had been misguided."

"I think she was afraid to go with Viner."

"You're right," said Grace. "As I came to know Augusta better, I began to understand her nature. I learned that she thrived on living on the dangerous edges of precipices, but that she would never be able to step right off the brink. She was full of enthusiasms, always taking up with new fads, then dropping them as quickly. She never really took feminism seriously; she was too fond of playing up to men. She flirted shamelessly, had men eating out of her hand; but Augusta was a child underneath it all: she desperately needed to be loved. Viner provided excitement, and I believe she loved him obsessively, but her husband offered her the kind of security she really craved."

"Did you know she had had other affairs?"

"No. But I am not surprised. She had so many men in love with her, and that place and the Farringdons would have driven anyone into the arms of a waiting lover."

"I think Aubrey cared for Augusta very much."

"Perhaps she loved him too in her way, when she recognised how much he meant to her. He was the parent, the father, the one who loved her no matter how badly she behaved. She had learned to understand her own frailties and she knew she was weak in not going to Viner. He had to come to her. He had to prove he loved her. I understand her better now," Grace paused, toying with her teacup.

"Why did she love him?"

"Why indeed? A peculiar fascination? Why do we women fall in love with any man? They are all flawed, and Viner was more flawed than most. I found out about him after Augusta's death. The diary does not exaggerate: he was a pig of a man; he had mistresses in every country in Europe. If he was murdered, he probably deserved it."

Nancy drew in her breath sharply. "So, you too think it was murder?"

"I know nothing that could prove anything. But there was the letter." Grace opened her handbag.

Nancy's heart leaped. "You've kept it?"

"You think me sentimental? I kept all the letters which reached me. Augusta was right, by the way: the family had intercepted my final correspondence with her, along with his. They would have known exactly what arrangements Viner had made to meet her." She looked down at the letter in her lap. "When I received this and knew that she was so ill I decided to go to Dorset. But it was too late. When I got there, she was already dead." She handed the letter to Nancy. "If, like me, you suspect Viner came to a bad end, I think you should read it."

Nancy took the letter.

Midwinter
Winchborne, Dorset
Sunday 18 May, 1902

My dear Grace,

Yesterday I had the strangest dream, I thought that John was on his way to me at last. I lay all evening in fear and trembling. All my desires centred on his coming, yet, now that the moment was here, what could I do? I felt powerless to act. Perhaps he came while I was sleeping? My mind wanders so. But, while I slept, I had another dream. I shall set it down and, Grace, you must tell me what it means.

I lie in bed in my dream but am

quite awake. I hear a sound from the wood such as the keeper makes when he is shooting. Then another sound, a cry, as if a hare is caught in a keeper's snare. No one stirs in the house. No servants run to investigate. I lie, hearing the echoes of the scream. It is nothing. The keeper is out shooting crows. Then another sound: the screech of an owl? The hare in its trap? But can a dumb beast cry out a name in its agony? "Augusta." Like a voice calling to me from hell. Then a second shot. I go to the window. Lights this time from below, and servants appear on the terrace; Aubrey's mama calls, "It is nothing. The keeper is shooting vermin. Go back to bed, everyone."

I wake, and my body is cold as ice. The night is silent. I am at the window and nothing stirs, but dimly I see Aubrey's mama; she has on her coat and a shawl over her head, and I know it is his mama, because for a second she looks up and seems to see me at the window before she is gone, not to the house, but into the blackness of the lawn.

What does it mean? Did he come while I was sleeping?

Another strange tale for you, this time from Aubrey's mama. She comes to me this morning and says that she has done for him once and for all, the vermin has been exterminated, he has gone away from me for ever. She laughs when I cry that it isn't true. She says, Oh Augusta. You fool. You would believe anything. Do you think a man would come, like a fox in the night, for your poor sick body? She says, do I think he would still want me if he could see me now? Do I believe Aubrey loves me, because he forgives my untold debaucheries? He has gone away. She repeats this very forcefully. I ask, Who has gone away? Aubrey? He is in London. Not Aubrey, she says, but John. The keeper has been out hunting vermin and now the fox hangs on his gibbet.

She denies all knowledge of the conversation this afternoon. But, Grace, I tremble at what this means. Tell me. I beg you, tell me. Have I done a terrible thing?

Nancy handed back the letter, her heart beating painfully. But what terrible thing? "Do you suppose she really thought that what she had heard was a dream?"

"She was confused. That much is clear. But Augusta was also adept at self-deception. Perhaps, somehow, Viner got a message to her. If so, and she knew he was coming . . . "

Nancy considered the implications. "If she knew he was coming and deliberately did nothing, it would be as if she had lured him into a trap." That would indeed have been a 'terrible thing', enough to turn Augusta's mind to the welcoming arms of death and provoke the desolate cry, *If only I had loved him just a little more*. She turned to Grace. "You went to Midwinter. Didn't you try to find out what had happened that night?" She paused. "Did you speak to the keeper?"

"I tried, but the story was that he had a severe chill and was confined to his cottage, too sick to see anyone. I quizzed the servants, and they said the man's son was taken with the same fever and was similarly confined. Perhaps the boy had heard or seen something of the shooting, *if* shooting there was."

"Oh, I think there was. Don't you?" Nancy thought of Ted's strangeness when she had asked how many men he had seen die, his, 'no one thinks about what it really means, how dirty and bloody killing really is', and his behaviour at Keeper's Cottage. She looked at Grace. "Weren't the servants suspicious about the gamekeeper's sudden illness?"

"I really think they were not. Servants as a class tend to accept what they are told. And there was a fever going about that spring."

"But didn't you do anything?"

"There seemed no purpose in it, once I knew that Augusta was dead. I was too full of my own sadness and moved by the anguish of those who had known her. Your husband was beside himself with grief. I soon saw that if Viner had been shot it wouldn't benefit anyone if I were to find out more, for it could only do Augusta's memory harm if her adultery became public knowledge. So, in the end I did nothing. Augusta was dead. Later, my investigations about Viner's career led me to believe that, if he were dead too, his departure would be no great loss to the world. Those I spoke to believed Viner had returned to Malaysia. What proof had I that he had been murdered, except the wandering writings of a sick woman?" Grace put the letter in her bag. She looked at Nancy. "You think I was wrong not to tell anybody about my suspicions?"

"In the eyes of the law you were."

"But was I morally wrong? Now that you know as much as I knew then, what are you going to do about it all these years later?"

"I don't know."

"And there are Augusta's children. If you were to drag it all up, wouldn't it harm them? Connie, is it — and Hugo?"

"Hugo is in France," said Nancy. "He is fighting on the Somme."

"Ah," said Grace. "At least Augusta was spared that."

* * *

Connie still missed Gus with a pain which had dulled but which never quite went away. The work at the Training Bureau helped during the day. One felt removed from the war in a way which had not been possible at the hospital: there were no wounded soldiers, no talk of the Front and dying. Everyone was keen and busy and talked of the future: how when the war was over women would continue to work in factories and offices and the Civil Service, and be inspectors and supervisors. In the evenings, at Nancy's flat, it was harder to ignore the pain, Nancy was kind and sympathetic, and Connie did not know what she would have done without her support at Midwinter, but it was so quiet and dull in the flat with just the two of them; it was almost as bad as living with her papa. Connie had found a new set of girl-friends. She had met them through one of the women at the recruitment office: society girls who were up in London to do their bit for the war effort. They knew all the best restaurants for jollies and they held studio parties, with wine and dancing almost every night. The atmosphere was gay and flirtatious; they talked about telepathy and table-rapping, laughed about betting and smoking and exchanged their favourite cocktail recipes; they discussed acquaintances with malicious abandon and things which her papa would think quite outrageous, such as Sapphists and sodomites and where one could get hold of cocaine.

She did not tell Nancy about the parties, but Nancy knew, she could tell; she was letting her 'have her head', hoping the novelty of her new friends would wear off. Connie hoped so too some mornings when, with a hangover, she ached for Gus and remembered his saying how small and petty London was after the intensity of being in the front line and how he disliked people who chased pleasure and money.

Stephen's letters helped, which surprised Connie sometimes, because Gus had been in the same battalion as Stephen and the association should have been painful. He had begun writing in the summer, to cheer her up she had supposed; but then he said once how much her replies brightened his day, that no one else wrote to him except his family and that Edith's letters were all about politics.

Stephen did not talk disparagingly of home: he wrote about missing Dorset. He did not say much about what was happening on the Somme, except that he was glad his company had been in reserve. It was strange for him to talk like that, as if self-preservation were the thing, when a year ago everyone had wanted to be in the thick of it and get at the Boche. He asked if she had news of Hugo, and she had. Connie thought of her brother's strange, bright accounts of stoicism under shell-fire and jokes about the squalor of trench life, suffused with an unconvincing, almost desperate patriotism. She tried to picture him in France, but she knew that no one in England could imagine what it was like on the Somme after the weeks of carnage.

* * *

War for Hugo had meant becoming a hero. He had invented a character, Hugo Farringdon, who would be indifferent to death and injury, who in some significant way might even singlehandedly change the course of the war. The Battle of the Somme was to have been his stab at heroism, just as for the commanders it was to have made history as the Big Push which won the war. The week-long bombardment before the combined attack was the heaviest the world had known: it would smash the wire entanglements and enemy guns so that the first and second waves of the attack could advance through the breached defences in an unstoppable rolling-up operation.

The men had gone down in their hundreds on the first day of July; whole battalions had crumpled under enemy shell-fire. Hugo, involved in the greatest adventure of all time, had seen all his boyish dreams shattered.

War had been the ground shooting skyward and raining clods of earth and lumps of human bodies; it was the sound of shells and the cries of the wounded. War was a wasteland of blasted trees and ruined buildings, of mud and shell-holes and barbed wire; it was a sense of helplessness and it was being afraid.

One early morning in September, three weeks since his platoon had been out in rest camp, Hugo waited for the signal to go over the parapet. Every nerve in his body was strung to its limit. He gripped his rifle to keep his hands steady, but every shell-burst made him want to scream out, "Not again, not again." What if he were hit this time? He was afraid of being ripped as he had seen others ripped by machine-guns and shrapnel. He was afraid of being a coward. He hoped that, if he were hit, it would not hurt, that he would die quickly and, if not instantaneously, at least quietly and not make a lot of noise, moaning and yelling. Their captain was sweating. You could see it ooze in globules and trickle down his face. His expression was strained and his mouth worked in anticipation of zero hour, his hand raised for the count-down, then, "Over the top. Good luck!" and they were moving.

"Keep up. Keep up!" Hugo ran. Keep up with the others, show them that he was not afraid, on towards the crack-crack of machine-gun fire and the grim concrete block of the strongpoint. He heard the man beside him moan as he went down. The sky was spattered with dark splashes as shells exploded in a burst of sound. He ran on. He wanted to go home. He wanted Papa. He heard the shout to take temporary cover and, tumbling into a shell-hole, lay on his back staring up at the sky.

There was an eerie silence and the sun was shining. It was a beautiful summer's day. From his cover Hugo could see nothing but the sky; it was as if the battle had disappeared. The silence began to prey on him. Where were the rest of the platoon? Had the destruction been so terrible that he was the only one left alive? A blind terror gripped him so that he could not move; his arms and legs felt too heavy and were slipping down into the mud and water. Perhaps he had been hit without realising it and his whole body was paralysed. No one would come to find him; he would be left there in the shell-hole to die.

The noise had started up again. Over the edge of his cover Hugo glimpsed men running, and then a bullet hit the earth above him and sent a shower of dirt into his face. He shook it from his eyes and spat out saliva. There was an explosion behind him, the side of the shell-hole erupted and he was scrambling clear of the cascade of dirt, pushing himself free and upward, out of the shell-hole and into the open.

⋆ ⋆ ⋆

It was a Saturday, and the sun was shining on the yellowing leaves of the sycamore trees outside. Connie was trying on a new dress, a daring, sheer, lacy thing with a beautiful low-cut collar. The telephone rang. She was still fastening up the buttons of the new dress when she lifted the receiver from its hook. Papa's voice sounded strange, as if he had a heavy cold, then she understood what he was saying.

She found Nancy in the kitchen, cutting up apples for a pie, her hair falling into her eyes. Nancy looked up with a distracted sort of smile, as if she had been thinking or worrying about something; she brushed a lock of hair away with a floury hand and her smile died slowly as she took a step towards her. "Connie? Whatever's wrong?"

Connie remembered when she was little, how she used to steal into the kitchens and beg pieces of apple from Mrs Cassell and then take them back to the nursery to share with Hugo. He had never dared go through the green baize doors with her, but sat upstairs, waiting for her to come back and empty her apron on to the counterpane.

Connie went to Nancy with dry eyes. "Hugo's missing. Believed killed. That means they're sure of it. It always means they're dead." She felt Nancy's arms hold her safe. She was the mother she had never had, the mother Hugo would never see again.

* * *

Stephen sat in the dugout and read Nancy's letter. She said the family were going to have some sort of a memorial service for Hugo next spring at Winchborne. The mud on his clothes had soiled the page and smeared the word 'memorial'. His hand trembled with weariness. The men had been clearing up corpses all day, digging them out of the mud and from shell-holes filled with ochre water; filthy, stinking bodies: some of them had been there since the start of the Somme fighting four months ago. He had felt no revulsion, not a shudder. His men, grey-faced with fatigue, dead-eyed, got on with the task of slipping around in the mud. The unreality of it helped: one became immune to the sights. He had delivered the dead men's paybooks to Brigade HQ, where officers, far from the front line, talked about 'pushes' and keeping up the men's morale and how frightfully overworked they all were. They issued edicts about dress, straps unbuttoned, untidy equipment. Standards were slipping. It had been noticed. Must keep the men up to scratch, old thing.

Missing believed killed. He would have to write to Connie, say all the right sympathetic things. He was used to writing letters to the relatives of men in his platoon: to mothers and fathers robbed of sons, and wives turned into widows. A fine soldier. Did his duty for his country willingly. He suffered no pain.

His name will live for ever more.

He tried to remember Hugo, a schoolboy, mad about his horse. What was it? Wellington? No, Nelson. Probably vanished long ago in the general slaughter. And he had been keen on fossils. There had been a row once because Hugo had gone fossil-hunting in the wood at Midwinter. That had been the start of the business with Nancy. His fault.

He wrote to Connie. He told her he had been promoted to captain. Once one got a name for being able to keep one's head one got marked for promotion. "See as much of Nancy as you can," he wrote. "She's a capital girl when you are low." He said he would remember Hugo as a fine young man. Then he did not think about him any more.

19

AUBREY drove along the road to Midwinter. He looked in the car's mirror at Nancy and Connie sitting behind him. He missed Browne, he thought, looking out through the windscreen. He missed the Wolseley and the luxury of being driven, yet he could hardly remember Browne's face these days. One found that happened after a while. He felt a chill come over him. Would it be the same with Hugo? Would his son become a dim memory, so that he had to rely on photographs to remind him of those features permanently sealed in their youth?

He glanced again in the mirror, Nancy looked pretty in a black costume and hat; much older these days, but the war had done that to young people. Connie looked about thirty instead of seventeen; she wore too much lip colour which was garish against her pale skin.

Strange, but he felt no bitterness

against Nancy any more. He supposed he had in the end believed her about that business over the Lennox boy, for Nancy was a different proposition from Augusta. What had he seen — a kiss between a girl and a young, war-torn soldier in need of human comfort? The boy might be dead, like Hugo, tomorrow; might be dead already for all he knew. Aubrey's mind was thrown back to the first time he had brought Nancy to Midwinter. How captivated he had been by her youth and innocent charm. Oh, he had been in love with her, had been confused by her, but he had never loved her as he had loved Augusta. The pain of losing Nancy had almost gone, but the memories of the terrible shock of that first loss still had the power to torture him.

He drew in his breath. The wood was gone; there was a clear, crisp view down the hill to Midwinter, an irregular slope of stunted trees and broken saplings with the quarry pool hidden in a dip of rough ground. So that was that. No more memories. Yet Aubrey felt uneasy: the house looked vulnerable, exposed. He avoided the mirror and Nancy's expression. She had not forgiven him for destroying the wood.

As he turned the car into the drive, Aubrey shrank a little from the prospect of greeting his mother. He had not been back to Midwinter since the previous summer. She had refused at first to believe that Hugo had gone, had held out against the final act of a memorial service. She was so damn blind about the war, glad that Asquith had been forced to resign that winter, scathing about Lloyd George's abilities as PM, but convinced that the military, and Haig in particular, knew what they were doing. She really believed that her rigid observation of 'meatless days', of economising on coal and turning Midwinter's acres over to the cultivation of potatoes would influence the course of the war. The new year had brought little hope in more informed circles; a weariness had set in at the War Office, a sense of dogged persistence without optimism. The slaughter of the Somme Battle had achieved nothing, and had tailed off in mud and ignominy.

His mama came on to the steps to greet them as they came to a halt on the gravel. She looked as she always looked, ageless and elegant and in command.

* * *

Nancy studied Mrs Farringdon. Could she really have been capable of arranging Viner's death? She remembered the pool, remembered Ted saying that his father had been a harsh but not a wicked man. His mother had had her favourites, Aubrey once said: she had paid her keeper well, had paid Ted well too, after his father's death, to watch the pool and keep his silence. Nancy looked at Aubrey, pale beside her. Had he been a party to whatever his mother had arranged with her keeper? She dismissed the idea. No. Not Aubrey, she was certain of it. In any case, he had been in London at the time. And yet, there was something, some memory of the wood and its pool which still had the power to haunt him. She stared up at the grim façade of Midwinter. Was she really any nearer the truth? Grace Hammond had decided to do nothing about her suspicions, and Nancy knew now that she too would do nothing — not because of Connie, nor even because of Aubrey, but because of her feelings for Ted.

He had not written for months, but she knew that he was in a tank battalion, the secret weapon which had excited everyone's hopes. She had seen a film of the machines in action: nothing faked, the film had promised, and she had seen the acres of mud in which horses floundered and men sank to their knees.

Nancy entered the house with Aubrey and Connie and breathed the familiar smell of the wards mixed with the oppressive smell of Midwinter itself. She had supposed that Aubrey's mother would ignore her, as she had on her previous stay. She had not expected an all-out attack, but Mrs Farringdon had a bee in her bonnet about spies. Did Aubrey know that there was a confederacy working in the country which was out to demoralise the nation? It had already infiltrated the War Cabinet and the Civil Service and it was now working through various organisations, including the women's war-employment agencies, spreading doom and gloom about the war.

Connie said she thought the nation did not need much demoralising: the government and the military had succeeded in doing that with their own incompetence.

"You must be vigilant, Aubrey," Mrs Farringdon warned. "The Unseen Hand is everywhere. It's a viper in the bosom which is eating at the nation's will to win." She cast a meaningful glance at Nancy.

"Do I by any chance embody this menace?" said Nancy. "The snake in the grass, the viper in the bosom?"

"The evidence speaks for itself. You've enticed Connie into your clutches and persuaded Aubrey to let you come back to Midwinter."

"Because of Hugo, Mama," Aubrey said wearily. "And Nancy did not 'persuade' me, as you put it. Might we avoid squabbling for the next few days, if only out of respect for Hugo's memory?"

Nancy glanced round the hall. There were hand-made bills posted up everywhere: 'Are we downhearted? No!';

'We shall grind them down!' and a bulletin board by the entrance, on which were pinned photographs and newspaper cuttings: 'Thrilling Story of Bravery . . .', 'Heroic Sons of Dorset', 'Pictures from the Firing Line'.

Nancy felt a grudging admiration for Mrs Farringdon's unshakeable faith in it all as she followed Roberts upstairs to the Yellow Room.

* * *

The rash of slogans had crept into the dining room: 'Eat Slowly, You Will Need Less Food', 'Eat Less and Save Shipping'. A pledge card — 'In honour bound we adopt the scale of voluntary rations' — stood in a frame at the centre of the table.

"Do you remember, Grandmama, when the war began, everyone was so sure it would be over in a matter of months?" Connie picked at her voluntary ration of one potato and thin fillet of haddock.

Mrs Farringdon frowned. "I won't allow defeatist talk here, Connie."

Aubrey gave an unexpectedly bitter

laugh. "I shouldn't be surprised if it doesn't go on for ever. It's become a war of attrition, of pointless slaughter."

Nancy glanced at him anxiously. The death of Hugo had depressed him so. He looked old and tired though he was only forty-seven. They were all so old in spirit. People were aware of the transience of life in a way they had never been before. Her own generation talked about being robbed of their youth, Aubrey's and the next generation had adopted a world-weary sense of hopelessness, except for Mrs Farringdon, who, though positively antique, hardly changed at all: she was as unyielding and uncompromising as ever. It occurred to Nancy, drawn back to the memory of Augusta's letter, that if Harry Powers had shot Viner he would have had little choice in the matter: Mrs Farringdon's orders were always absolute. It would have been a matter of duty, of loyalty, if not exactly to Country, then to Mrs Farringdon's embodiment of it at Midwinter.

Mrs Farringdon was still preoccupied with the unseen hand of subversion. She shook her head at Aubrey's pessimism and turned to Nancy. "This is your doing. All because he allowed you to worm your way into his affections again. Aubrey is weak. He was always weak. He would do well to listen to my advice."

"As I listened to it in the past, Mama?" Aubrey said with an odd bitterness. "If only I had followed my instincts . . . "

He did not finish, and Nancy looked swiftly at Mrs Farringdon, but she gave no indication that she had observed Aubrey's peculiar tone as she turned on him. "You were weak-willed over Augusta, and you let the pattern repeat itself all over again. Why couldn't you be like your papa? He was a splendid, honourable man. Or like Hugo, who died doing his duty — "

"Mama — please."

"What a courageous boy! Aren't you proud of him? To have served and died for his country. A glorious sacrifice. No man can do greater than this. Aren't you ashamed that people will say that your son was more of a man than you are?"

Nancy folded her napkin and stood. "I'm sorry Aubrey, I can't listen to this any more."

The colour had drained from Aubrey's face. He banged his fist on the table. "My son's death was a tragedy. There was no glory in it. All that promise squandered! Wasted!"

"Death is never a tragedy," said Mrs Farringdon with steely composure. "It is either noble, as in war, or it is God's just retribution on the sinner, or it provides a happy release at the end of a long and useful life when one goes to meet one's Maker. I am not afraid of death, nor of His judgement on me."

Nancy left the table.

Mrs Farringdon called after her, "Aubrey's papa would have done the right thing. He would have fought for his sovereign and his country. I hope you're satisfied with the way you have contributed to my son's degeneracy."

Nancy nodded to Roberts who, maintaining the expression of an automaton, opened the doors. She heard them close firmly behind her as she reached the stairs. There was a murmur of voices from the convalescent ward, muted. Upstairs, a gramophone played Gilbert and Sullivan. She went straight to Hugo's room, for in a sentimental way she wanted to say a last goodbye. The small dreary bedroom had been kept ready for his return. His books were stacked on the shelves by the fireplace, the bed was made up with a blue and grey patchwork counterpane, his collections of fossils and geological specimens filled a glass wall cabinet, and a few were scattered on the table by the window, as if he had left off arranging them suddenly.

How little she had really known the boy, Nancy thought as she walked about the room. A passion for Conan Doyle — had that been evident? Stevenson, *Ivanhoe*, *Tom Brown's Schooldays*, a photograph of Scott of the Antarctic propped by the bed and, above the plain oak bedhead, an amateur oil-colour of a horse, so badly done as to render the animal unrecognisable as Nelson; but she remembered Connie painting it, and the fossils and Hugo's ambition for a museum. She picked up a large piece of ammonite, neatly labelled in ink: "Upper inferior oolite, section of whorl, found near Sherborne, March 1915." She weighed it in her hand and then put it down. In an open box, on a bed of cotton wool, lay a number of small red square stones. The box was labelled: 'Clay tesserae. Roman? Found at Midwinter, July 1914'. Nancy picked one up and curled her fingers over its hard edges. Dear, dear Hugo.

She was startled when the door opened. She swung round to face Aubrey.

"Nancy!"

She put the tile in its box. "I just wanted to remind myself."

"Of course." He cleared his throat. "I've been meaning to thank you for travelling down with us. It can't have been easy for you to return to Midwinter."

"Hugo was very dear to me."

"I know. And I'm glad you wanted to come for the memorial service."

She looked round the room and said gently, "I'll leave you alone."

He held out a restraining hand as she walked past him to the door, "I'm sorry about the scene at dinner. You know what she's like. It's just Mama's way."

"For goodness' sake, Aubrey. You don't have to apologise for her. Even by your mother's standards, the outburst was unforgivable."

"The war has upset her, it has upset us all, and she was terribly fond of Hugo."

Nancy looked round at the poignant collection of fossils. "It's so unfair, and such a shameful waste. He had a good brain — and so much to look forward to."

Aubrey sat on the bed with its patchwork counterpane. "Mama had a point, you know."

"What? That I have contributed to your degeneracy? I can't think of anyone less deserving of the term 'degenerate' than you."

He looked at her seriously. "No, not that. Since Hugo's death I've been conscious of a sense of inadequacy. There are men older than me joining up."

Nancy felt a bleakness come over her. "Probably harassed by selfish old ladies who want to boast they have heroes for sons before they themselves die."

"Or men who have stood helplessly by and seen their own sons go to the slaughter."

"That's just bunkum."

He smiled. "Dear Nancy. You always

were so forthright."

"You think another pointless sacrifice would square things?"

He spread his fingers and stroked the counterpane and his look was despairing, "I don't know. I really don't."

* * *

Nancy hoped she had talked him out of it. She walked behind him with Connie into the plain little church at Winchborne. Mrs Farringdon held on to Aubrey's arm but walked erect as ever, in a long black coat with a fur collar and a hat trimmed with ostrich feathers, which was very large and slightly eccentric. Most of the village had turned out for the service; they swelled the congregation of family, friends and servants, along with a few of the Midwinter convalescents and soldiers on leave.

Edith had come from London to attend the service. She looked pale and tired. Since Gilbert had thrown her over and, it was rumoured, had asked Marjorie Benson to marry him, Edith had pushed herself relentlessly into the work of the Active Suffragists. She returned to Midwinter with Mr and Mrs Lennox after the ceremony. She kissed Aubrey and then Nancy.

"Poor Aubrey." Mrs Lennox's lips wobbled uncertainly as she drew Nancy aside. "I know how he feels. It could so easily have been our own dear boy." She fished for her handkerchief in a black-beaded reticule. "I have too vivid an imagination, I'm afraid, Nancy."

"Have you heard from Stephen?" Nancy asked.

"Yes. He was going to try to come home, but they have cancelled his leave yet again for some ghastly 'push' or other. Now the Americans are in the war, he was hoping the Army would take more notice of things like leave."

Edith interrupted her. "Stephen would so much have liked to have been here today. You must come to the house, Nancy. Tomorrow? Will you be staying at Midwinter until tomorrow?"

Nancy glanced at Aubrey. "No. I shall be going back to London tonight."

* * *

Nancy stayed in London all that spring. She heard that Aubrey had applied for a commission in the Army and, later, that he had been accepted. "Why won't someone stop him?" said Connie, after she had been to visit him one day.

"Perhaps we should try to be proud of him, seeing as his mind is made up," said Nancy.

"But Papa won't last five minutes in the Army," Connie wailed. "Whatever is he thinking of? By the way," she added, with a swift change of mood, "did you know that Edith has been visiting him at the house in Bloomsbury?"

"Edith?"

"Do you think they are having an *affaire*?"

Nancy stared at her. "Don't be ridiculous, Connie. You're talking about your papa. And anyway, Edith loved Gilbert."

"And Gilbert is back with Marjorie. They're going to get married. So why isn't Edith heartbroken any more?"

Nancy was thoughtful, Edith and Aubrey? It was true that Edith had always been fond of him, and true as well that she had changed in the past weeks. While one could not have said that she looked like a woman in love, it was clear that something or someone had begun to take her mind off Gilbert.

Stephen, his leave at last secured, came to see them at the end of May. He looked gaunt and ill, and had a disturbing resignation to the war going on for years.

"You must buck up, for Connie's sake," Nancy urged him. "She's still down about Gus and Hugo, and now Aubrey is to join up as well. I don't know what she'll do if you give up hope."

When Stephen went back to France, Connie cried. She said it was because he had made her think of Gus and Hugo, but Nancy, remembering Connie's adolescent crush on Stephen, wondered if there was more to it than that. Suddenly she felt very alone. Connie's story of Aubrey and Edith's friendship had disturbed her more than she was willing to admit. She thought of Ted, remembering the last time she had seen him. He rarely contacted her, and, when he did, it was usually a standard Army field postcard with its printed and impersonal message: "I am quite well. I have received your letter." His letters paid the same attention to bald facts: he was well, their conditions were 'not so bad', he wished the high-ups would give them some leave. Only occasionally would he allow a personal lapse, saying once that he wondered if his roses were blooming; and, on another occasion, with an unprecedented hint of sentiment, he wrote that he had pictured her walking along a French country track towards him. Nancy cherished these gems: her memories of him flickered to life again. She told herself that his father had been a murderer and that Ted had shielded the crime all these years, but she knew that it did not make any difference to the way she felt.

Gilbert married Marjorie Benson that summer. Nancy went to the wedding with Connie.

"Good Lord. Is that Edith?" Connie said. "I never thought she would come."

Nancy turned to see Edith talking with Aubrey. He was in uniform, but looked like an actor dressed for the part: too clean-cut, too conventionally heroic to be a real soldier. Could Connie be right about an affair? Edith had given no hint to Nancy of her friendship with Aubrey, but there was an obvious rapport between them. Nancy noted the swift intimacy with which they responded to one another: it was clear that even if they were not physically intimate — and the idea *was* preposterous — they had become close.

Nancy felt a perverse sense of betrayal. Connie, beside her, giggled. "People would start to gossip if it weren't so impossible for anyone to imagine Papa conducting an *affaire*."

What would they say, wondered Nancy, if they knew that Aubrey's mama had had a man murdered? Surely that was something for the imagination?

The wedding breakfast was a muted celebration. People made excuses about the food, saying that no one could get a decent spread any more. The talk was of Zeppelins and Gothas, daylight raids and near misses, fuel shortages, the ploughing up of parks for food crops and the likelihood of rationing. Nancy stood alone by the buffet. She disliked these affable occasions when everyone tried to pretend they were enjoying themselves in spite of the war.

Aubrey came towards her. "Marjorie looks happy."

"Why shouldn't she? She finally got her man." She smiled. "And so has Edith, unless I'm much mistaken. You look very handsome, Aubrey, in your uniform."

He frowned, blushing, and Nancy laughed suddenly. "Aubrey! You are a sly old thing."

He glanced round anxiously. "Do you have to put it quite so vulgarly?"

"Tell me I'm wrong then."

"Edith is a splendid girl, but there's nothing peculiar going on."

"Would it be so awful if there was?"

"You really are the limit." After a while he said, self-consciously, "You could take steps to divorce me."

"What shall I do? Hire a detective to follow you about?"

"It could be arranged discreetly through my solicitors, should either of us wish to marry again."

"I'll think about it. I certainly wouldn't oppose it at all. Now kiss me and say that you're happy."

Aubrey kissed her cheek. "Mama must not know about Edith, of course."

Nancy gave a dry laugh. "I'm sure she must not. Don't worry, I shan't breathe a word."

* * *

Aubrey came to see her one evening some weeks later; he said he was being sent out to France. Nancy showed him into the sitting room at the flat. "I'm afraid Connie isn't here. She's still at the Training Bureau. She gets so involved in the work."

"Is my daughter turning into a feminist?" he said with a brave attempt at lightheartedness.

"If she is, it's because of Edith's influence. You ought to approve," Nancy said.

Aubrey smiled. He looked sad and very dignified in his officer's uniform. "I'm grateful to you for watching over Connie, Nancy. There have been times — " He cleared his throat. "There were times when I judged you too harshly."

Nancy knew that he was thinking about Stephen. It was his way of saying that he had forgiven and forgotten.

"If anything happens to me you will continue to be a friend to Connie, won't you?"

"Of course." Nancy felt a wave of fear for him. He was very vulnerable, too old to be going out to the trenches.

"Don't feel too hard about Edith. If I come back — "

"Edith has been a good friend," Nancy interrupted him. "She always will be. And if you want to marry her, I told you, I shan't oppose a divorce."

"You're being very sensible about all this."

"I've not been very honest with you, Aubrey. There has been someone else."

He looked at her in surprise. "Good Lord. Who is it? Not Stephen?"

"No. And it hardly matters now, but I was in love with someone for a while."

"Is he in France?"

"Yes." She looked away and felt a pull at her heart, knowing she lied when she said that Ted did not matter any more. She was glad when Aubrey dropped the subject.

"Nancy, *if* anything happens to me — " he took an envelope from his pocket — "there are things — to do with Augusta — which I ought to have told you about, and — well, I just wanted to set the record straight."

Nancy took the envelope. It was sealed with the Midwinter insignia and her own name was written on the front in Aubrey's familiar hand.

"I loved her deeply, Nancy. Perhaps, one day, you will understand why I felt as I did about the pool."

"Because of Viner?" Nancy's mind lurched. Had she been wrong? Did Aubrey know after all about the murder?

He shook his head to silence her. "No. Not because of Viner."

Nancy held the slim envelope and watched him go. On a sudden impulse she ran after him to the stairs. He touched her cheek self-consciously, "I should have told you. It wasn't fair of me to expect you to live in her shadow."

Nancy returned to the sitting room

when he had gone. She stared at the envelope he had given her. What record? What else was there to tell? She was tempted to break the seal, but a superstitious regard for Aubrey's safety prevented her and she crossed the room and placed the letter on top of Augusta's diaries in her writing desk.

20

THE lorry jerked and ploughed along the track. Bright, the second-lieutenant in command of the tank crew, sat, bespectacled and thoughtful, with his arms wrapped round his knees. The men were buoyant with the prospect of some action after weeks of inactivity, but as the lorry approached the edge of Ypres they fell silent.

The place always had that effect on people, Ted reflected: the ruined streets and the rank, weed-filled canal had an atmosphere of desolation unlike anything one could imagine, except perhaps the entrance to hell itself. "Wipers." Ted hated the name. He hated the Salient and the fact that they were fighting over the same mangled villages, the same wastes of mud and shell-holes and shattered tree stumps over which men had died for the past three years. The place smelled of death for mile after mile; that sickly stench of unburied corpses.

They had been sent with the rest of the tank crews in B-Company to reconnoitre the area before the next day's show; not a battle, just a division of infantry and a few tanks, out into the wilderness to 'tidy up' a couple of German pill-boxes. A small affair. It probably all sounded very easy to the men who drew up the clean, crisp maps and gave out orders from their well-drained dugouts behind the lines.

Ted and one of the gunners followed the officers and the working party sent to guide them. They walked warily in twos on duckboards which floated on the sludge. The sky was grey and watery, as empty as the wastes of mud spread below it. Every now and then the heavy rattle of a German machine-gun would remind them that the pock-marked acres of mud, against all the evidence of their own eyes, concealed the enemy trenches and gun-posts marked in neat red ink on the map. They moved down the slope and made their way to the swamp of intersecting flooded shell-holes. Bright puzzled over the map. "There should be a couple of villages to the right." He was the youngest of them all, probably not even twenty yet, a cocky blighter when he was on form, but human, thank God. Ted felt a swift sympathy for him, There were no 'villages'. Every building for miles had been reduced to a patch of rubble in the yellow slime. It was obvious Bright hadn't a clue where they were.

The sound of guns was becoming more purposeful. The working party was scurrying back, and from their left came the rapid answering fire of a Lewis gun. They made their way up the slope and joined the rest of the crew.

"Let's get out of here," said Bright. "We'll be back soon enough."

* * *

They had been ordered to take up their position. "Christ Almighty!" A star shell lit up the road, jammed with infantry and ammunition limbers. "If they start going for us now we've had it," muttered Ted.

"Never mind the Boche. Get on. Get on!" Bright joined the crew inside the tank and scrambled into his seat, as near to panic as Ted had seen him. He turned and grinned suddenly, his spectacles glinting in the near darkness. "Let's get off this bloody road. We're nothing but sitting ducks."

The tank edged its way forward. Men scrambled out of the way. A gun limber went over and the tank slithered off the road and righted itself, then ploughed on. Ted was sweating. How much further? Had they reached their starting point? The artillery had opened up already and started off the enemy's counter-barrage. The shelling grew in intensity, but at least they were well away from the death-trap on the road.

A succession of huge crashes shook the tank and made the space inside throb with noise; it came in waves of fire, several stabs of sound together, which numbed the mind and made it hard to think, let alone understand what Bright was trying to signal. The roar of the engine was deafening; the blast and rattle of the Lewis machine-guns and the six-pounders filled the cramped space. It was some minutes before Ted saw outlines of tanks against the dawn sky through the front flap and realised they had officially gone into battle.

Minutes later they were sinking in the mud. The six-cylinder engine roared unsuccessfully. The shelling had eased a little, and Bright and the rest of the crew climbed through the tiny door leaving Ted and the gunners inside. A sick fear pulled at Ted's gut as he heard the men try to get the unditching beam in position. How could a handful of men pull twenty-eight tons of steel out of the sloppy mud? He loathed the war. He loathed the men who had made the war happen and made it go on and on, month after month. Stick to the duckboards, lads. Don't go off the track or you'll land in the soup. They were all in the soup this time. If they were not shelled to kingdom come they would drown outside in that brew of corpses and vehicles. Ted closed his mind to the images of death which came too readily when he was off his guard. There had been a time, long ago, when he had not known what a corpse would look like after being in water for months; it had been the stuff of his nightmares. He had imagined coming upon that thing floating on the surface of the pool. Well, now he knew what Viner would have looked like; he had seen enough corpses, broken and bloated, to form a fair idea, and the knowledge did not make it any better.

He heard Bright's shout. "I think that's it. We'll try again." They cranked up the engine and the tank roared and shuddered, but they were digging themselves deeper into the quagmire. Worse, they had come under fire from a machine-gun post somewhere to their right: as he obeyed Bright's order to cut off the power again, Ted could hear the five-point-nine's rhythmic chatter.

"Never mind the heat. Never mind the noise," someone quipped in the eerie silence, quoting from their official instructions. "Think of your pals in the Infantry and thank God you're bullet-proof."

"Bullet-proof!" laughed Smithy with his bitter humour. The enemy fire hitting the outside of the tank sounded like metal rain; every now and then 'splash' from the bullets flaked off the armour and shot across the inside of the tank.

Sooner or later the shelling would start up again and find its target. Ted thought of the ninety gallons of petrol next to him. What was it like to be burned alive?

There was a lull in the enemy fire. "Stick to your guns, Smithy, Thompson." Bright climbed out through the door, followed by the gearsmen and the other two gunners. The silence in the tank was unnerving.

Thompson began shouting, asking permission to fire the six-pounder to try to knock out the machine-gun post. There was something impersonal about firing from inside the tank. Not the same as shooting a man at close quarters. Stick with it Smithy, Thompson. Thank God you're bullet-proof. The Boche were firing again and Smithy had started up on the Lewis gun, giving cover to the men outside the tank. He was good at his job. Thompson had permission from Bright to fire; he prepared to open the breach. Ted wished he had something to do besides sit there and wait for instructions. At least the gunners could concentrate on blasting away blindly at the enemy. His dad had been a good shot once. Not now. Don't remember that just now. Think of something else. One of Smithy's stories: a man with his head blown clean off by a whizz-bang. No not that. There was this corporal, he had his arm torn away, flesh hanging down his chest and him trying to paste it back again. The blood, You should have seen the blood . . . Oh, Christ. It was too late. Viner was there, his arms outstretched, screaming. He was in the tank with him. Ted pushed him away, covering his head with his arms, away from the blood.

Smithy was shouting at him to close the breach and Ted brought himself to his senses and scrambled from his seat, avoiding the screaming Thompson; he could not look at the gunner who, opening up to load the six-pounder, had met the full force of enemy bullets bursting through the aperture.

* * *

The crew could see the infantry retreating. They abandoned the tank, making their way back to Advanced HQ. They were half dead with fatigue and had moved into a state where they no longer felt anything — not even fear — as bullets whined behind them. Sounds came at them as if from far away: the cries of the injured, the continuing roar of shelling. Men were carrying comrades. The two gearsmen carried Thompson between them, but he had passed beyond any help from the dressing station.

Smithy did not seem able to grasp the fact that they had lost Thompson and the tank. He kept saying that Thompson's butchered face would be patched up by the medical men, they would go back to retrieve the machine, they always had orders to salvage ditched tanks. He shook his fist at the air. "Bastards!" It sounded stupid, like a madman howling at his fate.

* * *

Stephen, wounded in the knee that autumn, came home to be nursed at a hospital in London. Connie went to see him every day.

"You've grown very fond of him,

haven't you?" said Nancy.

"He's asked me to marry him. I've said yes."

Nancy hugged her. "I'm so glad." And she was, though she knew that the marriage would alienate her from Connie, for her brief affair with Stephen would always be a dangerous secret between them.

Connie prattled on. "Of course we shall have to wait until I'm twenty-one. I expect Papa will insist on it. I shan't write to tell him in France. I shall wait until he comes home on his first leave."

It was later that afternoon when the doorbell clanged and, looking out of the window, Nancy saw the telegraph girl. Her heart leaped, for a telegram could mean only one thing these days, and she thought at once of Aubrey. She hurried downstairs and, returning with the telegram, handed it to Connie, watching her dumbly as she opened it.

She knew at once that Aubrey was dead.

* * *

The mourners gathered in the cold little churchyard. The family tomb was large and ugly, too ornate for the simple sandstone church, and Nancy felt instinctively that Aubrey's bones would not lie at ease there. She listened to the vicar's final words. *Dust to dust* . . . How little Midwinter had altered since its adaptation to the war: the same slogans everywhere, the same mutilated figures in the beds and corridors. Only the faces had changed. There were streamers across the main wards and Connie, glancing at them, had voiced Nancy's own thoughts, saying, "How incongruous, to have the funeral at Christmas."

Nancy looked at her, small and grieving next to Stephen. He had insisted on coming for the funeral, though he was barely used to the crutches they had given him. His injury would leave him with a permanent limp; Stephen's portion of the war was ended and there would be no question of his going back to France.

Connie had taken the news of Aubrey's illness and death with a brave resignation, saying she had expected all along that her papa would not last more than a few weeks in the Army.

If Nancy could have foreseen what would happen, she would have envisaged an act of futile heroism or a sniper's bullet, not that he would die a victim to dysentery.

Stephen moved to stand beside her. He shifted his leg uncomfortably. The parson's funeral oration about Aubrey's achievements had depressed him: the years of exploration, service to his country, an exemplary life. Words, words. The man had been a paragon. Stephen felt no emotion over Farringdon. While he had not disliked him, neither had he admired him. How could he mourn someone he had never really known? He doubted his sister would have been happy with him; Farringdon was not the sort of man who had the gift for making a woman happy. He felt constrained to say something to Nancy.

"He had not even seen action."

As if death at the hands of the enemy could somehow have lessened the blow of Aubrey's passing, thought Nancy.

"He said, 'If anything should happen', and I did not know what he meant," she told him as they moved slowly away from the grave. "He was rather sad and solemn the last time I saw him, and even then he looked rather frail."

"A premonition? The idea isn't so fanciful. Anyone who has been out there faces their own death to some extent or other. There are plenty of stories of men who knew they would be killed in the next action, slipping farewell messages for loved ones to a comrade at the last minute."

Nancy thought of the letter Aubrey had given her before he went to France. What was it he had said at the time? That he wanted to set the record straight?

Mrs Farringdon had not moved from the family tomb. She wore her funeral coat with its black fur collar and the ostrich feather hat, and leaned a little on a gilt-headed cane, with no other outward indication that she was grieving. She would reign alone at Midwinter, without son or grandson to carry the Farringdon name. Nancy felt no pity for her. She thought of Viner crying out in his agony, "Augusta," like a voice calling from hell, and of Aubrey's letter, which had at last revealed to her the final chapter to Augusta's story.

She left Connie and Stephen and walked back to the Farringdon grave. "You knew how terrible it would be for Connie if anything happened to Aubrey. Why did you push him to enlist?" She knew the attack was futile, yet she felt a need to release her anger.

Mrs Farringdon did not lift her glance away from the tomb as she spoke. "Country comes before any other consideration."

"Rubbish. What earthly difference could he have made to the war? Aubrey was an intellectual, a traveller, not a fighting man. He would never have made a soldier."

"You're wrong. My son at last saw where his duty lay."

"You know as well as I do that it had very little to do with duty." Nancy thought again of Aubrey's letter. "He would never have joined in the madness if he hadn't been haunted about the past."

"And what do you know about the past?" Mrs Farringdon said scathingly, still staring at the tomb. "You are of this new, shallow generation. You have no background, no breeding."

Nancy did not answer. The rest of the mourners had formed a straggling group around the church gates, leaving the two of them isolated among the graves. After a while she said, "I met a friend of Augusta's some time ago. Do you remember Grace Hammond?"

Mrs Farringdon gave no indication that she had heard.

"Did you know that she received a letter from Augusta, smuggled out from Midwinter shortly before she died? You knew, of course, that Viner was coming for Augusta?"

Mrs Farringdon turned slowly. Her face was white and hard and dry, her eyes as sharp as ever, uncluttered by tears. "Of course we knew. Aubrey said he was going to let her go with him."

"Perhaps he was right," said Nancy. "Perhaps Augusta could have been happy with Viner."

"Happy! What did happiness matter? What about the scandal if he had let her run off with the fellow? We could never have kept it quiet." Mrs Farringdon remembered that her son had cried. She had been ashamed of him. She had told him to be a man, they would think of something, they would tackle it together; but he had been a coward when the time came and she showed him Viner's letter with the message to Augusta to meet him. "He went to London. He left me to deal with the problem of Viner."

"I'm sure he didn't mean you to deal with it quite so conclusively."

Mrs Farringdon stared at her coldly. "Viner was the sort of man who could be appealed to with money. He promised not to bother us again."

"I don't believe you." Had Aubrey believed it? "I've read Augusta's letter — the one you never saw. She talked of hearing shots."

Mrs Farringdon's gaze did not falter. "Augusta was ill and suffering from a kind of hysteria. She imagined all sorts. She may well have heard the keeper shooting."

"I spoke to Ted Powers."

Mrs Farringdon rocked slightly on her feet. "Powers is in France." Her voice was almost a whisper as she gripped the handle of her cane and leaned on it for support.

She looked at Nancy and knew from her expression that the keeper had let something slip. If he had spoken to Nancy, who else might he not have talked to? She said in the same half-whisper: "I should never have let him leave Midwinter." Suddenly she felt tired, drained by the war which had destroyed so much. Things had been so very different in the old days: one knew where one was, one was certain of principles, values and traditions. She looked away, drawn again to the grave which held the bones of her husband, her grandson and now her son. "I never liked Powers. His look was insolent. He had none of the humility of the generation before him. If I had not needed someone to look after the wood I would have sacked him long ago."

"If he hadn't known so much, you mean." Nancy saw Mrs Farringdon's hands tighten again on the cane. "Have you never thought that if you had let Augusta go with Viner, Aubrey would not have grieved all these years as he did over her death?"

Mrs Farringdon looked up, and there was a strange, disquieted expression in her eyes. "Yes. We could not have anticipated that." She fell silent and, at last, Nancy thought she had moved her. Then Mrs Farringdon said coldly, "Well now, what are you going to do about it?"

"You mean, of course, am I going to tell anyone what I suspect?"

"I suppose that is what I mean."

Nancy laughed in disbelief. She turned to glance at the group of mourners drifting towards the cars. "Do you think that on top of all that has happened to her, I would want Connie to find out?"

Mrs Farringdon turned on her and her eyes were hard with anger. "You don't know the circumstances. Viner was evil. It was my Christian duty."

"You *could* have paid him money. You'd offered Viner money before and he had taken it. There was no reason why he shouldn't again. Why didn't you?" Nancy said despairingly.

"Because I knew he would keep coming

back, that sooner or later the affair would become a public scandal which would break us." Mrs Farringdon fell silent.

"So you got the keeper to shoot him."

"Powers was a good, religious man. He had seen them together: the memory was seared on his mind. He recognised evil when he saw it, knew the punishment such depravity deserved and where his Christian duty lay."

"You really believe it was his *Christian* duty?"

"It was mine. A divine responsibility. Powers carried out my orders to rid Midwinter of vermin, and, believe me, Viner was vermin: he was corrupt through and through."

"I don't suppose it even occurred to you that your keeper might have nursed a conscience about what happened?"

"He agreed to do it out of loyalty to the family."

"You mean he carried out your orders without any questions, because if he hadn't he would have been out of a job."

"Is that the sort of thing Powers has told you?" Mrs Farringdon said angrily. Her eyes glittered. "You say the keeper nursed a conscience. What about his son?"

Nancy stared and her heart leaped. "Ted? He had nothing to do with it."

Mrs Farringdon seemed to consider for a moment before her eyes took on a hooded expression. She turned away and began to walk from the grave. "I'm rather weary. I have suffered a great deal, Nancy — far more than you think, I am tired of these melodramatics."

* * *

"Are you coming back to the house?" said Connie, turning to Nancy as she approached the gates of the churchyard.

Nancy glanced at Mrs Farringdon, watching her lean on Roberts's arm and walk towards the waiting car, and saw, for the first time, that she looked frail and old. "No, I'm not coming back. I shall catch the next train to London."

She walked alone along the road to the station, where she sat on a seat on the platform, avoiding the crowded hot little waiting room. She glanced along the empty railway line. There had been so many arrivals and departures from this place, each with its own drama attached to it: boys going off to the trenches, Augusta leaving for Paris, her own departure from Midwinter.

A wisp of smoke appeared on the horizon, and she heard the heavy rumble of an approaching train. Nancy climbed into a carriage and found a seat. She wiped a clear space with her glove in the condensation on the window. It was growing dark outside as the train jerked into activity, and with a grinding of wheels moved off from the station. She watched the fields and woods of Winchborne slip by: there was a glimpse of Midwinter and its empty acres and then they were gone. Nancy closed her eyes and heard only the rhythm of the train.

After a while she pulled Aubrey's letter from her pocket and opened out the sheets of paper, seeing again the familiar handwriting, remembering with an unexpected rush of affection all the times in the past when she had corrected the syntax and rebelliously changed a word or a phrase.

My dear Nancy,
I know I shall not survive the war. I suppose I would act differently now, if I could step back in time a little, but the thing is done. Comfort Connie, be a friend to Edith if it is in your heart to do so. I think it will be; in recent years I have recognised a goodness in you. Had I been less rigid, more accessible, our marriage might have been different. But who can say?

There is one thing, however, which I must do: I have to tell you the truth about the pool.

I have always let you believe that I could not bear to talk of it because it is the place where Augusta met her lover. It was so much easier not to have to explain. But one unpalatable fact, Nancy, is that Augusta had entertained many lovers; there were many such 'sites' which could have held equally painful memories. Augusta needed her admirers from the early days of our marriage. When I discovered the kind of woman she was, I was filled at first with pain and disgust, and yet I could not stop loving her. In time, I learned to tolerate her indiscretions. I was prepared to tolerate Viner, believing it would not last.

They had been meeting and corresponding for over a year before they were discovered one afternoon by the gamekeeper in the wood. Mama persuaded me that I should put an end to the relationship. This was not like the other affairs: it was becoming too intense, too threatening to the family name. I sent Augusta away for a while and Viner was paid substantially to leave the country, but the affair continued, and I learned that Viner was preparing for Augusta to join him in Malaysia. Mama had discovered their correspondence and we watched over Augusta carefully. The strain was causing her to suffer nervous traumas; she was under constant medical supervision.

And then Viner arrived in England. Augusta told me that he was coming for her; she asked me to let her go free. In that moment I would have let her go, Nancy. I saw that I was wrong to hold on to her, that she truly loved Viner despite his all too obvious faults. But I let Mama persuade me that I was weak; I agreed that we should try to buy Viner off again. We concealed his letters, which told of the time and place where he would meet Augusta, and I went to London, leaving Mama to contact and arrange payment with Viner. I had no doubt that he would take the bribe. I began to believe that it was for the best.

But while I was in London I saw that my first instinct had been right: Augusta must be allowed to choose whether to stay at Midwinter or go away with her lover. I telephoned her. I spoke to her alone and told her where Viner was staying and of the plan he had made to meet her by the quarry pool in the wood. I told her that she must go to him if she was sure that it was what she wanted, but that she must be sure and make the best decision for her future happiness.

Imagine my joy when I returned to

Midwinter and learned that Augusta had made her choice and would stay with me of her own free will. I had behaved honourably, and Viner had taken our money and would trouble us no more. But Mama, knowing nothing of Augusta's decision and the moral struggle which must have preceded it, told her, very cruelly, that her lover had taken a bribe. Augusta wept a great deal. She kept repeating that she should be with her lover. She swore that she would go to join him.

I shall never know whether it was Viner's betrayal which finally unhinged her, or a false notion that she had betrayed her lover, but she slipped our attention the next day: she wandered to the wood and, in her deranged state, must have slipped or jumped into the pool. I was not alerted to the fact that she was missing until late that afternoon. I went in search of her and found her face down in the water. I pulled her out and carried her to the house, but she must already have been dead for some hours.

We kept Augusta's suicide secret:

Mama and the physician knew, of course, and perhaps some of the servants suspected, but Midwinter servants have always been loyal.

So, now you see, my dear Nancy, why, since the day I found her, I have not been able to talk of the pool except with horror and sadness, nor think of Viner save with loathing. Forgive me for the deception. It was not your fault. You were not to know.

Nancy folded the letter and returned it to its envelope. Augusta had made her choice, had known that Viner was coming, not in a drug-confused fantasy, but through a phone call from Aubrey, and she had done nothing. She had known the time and place and done nothing. Nancy slipped the letter back into her writing desk with the diaries. Grace had been right in that Augusta had recognised her need for Aubrey, but she was wrong about Augusta not having the courage, in the end, to step over the brink. Unable to live with the knowledge that she had betrayed Viner, she had followed him to the grave. How much had Viner loved Augusta? He had returned to England to fetch her. Would he have accepted another bribe if it had been offered? Nancy supposed she would never know. Such was the nature of love, that only within its charmed limits could one come near to understanding it.

* * *

At last had come the news Ted craved: they were going on leave for seven whole days. Not out in rest billets, but back to the clean, beautiful air of Blighty. And after that? Ted did not know how long his own luck would last. First Ypres, then Cambrai, where they had lost more than a third of the Tank Company, then Christmas — a cold and gloomy time, counting the dead, getting used to new faces. It was only a matter of time before his own unit copped it.

He was impatient with the walk to the railhead, the dragging wait for a military train and the slow journey to the coast; he wished his mind did not go over and over the events of the past year, instead of looking forward to the days of freedom ahead. There had been rumours that tanks were going to be abolished after the summer's Big Push: they were too prone to technical breakdowns and they got stuck in the Flanders mud. The Hindenberg Line had been easier, massively fortified, but perfect attacking ground for tanks, chalky and dry. No swamps of mud, no stinking corpses, but real woods, with real trees and the odd village with houses still standing. There had been a new and unfamiliar tank, then more breakdowns and wondering again whether Haig would order tanks out of the war. Ted looked around at the men beside him. The draughty hours waiting at Le Havre for a boat to take them across the grey, foggy sea had dampened everyone's spirits; they looked less like men going on leave, as they huddled on deck, than the sorry dregs of battle.

They arrived at Victoria, where Ted learned that he had a night and part of the following day to spare before he could catch a train for Dorset. He watched jealously as other men greeted sweethearts and wives, and he felt a sense of anti-climax. An old woman with a trolley of tea and an insulting world-weariness handed him a cup of brown liquid which bore an uneasy resemblance to Flanders mud. News-stands plastered some lie about an advance. 'Let 1918 be the Year of Victory'. Did these people in their clean civilian clothes believe it? How strange to see so many civilians, and women and children strolling about with bland expressions, instead of fear on their faces like the French. How unreal and stupid they all looked. Ted was conscious of his filthy uniform, his unshaven face and cracked and dirt-stained hands. He did not belong in this clean, insipid scene. He had grown used to the Army. He loathed it, yet he belonged there.

A draft of new recruits was lining up on the concourse. Clean uniforms, fresh faces. Smithy jeered. "Poor sods don't know what they're in for." One of their group yelled, "Go home, you bloody fools." Then they fell into a mood of depression as they came out into the street, to noise and traffic and yet more uncomprehending, stupid bloody civilians. "Let's get pissed," muttered Ted. They made for the nearest pub.

Two hours and several pubs later they were wandering along the Tottenham Court Road, their number reduced to three. The difficulty of finding a bed for the night began to loom. Smithy knew of a house in Soho where he was bosom pals with the landlady. Ted did not believe him: he had witnessed one of Smithy's bosom friendships once on a rare visit to a French *estaminet*, and it had ended in their being thrown out after a brawl. He said he would leave them to it, he had just remembered a girl who would be keen as mustard to see him in London. The others glanced at one another and winked, their suspicion that Powers was a bit of a 'dark horse' confirmed.

Ted waved them goodbye and, feeling an urgent need to pee, relieved himself in a shop doorway. He propped himself against the wall, then pulled Nancy's ragged letters from his top pocket. Unfolding one, he peered carefully at the address.

* * *

"Nancy. My best girl."

"Ted? Is it you?"

"I love you, Nancy. Say you'll ditch the other fellow. Give him the boot."

"You're drunk."

"Ever so slightly. Have you got a bed for the night, Nancy? Oh, lovely Nancy, you look — beautiful."

Nancy pulled him indoors and shut the door. "Be quiet. You'll wake Connie."

He leaned against the wall with his eyes closed muttering, "Nancy, beautiful Nancy."

Nancy tried to collect her thoughts. She had been on the point of going to bed. She pulled her dressing robe round her and tightened the sash. The shock of seeing him subsided a little. He smelled, not just of drink: his clothes smelled, an odd, sickly stench, like tramps on the embankment, river beds, sewers. "You could do with a bath," she said, telling herself not to be so insensitive. Was that all she could do after eighteen months, tell him he needed a wash?

"A bath." Ted giggled. "Bloody top hole. Haven't had one of those chaps in years."

"For goodness' sake, shut up, Ted." Nancy closed the door and bolted it.

Putting her shoulder under his arm and, with several halts during which he told her repeatedly that she was lovely and he loved her, she helped him up the stairs. Nancy prayed that Connie would not wake. She propped him on a chair in the bathroom and turned on the bath taps, then hurried into the bedroom and scrabbled in the wardrobe for her old grey wool dressing gown and a pile of blankets, then returned to the bathroom where Ted had begun to undress. She watched him struggle with his tie and collar and, putting down the blankets, went to help him, telling him in a brisk, tight voice all the while to sober up. He caught her arm. "Nancy — you *have* ditched that other fellow, haven't you? Aren't you even a little bit pleased to see me?"

His hands were scarred and filthy. He was conscious suddenly of the contrast with the light silk of her sleeve and removed his hand. "Sorry. Sorry — you're right. I'm drunk."

She said, "Oh, Ted. You idiot. Of course I'm pleased to see you."

She left him with the water running

and went along the corridor to the sitting room; the fire was not quite dead and she put on more coals and stood near the hearth, hugging her arms round her. After a while she unfolded the blankets and made up a bed on the sofa: she tucked the covers under the back cushions briskly, fiercely; she would not think about this turn of events; she would not analyse her feelings. But the feelings would not be pushed away as she sat on the made-up bed. Relief that he was safe? Oh, yes. And more than that: a pure gladness had radiated through her when she had pulled him, drink-sodden and stinking into the hall. He had come to her. He had seen her as a refuge.

He was after a bed for the night, she told herself coolly. But another voice stole into her thoughts more strongly. He needs me. He has come because he loves me.

* * *

Ted lay in the hot water and began to weep, slow silent tears. His best girl. She had taken him in. Lovely, beautiful Nancy. How could he have been so wrong about her? He let the hot water and steam soak away the months of wretchedness. A clock ticked softly on the landing. Peace, peace, peace. He heard it chime the half-hour, then the hour. One a.m. He woke with a jerk, like he did when on watch, guiltily, his heart racing. There came again a gentle knock on the door. He had been dreaming about her. God, she had been waiting up all this time for him.

"I've made you some coffee and a bed on the sofa," she whispered through the door panel. "Come to the sitting room when you're ready."

He washed swiftly with soap in the cooling water and dried his body on the large rough towel she had left for him: scented soap, Pears's Attar of Roses; a thick, clean towel; there was a carpet on the floor and a soft grey dressing gown for him to put on, draped over the back of the chair. Hers? He held it to his face and breathed in the faintly feminine smell.

She was sitting on the sofa where she had made up a bed of blankets; a good fire burned in the hearth. He wanted to weep again as she held out a cup of coffee. He could not meet her eyes. "Sorry to embarrass you like this."

"I'm not embarrassed."

"I was with some pals. We had a drink or two. I couldn't get a train to Dorset until tomorrow afternoon."

"I told you. I'm not at all embarrassed. I'm glad you're here."

"What about Farringdon's daughter?"

"Connie won't wake now. I always get up before she does in the mornings. I'll explain to her before she sees you."

"It's so good to be here. It's — it's like being in heaven." He swallowed the lump of emotion in his throat.

"Why didn't you let me know you were coming?"

"I never meant to. I wouldn't have except — "

"Except you were with some pals and you had had a drink or two. Why don't you come and sit down and drink your coffee?"

He sat beside her. Her hair was down on her shoulders, soft and tumbled. The sight of it was very erotic. She must have been going to bed when he arrived. What a bastard he was. What must she think of him, to come to her, filthy and half-pissed? But she was smiling at him, her eyes drowsy. God, he wanted her. He had forgotten what it was like to be so full of wanting a woman. He could hardly contain it, just feeling the heat of her thigh against him, smelling her warm scent and looking into those eyes. His head felt dizzy, as if he were still drunk, though he knew he was sober.

"Ted . . . " Nancy began. Her voice was unsteady. She knew she should move away but she could not bear to leave him now, after so long without seeing him, worrying about him, wondering about so many things. She felt sleepy after waiting for him while he bathed. They were sitting too closely together and were far too unsuitably dressed for decency. If Connie came in . . . but she was reluctant to move from the warmth of the fire and the comfort of the warm blanket against the back of her bare ankles. She wanted his tough hard body, incongruously clad in the inadequate grey dressing gown. So much had come between them since that day at the cottage, yet she still felt the same.

He touched her thigh and she sat very still, feeling the heat from his hand steal through her and desire for him pulse and pulse and pulse again.

She closed her eyes and waited for him, his fingers on her thigh exploring more firmly, his mouth seeking hers, and she felt with her hand for the back of his neck and pulled him closer. He slipped her robe from her shoulders and lowered his head to her breast, cupping it gently as if afraid to bruise her.

Nancy slid down on to the blanket and parted her legs for him, echoing his impatience as he tugged at the cord of the dressing gown. She reached for him to guide him, and he lifted her and found a rhythm, his hands beneath her. She cried out at his perception, then was consumed by sensation, her body separate in its moment of ecstasy, then at one with his as he came inside her.

He slept straight away, and she lay, cradling him in her arms. After a while she roused herself and, easing her body from his side, left the sofa. She tucked the blanket round him, put a guard in front of the fire and slipped from the room.

* * *

"But why should Ted Powers come here?" Connie stared at her.

"He was on leave and stranded for the night. I had written to him. You know — I used to write to Browne as well and some of the other Midwinter staff. I suppose he felt we would help."

"Well, I call it a gross impertinence."

Nancy's temper snapped. "I suppose if he had been an officer it would have been all right! The least we can do is offer the poor man a bed for the night."

Connie looked at her in surprise. "Keep your hair on. It's your apartment. Turn it into a doss house for Tommies if you like."

* * *

"She's gone."

Ted took the mug of tea from her. He pulled a face. "I heard. I'm sorry. I'll be out and off your hands as soon as I'm dressed."

Nancy went to the window and watched Connie cross the street. "You mustn't mind her. She's a product of Midwinter." She turned. "I'm extremely fond of her, though, and she's been through a lot. You know Hugo was killed?" He shook his head. She hesitated, not looking at him, saying lightly, "And her father — did you know Aubrey was in France? — he died of dysentery in November." She might have been talking about an acquaintance instead of her husband, she thought, wanting to challenge Ted, to say, What now — now that I am not a married woman?

He stared into his tea for several seconds then looked up. "What does that mean to you — him dying?"

"It was a shock. Even though we had separated I still cared. He should never have joined up, he had the wrong temperament for the Army."

"Tell me the right one." Ted sipped the hot tea, apparently dismissing Aubrey, yet the implications of her freedom were coursing through him. "What would he have said about what happened last night?" he said suddenly.

She hesitated. "Aubrey would have been shocked in the same way as Connie would find it shocking. The *gamekeeper*, my dear!"

"Not so bad if it was one of his own kind. Did he ever forgive you for that?"

"I think so." She looked at him steadily, "But I had hoped we weren't going to talk about Stephen." She sat beside him. "Aubrey never felt the same about me as he did about his first wife. I knew pretty early on that I would always take second place to Augusta." She paused, remembering the letter Aubrey had left her, to 'set the record straight'. "Did you know Augusta Farringdon committed suicide?"

He frowned. "You've got to forget that woman."

Nancy said quietly, "Have you forgotten things that happened?"

He looked at her, "They hushed it up, but we knew Farringdon had found her in the pool." He lowered his gaze. "I don't think of much when I'm out there. It all seems a long way away."

"You're too busy fighting the Hun, for King and Country. "'Remember Belgium'. Does anyone still remember Belgium? How ridiculous the old slogans seem."

"People will never again see war as a moral crusade. It's the foulest thing you can imagine."

"More foul than murder?" said Nancy.

"War is murder."

"What about the death of John Viner?"

He stared at her. "So you do know about that," he said flatly.

"I worked it out. Aubrey's mother ordered the execution. Your father acted as executioner."

"My dad was only carrying out his orders. Doing his duty. He did nothing worse than any ordinary soldier who believes, poor deluded idiot, that he's helping to stamp out evil."

"It was still murder, however you look at it. You can't free him from blame with words like duty."

A shadow crossed his face. "I can't tell you about it. You wouldn't understand."

"Why didn't you write to me more often?" Nancy went to the hearth and put more coals on the fire.

"Where was the point? Oh, I suppose I believed you about Lennox — but there would always have been Viner's ghoul between us."

"Did you really think I would stop loving you because of that?"

"The thought had occurred to me." He watched her return to sit beside him. "It's not even Viner any more. The war has killed everything off. Where's the use?"

"The war has destroyed lots of things, but people can't exist without love."

"We seem to have been doing that very nicely in tanks."

"I love you, Ted. I've loved you for a long time. The war hasn't changed that, nor has what happened years ago. And I won't let you become empty and deny that you need someone." She turned away in exasperation. "Oh, you're a difficult man to get through to. You're so thick-skinned and obstinate."

"You're wrong about that," said Ted. "I'm not thick-skinned. I've let you get to me. I kept all your letters."

She held his hands in hers. "Then let me in further. You were only a boy.

Whatever you witnessed, you weren't to blame."

"You're wrong about that too."

"Tell me what you saw."

"Not just now. When I've been back to Dorset. I want to see the place one last time."

"You're going to Midwinter?"

"To my uncle's farm at Melcombe, but, yes, I want to take another look at Midwinter. Call it laying a ghost if you like, but this time, when I go back to France, I want to go with my mind clear."

She felt a chill of anxiety for him, not wanting to hear him say, as Aubrey had said, "*If anything happens to me*." "Promise you'll come and see me before you go back?"

He kissed her, but he did not promise.

21

A WEIGHT of memories and guilt had been swept away once Ted had decided to talk to Nancy. The knowledge that her husband was dead had put a further seal on the past and let a chink of hope into the future; for she was right, people could not exist without love. He walked the bridleways and field paths to Winchborne and through the stunted wood to Midwinter's pool, where he stared for a long time into its murky surface, able at last to confront what had happened. The war had brought little good to most people, but for Ted it had brought about a release. He had grown used to living with the certainty that each day could be the one when he didn't make it. Such familiarity with death was frightening, it generated new nightmares, but it had also liberated him from old ones. Viner would be a skeleton. The wood had gone and the evil at its centre was reduced to a handful of bones with no further capacity to torment him. He remembered all those years of wanting to tell someone, of watching the pool after his father died in case the carcass bobbed up. The face would have decomposed quickly. How could he tell Nancy about that? But she would wait, patient, unshockable. He would begin and, having begun, it would be easy.

* * *

Ted had been gone two days when the telephone rang. Nancy, alone in the flat for the evening, ran to answer it, half hoping that he had rung her from Dorset, or was in London and was coming to see her.

It was some seconds before she recognised Mrs Farringdon's voice, shrill and with an unprecedented note of panic in it. "I have heard that Powers is in England on leave."

Nancy clutched the hand-set. "How do you know?"

"He has been seen." The voice paused, then continued impatiently, as if unsure whether Nancy was listening with proper attention. "I said he was seen. He was here, at Midwinter. Why has Powers returned, secretly, to his old haunts unless he is here to cause trouble?"

Nancy was silent, her heart beating swiftly.

"Are you still there? Hello!"

"Yes. I'm here, I don't see . . ." Nancy's mouth was dry.

"You said that Powers had once talked to you about Viner." Mrs Farringdon's voice rose even more shrilly. "He might try to find you. What if he tries to make a clean breast of it to someone — to Connie? For *Connie*'s sake, you must stop him. Threaten him. Tell him that if he talks too freely — "

Nancy gave a laugh of incredulity.

There was silence. Then Mrs Farringdon's voice softened; suddenly it became ingratiating. "Nancy, people change after they have been in France. You and I know how peculiarly the war can affect some men: he may feel vindictive towards us, or he may believe he had to come back because he has to — get things off his chest. Listen — he may try to get in touch with you, try to talk to you again.

You should be careful, Nancy. I believed you when you said you were concerned Connie shouldn't find things out. I did what I had to do years ago, to protect the family. But Powers doesn't share our concern for Connie."

"You're afraid he will talk to people and land you in it, is that it?"

There was a pause. "We have to impress upon him that, if he talks to anyone, it is he who will suffer."

"*We?*" said Nancy. "You want me to help you threaten him? With what exactly?"

Again there was a brief silence before the voice continued. "You silly girl. Do you really think Powers's father was alone that night, or that his son stood idly by?"

The disembodied, mollifying tone seemed to Nancy to be infinitely more menacing than any of the face-to-face confrontations between them in the past. She felt as if her heart had been clamped in a grip of iron. "I don't know what you mean."

"I mean that the keeper was willing enough, but he did no more than wound Viner a little."

Nancy's breath rose harshly in her throat. "The old man shot him. He *killed* him. What he had done haunted him to his grave."

"He lost his nerve. It was the son who did it for us in the end. He was glad to put that vermin down."

"I don't believe you."

"He shot Viner at point-blank range. I watched as they weighted the body with stones and threw it into the pool." There was a pause. "If he tries to contact you, Nancy — to confess what happened — "

Nancy's head was pounding as if it would burst. "I don't believe you," she repeated, but she knew that she did as she slammed the telephone back on its hook and stood trembling with it in her hand.

She imagined the scene in the wood, saw Ted and his father throwing Viner's body into the pool. Revulsion welled up inside her as she placed the phone-set back on the table. She went into the sitting room and sat feeling faint and sick.

Nancy went to bed early, before Connie

came home. All that night she went over and over her moments alone with Ted, closing each one with the image of Ted and a shotgun, of Ted weighting Viner's body with stones. She came to the recent memory of their love-making and wept into the pillow.

The next morning she got up early and walked for more than two hours, feeling exhausted and depressed.

"Where have you been?" said Connie. "I was so worried when you weren't here. I didn't dare leave for the office. You could have left a message."

"I'm sorry."

Connie said, "You look awful." She took Nancy's coat and watched her flop on to the sofa. "What on earth has happened?"

Nancy began unfastening her shoes. She pulled them off and put them on the floor, setting them very neatly side by side. She stared at the shoes and then looked up. "I'm sorry I worried you. Do you mind if I don't tell you about it?"

Connie stared at her, then looked away. "I'm going to the recruitment office. Are you coming with me?"

Nancy hesitated. "No. I'll go in tomorrow."

★ ★ ★

Nancy was asleep on the sofa when the door-bell clanged later that day. She stood up shakily and went to the window, seeing the top of Ted's uniform cap as he stood on the doorstep. He stepped back and looked up and she knew, before she could move from the curtain, that he had seen her. She heard him shout her name. He shouted again and she opened the window. "Go away, I don't want to talk to you."

He took off his cap and stared up at her. "Why not?"

"Mrs Farringdon knows you were in Winchborne. She telephoned me. She told me the whole story."

He looked up and down the empty street. "Look — I'm not going. I'm not moving until you let me talk to you."

Nancy hesitated. "There's no point."

"There's every point. I love you."

At last she went down and let him in. She stood by the fire in the sitting room, hugging her arms round her.

"Why did you listen to her?" he said. "Why didn't you wait for me. I would have told you."

"Yes, your own version of it, like you have up to now. I doubt you'd have told me you were a cold-blooded killer."

Ted looked down at the cap in his hands. After a moment he looked up again. "So the old girl has done her worst."

"She told me the truth, if that's what you mean. She has an idea you're suddenly going to start confessing to everybody. I expect she's frightened for her own skin and wanted to get to me first."

He looked at his hands, criss-crossed with lines of dirt which it would take more than a bath to erase. "Viner buggered her, you know, that afternoon, when we saw them. He tied her to a tree and then used her."

"My God. That was no reason to kill him."

"No. There are very few good reasons for killing."

"But you shot Viner? She said you

were the one who did it."

"Yes." He looked again at his hands. "I couldn't stop the nightmares. Not for months. It was even worse for my dad. Mrs Farringdon put out a story that he'd gone to stay with a relative and hid him away at Midwinter. But we got used to it after a while. Dad was supposed to watch the pool in case Viner's body appeared. When he died I became gamekeeper. I'd an aptitude for it and someone had to stop people from prying. It became a way of life, watching the pool."

They were silent. Nancy's heart beat painfully. She had wanted him to deny it; even at this late stage, she had hoped he would say that Mrs Farringdon had invented her story.

"Well, now you know," he said harshly. "All your questions answered."

"I don't wonder you wouldn't tell me."

He looked at her, and the anger in his eyes made her recoil from him. "Who are you to sit in judgement, Nancy? What do you know about killing? Viner's death was nothing compared to the millions who've been sent into the trenches. They're being murdered every day by the military. The slaughter in this war carries a huge, dirty guilt. How are the generals and politicians going to explain themselves after the Great War is over? With words like duty, necessity, patriotism. You can bet your sweet life on it."

Nancy had begun to tremble. "Go away. Just — go away."

* * *

The German offensive began in March. They advanced thirty miles in a matter of days, sweeping across the Somme battlefields, the carnage mounting week by week until there were as many dead as there had been at Passchendaele and the Germans were only fifty miles from Paris. Ted's company, billeted in a village for refitting, had been hurried back to the lines with orders to hold their position at all costs. And then, in April, relief orders came: the tank crew were back on route marches and training, and, for a while, it was no longer their war.

Sometimes Ted managed to get hold of English newspapers. At home everyone was obsessed about rationing, and talked about tightening belts and having their backs to the wall. "However bad it gets, we shall never give up hope." Hope. It was in short supply that spring, yet the word kept recurring. Hope had taken root in the fact that the German advance had been halted, but Ted's own aspirations, which had sprung from the blossoming of his love for Nancy, died that spring and summer as the war pushed on towards its conclusion. He had met a few of the colonial troops since he joined the Army; everyone said there was a good life to be made in Canada, Australia or New Zealand. He knew now that if he survived the war he would never return to Nancy; he would never be able to tell her how, in his thoughts, he had kissed her lips and breasts and held her lovely body to him.

He wrote one last letter to her, setting down what had happened on the night of Viner's death; it was a kind of catharsis, though he did not know whether he would ever send it.

* * *

Nancy knew after the summer that she had to get away from London. Connie had gone to live at her father's old house in Bloomsbury and was already planning her wedding; work no longer held any consolation, and the flat seemed bleak and lifeless in the long evenings. Besides, the war was over in all but name once the Hindenberg Line had been broken. The German allies were collapsing one after the other — Bulgaria, Austria, Turkey had fallen — and the British Army was at Mons, right back where it had all started. There was work still to be done, but suddenly it all seemed less urgent.

"I thought I would go up to Yorkshire for a few weeks. I need to get away somewhere for a while," she told Connie. There were other reasons why she had to get away. Now that Stephen and Connie were spending so much time together, Nancy felt an increasing embarrassment in their company. She added brightly, "I spend too much time playing gooseberry."

"Oh, Nancy — have we been selfish?" said Connie, at once contrite. She hugged her. "Don't go away because of us."

"I'm not." Nancy put her arm round her, glad that Connie was happy and had discarded her bright shallow friends, and that Stephen had at last begun to smile and joke again. She released her. "But you don't want me around all the time."

It was best that she should go away for a while. Aubrey had accepted her affair with Stephen, but would Connie if she ever suspected anything? Some secrets were unacceptable — she thought of Ted — murder, for one. She pictured him with a shotgun, saw him weighting the body with stones and colluding with Mrs Farringdon, and her heart felt frozen and numb. She had loved a murderer, might even now have been bearing his child. She supposed she should be grateful that at least fate had not dealt her that.

* * *

The journey north, though in a sense a journey back in time, was liberating. Nancy felt that she had been shut up for a long time. Marriage to Aubrey and the effect of the war with its restrictions and fears had stifled her.

She spent the whole of the autumn and early winter in Yorkshire, travelling the scenes of her childhood, visiting the town where she had been born, the places where she had grown up. She was in Yorkshire when the war came to an end.

People fell in love on Armistice Day. Others remembered loved ones with sadness and viewed the living with bitter envy. Nancy felt as if she were starting out anew, made wiser by the experience of war, but not melancholy, saddened by loss, though without any accompanying bitterness. She was a widow at twenty-three. Her life was before her.

She returned to London in January to sort out her affairs, for, as she wrote to Connie, she had decided to move back to Yorkshire. The flat was empty: the sitting-room curtains were drawn though it was not yet dark outside; the fire-grate was empty of ashes, and the room smelled of polish. Connie had left a note asking her to contact her as soon as she came home. There was a pile of letters on a brass tray on the table. Nancy picked them up and flipped through them: a number of bills, a letter from Edith, posted in London. The last letter in the pile was from France and it was dated November. It pulled her up with a jolt and wiped out the healing effect of the past weeks. Did she really think she had forgotten Ted, or could dismiss him like shaking off a bad dream? His very handwriting sent a flood of emotion through her.

She sat on the sofa with the letter unopened in her lap, and the flat suddenly felt cold. She laid her gloves on the cushion beside her, then, taking a deep breath, she opened the envelope and unfolded the pages. It was an account of what had happened the night Viner was killed.

Dear Nancy,
I feel I owe it to you and to myself to set down what happened. I don't know if you will decide to read this letter, but if you do, at least I shall have told it as straight as it can be told.

I had been given a load of work at the stables the night Viner came — the old lady's orders, I suppose, to keep me out of the way — but I was keen to finish early and worked like a mad thing through it and got home before dusk. My father wasn't there, nor was he anywhere near the pens, and I hung round the house for a while, then set off to look for him in the wood.

The wind was all in the tree canopy, and I didn't hear Viner until I saw him, coming down the path which led from the top road. He shouted, what did I want? But, before I could answer, my father stepped out from the trees and yelled out to me to get off back to the house.

"I'm here on my mistress's business," Dad told Viner, who stood with one hand in his pocket, as if we had all met on the road, instead of at night and hidden away in the middle of the wood.

Viner thought by 'mistress' he meant Augusta Farringdon. "A message," he kept saying, getting impatient. "Have you a message?"

My father was trembling. He said he had no message for him from that whore. There was something magnificent as well as terrible in the way he brought his gun up to his shoulder. He said God would bring His own vengeance to bear on Augusta Farringdon; this message was for the sinner who had corrupted her.

By this time Viner knew what was going on. He seemed to be going to protest, and then he moved away as the gun went off, and he let out a scream and fell on his knees. My father just stood there and let the gun slide to his feet.

Sights like that have become routine these past years. I've seen worse things over and over, but in those innocent days, I could never have imagined a man's face blasted half away, nor had I ever seen so much blood. My father was shaking and crying, asking Christ to have mercy on him, and then Viner called out Augusta Farringdon's name, as if he expected her to be able to come to him. He screamed out again, begging for death and for us to put an end to him.

I took hold of the gun. I told myself

it could not be much harder to put the barrel to Viner's head and squeeze the trigger than it was to put down a dying animal. That's what I thought when I did it, but afterwards, when I saw — I knew it was not the same.

My father said I was to run to the house for help, but not to talk to anyone except Mrs Farringdon. I kept thinking of what we had done. They hanged murderers, didn't they? I would swing on a gallows and so would Dad. I met Mrs Farringdon half-way across the meadow, all in black, with a hood over her head, and I thought the hangman had come for me already. I told her about my father not killing Viner outright, that I had been bound to finish it, and she hustled me back to the wood, telling me we had done well, it didn't matter if things had not gone as they should.

She spoke to us quietly, and her way of talking was reassuring. She told us we had eliminated a pocket of evil from God's good earth, and God would reward us one day for it. All we had to do was cover up what had happened and everyone could carry on normally as before. She watched us while we tied stones to Viner's ankles and slid his body into the pool. We stood there, the three of us, side by side, staring at the water until we could no longer hear the air bubbling out from the corpse.

I learned to live with the memory, the constant watching, watching that place in case Viner's body ever bobbed up again head first. But my father never got used to what he had done and what he had made me do, nor the fact that, because of it, Augusta Farringdon drowned herself. He took to strong drink and it killed him, slowly, and with the fear of hell-fire tormenting him.

I'm not asking anything of you, Nancy, only that you try to understand, even though you can't forgive.

I shall always think of you with love.

Ted

Ted was not demobbed until the spring of 1919. Then began the weary toil home. There were few celebrations, no crowds to welcome the heroes, and an air of pessimism infected the returning men.

Ted went to Dorset, hoping his uncle might offer some farm work until he could sort out his vague plan of going overseas. He took the train to Winchborne and heard in the pub there that Nancy Farringdon had gone up North the previous autumn.

"Went up to Yorkshire, back to her own people," said the landlord. "There's Farringdon's daughter left, but she's living in London — going to marry the Lennoxes' boy. They say old Mrs Farringdon's gone twisted and bitter. She's putting up fences all round Midwinter and won't let anyone in."

Ted did not go near the estate. He walked the few miles to Melcombe, where his uncle welcomed him uneasily. It did not feel right to be back, and Ted soon saw that he could not stay; the farm was already using as many ex-servicemen as it could take on. There were thousands all over the country looking for work.

"I'm sorry, Ted, but you can see how

it is. You're welcome to come back round harvest time, but now the spring sowing is over . . . " His uncle put a plate of bacon in front of him, then went to the dresser and took a scrap of paper from inside a Toby jug. He unfolded it and laid it on the table.

"What's this?" Ted looked at the paper and peered at a pencilled row of figures.

"It's a telephone number."

"And what do I want with that?"

"Thought there might be a job in it for you."

Ted shook his head and broke some bread from a loaf, dipping it in the bacon fat. "Where did you get it?"

"A woman came looking for you round about Easter. Said if you wanted you could get in touch with her."

Ted paused with the forkful of bacon in mid-air. "Did she give a name?" he said cautiously.

"She said you'd been writing to her and you'd know who she was. I kept the number just in case." He watched Ted's face.

Ted put the scrap of paper in his pocket and resumed eating.

"Do you know who she is?" said his uncle.

"Farringdon's widow."

"Maybe she wants a keeper."

Ted shrugged, as if the idea were worth considering, but the paper felt red hot in his pocket and his heart was beating as if it would burst.

* * *

She had bought a farm cottage in a moorland valley with some money Farringdon had left her. It was sheep country: there was nothing for miles except moor and farm and a ribbon of road linking the villages to the nearest town. She looked soft and pink and wind-blown. Ted's heart turned over when he saw her.

"I'd just been feeding the calf." She wiped her hands on her apron and took him into the house. A low ceiling, a fire in the grate — it was simple and homely and suited her. He felt as if he were seeing a side to her which he had never witnessed but which had always been there. She took off her apron and sat at a desk in a corner of the room, gesturing him to a seat by the window, as if she were conducting a formal interview.

"I need someone to help manage the farm."

He glanced at the muddle of papers on her desk.

"It's an account of the contribution of women to the war effort." She laughed as he pulled a face.

"Sounds high-faluting."

"It is. And I can't write high-faluting prose as well as run all this. I've talked to a few local men but nobody seemed to suit."

"You were waiting."

"I was waiting," she echoed. "Oh, Ted. It's so good to see you. I hoped you would get in touch again. Your uncle said you were still in France."

Ted leaned forward, his arms resting on his knees. "Have you thought this through? I killed a man. Not a ruddy Boche behind a machine-gun or a bayonet, with orders to get me before I got him. I shot a defenceless man through the head all because he had abused your husband's first wife."

Nancy shook her head, smiling gently. "No. When you shot him you did it because he was dying in agony, because you felt pity for another human being. You could have run away, but you did what your father couldn't finish. When I read your letter, I knew that what you did, even at fifteen, you did out of humanity."

"I did nothing to stop it happening. I could have stopped him when he had the gun levelled at Viner. I could have reasoned with him, but I thought, yes, that lump of vermin ought to die. I *wanted* him to die."

"What changed that?"

"When he screamed out for her. It was as if he had summoned up all his dying strength to call her, as if she were all that mattered." Ted looked out of the window restlessly. "Mrs Farringdon sent me out the next morning to hunt for the spent cartridge cases; she didn't want anything left lying around. I saw Viner's blood spilled over the bluebells. I smelled it on my hands. I knew then that the greatest evil lay in what had happened that night and not in anything he had done."

Nancy stood up. "Come and see over the farm."

They walked outside. Nancy stole sideways glances at him and her heart quickened. It was the same feeling. It always would be the same. They walked through the yard and up the slope of the field and stood looking down at the farmstead. The air was crisp and the baa-ing of sheep echoed distantly across the hill. Nancy breathed in deeply and linked her arm through his. "Well? Are you going to stay?"

He smiled. "You're serious, aren't you?"

"Never more so."

He took her hands and kissed the chapped knuckles. "Don't Yorkshire folk gossip?"

"That is a problem. I was relying on you to do something about it."

"You mean do the decent thing?"

"Something like that." She smiled at him. It was so good to be with him, to have him safe by her side. The death of John Viner seemed long ago, and his and Augusta's story was set in a time which no longer had any relevance. Ted had been right — wicked though Viner's murder had been, it was insignificant when set beside the four years through which they had come: after the slaughter of the innocents, what was the death of one miserable sinner? Insignificant? Irrelevant? No. That was not true, for if Augusta and Viner had not lived and died as they did, she would not be here with Ted. She touched the lines of his jaw tenderly. He looked older and harder, his hair greying a little at the sides, and the strains of past and recent horrors were etched in his face. Their relationship would not be easy.

He reached for her, and she kissed him. Their mouths were cold, their bodies at once hungry for one another. They parted and Ted wound his arm round her waist, and side by side they walked back to the farm.